This woman wasn't a nanny. This woman wasn't a fresh-faced twenty-something, overweight from too much snacking on kids' food throughout the day. This woman was tall and elegant, with a kind, understanding face.

She looks tired, thought Hope, and rather sad. I wonder why. Yet the children seem to have taken to her, and that is a definite plus. And she doesn't look at all like Mary Poppins.

"Excellent beach reading . . . By turns touching and amusing."

Library Journal

Also by Caroline Upcher

FALLING FOR MR WRONG
THE VISITOR'S BOOK
GRACE & FAVOUR

Coming in Hardcover

WITHIN A WHISPER

ATTENTION: ORGANIZATIONS AND CORPORATIONS
Most HarperTorch paperbacks are available at special quantity discounts for bulk purchases for sales promotions, premiums, or fund-raising. For information, please call or write:

Special Markets Department, HarperCollins Publishers, Inc., 10 East 53rd Street, New York, N.Y. 10022–5299.
Telephone: (212) 207–7528. Fax: (212) 207–7222.

CAROLINE UPCHER

DOWN BY THE WATER

HarperTorch
An Imprint of HarperCollinsPublishers

This is a work of fiction. Names, characters, places, and incidents are products of the author's imagination or are used fictitiously and are not to be construed as real. Any resemblance to actual events, locales, organizations, or persons, living or dead, is entirely coincidental.

HARPERTORCH
An Imprint of HarperCollins*Publishers*
10 East 53rd Street
New York, New York 10022-5299

Copyright © 2001 by Caroline Upcher
ISBN: 0-06-103152-6

All rights reserved. No part of this book may be used or reproduced in any manner whatsoever without written permission, except in the case of brief quotations embodied in critical articles and reviews. For information address HarperTorch, an imprint of HarperCollins Publishers.

First HarperTorch paperback printing: June 2002
First HarperCollins hardcover printing: June 2001

HarperCollins ®, HarperTorch™, and ❤™ are trademarks of Harper-Collins Publishers Inc.

Printed in the United States of America

Visit HarperTorch on the World Wide Web at www.harpercollins.com

10 9 8 7 6 5 4 3 2 1

If you purchased this book without a cover, you should be aware that this book is stolen property. It was reported as "unsold and destroyed" to the publisher, and neither the author nor the publisher has received any payment for this "stripped book."

Acknowledgments

I should like to thank the following people for their help while I was writing this book:

Sarah and John Lloyd
Beryl Holmes
Margaret Prince and all at Amagansett Taxi
Lynda La Plante
Cheryl Merser
Deborah Rogers and Michael Berkeley
Ann Patty
Sue "Susu" Delong and Julie Rhodes
Ann Patchett and Karl Van Devender
Emma Sweeney, Laura Bucko, and Camilla Stoddart
Mr. Harris, Gail, Stuart, and all at N. Harris & Co.
Richard Hughes, Anita Nair, and all at Lloyds TSB, Pall Mall St. James's Branch.
Bill Stoecker, Sandra Phillips Flax, Jeannine Friend, and all the East Hampton and Amagansett real estate brokers who have helped me.
Douglas Kane for giving me his idea for a children's book (a book he will probably never get around to writing himself although someone should encourage him to), part of which I have used as Harry's story in chapter 16.
Marie and Bob at the fish farm, Cranberry Hole Road.

And for superb fishing instruction, Stephen Reibel and Ellen Feldman.

For Rosie the Riveter.

For Harry, Claudia, and Caitlin Lloyd, otherwise known as Harry, Coco, and Booty, whose names I have appropriated for my characters, to whom they bear no resemblance whatsoever. Of course.

For Annabel, to whom the above also applies.

For DKNY (nothing to do with the fashion retailer).

And in memory of my mother, who died while I was writing this book and who was nothing like Marietta but, sadly, a lot like Hannah at the end.

DOWN BY THE WATER

1

Hope went downstairs to the kitchen at seven-thirty on a Monday morning and encountered an unfamiliar sight.

At least it was unfamiliar to her.

Normally by seven-thirty she was still upstairs trying to decide what to wear. With one ear tuned to the Weather Channel, she would be moving in and out of the bathroom with the phone clamped to her ear. The children would be downstairs, dressed and eating breakfast with Rachel.

But Rachel had quit the day before. As had Lisa, Karen, Julie, Maria, and Sandra before her. All in the space of two years. Today Hope found herself confronted with managing three children under nine and no help.

Only Harry had made it downstairs on his own.

He was a responsible little eight-year-old who took his position as the oldest very seriously. If Harry made her laugh from time to time, Hope kept it to herself. She knew how sensitive Harry was and she would rather die than upset him, but sometimes his behavior really was a little over the top. If someone had presented him with a T-shirt with the words I HELP MY MOM on it, he would have worn it with pride. In fact, thought Hope, given a choice, he would have requested an apron instead of a T-shirt. And while she knew she ought to be grateful for the fact that Harry loved housework, she didn't know whether to feel pleased or worried that she had scored points over her ex-husband Craig by giving Harry a vacuum cleaner for his last birthday. Craig's present of a bike had come a poor second. Hope was beginning to think about a cookbook for Christmas.

Harry had fixed breakfast, and Hope could only stand and stare in horror. There was a trail of splattered milk from the oversize carton he'd clearly dropped on his way from the fridge to the breakfast table. He'd poured the OJ into Hope's best wineglasses, miraculously still intact. Pancake mix that could have cemented the entire house congealed in a mixing bowl, surrounded by broken eggs. Harry was kneeling in the middle of the table, solemnly lighting candles.

Hope rushed over and blew them out.

"What have we taught you about playing with matches?"

"Sorry, Mom."

"Never mind," said Hope, picking up Booty, who had bumped down the stairs on her bottom, and putting her in her high chair. "Put Booty's bib on for me. Where's the Princess?"

"In her room watching *Beethoven*."

"Keep an eye on Booty for me."

Booty was her youngest, her two-year-old and, though she knew she wasn't supposed to have one, her favorite. Booty had been given her nickname by her father, Eddie, Hope's second husband. "You're my little Puss in Boots," he told her, so frequently that it became shortened to Booty.

Eddie was English, and he and Hope had very different views on how children should be raised. Coco was a case in point. She and Harry were the children of Hope's first marriage, to Craig Collins. Coco, as Eddie never ceased to remind Hope, was the perfect example of how an American upbringing could produce a monster child. By praising their children at every opportunity in order to build up their self-confidence and enable them to be successful and healthily competitive, American parents were spoiling their children outrageously. This was something Eddie was always telling Hope. But, she noticed, he never liked being reminded that the British were notoriously uncomfortable with success, preferring modesty, sometimes absurdly false, at all times. And this, she maintained, was nurtured in the early stages of childhood by British parental reluctance to highlight a child's achievements. She, an American, took pleasure in spoiling her children, seeing it as a sign of her love for them. Eddie, however, took care to restrict presents to birthdays and Christmas and gave the kids a pat on the back very occasionally, only when he genuinely believed they deserved it.

"Otherwise how will they know we really mean it?" he reasoned.

"But how will they know we truly love them?" Hope would counter.

Now she climbed wearily back upstairs to Coco's room.

Standing at the bedroom door, she surveyed her daughter for a moment. Coco Collins, six, white-blond bangs, turned-up nose, eyes the color of a Tiffany box, was sitting cross-legged in her pajamas on the floor of her bedroom watching *Beethoven* for about the twenty-fifth time.

And why not? thought Hope. She loves it. It keeps her quiet. I watch the Weather Channel, and if I could get someone to bring me breakfast in bed (as she knew Rachel had been doing for Coco for the past month, something to which she had deliberately turned a blind eye), I would. I love my daughter, and I love seeing her enjoy the things she's lucky enough to have.

Everything in Coco's room was pink. Satin, velvet, chintz. Furry, fluffed, flounced. It was like entering a miniature beauty salon. When Coco's grandmother, Maisie Hofstater, had arrived last Christmas with a giant plastic child's kitchen in offending shades of green, red, and yellow, it had been discarded by Coco the morning after Christmas, to find its true home in Harry's room.

Eddie thought Coco was a spoiled brat and should be made to toe the line and do things she didn't want to. "She's always been given to understand that she's this beautiful little girl who can get away with murder," he told Hope, over and over again. "You're always telling her how wonderful she is, and it's gone to her head. Soon you won't be able to handle her. Mark my words."

"But I *do* think she's wonderful, so why shouldn't I tell her so?" was Hope's eternal argument. "I adore her; it's important that she knows that."

"Well, there's no need to tell her so often that she becomes completely unmanageable," Eddie always grumbled.

Doesn't know what he's talking about, thought Hope. I can manage her fine.

"Coco. Breakfast, honey. Downstairs."

Coco didn't turn around. "Barbie's watching *Beethoven*."

"Well, leave her up here and come on down."

"I'm watching *Beethoven* too."

"Not when it's time for breakfast and then school and you're not even dressed." Hope hoisted Coco to her feet.

"*No!*"

Coco flopped back to the floor and faced the screen.

"Mommy, can I have my breakfast up here, please? Rachel always let me."

Hope tried to banish the sound of Eddie saying "I told you so" from inside her head. Eddie had dubbed Coco the Princess, and Hope had to admit Coco did live in an eternal fairy-tale world of which she imagined herself the ruler. She barely acknowledged the existence of her brother and sister but reigned supreme over a principality of Barbies, Kens, Shelleys, and a stable of My Little Ponies, most of whom accompanied her to school.

Hope's phone rang. She fished it out of the pocket of her robe.

"Coco. Be downstairs in five. . . . Oh, hi, Mom. Eddie told

you? . . . No, Rachel's still here," she said, glaring at Coco, whose eyes had strayed from the TV screen for one second as she caught her mother out in the act of telling a lie. "She won't be leaving for a week. . . . Sure. I'll be interviewing for her replacement all morning, just as soon as I've got the kids off to school. . . . I'm taking the day off. . . . Oh, sure, you'll be the first to know. . . . Of course I can manage. You take care of my husband. But don't forget to send him home to me on Friday. . . . You too. 'Bye, Mom."

"That was your grandmother," she told Coco's back. "She thinks you ought to go downstairs and have your breakfast."

Coco, who even Hope had to concede was abominably spoiled by Maisie when she went to stay with her in Manhattan, adored her grandmother. But she wasn't born yesterday.

"Grandma always gives me breakfast in bed."

"Grandma should be shot," muttered Hope.

Coco ejected *Beethoven* and ran downstairs clutching it, along with various Barbies and Kens, and resumed viewing in the kitchen. Hope followed with her clothes and poured her a glass of orange juice.

When *Beethoven* was finished, Coco looked crestfallen. "I want Daddy."

It was something she invariably said when things weren't going entirely her way. If Eddie thought she spoiled Coco, Hope hated to think what he'd do if he ever witnessed the way Craig catered to his daughter's every wish.

"Daddy said he'd take me to Disneyland," Coco went on. "He promised. When can I go?"

When you start behaving yourself, Eddie would have said. But Hope said instead, "The next time you visit Daddy, I guess." Craig lived in California.

"But I want to go to Disneyland in Paris!" moaned Coco.

"Naturally," said Hope. "Then you can take in the collections while you're there. Front-row seat at Chanel for the Princess. We didn't call you Coco for nothing."

The phone on the wall rang, the kitchen line.

"Daddy!" yelled Harry. Coco had already picked up.

"Daddy? This is Coco. Would you please take me to front-row Chanel? . . . Great. Here's Harry."

"Hi, Dad. Rachel's left and Mom's in a state. You should see her. She's really wired, and she's not even dressed yet. I made breakfast. I'm taking care of her so don't worry. . . . Sure, Dad. Here she is."

Oh, thank you, Harry. Thank you very much. Would it be so hard to wait twenty-four hours before you told your father yet another nanny has quit?

What was she going to do about her children? The recurring pattern of nannies leaving one after the other was taking its toll. The kids didn't really know where they were anymore, and the resulting insecurity was showing up itself in disturbing ways.

While his obsession with housework seemed funny at first, Harry was becoming clingy and a bit of a prig. In the beginning she had regarded it as his way of taking care of her and standing in for his father, but now she was worried. Harry had become a little too judgmental for her liking. She wondered what he had told his father about her over the last few months.

As for Coco, Hope had to admit Eddie was right. The child was becoming impossible. As much as Hope might tell herself she didn't discipline Coco because she loved her and showered praise on her to give her confidence, a more truthful reason would be that she just didn't have the strength to stand up to Coco anymore. It was easier to look the other way and let the Princess reign supreme. But she couldn't go on like that. Someone was going to have to take a firm hand with Coco, who had made mincemeat out of the succession of callow young girls Hope had been hiring.

Only Booty seemed as adorable as ever, but Hope knew it was only a matter of time before she too started to act up.

And, as if her children were not enough, now she had her ex-husband to deal with.

"Craig?" She took the receiver, prepared for the worst.

"Did I hear my son"—always *my* son, never *our* son—"tell me Rachel has quit? Is it true?"

"Would your son lie to you?"

"Cut the crap, Hope. Has she quit?"

"Yes."

"Why?"

"You tell me."

"Okay, I will. Same reason the others quit. You treat 'em like shit. You work all week and show properties all weekend. You give clients your home number so they call you all hours of the night. And you expect the nanny to be there for the kids. When do *they* ever have time off? I only gave you custody because—"

"Okay, okay." It was all right for him to talk. He'd left her with two kids under five. He'd had a call from the Coast and rushed off to California to pursue a career in Hollywood, leaving her holding the fort— and the babies. Harry had been four and Coco only two and a half. For three years before that she had supported him in New York with her real estate commissions, working mostly from home, while he'd developed, written, and polished his screenplay, closeted in the den of their tiny apartment in the Village, yelling at her if the kids cried or disturbed him. And all the time she'd fretted about what would happen when it was finished and no one wanted it and she had to support him for another three years. She'd been married to a loser—in her friends' eyes at least, if not in hers—and while these friends had been busy upgrading their houses and cars and vacations, she had been trapped, unable to further her own career.

She had even begun to rehearse what she would say to the outside world if the time came when they could no longer afford to live in Manhattan.

"Craig and I have decided to downsize. It's the way to go as we approach the twenty-first century. We feel it paints a healthier, happier picture for our children. It's all about integrity. Sharing. We couldn't live with ourselves if we didn't redistribute some of our wealth. We don't choose to raise our children in the city."

But she didn't believe a word of it.

Then Craig's script got the long-awaited green light. It was a go. He left for the Coast the following week and never came back.

It took Hope two whole months before she became suspicious. The first month it was: Had he found a house? No. Had he been looking? No. Was he coming back to New York soon? No. The second month the questions changed. Where had he been when she had called the night before? Should she leave the kids with Maisie and come out for the weekend? Should she renew the lease on their apartment in the Village? When she received no straight answers to any of these questions, she flew out to Los Angeles and confronted him.

He talked about a fresh start, better to do it now, and she wouldn't like California anyway.

And so he left her as soon as he got a lucky break in his career, whereas she, who had sweated blood to hold her own as a broker at Tudor Woods Realty, moving town houses, condos, and stylish co-ops all over the city, working feverishly from her home as much as from her office in order to keep the kids out of Craig's hair, would have to face total humiliation just when important clients were beginning to recommend that their friends ask for her by name when they put their homes on the market, just when it was finally, against all the odds, starting to go right for her.

She let the apartment in the Village go, took the children, and moved in with her mother to lick her wounds. And then, just as her divorce came through, Tudor Woods offered her a lifeline. There was a vacancy in their East Hampton office.

Relocation. A fresh start for her too. Move to the Hamptons. If Craig could begin a new life, goddammit, so could she.

All that changed were the properties she dealt with. Instead of town houses, condominiums, and co-ops she was now dealing with waterfront homes, traditional clapboard farmhouses, beachfront building parcels, and former fishermen's cottages. She worked just as hard. She was never home.

And all because of what Craig had done to her, all because she wanted to prove to herself that she wasn't a failure just because her husband had left her. But sometimes, lying awake in the early hours of the morning, she admitted the awful truth to herself. If Craig ever wanted to come back, Eddie would be history.

She had discussed it endlessly with girlfriends. She was in denial about Craig, about the fact that he had left her. Despite the fact that she had remarried and had a new baby girl, she was still not completely over him. She still answered the phone at Tudor Woods with the words "Hope Collins" instead of "Hope Calder," much to Eddie's irritation. It was a source of enormous comfort to her that she still had the same initials. If anybody were to pin her down and demand the truth, she would have to admit that there were times when she still thought of herself as Craig Collins's wife.

The one thing Eddie must never find out was that she had married him on the rebound.

She had married him for a number of reasons, and all of them had seemed valid at the time. He was incredibly cute. All her friends told her so. He was so different from Craig. He made Hope laugh. He was adorable with Harry and Coco. He made them laugh; they accepted him as a kind of funny English uncle. In fact, it was Harry who more or less settled her on the idea of marriage.

"Mom, c'mon. Uncle Eddie's here all the time. Why don't you guys get married?"

And then there was the sex. When she married him their

affair was really still at the infatuation stage. She was so grateful to him for taking her mind off Craig that she probably would have taken Harry's suggestion and proposed herself if Eddie had not done so first.

Plus she was becoming very fond of him. He was so easy-going compared to Craig, who was like a rat in a trap all the time, fueled by the same nervous energy as she was, drumming his fingers and constantly looking at his watch. With Eddie she was able to relax for the first time in years. And she had a horror of becoming like the hard-bitten divorced women brokers she saw littering the business.

Yet here she was, too tired to fuck her husband even when he was home. Their lifestyle was crazy. Eddie lived in New York during the week, earning a pathetic publishing salary, while she more or less bankrolled them, working at a frenetic pace in the Hamptons. But she couldn't face moving back to the city and starting all over again.

And then of course there was Booty to consider. Eddie had succeeded in getting her pregnant almost immediately and for a little while after Booty was born, Hope wondered if she might not be falling in love with Eddie after all. Then she realized it was Booty she was falling for, not Eddie.

Eddie was just hopeless.

"What are you doing about it?" Craig's voice penetrated her thoughts, tense, urgent. He was so driven. Why else would he get up at five every morning so he could call his kids before they went to school and still have an hour to work out at the gym before driving forty minutes on the freeway to arrive at the studio by seven-thirty?

She wondered what her father would have made of Craig if he could see him now. Her father's approval of Craig had had a lot to do with her decision to marry him.

Mel Hofstater had died of a coronary a couple of months after the wedding. He didn't live to see his grandchildren, and for that Hope was eternally sorry. Mel would have made a wonderful grandfather. She named Harry for him. Her father's real name was Harold Melvin Hofstater but he was always known as Mel. He had been a journalist, a staff writer on *The New York Times*, then a freelancer, eking out a precarious existence, writing a piece here, a feature there, closeted in his study, pecking away at his battered old manual typewriter, and driving Maisie mad. Hope had grown up with a writer in residence. Having Craig at work on his screenplay had seemed comfortingly familiar to her.

From Hope's early teens Maisie had exhorted her to marry a rich man. "Make sure you get some security, honey. Don't pick a man like your father." So when Hope produced Craig, a struggling young writer, Maisie was unimpressed.

Mel, on the other hand, was delighted, sweeping Craig into his den and holding him hostage for hours, engaging him in lengthy debate, writer to writer.

"He'll go far," Hope overheard her father telling Maisie. "He's a serious young man with an agile mind and plenty of energy. What's your problem with him?"

Maisie's real problem was that while Craig had been born a nice Jewish boy, his family had changed their name from Kallinsky to Collins in an effort to become assimilated.

"He was born Chaim Kallinsky. Why didn't he stay Chaim Kallinsky?" Maisie grumbled.

"Hope and Chaim. It doesn't sound right. Why didn't you call me Rachel or Rebecca? Or Hester, for that matter?"

"Your father liked Hope," muttered Maisie. "Ever the optimist. But look where it got him."

Hope had adored her father, and losing him when he was only fifty-two had made her more emotionally dependent on Craig than she had at first realized. Mel Hofstater had always been there for her. She always knew, without having to hear him say it every five seconds as Maisie did, that he believed in her and it gave her confidence.

"What do you want out of life, Dopey?" he'd ask her every

now and then, using his pet name for her. She'd seen *Snow White and the Seven Dwarfs* and dubbed herself Hopey-Dopey.

"I don't know, Daddy," she'd say. "What should I want?"

"Whatever it takes to make you happy," he always said. "And I mean you," he always added. "Not what makes other people happy, and not what they think makes you happy. Just take your time, work it out, and go for it."

"What do you want out of life, Daddy?" she'd ask him when she was older.

"Oh, just a long and peaceful retirement like a regular office worker so I can write my novels," he'd tell her, and tap his head. "It's all up here. As soon as I'm sixty-five, I'm going to quit writing this crap and turn out my masterpiece."

He never made it. It nearly broke Hope's heart every time she looked at his battered old typewriter, gathering dust in the study Maisie now used as a junk room.

If Mel had lived, would Craig have left her? Hope often wondered. Craig had respected her father. But would her father have embraced Mr. Hollywood, the Craig of today? She suspected not.

He was a producer now. His name was going to be up there on the screen in movie theaters. But she couldn't amaze her friends. She couldn't point and go, "Look, there's my husband." She'd lost him.

And where was Eddie? Nowhere.

"Doing about what, Craig?"

"Hiring another nanny. Maybe I'd better put somebody on it. I'll have my assistant look into some agencies in New York."

"I'm quite capable of hiring a nanny, thank you. Now I have to get the kids to school."

She had six potential nannies coming for interviews that morning, and as soon as she had delivered Harry and Coco to the school bus, she would call Tudor Woods and tell them she was working from home and would be checking her voice mail.

But Craig wasn't finished.

"Hold on a second, Hope. Haven't you forgotten something?"

Now what? She hadn't told him about Harry's progress with math at school (always dreadful so why mention it?) or given him an update on what Coco wanted for her birthday (over a month away and already the list was two pages long).

"Your father's anniversary is coming up. He died over the Easter weekend, right?"

"That's right," she said softly. How sweet of him to remember.

"I thought I'd fly back, spend the weekend in New York, take you and the kids to the cemetery, lay some flowers on your father's grave, pay some respect. He was a good man."

"Take Mom too?"

"Maisie? Sure. If she'll speak to me."

"Oh, she'll speak to you, all right. You're Mr. Big in her eyes now."

It was true. Craig's success in Hollywood had made a huge impression on Maisie. Lately she'd begun to say his name with a new reverence that Hope teased her about.

"He's the father of your children," Maisie said. She didn't like being teased.

"Only two of them," Hope reminded her.

"More's the pity." Maisie had never got the point of Eddie.

"So," said Craig. "I'll be in touch about the arrangements nearer the time."

"Fine," said Hope, hardly believing what she was hearing. "Fine. I'll look forward to hearing from you. Craig . . ."

She stopped. Should she say it?

"Yes?"

"Daddy would have been so pleased you remembered."

"Of course I remembered. He was like a father to me."

Craig's parents had died when he was very young, but this was a bit strong. Nevertheless, she was moved. Any minute now she would start to cry.

"Gotta go." She gulped. "Talk to you later." She hung up.

Why couldn't Craig always be like this? Why did he still have the ability to set her heart pounding at the thought that she would see him again in a week or two?

She still loved him.

She'd married adorable hopeless Eddie on the rebound and she still loved her first husband.

The phone rang again.

He'd caught the break in her voice, she thought. He was calling back to see if she was okay. Wrong.

"It's happened," said her friend Judy. "We were over there for dinner last evening. They're going to relocate from New York to Boston. His new job came through. They're through with the Hamptons. They'll be summering at the Vineyard or Cape Cod from now on. Go, girl."

"You mean—"

"They're selling their house. They're putting it on the market later today or tomorrow. The husband's going to call everyone from his car while he drives to the city. Here's the number at the house. Move!"

Hope's friend Judy O'Neal lived on Further Lane, East Hampton, in a house her husband's family had owned for generations. The O'Neals had something in the area of seven or eight acres of prime real estate, and when Judy "popped next door" to see the neighbors she usually drove.

As Hope took down the number, she was already writing the copy for the ad in her mind:

Oceanfront exclusive. Short walk to village and five min-utes from the Maidstone Club. 200 feet direct frontage of wide sandy beach. New to market. $1,500,000. Tudor Woods exclusive. Contact Hope Collins.

Six percent commission split fifty-fifty with the agency. Hope shivered. She could make $45,000.

She dialed the number, mentally slapping her wrists to stop her hands from shaking. She had to get this house as an exclusive for Tudor Woods, better still with herself as broker, before the other agencies knew it was on the market.

A woman answered.

"Mrs. DeLane? It's Hope Collins, Tudor Woods Realty. How are you? Your husband just called, and I'd like to come right over and get all the details—if that's convenient?"

"This is the housekeeper, ma'am," said a disdainful voice. "If you'd just care to hold on for one second I'll see if Mrs. DeLane is available."

"Hello. This is Nancy DeLane. Douglas only left for the city five minutes ago. He must have called you from the car."

"I just got the message," Hope said. It was almost the truth.

"Well good for you. Tell you what, why don't you come over around ten-thirty this morning?"

There was one small problem and it was staring at her from the high chair.

She looked adorable in the little bonnet that allowed a few of her dark curls to escape and frame her face. Hope tied the strings under Booty's chin, dressed her in her blue coat from Harrods sent by Eddie's mother the year before, and placed her in the baby seat in the back of the car.

Driving to Further Lane, Hope realized she'd been so busy dressing Booty, she'd taken less care with her own appearance than she normally did. Still, the jacket was Italian and the trousers Ralph Lauren. Did it really matter that she hadn't had a haircut for six weeks?

Yes, of course it did, and her nails were a disgrace.

"Oh, she's so cute!" exclaimed Nancy DeLane, when Hope had made the introductions. "Let's go into the kitchen, Caitlin, and Clara can find you something to drink."

The house was beyond Hope's wildest dreams. She'd never had anything like this to sell before. Shingled, traditional, vast living rooms with twenty-foot cathedral ceilings and tall stone chimneys, seven bedrooms, each with their own bathroom, clay tennis court, thirty-foot pool, decks, and a separate two-room gatehouse that could be used for an overflow of guests. Hope revised her asking price every five minutes: Two million. Two and a half. Three.

As she scribbled down the details and ran her measuring tape across oceans of floor space, she watched her commission climb higher and higher.

It was only when Nancy DeLane showed her a nursery complete with built-in bunk beds and a child's miniature beauty parlor with a mirror framed by spotlights that Coco would have died for that Hope remembered Booty.

Guilt set in immediately. Poor little Booty, abandoned downstairs with a stranger while horrible selfish Mommy thought of nothing but how much money she could make.

She moved swiftly to the top of the stairs and then ran down them as she heard Clara calling.

"Mrs. DeLane! Mrs. DeLane! Could you ask the lady to come down please? Quickly."

It was clear what had happened. The housekeeper had taken a phone call. Booty had seen her chance to escape and go looking for her mother. Her juice—it looked like cranberry or black currant—was in a small glass tumbler. Booty was used to drinking from a plastic cup with a lid on it, a cup Hope would have brought with her if she hadn't rushed out of the house thinking only of herself. The housekeeper had not anticipated the speed with which a determined two-year-old could travel.

The swinging door to the kitchen had been left open. From the dining room it was all open plan, and Booty had had a clear run to the largest of the reception rooms. She had got as far as a beautiful white calico sofa before she dropped her juice.

Clara, an overweight Hispanic, was lumbering around the room trying to catch Booty, who was screaming her head off.

"Oh, Mrs. DeLane, I think she cut herself. I think it's blood."

Hope panicked.

My baby. Bleeding, hurt, how could I have left her, I'll never do this again, I'll give up Tudor Woods, I'll stay home for twenty years, I'll—

Booty was fine. She was having a ball, hiding behind the bookcase playing peekaboo with a now very nervous Clara. But the two white calico sofas on either side of the fireplace were ruined.

Nancy DeLane brushed aside Hope's promises to take care of the dry cleaning. She smiled. She admonished her housekeeper for not keeping an eye on Booty. She was utterly charming about the whole affair.

But she didn't say another word about the sale of the house, and within five minutes Hope and Booty were in the car halfway down the drive.

"Oh, Booty." Hope sighed.

Who would get it now, Sotheby International? Allan Schneider? Was Mrs. DeLane even now on the phone? Would she tell everyone what had happened? Would it get around that she, Hope, had been so unprofessional as to take her two-year-old with her to assess a house?

How she hated this never-ending dilemma. Her resolution of five minutes ago to stay home with the kids was now history. She had meant it at the time. She meant it every time she said it. She adored the kids. But she had to work. She had to show Craig she was just as much a player as he was; she had to impress him, make him see what he'd lost.

Without realizing it, Hope had driven straight to the office. Oh, well, she might as well check her voice mail.

"Hi, sweetheart," chorused all the other brokers as Booty trotted in after Hope. "Hope, you got trouble."

How did they know already?

It wasn't what she thought. There were no potential clients on her voice mail, just the four nannies she had asked to come and be interviewed at the house that morning calling to find out where she was.

She had forgotten all about them.

She sat down at her desk and placed her head on her arms.

"I heard two of those girls leave their messages." Doris, one of the older brokers, had the desk next to Hope's. "You wouldn't have wanted them. I know families they've worked for. They've been through too many jobs for you to be able to trust them. Which agencies are you using? They're sending you the dregs."

"That's because my children are crazy. Harry's as good as gold but as soon as he has their trust he starts acting up and leading the other two into trouble. Coco's a little terror. And Booty's just Booty, fine except for her tantrums. Eddie's in the city all week. And I'm out working all the time. I can't win. Every night I pray Mary Poppins will come flying through the stars with her carpetbag to rescue me."

"Well, have you tried looking for her?"

"Very funny."

"No, I'm serious," said Doris. "Mary Poppins was English—in the movie anyway. The English are the best, but they have to be Norland nannies. I rented a house to a family from London recently, and they brought their nanny with them. She was a living saint and the children were beautifully behaved. And those accents! She said she was a Norland nanny. She gets work by placing an ad in a British magazine called *The Lady*."

"*The Lady*," repeated Hope. It sounded too good to be true.

It was.

She had no difficulty getting the number in London from international information, but *The Lady* told her, very politely, that they didn't accept advertisements from parties from the United States.

I am not going to be beaten, Hope told herself. I am going to find Mary Poppins. I am going to continue working, and my commission by year end is going to total more than $300,000. I am going to show Craig what he's lost.

But how?

Doris kindly got a copy of *The Lady* from her British client, and as Hope read it, a plan began to form in her mind. She picked up the telephone again.

"Eddie? I want you to do something for me for a change," she told her husband. "I want you to call your sister Maud in London, and here's what I want you to say."

2

I could kill my mother.

She's done it again.

Just when I thought I was turning a corner, she has to go and show me up as a really hopeless case. In her eyes, at any rate.

I have a bit of a problem with men. I'm the first to admit it. You'd have thought now I'm well into my forties I'd have learned a thing or two, but no. In the middle of the night when I can't sleep I face up to the truth. I take one look at the kind of man people like my mother seem to think would be perfect for me, and I want to run a mile. But if a man came toward me wearing a T-shirt emblazoned with the words I'M TROUBLE, I'M MARRIED, I HAVE A DEGREE IN WOMANIZING, GET OUT WHILE YOU STILL CAN, THERE ARE PLENTY MORE LIKE YOU WHO WILL MAKE COMPLETE IDIOTS OF THEMSELVES FALLING FOR ME BEFORE I DUMP THEM, I'd be instantly attracted. And of course I'd be convinced none of the above applied to me. You know what they say about falling off a horse? You've got to get right back on before you lose your nerve. That's a bit like me and men. When a man proves to be a disaster, you can be sure I'll walk straight into an affair with his clone.

Of course I don't do it consciously. And it's only in the dead of night when I can't sleep that I realize I do it at all.

It fascinates me that these days it's all about thirty-somethings and how they can't get a man to commit to them. Why does everyone seem to think it stops there? Some of us are still assuming we'll meet Mr. Right when we're forty, fifty, sixty. And in my mother's case—if she didn't have my father—seventy.

Sometimes I look at my mother and wonder if she's Wallis Simpson come back from the dead. It's a cinch they came from the same planet originally. I can't remember if it was Wallis or that legendary editor of *Vogue*—what was her name, Diana Vreeland?—who said you could never be too rich or too thin. Probably neither but it's certainly my mother's philosophy, although as far as the too-rich bit's concerned, she must have taken her eye off the ball when she met my father. But my mother looks like Wallis Simpson. Same black hair and penetrating eyes. She's always immaculate. And very thin.

I'm the complete opposite. I'm tall and big-boned, and while I'm not exactly fat, you couldn't say I was thin either. The nicest thing I ever heard anyone say about me was a fisherman from Brittany who remarked to a chap he was having a drink with in the pub in the village that I was "*bien proportionée.*" At least I think he meant me. He might have been talking about Gussie, my father's thirteen-year-old Labrador who was lying on the floor beside me.

But *bien proportionée* or not, tonight a man had shown a smidgen of interest in me and my mother had knocked it on the head.

We'd been asked over for drinks at the McIntyres, who lived in a rambling old house sprawled along the top of the cliff like out-of-control bramble. I liked going there. The McIntyres accepted me for who I was. They didn't invite a single man for me. They knew I still lived at home and that I worked for my parents, and they didn't seem to think there was anything too sad about that. They never made me feel odd or different because I wasn't married and didn't have any children. Ronald McIntyre was the local vet, and he was always delighted that I appeared more interested in his patients than I did in his guests.

But tonight there was a man for me. Of course, he wasn't single. He'd arrived without his wife, who had remained in London sorting out some crisis. Ronald propelled me toward him, and my heart started to go *thump thump thump* because he was very much my type. Dark hair. Sad brown eyes. Fine features. Straight nose. Thin mouth. Yes, I know thin mouth is bad, says they're mean and cruel, but it's what I always go for.

Tall Dark Stranger (of course I was so covered in confusion when Ronald introduced us, I missed his name) and I talked for over an hour, and with each sentence I could feel self-esteem seeping back into me. I am attractive. I am interesting. I have read the books he's read and I've watched the television programs he's watched and he probably thinks I live some madly exciting life in London instead of . . .

My mother appeared at his elbow just as he asked me, "So what is it you do?"

"What do you mean, what does Annabel do? She doesn't do anything."

My mother moved to stand beside me. She had twenty-five years on me, but I could see him making comparisons. She applied her makeup like an expert. Her hair was freshly cut. Her jewelry was real—and so were the lines on her face, but it didn't seem to matter. Beside her I felt dowdy and old even if I didn't look it.

"Maybe you'll take her off our hands. High time someone did. I'd pay handsomely. Name your price."

There it was. The same old tired line she trotted out to all stray men who uttered more than half a sentence to me. Of course she'd hit the roof if someone actually did lure me away. She depended on me more than she cared to admit.

She made me sound like an old car that was in danger of being towed. And she actually winked at Tall Dark Stranger.

Well, after that there was nothing I could do. He switched his attention to her and never gave me another thought.

Now I'm really hopeless. I'm going to have a cigarette before I go to sleep. I know I'm supposed to have given up for the fifty-sixth time but what the hell. I even resisted when Tall Dark Stranger offered me one. We laughed about it. He said I ought to go and live in New York, when it seems they've banned smoking just about everywhere. Fat chance. How does someone like me ever get to go and live in America?

No, I'll have one last cigarette to console me and then I'll go to sleep and dream about Tall Dark Stranger.

I could kill my mother.

Be careful what you wish for.

3

Eddie Calder's wife thought he was hopeless. Well, he was—literally. He was without Hope, his wife of two and a half years, from Monday to Friday every week. She was on Long Island and he was in New York.

In Manhattan he stayed with her mother, Maisie Hofstater, in a rambling rent-controlled apartment in a prewar building on the Upper West Side, the same apartment in which Hope, the Hofstaters' only child, had grown up. It made sense, at least to the two women. Why should Eddie pay rent to someone else when he could stay with his mother-in-law for free? Why indeed? Except to have a little longed-for privacy.

Which he was never going to get while he was living with Maisie, on opinionated elderly woman with sagging jowls and dyed black hair who spoke endlessly on the telephone every evening to her friends, talking so loudly that quite often Eddie found himself driven to take a walk around the block to preserve his sanity. He had begun to view his own mother in a rather more appreciative light, she who had always told him to be more aggressive. He could hear her now: "Edward, honestly, you always settle for an easy life. It'll get you nowhere. You've got to fight for what you want."

She was absolutely right, bloody woman, Eddie thought affectionately, as he trundled down Riverside Drive on the

M5 bus on his way to work, occasionally tracking the progress of a steamer moving slowly up the Hudson to dock at a midtown pier. He really ought to stand up to Hope and her mother and insist on getting his own apartment in the city. Right now he was in deep shit. Hope had called the day before and asked him to ring his sister in London, and he'd forgotten. Hope's language on the phone that morning, when she'd called to ask him what Maud had said and discovered he'd done nothing, had been colorful. Eddie had felt tempted to call out to Maisie that she should tear herself away from her favorite radio program, *Imus in the Morning*, for half a second and pick up on the extension so she could get an earful of her daughter in full flow. But that would only present evidence of what Maisie was constantly hinting at in a none too subtle way: Her daughter had married a loser.

"What would you do, Mrs. R?" he asked the statue of Eleanor Roosevelt as the bus turned left on 72nd Street and continued its journey down Broadway. Eddie loved his bus ride to work. Sometimes it took as long as an hour to get from 105th Street to 22nd Street where the offices of the Gramercy Press were located, but the longer it took the better he liked it for it was the only time during the day when he was by himself.

He owed his job as a senior editor at GP to Hope. She hadn't got him the job as such. She wasn't in publishing. But it was because he was married to her, an American citizen, that he was able to stay in the United States without Immigration giving him any trouble.

He had come down from Cambridge with a 2.1 in English, feeling rather useless, and no one was more surprised than he when he landed a job as an editorial assistant at Random House UK. He strongly suspected it was his ability to drink other editors under the table in the pub at lunchtime that had brought him to the attention of the powers on high. Whatever, it had resulted in a meteoric rise to the position of junior editor.

On the strength of these numerous assets young Edward Calder found his name being put forward for the Tony Godwin Award. He won it and as a result was sent to New York to spend six weeks in the publishing house of his choice, observing what went on (a similar winner in New York came to a London publisher), and overnight he became Fast Eddie Calder.

Of course, underneath he was still dozy and dreamy and without much ambition other than to have himself a good time, helped along the way by as much alcoholic refreshment as was available. But the Americans in his office took to him and in their enthusiasm assumed he was as driven and focused as they were. Eddie, always happy to follow where others led, played the ambitious young publishing executive wannabe—with the added attraction of an English accent—for all it was worth, cheerfully assuming that since he was only going to be there for six weeks no one would notice that he wasn't doing a stroke of work.

He was right. Everyone thought he was a whiz kid in the making. Women literary agents took one look at the soft sandy hair flopping over his brow, his pale freckled skin, his kind brown eyes, and his engaging boyish grin and went wobbly at the knees.

"What a sweetheart," they told Clement Springer, the publisher at the Gramercy Press, "and so talented."

"Who's your favorite author on the Gramercy list?" Clem asked Eddie over a martini in his office during Eddie's penultimate week.

Eddie's mind went completely blank. He couldn't for the life of him remember a single author they published whom he'd ever read. He'd only chosen to go work at the Gramercy Press as his prize because he'd once had a drink in London with a pretty young female editor from there while she was on a trip to England. She was the only person in American publishing he'd ever heard of. But when he arrived in New York, anticipating with pleasure the notion of a follow-up drink with her, he discovered she'd married an author and gone to live in D.C.

His eye alighted on a slim volume bearing the Gramercy logo on the shelf just above Clem's head.

"Will Washington," he said quickly, and then deliberately spilled his drink so he wouldn't be quizzed further.

And he would have been, because Will Washington was a little-known African-American writer from Mississippi whose pathetic story about a sharecropper's son befriended by a civil rights poseur who took him to New York and left him to flounder had netted Gramercy close to zero sales.

What Eddie couldn't possibly have known was that Oprah Winfrey had been told about the book and it would later be her book club selection, thus catapulting it onto the best-seller list. At this point Clem told Eddie that if only there wasn't the small problem of securing a green card, he would be offered a position as senior editor immediately, given his obvious talent at spotting a winner.

"You gotta take it, man," said Larry Fredericks, who also worked at the press. "Hell, you gotta grab the opportunity with both hands and ride the fucker. Senior editor at GP. Way to go."

"Yes, of course," said Eddie politely. As far as he could make out, Larry was a cowboy from somewhere like Montana who could also read a book. Eddie was never quite sure during their many conversations about literature whether Larry was talking about a book or a bronco. Larry took him line dancing and paid him in bottles of Southern Comfort to write reports on manuscripts and put the initials LF at the bottom.

"Susie and I are taking a house in the Hamptons for the summer, so you come out and stay for a weekend. Say yes. Only thing to do."

Eddie said yes, please.

When he arrived one August morning he found paradise.

The house was a wooden shack right on the beach with no furniture except for beds, night tables with reading lamps, a large wooden table, and six giant chaise longues outside on the deck. The oven didn't work and the fridge contained no food, only six-packs of Budweiser piled on top of each other.

"We're house hunting," Larry told Eddie. "no more summer rentals. Fuckin' hassle, man. We're buyin'. We'll be out most of the day lookin' at properties. Brokers got us pooped outta our fuckin' skulls lookin' at places. Sorry to leave you on your own, but we'll take care of you in the evenin'. Count on it."

Eddie walked along Atlantic Avenue Beach from Amagansett to East Hampton and had to concede it was a step up from Margate and Cromer, the sum total of his beach experience back home. He walked back and was so exhausted he lay down on one of the chaises with a manuscript and a margarita (Larry had thoughtfully left a pitcherful balancing on top of the Buds). He had reached page 5 when the phone rang. Eddie stumbled about the deck, eyes blinking in the glare of the sun (he might have turned over five pages of the manuscript but he hadn't had his eyes open), trying to find where the outside phone was plugged in.

"Larry?" The voice was female, breathless and hurtling down the line at breakneck speed. "It's Hope Collins from Tudor Woods Realty. I'm so pleased I caught you. I'm running late. I'll explain when I see you. You walk right on over there and I'll be with you in twenty. You have the address. See you there. 'kay?"

"Wait a minute. They're not . . . I'm not—"

She'd hung up.

Shit, thought Eddie. Now what was he supposed to do? Through the haze of half a pitcher of margaritas he employed a little lateral thinking. Hope Somebody from Tudor Woods Realty. That was easy enough. He staggered indoors and opened the only closet he knew to contain objects other than liquor. Underneath a year's supply of toilet tissue he found a phone book.

"Tudor Woods International."

"I'd like to speak to Hope, please."

"She just left. Can I give you her voice mail?"

"No, please don't. Thank you," said Eddie quickly. "It's just she's gone to meet some friends of mine, Larry and Susie Frederickson, to show them a house, and they can't make it, and I thought maybe you could reach her on her mobile or something and head her off at the pass."

He was rather pleased with "head her off at the pass." He felt Larry would have approved.

"Sure thing."

He had just made it back to the deck and freshened his margarita when the phone rang again.

"This is Tudor Woods. We're sorry to have to tell you, but Hope seems to have switched off her mobile and we can't reach her right now. We rented you the house on the beach where you're calling from. Could you walk to the property she's on her way to and maybe, like, explain the situation to her? You could even look at it for your friends. It's not far. You just have to walk ten minutes along the beach. . . ."

I just did, he thought. I'm bloody knackered.

But Easy-life Eddie did as he was told.

He found the house without any problem and walked up the steps from the beach and around the deck to the front entrance. No sign of a car. He rang the doorbell. No answer. Hope whatever-her-name-was wasn't there yet. He settled down on the front porch to wait.

Half an hour later he was still there and just about to give up and stomp back through the dunes to finish off the margarita when a black two-seater Toyota screeched up the drive.

A tiny whirlwind in the shortest skirt Eddie had ever seen was out of the car and racing past him into the house before he could even get to his feet.

"Larry, I can't tell you. I'm so sorry. I am just so sorry. It's the fourth time this year. I am fit to be tied. I had to go back and check they're okay. They're with a sitter and they've never had her before and who knows? You and Susie have kids?"

"No. I'm not—"

"Well, anyway, I'm sure you understand."

"I'm sure I do but what do I understand?" asked Eddie in despair, suddenly realizing that he was still in his bathing trunks and feeling like a complete nerd. She was standing there staring at his bare chest and knobbly knees.

She was sensationally pretty. Petite. Dark curly hair about her head like a poodle's. Her tan was dark gold, accentuated by a little white sleeveless shift that barely covered her thighs. Eddie thought she was wearing an unnecessary amount of gold jewelry. He had always found bangles particularly distasteful, and the large crucifix was surely a bit over the top. But the thing that really horrified him was her black nail polish. Fingers and toes.

"My nanny's quit," she wailed. "Again!"

She looked completely helpless and Eddie, like an idiot, felt an overriding urge to protect her for the rest of her life.

"Your office obviously didn't reach you. I'm not Larry Frederickson. I'm his friend, Eddie Calder. I'm staying with him, and I came over—"

"So you're not the party interested in this property?"

"No, I—"

"Shit! This is a totally wasted trip."

"No, it isn't," protested Eddie. "You could show me and I could tell them all about it."

She shrugged.

"What can it hurt? You have sand on your feet. Let's start with I show you the outside shower, and you can rinse them."

She led him around the side to a wooden platform with a nozzle above it protruding from the wall of the house. Eddie turned one of the faucets.

"Here." She reached out and grabbed Eddie's left leg and guided his foot under the water. Her touch was unexpectedly gentle, and her fingers on the sole of his foot sent an instant signal to his penis. Eddie hoped she'd think his blushing was due to the sun and not his embarrassment about the erection that was fighting to escape from his swimming trunks. That was the trouble with having fair freckled skin. He turned bright red at the slightest provocation.

He turned away hurriedly so she wouldn't see and in doing so brushed against her so she half fell and landed under the falling water. The white shift was immediately drenched.

"*Shit!*" she yelled again, reached behind her neck, and unzipped the dress, stepping out of it in the same single fluid movement with which she had got out of the car.

Her bikini was pink gingham with a white *broderie anglaise* frill. Half-cut bra. High-cut panties.

Shit! thought Eddie, as she scrunched up her dress and disappeared into the house as if nothing had happened, leaving him to wash his right foot on his own and follow her through the kitchen, the breakfast room with its view of the ocean, the family room, the laundry room, the downstairs bathroom, the split-level living room with dining area, the hallway that ran from front to back porch. Upstairs were four relatively small bedrooms overlooking the drive, a bathroom, a shower room, and, at the back of the house, the master bedroom and bath.

"The pièce de résistance," she said, throwing open the door to reveal a king-size bed and a breathtaking view of the ocean.

And then her mobile rang.

He jumped, lost his balance, and put his hand out to steady himself, and it landed on her bare waist. He found himself caressing her hip as she answered the call.

"Yeah, I know. I found him. I'm showing him the house now. . . . Oh, they are?. . . . Well, fine, we'll expect them. Terrific. 'Bye."

While she was talking Eddie had moved his hand slowly downward and inside the elastic of her bikini bottom.

"Okay," said Hope Collins, looking him straight in the eye, "you have a finger almost inside me and that was my office on the line to say your friends, my clients, are back and they're walking along the beach to join us. What are you going to do?"

Now was not the time to think of his mother, but Eddie couldn't help remembering her pleading for him to be a little more aggressive. Mum, he thought, if you could see me now.

He withdrew his finger and pressed himself against Hope, who obligingly opened her mouth, allowing him to plunge his tongue inside it.

There was a full-length mirror on the wall beside them, and Eddie could see them reflected in it. It was an image he would never forget. A tiny frantic little poodle in a pink gingham bikini clinging to him as if she couldn't get enough of his fair sunburned body. As they collapsed on the bed he saw the magnificent view of the ocean replace them in the mirror.

Eddie was secretly relieved that Larry and Susie arrived before they could actually have sex. It was pathetic of him, he knew, but he didn't think he could have handled it if it had been wham-bam thank-you-ma'am, and then have to pretend total innocence to Larry and Susie. It wasn't his style. He wasn't Cool Eddie. He was a rough-and-tumble overgrown schoolboy, "really rather sweet" Eddie (in the words of his last girlfriend back home in London), who was no match for the likes of Hope Collins.

He had enough presence of mind to know that even if they stood up and dusted themselves off and were standing miles apart, they probably wouldn't fool Larry, so he grabbed Hope's hand, led her into the walk-in closet, and shut the door.

This was fun. This was more like it. This was schoolboy prankster stuff and he felt quite at home. They stood in the closet holding hands very tightly while Larry and Susie wandered through the house, Larry going "Hey! Anyone here? Nope. Car's still here. Guess she must have gone for a swim. Her dress is on the porch. I've heard that's what they do, these brokers. You have a house on the beach; they ask to use the bathroom to change; then they go right out and swim while they're here. Let's go look. Wonder if Eddie made it over."

Eddie knew that most guys would have flung her straight back down on the bed once they were alone again. But by that time the moment had passed. He'd gone back to being the old Eddie, so he escorted her politely downstairs.

And he had no idea that by the time he had opened the car door for her he'd unwittingly negotiated himself a potential role in Hope Collins's life. Eddie imagined she'd think him a nerd. He little knew that she felt quite the opposite, that for the first time since Craig had left her she found herself attracted to another man. There was something different about this one that she couldn't quite put her finger on. All she knew was that she was aching to finish things off with this unusually shy creature with silky hair and baby skin.

But of course she knew better than to let him know.

Instead, she stuck her head out the window and yelled, as she drove away, "By the way, tell your friends the asking price is eight hundred thousand."

Luckily only the male Calders were hopeless. Eddie's father had been fired from his job when Eddie was ten, but he hadn't dared tell Eddie's mother for six months. He had had to confess when they ran out of money. Eddie had never known whether his mother had thrown his father out in disgrace or whether he had left of his own accord. All he knew was that his sister, Maud, was a complete star in their mother's eyes and he was nowhere, despite the fact that *he* had produced a grandchild.

Maud was the opposite of Eddie. Tough, chain-smoking,

twice engaged to be married but never made it to the altar. No children. At least two abortions. She was a newspaper columnist and had once written a Dear Abby column for a woman's magazine. For this reason, Eddie assumed, his request was something she could easily cope with. Not so.

"Hope wants me to do *what*?"

For the second time that day Eddie held the phone at arm's length to avoid the perforation of his eardrum by female screeching. He was trying to scrape his lunch—takeout pizza, extra pepperoni—from the pristine photocopied first page of an extremely important manuscript that had just arrived on his desk. As he did so he realized that the sogginess of the pizza had penetrated much deeper than the first page. The entire manuscript was now slightly damp and smelled of onions. What on earth had induced him to take it out of the box?

"Maud, hold on a sec."

"Edward, why me?"

"She thought you'd know about stuff like that. We need a new nanny. Hope wants an English one. Don't ask me why. The fucking *Lady* won't run an ad for an American. Hope wants you to place the ad and interview for her. Easy."

"Don't be absurd. That woman you're married to has some nerve."

As much as Maud claimed she didn't want them—"You know my views on children. Find some magic ointment to make them invisible at birth and I'd be happy"—Eddie knew there was a part of his sister that felt she had failed by not having any.

"Maud," he wheedled, "do it for me. Do it for your nieces, and nephews. You adore them. You want the best for them. You know you do."

But not as much as you adore me. Eddie knew he could wind his big sister around his little finger. He was the child Maud had never had. It was a trump card he played for all it was worth.

"I only have a niece," Maud told him tartly. "The other two are hers, not yours. She's really taken you for a sucker, Edward. Why you ever married her is beyond—"

"All right, Maud. Don't start."

"Now you sound like your mother-in-law. You've let that family take you over, Edward. By the way, have you rung your own mother recently?"

"What's wrong with Mother?" he asked nervously. He lived in terror of being lectured by either his mother or Maud but at least he could win Maud over pretty quickly. His mother was a different story.

"She wants you to come over with Booty this summer and see her."

"I'm not sure Hope can get away. It's a very busy time of year for her, the summer season."

"Who said anything about Hope? She wants you and her granddaughter. I thought I'd better warn you. I don't think Hope's invited."

"Shit. She's not starting all that up again."

"Well, maybe you'd like to call her and ask her to place the ad and do all the interviewing stuff?"

"Maud, please. I'll owe you. Name your price. What's it worth?"

"Don't worry. If I find myself devoting another second to this knotty little problem of yours you'll owe me big time, to use one of your wife's vulgar expressions."

"Maud. She did specify a Norland-trained nanny."

"Edward, as I think I've told you for the last thirty years, don't push your luck."

To Eddie's astonishment, she called back a week later.

"Edward, you're in luck. I've found you one."

"One what? Oh, a nanny. Christ. Have you really? What have you done with her?"

"I've done damn all with her except note her particulars. I think the rest is up to you. Her name is Annabel, Annabel Quick, and she's from Cornwall. Here, let me give you her phone number. She's expecting to hear from either you or Hope ASAP. Tell Hope to call me herself and I'll give her all the details. I can't tell you the time I've had finding her."

Eddie settled back in his chair. Maud was going to make a real meal out of this, he could tell.

"I placed the ad. I've been interviewing nannies all week. You wouldn't believe the demands they make. They want a car, their own flat, full membership in a gym where they can dump their charge in a nursery and go and lie in the steam room, weekends off, and, in London, three hundred and fifty pounds a week. And most of them are total idiots. They sit there nattering about Crescendo classes, Gym babes, YMCA Tumble tots, play groups, recreational centers. I mean, have you ever heard of Bunny Parks or Snakes and Ladders? The only highlights were when they ratted on their employers. Of course I only probed when I knew the people they worked for."

"Of course," said Eddie. Maud was the most indiscreet person he'd ever come across. She couldn't keep a confidence to save her life. To give her her due, she wasn't really aware of what she was doing half the time. She just opened her mouth and out it all came. The request "Maud, you must promise to keep this to yourself" was a complete waste of time.

"Yes. There was this girl who worked for the Greers, people I know socially, and she told me they have separate rooms. They don't sleep together, haven't for three years apparently. He sleeps in a dreadful loft conversion they had done at the top of the house every night, but when you go into their bedroom you'd never know. And there was this other girl, who worked for a woman on the paper. A single mother—divorcée—and she's having an affair with the husband of another woman who works on the financial pages. The girl said he comes round every weekend and she has to take the children out for a couple of hours. He tells his wife he's at football. The mother told her all about it."

"But this one, what's-her-name, Annabel? You don't think she'll be like that?"

"Not at all. She's sweet. Adorable. Exquisite manners. Loads of experience. Just what you want. And by the way, Edward. . . ."

"Yes?"

"She's Norland trained."

"So I owe you . . ."

"Big time. No. More than that. You owe me *mega* time, Edward." And with that she hung up.

Eddie put the phone down slowly. There was something very fishy going on. He knew his sister. She detested Hope. He'd always thought they were two of a kind—driven, ambitious—but Hope had several advantages over Maud that Maud would rather die than admit. She was younger than Maud, prettier, and worst of all she'd pried him away from his family.

Suddenly Eddie felt rather uncomfortable about the fact that Maud was in the process of planting what amounted to a spy in his household. Would this nanny repeat back to Maud everything she witnessed between him and Hope?

Pray God that Hope knew what she was doing in allowing Maud to get involved in their lives.

Pray God.

4

They say a woman never really grows up until her mother dies. If this is true—and if it can apply to someone whose mother was burned to death in a horrific fire—I didn't become an adult until I was forty-seven. But I honestly believe that Hope and Eddie Calder had a lot more to do with it than my mother's death.

I first heard about Hope from my friend, Maud. I say friend. Most people would rather die than acknowledge Maud as their friend, but I've always been fond of her in some weird way I can't quite figure out. We're not remotely alike. Maud is tough as hell, or at any rate she likes to give that impression. She works in the media and I think I'm right in saying that she's currently a print journalist. I'm never entirely sure which paper or magazine she's writing for, and this drives her crazy so I generally keep quiet about it. What I do know is that she once wrote an advice column, but that's one thing she never wants to be reminded of.

She's the most competitive creature I know. A cozy post-prandial game of Scrabble will turn into a nightmare fight to the death with Maud. She berates me every time I lose a single game, accuses me of not trying hard enough. When I protest, "It's only a game of Scrabble," she just doesn't get it. I have to want to win—whatever it is.

I suppose that's part of my trouble. I'm a touch lazy. Why,

you may well ask, was I still living at home with my parents at age forty-seven? The truth of the matter is that there seemed no reason to change things. Until now. I lived in a beautiful house on the Cornish coast. I had a job. I had a man. Why rock the boat?

Then, in the space of one horrendous week, it all fell apart. I lost my parents. The house was nearly burned to the ground and became virtually uninhabitable. With the house I lost the job. And then I lost the man. But I'm not about to go into that now.

I suppose I should fill in the background. I worked for my parents. I suppose you could say we had a family business. My father, Colonel Felix Quick, DSO (he was honored for holding a bridge in Normandy in World War II, thus preventing the Germans from advancing and capturing a lunatic asylum on the other side), retired from the army just as I was wondering what to do with my life. Although why I wasted any time wondering is beyond me. My mother, Marietta Quick, was sensationally bossy. The day I left school she presented me with a plan.

"You're going to nanny school, Annabel," she announced.

"I thought I was going to art school," I protested. I rather fancied myself as the artistic type. Bit of a free spirit. Translation: no responsibilities.

"With no academic qualifications whatsoever?" Marietta's retort had a decidedly triumphant tone. In those days you needed at least five O levels. I had three. All languages. "At least she'll be able to speak," commented my father, grumpy as ever. To be honest he wasn't really grumpy. It was kind of a self-defense mechanism that kicked in whenever Marietta became particularly overpowering.

"I could re-sit my exams," I suggested.

"Waste of time." Marietta dismissed me cheerfully. "Norlands. You can start in the autumn."

"But why?" The thought of looking after other people's

children filled me with dread. I was an only child, but some of my school friends had younger siblings and they were little pests.

"Because when I've turned Rosemullion into a bed and breakfast and the guests bring their children, your experience will be invaluable. I can offer a baby-sitting service by a Norland-trained nanny—at a price, of course."

I suppose it was around this time that I realized what my father had had to put up with all those years. Marietta had an irritating habit of forming a grand plan in her head and only informing all other affected parties once she was about to put it into action.

Talking of action, my father missed it dreadfully. During the postwar years he went into a deep depression. He simply could not exchange his army uniform for a business suit. And although it irks me to admit it, we would have been lost without Marietta's resilience, not to mention her entrepreneurial skills.

They'd bought Rosemullion, an eighteenth-century house standing above thatched fishermen's cottages in grounds leading down to the rocky inlet of a cove below, on my father's retirement, but it was clear they didn't have the means to keep it going, so Marietta blew the last of her capital on transforming it into a small hotel. I can still recall the evening she spent sitting at the kitchen table in her housecoat agonizing over the wording of the brochure she was going to have printed to lure potential guests from all over the country for their summer holidays. Finally she settled on:

Felix and Marietta Quick welcome nonsmoking guests into their beautiful house, where they hope its relaxing atmosphere amid antiques, log fires,

Blah blah blah! I wanted no part of it. But a few years later I really didn't have much choice.

I went to Norland. I wheeled a Silver Cross pram round and round the grounds at Hungerford as part of my training. It was a bit like what I imagined I would have encountered had I been sent to boarding school. We slept in dormitories with cubicles with the baby in a cradle beside us. We trained with real babies. People actually left their infants with us to use as guinea pigs. My baby's mother had had to move unexpectedly and she couldn't handle taking care of an infant at the same time. So he came to Norland to be entrusted to my tender care. Poor brat. He's probably scarred for life. The other reason it was like boarding school was that everything had to be marked with name tapes. Flannelette nighties. No Babygros in those days. Even the diapers had to be name-taped. Twelve gauze and twelve terry-cloth ones, all marked with baby's name.

And when I graduated I was employed right away. Marietta was thrilled. Everything was going according to plan. I'd work in London for a few years, and if I didn't get married right away—marriage was part of Marietta's plan for me, provided he was a suitable catch—I'd come home and help run Rosemullion.

The only problem was, I screwed up in a major way. I caused a scandal. It went like this.

My first job was fine. I looked after a newborn baby and then the family moved away. Then I took care of a sullen eleven-year-old whose family had so many servants running around after her there was very little for me to do. Fine by me. It was the height of sixties London and I was out discovering sex.

I came unstuck on job number three. He was called Jasper. I was hired to look after Marcus, age four, Marybelle, seven, and Arabella, nine. Jasper was twenty-two and a son from the father's first marriage. From day one I was completely out of my depth with Marcus, Marybelle, and Arabella, and it had nothing to do with having to call out their ludicrously pretentious names every five minutes. They were little terrors, but I think I would have coped if I hadn't started having sex with Jasper on my second night in the house.

He had his own apartment on the top floor, and he had me creep up the stairs in the middle of the night and crawl into bed beside him. I thought it was love. I assumed we'd get married. I believed it was only a matter of time before I would be welcomed into the bosom of the family, not as the nanny but as the young bride. I put Jasper's reluctance to announce our future together down to shyness. Rather sweet!

When the parents summoned me to come downstairs one evening and drink a champagne toast to Jasper's engagement I still didn't get it.

She was a blonde. She wore a blue hairband, pearls, and a pale blue sleeveless shift. I have come to terms with the fact that I will remember these details till the day I die. I suppose any normal person would have grown up there and then. Wised up, more likely. Men are bastards. Men aren't what they seem. Men lie.

But I didn't grow up. I just ran home to Mummy and clammed up. The only people I talked to were the fishermen down at the cove and, like the crabs they caught, I developed a protective outer shell. Inside I was a mass of vulnerable quivering crab meat, but I was damned if I was going to let anyone have a taste. I didn't know all of this at the time, of course. It is only now, years later, as I face a major turning point in my life, that I realize that this was the experience that would inform my decision to hide away down in Cornwall, using my parents and Rosemullion as protection.

Protection from what? They couldn't protect me from Guy. From being loved by him. And being hurt by him.

But I cannot bleat about a broken love affair when my parents have just died.

Yet I can't stop thinking about him. I was wondering where he was, what he was doing, even as I was traipsing around the ashes of Rosemullion with the miserable bureaucratic character from the insurance company. What do they call them? Adjusters. He kept going on about waiting for the report from the fire department and how it would take weeks, maybe months, and I mustn't worry.

The fire had started in the middle of the night. There had been no guests. Only Felix and Marietta, asleep in their bedroom, and me in mine at the other end of the house.

They died: burned to death, smoke inhalation—I couldn't bear to dwell on the details.

I survived. The first I knew the place was ablaze was when a burly fireman smashed the glass of my bedroom window and climbed in to rescue me. Now I understand why firemen have to be big and strong. He needed the strength and the grip of a gorilla to hold me in his arms and keep me from running back into the house to try and save my parents.

Rosemullion was an old rectory. It stood right beside the church, and I buried Felix and Marietta in the walled graveyard at the top of the cliffs. They carried the coffins out of the church, past the blackened ruins of the house, to twin plots in with the rows of fishermen drowned at sea.

Some of Felix's brother officers traveled from all over the country, but I noted that Marietta's grand girlfriends from her former life merely sent flowers. Cornwall was just too far away—except in August, at Rock, when Prince William and Prince Harry went there for a week's surfing.

Maud didn't come either. Well, that was no surprise. Maud hadn't been back to Rosemullion since she and her mother and brother had come as paying guests one summer. That was how we'd met. Teenage girls giggling together and flirting with the fishermen's sons learning from their fathers, attempting to strut about in front of us in their great big rubber waders and then pushing us up against the boathouses for some awkward groping under cover of darkness.

I recalled there was some scandal about Maud's father

that Marietta had sniffed out almost immediately, as was her wont. He'd run away or something. I never understood whether Maud's mother had thrown him out in disgrace or whether he'd left of his own accord.

I had never forgotten Mrs. Calder. In those pre-Jasper years, it was the first time I had seen what being hurt and betrayed did to a person, how it hardened the face and embittered the spirit. But Mrs. Calder was determined to see that her children were successful despite what had happened. Maud, unlike me, had turned out according to plan. I might not fully understand what it was she did, but she was clearly good at it. And loyal. She held my hand throughout the whole Jasper crisis and was the only one of my London friends to stay in touch. Even if she did always insist I go there. Maud didn't operate outside major cities, so a trip to Land's End was out of the question.

She telephoned me about a month after the fire and summoned me to London to stay with her in her little bijou house behind Kensington High Street.

"I've got you here under false pretense," she shouted at me, as she opened her front door. Maud always shouted. She had a plastic cigarette holder dangling from her lips. "Don't look at me like that. There's no need to go all high and mighty on me just because you've given up. I'm trying, God help me. These things collect the tar or the grunge from cigarettes that kill you. I'm supposed to look at it and go *aaaargh! I'm stopping smoking at once!* But of course all I do is look at it and throw the bloody thing away and light another. I'm sorry I didn't make it to the funeral."

"I never for one moment thought that you would." It was a bit like that, our friendship. Maud throwing out superficial apologies, promises, and compliments she didn't really mean and me throwing them back at her with rather bad grace. "What are the real pretenses if you've got me here under false ones?"

"I know I'm supposed to commiserate with you about your parents but as you know I'm pretty useless about that sort of thing so I'll just say very quickly that I'm sorry and move on swiftly to tell you my latest Hope horror story."

I knew all about Maud's loathing of her sister-in-law, "that woman" who had got her hands on Maud's beloved little brother. Edward, as far as I could make out, was an afterthought, born fourteen years after Maud, and the closest thing Maud had ever had to a child of her own. I could just about remember a toddler clinging to Maud's mother when they'd come to Rosemullion. One of the things I had always loved about Maud was her unconditional love for her brother. Maybe it had something to do with the father leaving.

"You won't believe what she's done now," Maud went on. "Come in, put your bags down. I'm taking you out to lunch. There's a new Japanese opened just round the corner."

"I don't like Japanese."

"I know you don't. High time you did." Typical Maud reaction. "She called and asked me to put an ad in *The Lady* for her."

"What on earth for?"

"A nanny. She wants an English nanny and they don't allow Americans to place ads. Can you imagine? If I didn't want the best for my brother's child I'd have Louise Woodward cloned and send her over on Concorde."

"I thought Louise Woodward was okay in the end."

"That's a matter of opinion. But I'd make sure her clone was really evil. I'd program her to annihilate Hope."

"So did you place the ad?" I asked once we were seated. "I'm not having raw fish, Maud. And I don't want any of that green stuff that makes your nose run."

"Wasabi. Horseradish. That's all it is. All right. No sashimi. I'll order you some tempura."

"What's that?"

"Don't act so suspicious. Just because you insist in living

out in the sticks, there's no need to behave like a complete hick. . . . My guest will have the tempura dinner and I'll have some yakitori, miso soup, ten pieces of *maguro*, and a salad. And we'd better have some sake. Oh, and a packet of Marlboro Lights. Yes"—she turned back to me—"I've been seeing girls all week. But I haven't hired any of them."

"Why's that?"

"Because I've had a better idea, and I'm looking right at her."

"You think I might be able to find you a nanny just because I was one over twenty years ago?"

"No, darling, I think you could *be* one again."

In many ways Maud was rather like my mother. She had Marietta's nasty little habit of forming a plan in her head and then springing it unexpectedly and assuming you'd fall right in with it.

"Don't say a word till you've heard me out." Maud was holding up a warning finger even though I hadn't even opened up my mouth. "I need someone I can trust to tell me about Hope and Edward. All about Hope, anyway."

"You can't!" I was horrified by this notion of Maud's recruiting a spy, whether it involved me or not.

"I bloody well can. Hope's a little tart. I know it. Sticks out a mile. I bet she's having it off on the side while Edward's in Manhattan all week. Nympho. Flighty trollop."

"You're talking about your own sister-in-law."

"Precisely. Mummy and I agree. We've got to get Edward away from Hope."

"You want to break up a marriage? Don't they have a child?"

"They have three. That's half the problem. Two of them are Hope's by her first marriage. Edward doesn't seem to realize what he's taken on. The nannies leave one after the other, and I worry about Booty."

"Booty?"

"Caitlin. Edward's baby daughter. So that's what I wanted to have a moan about. The last thing I want to do is help Hope out, but this is a golden opportunity for me to place a spy in East Hampton by finding her a nanny. She's so obsessed with status she thinks an English nanny's just the ticket, and she's got this idiotic notion that I can find her Mary Poppins just like that and it'll be the answer to all her problems."

"Well, you wrote an advice column, didn't you? How did the letters start? Dear Auntie Maud?"

"Shut up. We all have to start somewhere."

"Has she specified any particular requirements?"

"She wants a Norland-trained nanny. Now do you get the picture? Who else could I think of but you? I mean, what are you going to do with your life now, Annabel? Did you plan on taking over the running of Rosemullion yourself?"

"There's nothing to run at the moment. All the bedrooms were destroyed in the fire. I can't just offer breakfast."

"It might be a blessing in disguise if you stop to think about it. You can't bury yourself down in Cornwall all your life—what's left of it anyway. It's not as if you're bloody Daphne du Maurier writing best-sellers at Manderley."

"Menabilly."

"Who Billy?"

"Menabilly. It's the name of the house Daphne du Maurier rented for twenty-five years. It wasn't called Manderley in real life, it was called Menabilly."

"Well, whatever." Maud didn't like to be corrected on the lives of celebrities. "Look, I'm not knocking Rosemullion. Jolly good billet if you're in that part of the world. But don't you feel the need for a bit of excitement? Fun and games in London? Get in touch with the youth culture? I get more from the kids in the office, frankly, than any of my boring old girlfriends. All women our age seem to talk about is how they're getting on with the Kensington diet, whether their upper arms are flabby or can they still wear sleeveless dresses, and can they still get away with short skirts when their knees have fallen to the extent they have more folds than a bloodhound's face. It's either that or an even more boring discussion about what stage one's parents have reached on the dementia scale. Is it time to put the old dears in a home or convert the basement into a granny flat? Not that they'll ever agree to do either, of course."

"That's one problem I won't have." I couldn't resist. It was the only way to be with Maud, who was even less aware of her lack of tact than she was about her inability to be discreet. "Maybe they should all start accidental fires."

Maud had the grace to look a little ashamed. At any rate she didn't mention the stupid nanny idea again and began to talk, quite sweetly for Maud, about my parents and how much she'd always liked them. It was only as I was huddled up in a corner seat on the long train journey back to Penzance that I remembered she'd only met them once.

Something happened while I was in London. Normally I was thrilled to get back home to Land's End. I had never craved London life. But this time I was restless. Maud's conversation over lunch rumbled through my head day and night. "Don't you feel the need for a bit of excitement?" she'd asked. I knew what she meant, but the truth of it was that I needed to get away from excitement. I'd had excitement in spades. Your house burns down, your parents die, your man gives you grief? You need a rest.

But it was much more than that. There was a great deal I hadn't told Maud. True, I was mourning my parents and a change is as good as a rest, as they say. The trouble with death is that once it enters your life you see it everywhere. Like love. Only instead of realizing that the lyrics of dumb love songs suddenly speak to you for the first time, you turn on the television and there's *NYPD Blue* and death all over the sidewalk. You pick up a thriller to take your mind off

things and of course there's a death on the first page. You begin to notice hearses. You trip over dead birds.

And while I was grieving for Marietta, and it was true her
absence left a giant hole in my life, I couldn't help feeling a
rather guilty sense of being liberated in some way. I had lived
in her shadow for so many years. A psychiatrist would probably have a field day with me. I'd had a terrible shock and I
still couldn't look at anything of Felix's without bursting into
tears, but suddenly I had been granted my freedom. Not in a
textbook way perhaps but even so, if there was ever a time
when I could become the free spirit I had always dreamed of
being, this was it.

Except of course I was running away. I had always had a
hard time facing up to my problems, and, boy, did I have a
few now! It was pathetic, but one of the good things about
Marietta was the way she'd always sorted out all the things
that went wrong in my life. She would try and make me deal
with them, but she always became so infuriated by the way
I'd let everything slide in my dreamy fashion that she invariably wound up taking care of business herself. Along with
everything else. At seventy-two, she might not have been in a
position to go nipping up ladders inspecting roofs at
Rosemullion, but she was still capable of picking up the telephone and summoning whoever—or whatever—it took.
Marietta was never one of the world's delegators. She'd kept
just as beady an eye on the people who worked for her as she
had on her paying guests at Rosemullion. But she wasn't
around anymore. I'd have to face up to the mess I was in and
sort it out myself. I wasn't seventeen, twenty-seven, or even
thirty-seven. I was forty-seven. A forty-seven-year-old innocent about to go out into the world on her own for the first
time.

Because that's what I had known I would do from the
minute Maud started talking. I looked up East Hampton in
the atlas. There it was, on the eastern end of Long Island,

sticking out into the Atlantic like a long arm summoning me. Land's End on the opposite side of the ocean. I hadn't realized it was by the sea. It was as if it was meant to be.

If I was going to grow up, now was the time. I'd been given a golden opportunity. I'd been to America a few times with Guy: New York, Boston, Washington, D.C. It wouldn't be a total shock to the system. I'd go to East Hampton and do the nanny thing for a few weeks and then jack it in and come home to deal with the reopening of Rosemullion. By then I'd know if I was safe. If I was in the clear. And if I had got Guy completely out of my system.

But when I called Maud and told her yes, I would go and be Hope Calder's nanny I didn't tell her it would only be for a short time or that I was leaving behind a trail of dangerous loose ends. In fact, I didn't mention any of my problems, not least the fact that I had just lost my driver's license.

Or that if anybody needed a nanny, it was me.

5

"No," said Booty firmly.

Oh, shit, thought Hope. This was going to be one of Booty's "no" days. There were days when she just said no to whatever she was asked.

"Is the Princess up?"

"No."

"Coco! Out of bed, sweetheart."

"I *am* out of bed. I'm dressed." Coco appeared at the door of her room, extremely indignant. This was a major first. Coco up, dressed, and no mention of *Beethoven*. That had never happened before, not even when Rachel had been around. Of course she wasn't dressed for school. That would have been too much to ask. She was wearing her tutu with pink tights and her pink satin ballet slippers.

"My lippers," said Booty immediately, pointing at them.

"No," said Coco. "Mine."

"No," said Booty, furious. "No! No! No!"

Hope could see a major incident brewing. The problem was that when Coco was at school, Booty wore her pink ballet slippers all the time. Booty thought they were hers. Rachel had discussed it with Hope, and Hope, rushed and preoccupied by work as usual, had said, "Oh, let her wear Coco's slippers if she wants to." Coco only wore them for her ballet lessons. The trouble was, Booty now wanted to wear them all the time. It was getting to the stage where she wouldn't go anywhere if she didn't wear the slippers, or at least got to take them with her in the car. Booty's going to be tall, Hope reflected, because she has such big feet already that Coco's ballet slippers almost fit her. But right now, she decided, no one was going to wear the damned slippers.

"Coco, honey, put your clothes on, please."

"But I have to look special. We're going to the airport to pick up Mary Poppins."

"No one wears tutus to airports," said Hope, wondering if other mothers had this kind of dialogue with their children first thing in the morning. "And besides, you have to go to school first. Annabel's plane doesn't get in until this evening."

Normally Philomena only came in the mornings, but since Rachel's departure she had agreed to stay on until Hope came home from work. Hope's one small blessing was that Booty adored the housekeeper and was happy to be left in her care. Philomena was a Filipino and the most docile, subservient creature Hope had ever encountered. She drove Hope insane. She padded about the house picking up after everyone, cleaning, polishing, and humming. It was the humming that Hope couldn't stand. Philomena always sounded so happy in her work, but how could she be? Hope had once sat Philomena down and told her that she did not expect her to stay with them for longer than six months and after that she, Hope, would personally help Philomena find a "proper job." Philomena had promptly burst into tears. She wanted to stay with Hope. She didn't want to be sent back to her country. She had her mama and her papa to support, and her little brothers and sisters.

Mortified at what she had unleashed, Hope had been assuaging her guilt by giving Philomena almost monthly raises. Now at least she would be earning them by taking care of Booty.

Spring was a frantic time for Hope, especially the weekends when people were driving out to the Hamptons from Manhattan to find houses to rent for the summer season. They were a fickle lot, the renters. Hope found that she was always landed with the meanest clients, the ones who wanted a waterfront property with a pool and at least four bedrooms but only wanted to pay $15,000 for the entire season. In their dreams!

Why did she always get these people? Hope was deeply suspicious of the up-call system that was in operation at Tudor Woods. Incoming calls to the switchboard were rotated by the receptionist to the next broker available to take a call, which was supposed to mean that everyone took pot luck, everyone got a crack at the big sales, and in turn everyone had their fair share of difficult clients. It was just a matter of chance. Or was it? How come I never get to deal with straightforward upscale clients who know what they want and have the money to pay for it? How come I always get the clients from hell? Hope suspected it had something to do with a new young male broker called Mark. She had a hunch that Mark stole clients from her, but so far she had been unable to uncover concrete evidence.

At least she had Eddie on the weekends to help out with the kids. Not that he was much use. Although he was always complaining about the way she spoiled them, Hope couldn't help noticing he gave them as much ice cream as they wanted, let them watch totally unsuitable videos, ensured their clothes became completely filthy within seconds, and made rash, unrealistic promises, leaving her to deal with the consequences during the week. She'd had to renege on so many of his promises it made her seem like a monster in the kids' eyes. The worst was the time he'd told them they could have a puppy and Mommy would take them to the pound to choose one. Hope told him if he tried that one more time, she would take *him* to the pound and leave him there. The kids overheard her. From then on, if Eddie made any attempt to discipline them, they turned on him. "Mommy's going to take you to the pound! Mommy's going to take you to the pound!"

Hope knew she shouldn't be asking herself such a question but she couldn't help wondering what Craig would do with the kids at weekends. Whatever he did it would be a far cry from the lovable chaos Eddie went in for, which, despite his determination to maintain the English way of parenting, involved more hugging and affection than discipline and structure. Craig was always going on about structure, and Hope never really understood what he meant except that, whatever it was, Eddie didn't provide it.

She reflected that since her ex-husband called every morning to speak to Harry and Coco, and Eddie only called on Fridays to say which bus he was taking from the city so she could meet him, and given that she was usually showing houses all weekend, it could be argued that she actually spoke more to Craig than she did to Eddie.

And now Craig was coming to New York.

She hadn't told the kids yet.

And she certainly hadn't told Eddie.

The kids. Harry and Coco.

Booty presumably wasn't included in the invitation.

It was in two or three weeks' time. Annabel Quick would be there, broken in and ready to cope with Booty at the weekend. Wouldn't she?

Which left Eddie.

Well, Annabel could be a nanny to him too. God knows, he needed one.

But what about all those renters coming out on weekends to look at houses? Mark would step in and take all that commission away from her.

How on earth was she going to explain her children to Annabel Quick? For the first time, Hope began to wish she knew a little more about her new nanny. The references Maud had sent were impeccable. Almost too good to be true. Something funny about that, Hope thought. And Maud had said she was as close to Mary Poppins as Hope could possibly get, and then laughed. What was that all about? Hope had had a letter of acceptance from Annabel, handwritten in elegant script on very smart stationery, thick gray vellum with the name ROSEMULLION at the top. It had been a simple letter, notable in its absence of girlish overstatement. Nowhere did Annabel say that she was "so thrilled to be coming to America to look after Hope's wonderful family" or that "the pictures of the kids were the cutest she'd ever seen." The sort of thing, Hope realized, she would have written at that age. Annabel Quick sounded like a very mature young woman. Well, Hope reflected, she would just have to rely on Maud, who had assured her that she'd taken care of all the proper details. There was no point in bothering about applying for a work permit until the three-month trial period they'd agreed on was over.

Then of course Hope had been showing houses when Annabel had tried to call her, so Eddie had spoken to her.

"What did she sound like?"

"Fine."

"Fine? What do you mean, fine? Fine how? Fine as in bouncy and cheerful or fine as in looking forward to meeting us or what?"

"None of the above especially. She just said Maud had asked her to call you with her flight details so you could meet her at JFK."

"Oh, okay. When's she coming? Where did you put the flight details? Because if it's during the day, forget it, Eddie, I'm—"

"I didn't get the flight details. I said you'd call her back."

"Eddie, you are such a nerd. Can't you do anything? Not even something as simple as take down a phone message?"

"I was reading a manuscript. I was concentrating. I didn't have a pen. It was inconvenient. You were the one who wanted to hire a nanny from England. You take care of it. Call her back. Here's the number."

"Well, at least you wrote that down. Whereabouts is it?"

"Cornwall. Land's End."

"Land's End. We've hired a nanny from somewhere called Land's End? Eddie, is this a joke?"

"Call her and find out."

But when she called, Hope spoke to a woman who made no sense at all.

"Oh, no, Annabel's not here at the present and I'm afraid we've no rooms available. None at all. In fact we're closed for a while. Annabel's going away to America."

"Yes, she's—oh, never mind."

Hope left her number.

Rosemullion. Land's End. Had she got the right Annabel?

But it was Annabel's voice on the answering machine that intrigued Hope the most. It was low and purring and so terribly British it gave Hope quite a shock.

"Message for Hope Calder. This is Annabel Quick. I shall be arriving at 19:30 at John F. Kennedy airport on Monday on Flight BA 176. I do hope it will be convenient for you to meet me. Please confirm. Miss Calder has given me a photograph of you all, so I shall recognize you."

Then a click. No goodbye!

And shit! Hope had just remembered she hadn't called to confirm she'd meet her. She'd just noted down the ETA in her datebook and rushed out the door. Well, now it was too late.

Miss Annabel Quick was on her way.

In the meantime there was a lot to do. After seeing Harry and Coco off to school, Hope drove at her usual breakneck speed to an ultramodern house buried in the woods between Amagansett and East Hampton. She'd had a call from the of-

fice to say the owners wanted to rent it out for the summer
season.

Personally Hope thought the owners, a woman named
Marcia McNair and her husband Billy, had overpaid for what
was essentially just a four-bedroom one-story house done
over by a tacky decorator before it went on the market. Situ-
ated as it was in the woods, it was dark and gloomy. Some expensive landscaping at the back had created a terrace with
some hideous stone urns and steps leading down to a pool
that barely got any sun. There was a lot of marble around the
place, gold taps in all the bathrooms, and uncomfortable-
looking minimalist furniture in the living room. Hope had
always thought it was the least child-friendly house she'd
ever been in. Not suitable for a family rental. Strike one
against it.

She knew the house had been built by a parvenu from
New Jersey who had acquired a vacant plot of land sold off
by one of the old-money owners of the neighboring estates.
Foolishly the man had thought he would be accepted by his
neighbors, who took one look at his ugly new house and
steered clear of him. When the house was up for resale, the
brokers pitched it as being in a quality area inhabited only by
the elite. Hope could imagine the line Billy and Marcia had
fallen for: that the broker had had to screen all prospective
buyers and accept offers only from the "right people,"
whereas Billy and Marcia had probably been the first suckers
to come along.

Hope encountered a lot of snobbism in the real estate
business, particularly since her catchment area was right in
the middle of the so-called glamorous Hamptons. People
were prepared to pay far more than usual just in the hope
that some of the glamour would rub off on them. Fine,
thought Hope, more power to them, let them waste their
money on overpriced properties. All the more commission
for me. Yet she felt bad about it. Why were people so stupid

that they'd pay a premium for an ugly uncomfortable house just so they could say they lived near celebrities or rich people and amaze their equally stupid friends? Why not buy one of the pretty farmhouses going for a song in unfashionable areas and do them up? But no, whenever she suggested it, the clients looked at her as if she were nuts. And maybe she was. She was in this business to make a healthy commission, wasn't she?

But then there was the other aspect of it: the satisfaction of finding the perfect house for each buyer. The truth was, and Hope knew this was the real downside of her job, she just did not like that many of her clients. Whatever anyone might say about the Hamptons, they attracted an avaricious, arriviste real estate clientele, people she didn't much enjoy dealing with. In fact, she preferred the locals, the people who lived there year round, whose families had been there for hundreds of years, probably since East Hampton was first settled in 1648, not long after the *Mayflower* landed at Plymouth Rock. But all that was left of these families were people struggling to make a living while having to pay the ever-increasing taxes on their land, people who invariably had to work as carpenters, caretakers, builders, or gardeners for the same autocratic, insensitive clients she dealt with every day. Hope was, she often reminded herself, responsible for disposing of land once owned by the ancestors of these decent hardworking people for vastly inflated prices that went not to them but to those to whom they had been forced to sell for a pittance years ago to survive life in the Hamptons.

Hope shook herself and rang the doorbell. A girl appeared: Pristine white T-shirt, short cropped hair, jeans with a crease in them, double deer moccasins, and a tiny baby clamped to her shoulder.

"Is Mrs. McNair here?" asked Hope.

"Yes. I'm the nanny. Mrs. McNair is in the shower. She'll be right with you."

"You're English?"

"Yes, I am," said the girl.

"I have an English nanny coming today," said Hope pleasantly.

"There are a lot of us about," said the girl, almost curtly, Hope felt. "Please wait through there and I'll tell Mrs. McNair you're here. I'm about to take Samuel for his daily visit."

"Where?" Hope didn't understand.

"To see his mother. He visits with her at ten in the morning and four in the afternoon. If she's here."

Hope had heard about these kinds of mothers—the ones who lay in bed until midmorning, lunched, shopped, and saw their children by appointment only—but she'd never really believed they existed until now.

And to think she felt guilty about the amount of time she spent with her kids!

Marcia McNair was enormous. Hope hadn't seen her for some time and she was a little shocked. Obviously Marcia didn't have time to go to the gym to take off the weight she had put on during her pregnancy, Hope observed, feeling rather smug about her own slenderness. She had never had a problem with her weight. Her body seemed to be made of elastic, snapping back into shape within weeks of the birth of all three children.

"I've hired an English nanny," she tried, after Marcia McNair showed her around the house. "I hear they're the best."

"Well, I hope you've got impeccable references," said Marcia. "You know what's happening this week, don't you? Louise Woodward goes to the appeals court."

Great, thought Hope. Just what I needed to be reminded of.

"Let me know what you decide," said Hope evenly as she left. "But I'm telling you right now, Marcia, you're going to have to drop your price. Thirty thousand for the season is too much. You're too far from the ocean."

"But what about the new pool? That cost thirty thousand to put in. We expected to get it back on the summer rental."

"Well, you'd better put a child safety fence around it if you want to rent this house to a family. It's not safe as it stands. Give me a call, and I'll put the details on our computer. 'Bye."

And she left before Marcia could start protesting further.

"Praise the Lord," said Doris, when Hope walked into work. "I'm here on my own. Everyone's out with a client already. The phone's ringing off the hook."

"Where's Petra or whatever her name is?" Tudor Woods had a high turnover of receptionists, a fact that infuriated Hope, who felt it was important to have someone who knew their operation inside out and could direct calls to the right broker.

"She quit last night. Some story about the clients treating her like dirt on the telephone and she wasn't going to take it anymore."

"Treating her like dirt. What about us?"

"I know, I know, but she's young."

"And we're old?"

"Speak for yourself. Uh-oh, here's another one. Tudor Woods. . . . Yes. . . . Oh, really? . . . Well, sure, hold on, I'll give you our top broker"—she winked at Hope—"Hope Collins."

Doris flicked a switch and gesticulated at Hope.

"You have to take this. It's a big one."

"Who is it?"

"Anita Mayhew."

"Do I know her?"

"Hope, where have you been? She's got the whole town excited. Looking to buy herself a fancy waterfront house. She'll pay top money. Comes from Texas. Husband died and left her a fortune. She's on everyone's books. Only a matter of time till she came to us."

"Oh, her. Why didn't she come to us first? We're supposed to be the best, aren't we?"

"Who knows? Anyway, she's still holding. Take the call, Hope, please. For me."

Hope sighed. A rich widow. Big sale. Big commission. Start pitching big. Why did this opportunity have to come when her mind was on the arrival of Mary Poppins? Maybe it was an omen.

"Hope Collins, hello. . . ."

By four o'clock that afternoon, Hope had decided that the last person she needed in her life was Anita Mayhew. She turned out to be a reasonably attractive woman in her early forties, wearing an expensive camel-hair coat, whose hair was totally at odds with the rest of her. Hope knew a botched home-coloring job when she saw one, and this one was a beauty: bright red with streaks of dye staining the temples. Why had Anita Mayhew attempted such a thing? It wasn't as if a woman who barely blinked at an asking price of $4 million couldn't afford to go to a beauty parlor.

But Doris had been right when she said that Anita was on everybody's books. She was the kind of client everyone hated. She was all excited when she sat in the office and looked at the particulars; then, when Hope took her to see the properties, she announced, "Oh, I've seen this already. It's totally wrong. What are you thinking of?"

The problem with someone like Anita Mayhew was that she didn't know what she wanted. One minute she said old, shingled, traditional. The next minute it was contemporary, glass, architect-designed. She insisted on using her own car, a surprisingly battered Toyota, whose interior, Hope felt, did not smell or look entirely clean. And once she was in the car, Hope was Anita's captive. Next time, if there was a next time, she would insist on taking her own car to look at properties or have Anita follow her.

Hope glanced at her watch as they left the driveway to the sixth house. It was getting close to thinking about picking up the kids. Hope badly wanted a spare half hour to go home and check that Annabel Quick's room was absolutely as it should be before they set off for the airport.

But Anita had other ideas. "I want to stop at the nursery and pick up a plant. We'll go to Whitmore's on Twenty-seven."

Finally, however, Hope was on the Long Island Expressway on her way to JFK, with the kids more excited than she'd seen them in ages.

"Now her name is Annabel, Annabel Quick," Hope told them. "Can you all remember that? Do we have a spare piece of paper anywhere in the car? We could write her name on it and hold it up at the gate. I should have thought of that before we left."

"Annabel Quick, Annabel Quick!" yelled Coco, wriggling in her tutu.

> *"Quick, quick, the cat's been sick.*
> *Where? Where? Under the chair.*
> *Hasten, hasten. Fetch a basin.*
> *All in vain. All in vain.*
> *The cat has licked it up again."*

"Harry! That's disgusting. Where did you get that from?"

"Eddie taught it to me last weekend. It's really helped me to remember her name."

"I'll bet. Listen. I never want to hear that rhyme again. Just don't listen to Eddie when he tells you stuff like that. It's gross."

"I don't have to listen to him because he's not my father, right?"

Oh, God, now what had she walked into? She shouldn't tell the kids to ignore Eddie. He'd taken them on as part of her package without a hint of complaint. The least she could do was try and see they respected him. But how could she, when half the time she didn't respect him herself?

"Mom?"

"Harry?"

"You know that rock we have in the front yard?"

"I do."

"You know what? I figure it's part of the Ice Age."

"Do you, Harry? Why?"

"Well, it's like there was this glacier in the Ice Age, the ice flowed south, and when it retreated it left all this residue of sand and gravel and clay, and then this new ice sheet formed. Long Island's like this moraine, a line of hills that was pushed up by a kind of Ice Age bulldozer. Our land was once the edge of an ice sheet where it came to a stop and then began to retreat."

Hope smiled to herself. He would go on about his glacier till they reached the airport. He was fixated on it ever since he'd learned about it in school. It was true, they did have a huge boulder in front of the house. Who knew? Maybe he was right.

Booty was fast asleep when Hope put the car in short-term parking, and she wished she could leave her there. As it was she barely stirred when Hope put her in her stroller and wheeled her into Terminal 3 arrivals. Harry and Coco were fighting over who was going to hold up the sign they'd managed to make with Annabel Quick's name on it. In the end Hope took it.

"It makes sense. I'm the tallest. I'll be able to hold it the highest so she can see it. Now, we'll all stand here and wait."

"How will we know what she looks like?"

"She'll find us," said Hope. "She'll see our sign. She'll be the best-looking person to come through customs. Keep looking now. Those people there were on her flight. I can see the labels on their baggage."

"Will she look like Barbie?" Coco asked.

"I hope not," said Hope.

And then to her horror, a Barbie clone came flouncing toward them and Hope heard Coco give a little squeak. Mercifully the woman ran past them into the arms of a swarthy man.

Women of all types went past them.

"There she is!" yelled Harry and Coco, over and over, only to be proved wrong. They were beginning to look a bit dejected, and indeed Hope was growing worried. Maybe Annabel Quick wasn't on the plane. She should have called her back. She should have confirmed. Why did she always screw up like this?

Booty woke up.

Hope would have believed it if someone had told her they could hear Booty over the sound of all the jet engines at JFK. Booty opened her eyes in a towering rage.

"No!"

Hope took her out of the stroller, and she began to pull Hope's hair.

"Stop it, Booty. Please. That hurts Mommy. *Stop it!*"

Booty screamed. It was rare that she did this, but when she was angry Booty was a force to be reckoned with.

"Shall I hold her for you?" said a voice at Hope's elbow.

"No, it's okay." Hope barely glanced at the woman beside her. "She gets like this sometimes. She'll be fine. But, hey, thanks."

"No, let me take her." The woman was quite insistent. "She'll have to get used to me sooner or later." And very firmly the woman removed Booty from Hope's arms. To Hope's amazement, Booty quieted down almost immediately.

Suddenly Hope realized the woman had an English accent, and she was looking at the piece of paper in Hope's hand. It couldn't be. This woman wasn't a nanny. This woman wasn't a fresh-faced twenty-something, overweight from too much snacking on kids' food throughout the day. This woman was tall and elegant, with a kind, understanding face and a good haircut.

"But you're . . . you're . . ."

"You're old!" shrieked Coco, before Hope could silence her.

Annabel Quick wasn't old. But neither was she a young girl like the previous nannies the kids had known.

Yet Booty seems to have taken to her and that is a definite plus, thought Hope.

"I'm Hope Calder." She held out her hand and then withdrew it quickly when it was obvious that if Annabel Quick attempted to shake it she would drop Booty.

She looks tired, thought Hope, and rather sad. I wonder why. She looked down. No wedding ring. This woman wasn't married. But then she knew that. She'd had her references as Miss Annabel Quick. Not even Ms. But she was beautiful. That soft English skin. Could it survive the sun and the wind in the Hamptons? And she wasn't wearing rouge. She had naturally rosy cheeks.

She looks different, mused Hope. She stands out. And she doesn't look at all like Mary Poppins. I'd better get her out of here before my children annihilate her. Harry and Coco were clinging to the poor woman's arms, fighting to be the one to take charge of her luggage cart.

Harry and Coco chattered nonstop all the way to the car, firing questions at Annabel about England, about her trip, did she have any pets, had she brought them with her, what did she watch on TV? On and on it went until finally, just before Hope turned off the Long Island Expressway at Exit 70 and began the home stretch toward Montauk, one by one they fell asleep.

And then Annabel Quick surprised her.

"This," she said, pulling something out of her raincoat pocket, "is a flask of some excellent scotch whisky. I know you're driving, but you might like a drop. Tell me about yourself, Hope. I've heard all about you from Maud, but I'd rather hear it from you. And while we're at it, we might as well have a cigarette. I bought some in Duty Free."

"I don't smoke," said Hope, "but thanks anyway."

"And I expect you're thinking a new nanny shouldn't either. Well, I swear this is absolutely the last cigarette I'm ever going to have in my entire life. I'm going to take just one from this Duty-Free carton and throw the rest away. Truly I am."

"I imagine they all say that." Hope laughed. She's nervous, she thought. Her hands are shaking.

"I imagine they do, but in my case it's the truth. Unless of course you object to me having this last one."

"Oh, no, please, fire away," said Hope, and then nearly lost control of the wheel as Annabel Quick burst into tears beside her.

What in heaven's name did I say? she wondered. And what's wrong with this woman I've hired to look after my precious children?

6

I awakened to the sight of Coco standing over me, dressed in a pink tutu.

Coco was a brat. That much I had established in the car during the drive from the airport the night before. And if she was like this now, heaven only knew what she would be like when she was older. Her looks were sensational. I wondered where the white-blond hair came from, since Hope was dark. And the turquoise eyes would make her a total knockout later on. But she was a handful. My instinctive reaction was to tell her to shut up and behave, but that wouldn't make a very good start to our relationship.

Now she was prancing about on the bed. I don't need this, I thought, as I hugged my knees under the bedclothes to avoid being pulverized by her feet bouncing up and down. I just do not need this! Coming here was the most insane thing I've done in my entire life.

Coco's feet landed on my stomach, making it heave.

"Stop that at once," I hissed. "Have you any idea how fragile I feel?"

She probably didn't even know what the word *fragile* meant.

"You're jet-lagged," said a voice from the doorway. "My dad gets it all the time."

I peeked out from under the bedclothes and saw the boy

standing there in his underpants. I had warmed to him the night before. He had been the least talkative of the three kids. The baby, Booty, had yelled for a while and then fallen asleep. Coco had directed a string of questions at me— "What's your favorite color?" "How old are you?" "How long are you staying," "Did my dad send you?"—totally ignoring Hope's demands that she not interrupt. But Harry, the eldest, had been sweet and polite. "Where do you live in England? What's it like there? Are you very tired? May I show you my stamps when we get home or will you go straight to bed?" to which Hope had replied, "You'll be the one going straight to bed, Harry honey."

"I am not jet-lagged," I told him, "at least not yet. I have a bloody awful hangover. Now scoot. Would you? Please?"

"Coco. Up. Now. Quit watching *Beethoven*," called Hope.

"I'm not watching *Beethoven*. I'm watching Annabel. And I'm dressed."

"No, she isn't," I called out to Hope, "unless you call a tutu dressed."

Coco glared down at me, and I had the distinct feeling some kind of war had just been declared.

I sat up when Hope came into the room. The woman was a complete marvel. How could she drink as much as she had the night before and still appear fresh, chic, and pretty at seven-fifteen the next morning? I didn't know much about clothes, but that looked like an expensive sweater and those trousers were beautifully cut. Not that Hope's petite figure needed any help.

She reminded me of someone and in one ghastly second I realized who it was. Marietta was immaculate in the mornings. She had always put me to shame by sitting up with the most boring guest, talking away into the night, while Felix and I scuttled away to our beds only to emerge bleary-eyed at the breakfast table. And there she'd be, already up and about, attending to detail and in control. Sometimes I felt like a bumbling idiot beside my mother. Why did I have the feeling Hope was going to make me feel the same way? And yet look at the way she'd behaved last night. Something was definitely not right with her world.

"Harry has breakfast on the table, but don't feel you have to get up your first morning. The thing is, I do want to run through a few instructions about Booty, but you know what? I have everything written down so I'll leave it all in the kitchen and I'll call you from the office and we can go through everything you don't understand on the phone."

Well, this sounded familiar. Marietta wrote everything down, pinned up lists all over the kitchen at Rosemullion, left me instructions right, left, and center, never trusted me to act on my own initiative. At least that's what she thought was happening. I pretty much followed my own schedule but let her think she was directing me. Things went better that way.

"Philomena hasn't turned up this morning," continued Hope, coming in and out of the room with various items of the kids' clothes that she attempted to get them to put on. I should be doing this, I thought. I should be up and about and showing how capable I was. "Philomena's my house-keeper. She's been a bit erratic lately, but never mind. Harry and Coco are picked up by the school bus, and I'll bring Booty up here when I leave for work so you can keep an eye on her while you unpack your stuff. I'm sure she'd love to help you. Harry and Coco, downstairs! Now!"

She was like a whirlwind, blowing in and out of my room. She was one of those people who are on the go every waking second; obviously that was what kept her so thin.

Harry was lurking outside on the landing, and I asked him for directions to the bathroom.

"Go down the back staircase. It leads directly into the kitchen. Take your stuff. You can leave it all down there."

I helped myself to some fancy moisturizing bath oil and

soaked my aching body in the tub. I was behaving more like an honored guest than a new employee. My body felt about three paces behind my brain. Jet lag and hangover, what a great way to start a new job. Getting drunk with the boss. But at least I now knew just about everything there was to know about Hope.

And she knew next to nothing about me. I had blamed my sudden bout of weeping in the car on exhaustion from the flight. Well, the longer it stayed that way the better. Maud had clearly omitted to mention the fact that I had just lost my parents. Typical Maud. But the truth was, right now it suited me to keep these things to myself. In a way I was desperate to unburden myself, to tell someone my secrets, to share my fears for the future with a friend, but I couldn't very well start dumping on Hope. Although God knows she seemed to have no compunction about bending my ear.

I heard her shout out, "Goodbye, catch you later!" But by the time I had wrapped a towel around me and peered around the bathroom door she had gone and there was Booty crawling between my legs.

I don't think it's meant to happen like this. Aren't mothers supposed to stick around for a kind of breaking-in period while their kids get used to the new nanny? Mercifully, the sight of my gleaming pink wet flesh seemed to have silenced Booty for the time being. She was staring at me with her mouth open.

But when I bent down to pick her up and take her back upstairs, she began to howl with the same intensity with which she'd greeted me at the airport.

Now what did I do? It was only a fluke that she had stopped crying the minute Hope handed her to me the night before. How long could I fool Hope into thinking I knew what I was doing with her kids? I didn't have the first clue.

Booty continued to scream while I dressed. That was the other thing. What constituted an appropriate nanny uniform these days? Would the jeans and T-shirt I wore day in and day out in Cornwall do? They'd have to.

"It's a waste of time making that noise," I told Booty. "I'm not going to take any notice of you. I'm too exhausted, plus I don't understand a word you're saying. I'm going to treat you like a little puppy. I'm going to chatter away to you, and maybe the soothing monotony of my voice will persuade you to shut up and relax. Are you a speedy little creature like your mother? Too crazed and busy even to stop and tell me what to do with you?"

Downstairs I found Hope's lists. They were stacked in pages on the table, taped to the fridge, the stove, even the dishwasher. I might have guessed Hope would be a fanatical list maker. A guilt-ridden displacement activity of the mother who wouldn't be doing the actual work. Write it all out in detail, the next best thing to doing it oneself. I made myself a cup of tea and began to wade through the notes.

> *Booty doesn't drink enough so offer her juice or milk (warmed up, heat in pan to lukewarm temperature) regularly.*
>
> *She has a nap around 11 (change diaper first) for about half an hour. Put her in her crib with her doll and milk or juice (whichever she wants). Put her in our bedroom, curtains closed, with the white blanket behind her head, crib tipped back.*
>
> *At about 1 o'clock, lunch. Fresh spaghetti in fridge— put in boiling water for 3 mins. Grate cheddar cheese. Mix drained spaghetti with butter and pour cheese on top. Cut up spaghetti with scissors . . .*

Oh, Jesus! What would happen if I tore it apart with my fingers? Would Hope come rushing back from the office in a fit? And where did Hope work? What had Maud said? Real estate or something. Where was the number?

Of course Booty wouldn't go to sleep, so I turned on the TV and surfed awhile until suddenly there they were: Teletubbies.

"Look, Booty. Laa-Laa, Po, Tinky Winky, and Dipsy."

It was ironic that I was more familiar with them than she was, but like millions of English children on the other side of the Atlantic she was soon transfixed. The controversy over these strange brightly colored little creatures was mind-boggling. A series created for one-year-olds upward—but should toddlers that young be encouraged to watch television? And wasn't there something of a throwback to the hallucinatory drug era about the dippy Tubbies floating dreamily around the garden as if they were on acid?

But if they could silence Booty the way they had, they were a definite plus. And when she fell asleep in front of the television, somehow I knew I would be putting her down for her nap at Teletubbies time every morning, whatever Hope's notes instructed. I'd pretended to defer to Marietta all these years and she'd been there on the spot. Hope at the office was a piece of cake.

I knew I should call the airline and book myself on the first flight home. I was on Long Island under false pretenses. I was a fraud. It wasn't fair to Hope.

But then I recalled Hope's anguish the night before. Once the kids had fallen asleep in the back of the car, she had embarked upon what seemed like a two-hour monologue all the way home along the Long Island Expressway.

She began relatively calmly.

"I can't begin to tell you how relieved I am you're here. Do you have any idea how many nannies I've had in the last two years? Take a guess. No, don't bother. You'd be way off. Eight. And their father says they leave because of me."

That was when her voice began to rise.

"Not the kids, me. I work too hard. I'm never there. Blah-blah-blah. He's always criticizing me. Why do I let Harry do so much housework? He's going to grow up to be a faggot. Why does Coco watch so much TV? Why don't I sit and read to her? Well, when does *he* sit and read to her? you ask. He's never there. He's far away in California. Okay, so he calls every morning when they've just woken up and they're all grouchy and he gets the moans and groans from them, but I'm the one who has to deal with them afterward. I'm sorry I'm going on like this, but there's just no one I can talk to about the kids and how I'm coping—or rather not coping— as their mother. They don't want to know at the office. You're going to be helping me with the kids; I feel I have to be up front with you from the start, otherwise it's not going to work. And it has to work.

"I love my husband. I feel we have so much history to-gether. He knew my father. That's important to me. And we're so alike. Deep down we want the same things. I know it. And I haven't changed. I'm still the same Hope he mar-ried. I know I'm obsessive. I know I want it all—the job, the kids, everything—but why not? No, he's the one who's changed, and in exactly the way I always wanted him to. Now he's successful and driven, and I'm not around to share it with him. It's just not fair."

About halfway through I realized she was talking to her-self. I think she'd forgotten I was there. The woman is an even bigger mess than I am, and she was dumping it all on me because I was a stranger. Maybe I should have done the same thing. Maybe I still would, if we got to know each other well enough. And I hoped we would, because already I rather liked her. She wasn't at all the monster Maud had made her out to be.

But something worried me. When she said, "I love my husband," she wasn't talking about Maud's brother Edward. She was talking about her first husband, the one in Califor-nia. So what was that all about?

I can see that she genuinely wants to be a wonderful

mother. She loves her kids. She just never has the time—or makes the time—to follow through. If I deliver everything that Hope expects of me, it'll take the pressure off and she'll calm down. Maybe she'll find the time to take stock of her life and sort herself out and the kids will benefit. I can't walk out on her. She's depending on me too much.

So when she called from work I told her everything was fine and tried my hardest to sound alert and confident even though I was asleep on my feet.

"Did you manage to unpack, get your room sorted out?"

"Oh, yes."

Lies, lies, lies. My suitcases were still lying open with half my clothes still in them and the other half strewn around the room. Hope would have a fit. I'd peeked into her room. Pin neat. Bed made. Scatter cushions arranged just so. By Hope's bed there was just one book: *No Time to Die* by Liz Tilberis, an account by the editor-in-chief of *Harper's Bazaar* of her battle to overcome ovarian cancer. How ironic, when it looks as if the main problem in Hope's life is that she has no time to live.

I was pretty relieved to find Coco's room full of unmitigated chaos. But Harry's room was a shock. It was even neater than Hope's. Nothing was out of place. His bed was made and his pajamas folded on the pillow. It was a little scary somehow to see such meticulous order in one so young. He was his mother's son in that respect.

"So, did you try the car yet?" asked Hope.

"Not yet."

"The school bus drops the kids off at the end of the road, but you're going to need the station wagon to take them to play dates and stuff. And shopping—if you could take over the weekly marketing?"

"When I'm less tired, maybe." And when I've worked out what the hell I'm going to do about the fact that I don't have a driver's license.

"You mean you wouldn't mind doing the marketing for

me once in a while?" Hope sounded like she couldn't believe her ears. "I thought you'd call me on that one right away. The other nannies always did. It's not part of their job description."

I hadn't even realized I had a job description. Needless to say, Maud hadn't mentioned one.

Harry and Coco arrived home together. Coco ignored me and rushed straight upstairs to her room. Harry hovered in the kitchen.

"We usually have pizzas when we get home from school. Mom keeps them here, in the freezer. I can warm them up in the microwave if you want."

"Thanks." I smiled at him. He was such a serious little boy. He needed to lighten up. "What about Coco?"

"You need to bond with her." I nearly exploded with laughter. He was a listener. He overheard these expressions and adapted them to his own opinions, unaware that they sounded ridiculous coming from someone his age. "How about you take her pizza up to her and have a chat, get to know her, watch *Beethoven* with her. She'd think that was really cool. I'll keep an eye on Booty."

He had a point. And already he was aligning himself with me, placing himself squarely on the side of responsibility. If only he knew he was teaming up with one of the most irresponsible adults around.

"Can I bring you anything while you're up there?" he inquired politely.

"I'd love a cup of tea," I said and watched his face light up. He was a people pleaser. Let me do things for you and then you'll love me to pieces.

Beethoven had got to the part where the mother goes back to work and hires a nightmare baby-sitter for the kids who forces them to listen to her repertoire at the piano. Little Emily gets bored, runs outside, and falls in the pool, whereupon Beethoven rushes to the rescue and saves her.

"You're not going to be like that, are you?" Coco asked. "You won't play the piano for us all day?"

"Do you have a piano?"

"No."

"Well, it looks like you're safe."

"But what if Booty fell in the pool? We don't have a Beethoven to save her. I keep telling Mommy we have to get a puppy. Annabel, you'll help us make her get a puppy, won't you?"

"But even if you get a puppy it wouldn't be able to save Booty if she fell in the pool," I pointed out.

"Oh, yes, it would. I'd choose the right puppy."

"There's just one problem, Coco."

"What's that?" she asked suspiciously.

"You don't have a pool."

"Well, the puppy could save her if she fell out of her high chair in the kitchen—"

I hadn't moved so fast in years. Harry hadn't come up-stairs again. I'd left a little boy in charge of a two-year-old with a request that he boil water for my tea.

Was I out of my mind?

I found him on the phone. Booty was sitting in the middle of the kitchen floor with upturned pizzas splattered all around her. She was sticking her fingers in them and happily licking each one in turn.

"It's Dad," mouthed Harry, "in California."

I hadn't even heard the phone ring.

"No, Dad, everything's cool. She arrived last night. From England. I'm sorry no one picked up this morning. I guess we were all busy getting Annabel settled. Mom'll find your message on the tape when she gets home. She always tells us not to play with the machine in case we wipe out the messages from her clients. . . . What did you say? . . . Hold on, here she is."

I took the phone with some trepidation.

"Hello. This is Annabel. Annabel Quick."

"Hi, there. It's Craig Collins, Harry and Coco's father. Calling from Los Angeles. You just arrived?"

Breezy voice. Very American.

"Last night."

"From London? And Hope left you alone with the little apes on your first day? Jesus, that woman only thinks of herself and her work."

"No, really, I'm perfectly fine, and they're behaving like little angels."

"Angels? My kids? Since when? Listen, take a tip from me. Don't let Hope get the better of you. Make sure she pulls her weight. They're her kids. She oughta spend time with them."

What about you? I thought. When do you spend time with them? I didn't like this man's brash tone.

"And don't let her talk you into doing all the marketing. I'm not paying you enough for that."

I winced. I'd already fallen for that one, and nobody had ever mentioned that Craig Collins paid my wages. I wondered if Maud knew this.

"You pay . . . ?"

"Yeah. Who else? You can't count on What's-his-name. So, are you all set for Easter weekend?"

"Easter weekend?" I was so tired I couldn't even remember what day it was.

"This weekend. I'm coming east and she's bringing my two into the city to meet me. Bit heavy of her, leaving you alone with What's-his-name and the baby your first weekend. She did tell you, didn't she?"

No. Hope hadn't said a word about running off to meet her ex-husband in New York. But something told me to keep that under my hat.

"Yes. Yes, of course. But to be honest, I'm not sure she's told the kids yet."

True enough.

"Wants to keep it a surprise, I expect. Well, would you please ask her to pick up when I call in the morning? I'd call her at work but she gets mad when I do."

"Maybe you should pretend you're buying a house."

"You know what? That's not such a bad idea." He chuckled. "Nice talking to you, Annabel. Hey, I almost forgot, you're from England. Mary Poppins to the rescue."

"Beats the cavalry," I said, thinking this kind of pathetic humor might be right up his alley. I was right.

"Beats the cavalry. That's terrific. Do me a favor, Annabel, teach Hope to laugh at herself. She could use a sense of humor. Talk to you later. 'Bye now."

"What hasn't Mom told us yet?" Harry confronted me the minute I got off the phone.

"That's for me to know and you to find out when she gets home," I told him. "Now, Coco, the rest of *Beethoven*. All three of you upstairs."

I sat down in Coco's flouncy boudoir with Booty on my lap. Within five minutes I was fast asleep.

The kids' shrieking woke me up when Hope walked in.

"Mommy, Mommy, Daddy called and said you had a secret! He spoke to Annabel. Something you haven't told us yet about this weekend."

Hope looked at me.

"Craig called?"

"I'm sorry. I was so tired I fell—"

"It doesn't matter. Craig called?" I could see she was nervous.

"Yes, he did, and—"

"He told you about the weekend?"

"I pretended I knew all about it," I told her evenly.

"What's happening?" screamed Coco.

"Daddy's coming to New York. I'm taking you and Harry to see him. Isn't that great?"

"And Booty?"

"No. Booty stays here with Annabel and Eddie."

The first time she'd said his name since I arrived. Extraordinary.

"I'm sorry about this, Annabel. I should have told you. You'll be okay, won't you? It's only little Booty, and she adores you already."

How could she tell that? Booty was fast asleep in my arms.

"And Eddie will give you all the help you need. It's only for two days."

"What's-his-name," I said.

"You really have been talking to Craig, haven't you? Well, I'm not going to worry about you. You'll be fine. I'm leaving my baby with a Norland-trained nanny. I understand they're the best in the world."

No, you're not. Not really. You're leaving her with a spy for your sister-in-law and you're providing plenty of ammunition to fuel Maud's battle against you. And you're leaving your baby with someone who is so out of touch with child care that, quite frankly, she's terrified at what she's let herself in for.

Sooner or later, Hope Calder, you're going to find out you've been had.

7

On the Thursday before Easter, everyone at the Gramercy Press was working flat out before they left for the holiday weekend.

Eddie was writing jacket copy, or trying to. Trying to beat the clock, too. The deadline for all copy to be in for his books on the Gramercy Press winter list had long since passed and the managing editor, an old battle-ax named Peggy, was hounding him. Eddie had always managed to get out of writing jacket copy up until now, but he wasn't about to reveal this to Peggy. He knew Peggy already suspected him of being a fraud, and there was no point in delivering concrete proof of this into her lap any sooner than he had to.

Larry Fredericks, on the other hand, was a different story. Larry didn't care two hoots about what Eddie did, providing Eddie was willing to accompany him to the Mesa Grill each evening for a few stiff drinks at the bar.

"Piece of cake, man," said Larry, when Eddie appealed to him for help. "Here's what you do. First you find another book—make it an established best-seller just to be on the safe side—and you rewrite that book's copy to suit your own. See, here's *The Horse Whisperer*. Wait a sec, it's the UK edition, but what the hell. It starts out, 'In the still of a snow-covered morning in upstate New York, a girl out riding her horse . . .' Is that lyrical or what? So rip it off, man. Say your book's a downtown thriller, you put, 'In the still of a rain-drenched Bowery alley, a man falls to the ground with a knife in his back'—or with blood running from his ears, whatever. Then you carry on until you have to write a paragraph of garbage about how good your fucking book is, so you go for the comparisons. The salesmen love that. You go, 'Not since John Grisham has there been a writer with such an extraordinary power to blah blah blah.' See, they've done it here: 'Cross *The Bridges of Madison County* with *Black Beauty* and you have *The Horse Whisperer*.' I'll pick you up at five-thirty and we'll go down a few whiskey sours."

"Better make it six," said Eddie glumly. "I've got a ton of books to get through. I inherited all the first novels that girl who went to Simon and Schuster bought. They're not replacing her."

"Boy, oh, boy, she commissioned a lot of crap. She surely did." And on that note of encouragement, Larry wandered out of Eddie's office.

Eddie sucked on the blue plastic of his Paper Mate pen as he approached the copy for a pseudo-literary romance he had inherited. *The Horse Whisperer* had proved a surprisingly adaptable base for several blurbs so far, and he set about reworking the opening line for the fifth time that afternoon.

In the heat of a sun-drenched Texas afternoon . . .

All went well until he reached the final paragraph.

Not since Edith Wharton, he wrote confidently, and then paused. Edith would have turned in her grave to have her prose compared with this torrid panhandle blockbusterette. There were limits.

Not since Jackie Collins . . .

He paused again. The Gramercy Press was perceived to be a literary house, and this trashy potboiler was being packaged as a sensitive first novel. If he had any sense at all he'd alert them to the fact that the departing editor had been publishing cheap thrills masquerading as literature and get rid of them. But it was too late now. The books were all in the catalog. He was supposed to have read them months ago, but as usual he'd left it till the last minute.

Not since . . . but the appropriate name eluded him. His mind strayed. He should call Hope. Tell her which Jitney he was catching so she could meet him. And he should tell Larry a drink at the Mesa Grill was out. He'd never catch the bus for the weekend.

A strange voice answered the phone, an English voice. For one ghastly moment Eddie wondered if his mother had arrived unexpectedly.

"It's Eddie. Is Hope there?"

"Er, no."

"Oh. Who's this?"

"Annabel Quick."

Even as she said her name, Eddie remembered that the new English nanny was arriving that week. Eddie felt awkward. He didn't like nannies. He never knew what to say to them, and he felt they came between him and the children. They were Hope's people, ganging up on him. Hope probably bitched about him all week to them. He had pleaded with Hope to have them disappear at weekends but to no avail. Then again, he was probably being paranoid as usual. They were just young girls after all.

Although this one didn't sound much like a young girl.

"Well, good. Hello. Welcome. I hope you're settling in. Do you know when my wife will be back? It's Edward Calder, Booty's father."

"Yes, of course. Hello. I don't know when she'll be back. Is there anything I can do? Are you coming out tonight?"

"I'm aiming to. That's what I was calling about. I'll try and get the six o'clock Jitney, gets into Amagansett around eight-forty. Could you get Hope to meet me and let the kids stay up? Okay?" He'd better get off the phone before she said it was out of the question like all the other nannies under Hope's thumb. "Thanks a lot. Gotta run. Look forward to meeting you."

Like hell! Woman sounded most odd. Nervous. He should never have allowed Hope to go ahead with such a mad idea. Not that he could have stopped her if he'd wanted to. Nor did he want to be the kind of husband who dominated his wife. It was just that he wished she'd consult him a little more sometimes. He had opinions. Booty was his daughter too. Once he had done all the initial legwork for her, Hope had just charged ahead as usual and arranged it all with Maud as if he didn't exist. He'd heard a junior in the office talking about an assertiveness training course she'd read about in *Cosmopolitan*. Maybe that was what he needed to enable him to deal with his wife.

And there was another thing. Maud hadn't returned his calls all week. What was that all about? Was there some kind of conspiracy going on? Were she and Hope up to something?

There he went again. Talk about paranoid. Get a grip, Eddie, he told himself.

"Say what?"

He hadn't realized he'd said it out loud.

Arlene was looming over his desk. Arlene was his assistant. If he had known he would have to interview assistants, Eddie would never have accepted the job at the Gramercy Press. The idea terrified him. When the personnel manager handed him a bunch of résumés from prospective candidates it didn't take him long to see that most of them were better qualified than he was.

Which is why, much to everyone's horror, he picked Arlene Kowalski.

When she came for her interview, Arlene was employed as a waitress. She was a single mother who had put herself through college working odd jobs. She was, Eddie discovered, a better manuscript reader than anybody else at the Gramercy Press because she assessed them like a regular book buyer. If a manuscript made Arlene cry or laugh, or if it held her interest for more than fifty pages, Eddie took it seriously. If she said it sucked, he rejected it without reading it himself.

Arlene chewed gum incessantly and was invariably inappropriately dressed for the office. Skimpy dresses with shoestring straps in summer were exchanged for oversize sweaters and leggings in winter. But Arlene knew the city backward and forward. She knew the best place for sushi, the best bars, the best pizza parlors, the best barbers, dry cleaners, anything Eddie wanted she knew where to get it or how to fix it. The only thing that ever threw her was when her kid, Max, got sick. He was a two-year-old; they figured out he must have been born only a couple of months before Booty. Her mother took care of him during the day. Eddie felt guilty knowing he had more conversations about Booty with Arlene than he did with Hope. They talked halfheartedly about getting their children together one day, knowing it would probably never happen.

Arlene took care of Eddie exclusively. She wouldn't lift a finger for anyone else. She barely even spoke to anyone in the office. But that didn't mean she would pass up the opportunity to give him a hard time.

Now here she was looming out of nowhere like she always did. Eddie often wondered if she had a hearing problem, since the two phrases she uttered regularly were, "Say what?" and "Excuse me?"

"I assume you have something to convey to me. Go on then, spit it out."

"You're so snotty Brit pompous, Eddie, that's your trouble." Arlene could always be relied upon to say what was on her mind. "As a matter of fact, Mr. Springer wants to see you. Right now."

"What about?"

"What am I, clairvoyant?"

"Well, can't it wait until after Easter?"

"Absolutely not. Get the fuck up there. You've been summoned. You've been chosen. Don't mess with the powers on high."

"Arlene, do you know the meaning of the word respect?"

"I respect you, Eddie. I work for you, don't I?"

"Do you?"

Clem Springer offered him a glass of chardonnay. Eddie accepted with alacrity. Things were looking up.

"Are you a Knicks fan, Eddie?"

"No, can't say I am." Had he been hauled up here to talk about the Knicks? Things were looking down.

"No. Neither am I. Pacers man myself. Think I might have a bet on tonight's game."

"Good idea."

"But first I want to talk to you about Josephine Gardiner. Want you to be her new editor."

"Me?" Eddie jumped. Josephine Gardiner was a big name on the Gramercy Press list. "Why?"

"She's English."

"Oh."

"Well, so are you. She needs delicate handling. Who better than a fellow Brit?"

"But I've never read any of her books," said Eddie, in a rare moment of candor.

" 'Course you haven't. Nether have I. Who needs to? Woman's made us a shitload of money ever since she won some Mickey Mouse literary prize. She's been nominated for your Booker Prize. We need to keep her happy, and she says she doesn't like Francis O'Halloran."

"Ah," said Eddie. Frank O'Halloran was about sixty and played the lofty patriarch to a number of nubile young females, some of whom had complained that his breath smelled foul.

"So I figured we'd try her on you. Take a couple of her books home over the weekend. I'll get her to call you. Meet with her. Bond with her. Keep her happy. Do what it takes."

"Maybe Larry Fredericks could—"

"Nope. She wouldn't want a cowboy. You've got the right look. Her agent adores you. Could make your career. You ought to be on your knees thanking me."

"Thanks awfully," said Eddie, wondering if he could politely make a run for it before he missed the six o'clock bus.

"Oh, you poor fuck," said Arlene with feeling, when he told her why he'd been summoned upstairs.

"What do you mean? I thought I was getting a boost to my career."

"With Josephine Gardiner? You're way wrong, buddy. Didn't they teach you anything at Oxford?"

"Cambridge," Eddie corrected her for the umpteenth time. He knew deep down that a put-down by Arlene was really a term of endearment, but there were times when it was hard to remember this. Now was one of those times.

"Maybe you haven't read her books, Arlene," he said carefully. He might respect Arlene's opinion on the slush pile but he couldn't help feeling a little patronizing toward her when it came to so-called literary fiction.

"Sure I have. All of 'em," said Arlene, surprising him as usual. "Nothing wrong with her books other than she writes about mega-boring tight-assed WASPs with more money than they know what to do with. If she wrote about real people who load their own dishwashers and sweep their own floors I'd have more respect, you know what I'm saying? But she can tell a good story. Her books aren't the problem. It's her."

"How come?"

"She's the most difficult author we got. I bet old Springer-dinger fooled you with some line about her being a very important author and we gotta keep her happy and you're the person to do it. Say what? You're not saying anything, so I hit the nail, didn't I? He used the same old line."

"He said it was because we were both English."

"Takes one stuck-up Brit to know another, right?"

"So what's wrong with her?"

"She's the most demanding bitch we ever had. She gets on the phone and it's yada, yada, yada in your ear, all the things she wants you to do for her. Trouble is, it won't be you who has to do the doing, it'll be me. I can see it coming. She'll be on the phone to me night and day with that prissy accent of hers."

"You mean English."

"Yeah."

"Like mine."

"No, yours is kinda cute. Pompous. Snotty. But cute."

"Thank you, Arlene. Oh, shit!"

"You just realized you missed the six o'clock bus. I coulda told you that twenty minutes ago."

"So why didn't you?"

"You were still up there with Springer-dinger. So what's the problem? Catch the next one."

"Booty will be in bed and there's a new nanny I'll have to negotiate with to be allowed to say good night to my own daughter."

"If you don't mind my asking, why do you guys have a nanny at all? All they ever seem to do is keep you away from your kid."

"Because Hope works, like you."

"Well what about Hope's mom? What are grandmas for?"

"Maisie's not that type of grandmother."

"What you mean is your wife is too snotty to mind her own kids and that goes for her mother too."

"Arlene, please," Eddie protested and as usual immediately began to wonder if she was right. However much he might make excuses for her, Hope didn't spend enough time with the kids. "You chose to work too, Arlene. It's not as if you spend much time with Max."

"I spend two hours in the morning and two hours in the evening and all weekend with him. And I do not choose to work, I have to work. I don't have a husband to support me and my child. The only thing I chose, as you put it, was not to go on being a waitress. I love to read. I can't write worth a damn. So I get to work as your assistant. So what's with the new nanny? What happened to What's-her-name?"

"Exactly. I don't think even I recall her name. She left. This one's called Annabel. She's English, and my sister found her in London."

"Which means . . . ?"

"Which means she'll probably give me a hard time, just like Maud. Just like Hope. Just like my mother. Just like you."

"Eddie, have you ever stopped to think why we give you a hard time?"

"Because you love me?"

Arlene had her back to him. She didn't say anything.

"Arlene?"

"I wish," he thought he heard her say very quietly. Then, "I gotta go. It's Mom's bowling night tonight. Gotta go relieve her of Max. Have a great Easter."

Eddie watched her walking away down the aisle between the work stations. Long legs in skin-tight leggings tucked into high-heeled boots. He wondered how old she was. He ought to know. It was on her résumé buried somewhere in his desk. Probably younger than she looked. He wondered who Max's father was and what had happened to him. He went and looked for a picture of Max and didn't see one. In fact, now he came to think about it, he had never seen one on her desk. Arlene had guts. She deserved to find a new father for Max.

He sat at her desk and rang home. It made him smile to see she had been trying to finish his jacket copy for him and had clearly given up in despair. At the bottom of one page he saw the words *Not since Donald Duck has there been* . . .

"Hope home yet?" he asked Annabel Quick.

"Not yet."

"Where on earth is she?"

No answer.

"Well, would you please tell her I'm getting the seven o'-clock bus, which gets in at nine-forty, and would she please meet me?"

"Of course."

"Can I say good night to Booty?"

"She's right here."

Eddie almost dropped the phone in shock. Normally he had to plead for Booty to be fetched from the bathroom, the bedroom, wherever.

"Hello, my Puss in Boots. I'm going to be late so I won't be there to kiss you good night, so you go to bed and I'll see you in the morning. Okay?"

"Okay, Daddy," he heard her say, in her adorable little voice.

"And you be good for Annabel."

"Annabel good. Love Annabel."

"Really? Is Coco there?"

"No."

"Harry?"

"No."

"They're out with your wife." Annabel came back on the line.

"Where?"

"I don't know."

"Well, that sounds like my wife. You'll have her meet me, won't you?"

"I'll do what I can."

I'll do what I can. What was that supposed to mean?

Inevitably he went by the Mesa Grill as he wandered along Fifth Avenue in search of a cab and inevitably he wandered in to say good night to Larry.

"Hey! Over here," yelled Larry from the bar. "What took you so long? You know it makes me so mad. They pretend they have a million bookings for dinner at six-thirty and they won't let us sit at a table to enjoy a quiet drink in the cocktail hour. They insist on cramming us all up against the bar like sheep in a pen and what do you see all around you? Empty tables. The guy has some stupid line like, 'Sir, I'd love to seat you. I know you won't be long. But if I seat you I have to seat everyone.' So why doesn't he just go ahead and seat everyone? Crazy."

"Get me a double vodka on the rocks, Larry, and shut up," growled Eddie. Larry said the same thing every time they came to the Mesa Grill.

"What's eating you?"

"I've missed the six o'clock and I have to face a new nanny and I didn't finish writing my jacket copy and Clem wants me to take on a new author."

"He does? Who's that?'

"Josephine Gardiner."

"Oh, jeez. I hear she's a real piece of work."

"Don't you start."

"Someone already told you?"

"Arlene."

"Aw, don't worry about it. You'll be fine. You're terrific with people. Clem knows what he's doing."

"What did you say?"

"I said you're terrific with people. In fact I've been meaning to tell you, I think you're in the wrong job."

"Oh, thanks, Larry, now you tell me."

"No, I mean you'd be better off in publicity. You're maybe not a natural editor. I can tell it bores you just a little. You want to be out there schmoozing, charming people. What you do best."

"Me?" Eddie couldn't believe his ears. He couldn't remember a time when anyone had ever told him he was good at something. He had grown so used to his mother thinking he was useless, to Maud being the successful one, to Hope more or less running his life. It was years since he'd actually stopped to think whether he had anything to contribute to anyone else's life—except, of course, his little Booty's.

"You don't have too high an opinion of yourself, do you?" said Larry. "Why is that? you're such a good-looking guy. I envy you all the time. People are crazy about you, and you don't even seem to notice."

"Larry, what are you talking about?"

"I'm serious, man. Look at Arlene. She'll do anything for you. And when did Clem Springer ever summon me up to his office and hand me an author on a plate? Susie thinks you're terrific. All those women agents are drooling over you, and it ain't just because of your English accent."

"How *is* Susie?"

"Well, we're back to having that conversation again and things are getting a little tense."

That conversation was the one about adoption. Susie couldn't have children. She wanted to adopt. Larry was happy as they were.

"It's crazy," said Eddie. "There's Susie desperate for a kid and there's Hope with three she hardly ever sees and I don't know what to do to make things better. She just never seems to listen to me."

"You've gotta tell her, man. I know it's hard, believe me. I'm having a problem getting my view across to Susie. I don't think women realize that us men don't have much confidence in ourselves. I mean, look at you, you think you're shit and you're not. And everyone expects me to be so take-charge and all but no one realizes how difficult it is; it just doesn't work like that automatically. Women are tougher than we are. I think they have been from the get-go, but somehow the message got handed down all wrong over the centuries and we're supposed to keep it all together and not get any of the credit and—"

"Larry," Eddie interrupted. Larry was one of the most repetitive people he knew. "I have to run or I won't make the eight o'clock bus, let alone the seven o'clock. I'm glad we had this little talk."

"Don't listen to me. I'm drunk as a skunk." Larry was looking very morose. Eddie didn't like to leave him like that especially after he'd been so supportive, said all those flattering things.

Supportive.

That really was a woman's word. Maybe that's what women did, supported each other through lengthy baring of souls. Maybe that was why they were so resilient.

He thought about it on the bus. Was that the way to get through to Hope? Talk to her like a woman? Why not? He felt surprisingly confident. Arlene thought he was terrific. Larry had said all those great things. Maybe even Clem Springer saw some potential in him.

He never made the bus. As he and Larry were about to leave, they bumped into Hamish "Under the Table" McVitie, (a Scots publisher so called because of his ability to drink everyone else under the table), on his first business trip to New York. So far Eddie had challenged Hamish to drinking contests only in London and Glasgow. New York had yet to be conquered. At some point during the evening Eddie remembered to call Hope and thanked his lucky stars the answering machine was on. He left a blurry message to the effect that he would be on the ten o'clock bus in the morning. And woke up on the couch in Larry's apartment at noon the next day. By Good Friday afternoon his head had finally cleared sufficiently for him to stumble off to make the four o'clock. Three hours later, as the bus plowed through the rain past the two swans on the pond to East Hampton, past the Guild Hall and the movie theater and on to Amagansett, Eddie began to get excited at the thought of seeing Hope and what he would say to her. He got off the bus ready to give her a big hug and whisk her off for dinner somewhere.

Only she wasn't there.

"Hi, Mike," he called, to a man getting out of a beat-up station wagon with a green light and a sign saying AMA-GANSETT TAXI. "Seen Hope?"

"Hope? Nope. I'm here to pick you up. An English lady called and asked me to come get you. I thought maybe you had company for the weekend."

Eddie got into the taxi feeling very deflated.

"So," said Mike, "you guys are not spending Easter together."

"What do you mean?"

"I took Hope to the Jitney yesterday. She went into New York. She had the two older kids with her. How come you didn't know?"

How come I didn't know? Eddie asked himself. How come I have to find out from the taxi driver what my wife's weekend plans are? And now I have to face a new nanny and spend the entire weekend alone with her. What the fuck is going on? What on earth am I going to say to her?

Never in a million years would he have predicted what his first words to Annabel Quick would be.

When she opened the door to him he was pleasantly surprised. For a start she didn't look like a nanny at all, more like an attractive, composed, middle-aged woman. She looked different, and for a moment he couldn't quite figure out why. Then it dawned on him that she looked English. Beautiful fresh skin with slightly flushed cheeks like the proverbial English rose. He recalled what a particularly unpleasant woman he'd encountered in Hope's office once had said about English people: "Good skin and bad teeth." He looked at Annabel's teeth as she smiled at him. They weren't perfect. They weren't a typical American orthodontist's pride and joy. But they were fine. And as for her skin, she was in bloom. There was no other way to describe it. Soft brown eyes, and already she had the hint of a healthy tan. It was a relief to see a woman looking so natural with none of the Hamptons beauty parlor makeover about her. Okay, so her fair hair was a little gray at the temples, but it was thick and glossy and her figure was trim.

Even better, she was clutching a large tumbler of scotch.

In response to her greeting, "You must be exhausted, what can I get you?" he said, "A double vodka on the rocks would be just wonderful," and stumbled gratefully through the front door.

Once again, things were looking up.

8

.

If I had been in a panic about taking care of three young children, it was nothing compared to the nerves I was experiencing at the thought of Eddie Calder's imminent arrival. I had absolutely no conception of what he might be like. I cursed myself for not having quizzed Maud more about him. All I knew was that he was Maud's adored little brother. I didn't even know what he looked like. Seeing him as a baby at Rosemullion wasn't much of a clue.

And then there was the additional problem that his wife was deceiving him. Hope had gone off on a secret assignation with her ex-husband, and I knew and could say nothing. Well, I could. I could even call Maud and spill the beans, but I wasn't going to. Be loyal to the one you're with, that's my motto this year. Maud's miles away and Hope's right here. But then how am I going to feel about Eddie? And his constant phone calls postponing his arrival didn't exactly inspire my confidence in him.

Having said I had no idea what to expect, he wasn't a bit like I'd expected, if you know what I mean. I suppose, subconsciously, I had thought he would be a male version of Maud: dark, beautifully groomed, the image-is-everything type.

My first feeling on seeing him standing there on his own doorstep was maternal. I wanted to mother him in a way I hadn't even wanted to mother the children. I wanted to run him a hot bath, read him a bedtime story, tuck him up in bed. And no, not like that. I didn't find him attractive. He wasn't my type. I liked dark, brooding, intellectual types like Guy.

Eddie was a sandy-haired little boy lost, very English-looking, slightly effeminate, appealing but only if you liked that sort of thing. But when he smiled at me I got a load of his unmistakable charm.

"You must be exhausted," I said. "What can I get you?"

"A double vodka on the rocks would be just wonderful," he said, and almost fell into my arms as he stumbled through the door, dropping a battered briefcase that was coming apart at the seams. He looked totally disheveled. I had a feeling that his having been caught in the rain had nothing to do with it. He probably always looked like this. Baggy sweater, home-knitted by the looks of it. Equally baggy corduroys. Scuffed loafers. No relation to Maud whatsoever.

"Would you like to have a bath before dinner?"

"A bath before dinner?" he echoed, staring at me in astonishment.

"And please take your shoes off before you go any farther," I said, without thinking. Hope's housekeeper hadn't turned up again. I had taken advantage of having the extra day to myself and spent the entire afternoon attempting to clean the house in readiness for Eddie's arrival. Marietta would have been proud of me, although if I had known he was such a ragamuffin, I wouldn't have bothered.

"Do you want to go straight up and I'll leave your drink on the landing table? Your room's the one on the—"

I could feel myself going red. I realized I was back at Rosemullion, welcoming a new guest who had arrived for the weekend, someone who had driven through the rain over Bodmin Moor and arrived hungry and cold, anticipating burning log fires, piping-hot water, and a comforting bowl of soup with Marietta's freshly baked bread. I had gone into my automatic bed-and-breakfast welcome for a man walking into his own house.

"I know where my room is," he said, in, a grumpy little-boy tone of voice. "What I want to know is where is my wife? I get off the bus, and the cabdriver tells me she's gone to New York and taken Harry and Coco with her. Not a word to me. I assume you're Annabel Quick. I don't mean to be rude, but I'm really pissed off. Have you any idea what's going on?"

He hadn't even known Hope wasn't going to be there. I felt absolutely furious with her. My only option seemed to be to deflect him with a bit of my own charm.

"Yes, I'm Annabel. It's so nice to meet you at last. I can't tell you how thrilled I was to come out here." Really laying it on thick. Total fabrication. "Look, first things first, a bath and then I'll have some food waiting. Just soup and a cheese omelet, I'm afraid. But I've made some banana bread. Booty loves it."

That brought back his smile.

"Booty asleep?"

"Fast asleep, but I expect if you crept in and kissed her on the forehead it would give her sweet dreams."

"You'd allow me to do that?" He sounded surprised.

"No *allow* about it. She's your child."

"And it's my house."

"Oh, God, I'm sorry." In my nervousness I took a swig of the scotch I'd had in my hand when I opened the door.

"And presumably my whisky."

"I don't know what to say. . . ."

"It's okay. Go right ahead. A cheese omelet would be great. And no tonic with the vodka. Straight up."

He bounded across the hall and up the stairs without taking his shoes off.

"My floor," I wailed.

"*My* floor," he called from upstairs.

I rushed around the kitchen, opening drawers, looking in

cupboards for what I needed to throw together a meal for him. Hope had left me a carton of clam chowder which she said was his favorite, but making an omelet in someone else's kitchen was harder than I'd expected. Still jet-lagged, I needed more than a few days to acclimatize myself, but Hope had arrived home yesterday, thrown a bundle of things into a couple of bags, shouted some garbled instructions to me about chowder, and disappeared in a rush to catch the bus to New York, with Harry and Coco running after her. I had spent the afternoon cleaning the house, to get to know where everything was as much as anything else. And Booty, bless her, had been adorable, trotting around behind me, vastly amused by the sight of me doing housework. But I was good at it, however funny a picture I presented. It was the one thing Marietta had left to me: the overseeing of the cleaning of Rosemullion.

"I must say I've never seen the place so organized," Eddie commented, when he came downstairs. "Our bedroom's always immaculate because Hope's obsessively tidy, but when you go into the bathroom there's no toilet paper, no towels, no Kleenex."

"I've been well trained," I confessed, and told him about Rosemullion.

"So when I walked through the door you looked upon me as a kind of paying guest. Room Thirty-nine's checking in, better make him feel at home."

"Something like that." I wondered whether to tell him we'd once met. Perhaps I ought to leave it alone. But I couldn't resist bringing Rosemullion into the conversation.

"Actually, Eddie, we've met before. You came to Rosemullion for a summer holiday when you were a baby. You couldn't be expected to remember."

"Tell me something." He looked mischievous. "Did Maud start bitching about Hope?"

"Just a bit." I grinned.

"And has Hope driven you nuts yet?"

This surprised me. "Not at all. Why would she?"

"She's manic. Never stops. I have to book time with her way ahead. But I can live with that. What I can't live with is how little time she gives the kids. You know, it's funny. I was totally freaked by having to meet you. But now we've come face-to-face, I'm encouraged to know you'll be with the kids. They need some kind of continuity, especially Harry and Coco. Their father walked out, and then I appear and Hope decides to start running the world. All they've had is a succession of young girls posing as nannies to look after them. It's much better to have an older—whoops!—"

"It's okay."

"Hope kept finding this never-ending stream of American bimbos with maple syrup for brains. That's maple syrup lite. But don't get the wrong idea. I adore my wife. The way we got married was insane—and please don't repeat this to Maud, the less ammunition the better—it was almost an arranged marriage. I needed to stay in the country; she needed someone to help her get over the Creep. It just so happened we fell in love. She infuriates me. She infuriates everyone. But that's the kind of person she is. She gets under your skin and you can't forget her. The thing about Hope is, she's never boring. So tell me, why has she gone into New York?"

"She's taken the kids to her mother's for Easter." It was half true, the best I could come up with. I couldn't stand it. He so patently adored her, and she had gone off to the city to see her ex.

"Oh, God, I haven't bought any eggies and bunnies and all that shit! Well, Booty won't be hard to fool. I'll pick up something for her tomorrow. But you see, Annabel, this is typical Hope. If the appalling Maisie's invited them for Easter, Hope's known about it for ages and yet she never said a word."

"Maisie's Hope's mother?"

"Correct. To understand Hope you have to meet the mother, although personally I wouldn't recommend it. It's all about Hope's rebellion. She had this typical New York Upper West Side upbringing. She went to Columbia Prep, a private school funded by Columbia University, very conservative. I never met the father, he died pretty young, but I suspect he was a gent. Maisie was this liberal sixties person who had Hope sitting on the floor cross-legged—I've seen pictures—separating the seeds out of marijuana instead of doing her homework.

"You know what Maisie is now? A reflexologist. The fucking apartment's always full of people wandering around in bare feet waiting for their massages. Place gets pretty cheesy. But at the same time Maisie wanted nothing but the best for Hope. I got the message loud and clear. Even though she'd already been married once before, everyone expected me to go and blow ten thousand bucks at Harry Winston for a ring out of my pathetic publishing salary, so I did.

"I still don't make very much. Every time I look at little Harry I think of that ring. I call him Harry Winston. He thinks it's got something to do with Winston Churchill. Just as well. Anyway, Hope's doing okay financially, and of course her ex contributes quite a bit."

This was too much. I couldn't hold out on him any longer.

"Eddie, Maud's my friend and you're her brother and I'm going to tell you something I probably shouldn't, but I'm going to anyway. Hope hasn't exactly confided in me, but I happen to know she's taken the kids into New York to see their father."

"The creep? She's meeting up with him?"

"Yes."

"No, you're mistaken. She wouldn't. Not behind my back. How do you know?"

"I spoke to him on the telephone. He told me he was coming to New York."

"Oh, shit, that's okay then. He was winding you up. Hope's not meeting him. He sounds like a real creep, doesn't he?"

"You've never met him?"

"Not on your life. Wild horses, et cetera, et cetera."

"You really think she won't see him? The kids are expecting to see him."

"The kids? Of course they'll see him. If he really is coming. Which I doubt. But just because he wants to see the kids that doesn't mean he gets to see Hope as well. Oh, no."

Well, maybe he was right. How did I know? Hope had seemed a little shifty to me, but maybe that was because she'd forgotten to tell Eddie she was going to New York. Forgotten on purpose?

"Come on, have another drink. Let's get drunk. Hope never gets drunk."

Oh, yes, she does. I wanted to tell him. We both had too much that first night I was here. But I'd said enough for now.

I liked Eddie. We amused ourselves trashing Americans for a while—in fun, of course—because of their complete lack of irony.

"But I love their enthusiasm," said Eddie, suddenly serious, "their positive attitude to life, their confidence. Over here you're allowed to be confident and boast about your achievements, real or not. I mean, for someone like me who was generally considered a lost cause in London, America is heaven. I'm bullshitting everyone into thinking I'm worth taking seriously."

"Eddie, does that include you? Do you take yourself seriously?"

"Good gracious, no. Maud got all the brains in the family."

"Well how can you expect Hope to do it?"

"How can I expect Hope to take me seriously? Christ, I don't know. I'm drunk and it's late and frankly I'm exhausted.

I'm probably boring you to death. I'd better go to bed. No doubt you have the usual preconceived opinions of me, based on what Maud's told you. I know who I am, Annabel. I know I'm a bit of a fool, and I know I'm lucky to have Hope."

"Then fight for her," I said quickly.

"What do you mean, fight for her? I haven't lost her, as far as I know."

"Go into New York and fight for her. Tell her everything you've told me tonight."

I don't know what came over me. I was probably as drunk as he was. But I couldn't help feeling that I wasn't wrong about what Hope was up to. What a situation I'd walked into. Talk about out of the frying pan.

Eddie stood up and started dancing drunkenly around the room, punching the air like a boxer.

"Gotta fight for her, fight for her, fight for her." He landed in front of me and leaned over to give me a kiss on the cheek. "Friends for life?"

"Friends for life," I confirmed, laughing. There was nothing else to do. He was a clown. He relied on his ability to make people smile to keep him going.

The next morning Booty woke up in a fury. She had suddenly realized that not only was Hope not there but Harry and Coco weren't either.

She wouldn't be comforted. Eddie appeared, touseled and sleepy, in a dressing gown so old and tattered—and so short—I assumed it must be a relic of his prep school days.

"Oh, Christ, what are we going to do with her? What's wrong? Shall I call the doctor? Booty, please don't make that terrible noise. Oh, God, this is awful. Annabel, please don't worry. I'll handle her."

Oddly enough I wasn't remotely worried, and the more I observed Eddie's attempts to calm her, the more I believed he would have been incapable of handling her had she been comatose. There wasn't a great deal of difference between Eddie's ineffective rantings and Booty's tirade, which she hurled at us from the center of her cot, where she sat with her little fists tightly clenched.

I began to speak to Booty in the same even tone I had used my first morning with her, and it worked. She allowed me to take her tiny nightie off in one quick movement, pulling the sleeves quickly over her chubby little arms. Gradually her sobs diminished into muted whimpers of protest, halfhearted at their loudest. And by the time I had her out of her cot, she was giggling.

"Amazing," said Eddie. "No one's ever been able to win her over that quickly. What's your secret?"

"I just didn't worry about it. If she had sensed that I was at my wits' end, it would have only made things worse. The secret is just not to care."

Where did that come from? I sounded like an expert, as if I had been taking care of toddlers for years and years, and yet it was really just good old-fashioned common sense. I began to feel a little confidence growing inside me. I had lost my mother, but at the same time I could kiss goodbye a lifetime of being put down at every opportunity. Now I was acting according to my own instincts without someone shouting instructions from the sidelines.

Unlike Marietta, Eddie had no qualms about having me deal with things that needed doing around the house. We took Booty for a walk down to the bay beach, let her scamper in and out of the water, paddling barefoot, even though the early April water was pretty chilly, and once she'd walked all the way back she was exhausted and ready for a nap. Eddie took the opportunity to go around with me looking for— and finding—work that needed to be done. And at every instance he found an excuse to blame Hope for the neglect of their property.

"She's in the bloody business, for Christ's sake. She's all too happy to sort out other people's problems with their houses, but when it comes to ours, forget it. You have no idea the amount of people who call here asking if she can recommend a plumber, a carpenter, their roof's falling apart, the glass in their patio doors needs repairing, their drains are blocked, who's good at driveways? And all because Hope's the agent who sold them their house. She's always got an answer for them, but look at our place."

As it happened, I had been looking at "our place" with increasing admiration in the few days I had been there. As Hope had explained to me, it was called a saltbox, built sometime in the fifties and modeled on the original rickety versions of the early settlers. But right away I had seen that the house was not practical for a family. When Hope had bought it she had been a young single mother, straight from the big city, a girl in a hurry, a woman on the rebound. She hadn't been thinking long-term. The place was stylish. The living room had a cathedral ceiling with plate glass windows looking out over a forty-foot deck to the woods beyond. The fireplace was magnificent. At $169,000 for three bedrooms and two bathrooms, it was, she told me proudly, a steal. Then.

Now it was a cramped impractical nightmare. Three bedrooms—for Hope, Harry, and Coco—were fine, but the arrival of Booty and a live-in nanny created instant problems. Booty now slept on the landing outside Hope and Eddie's room and her playroom extended all over the house. I was in a small spare room that was probably meant for an upstairs study or sewing room.

"I mean, look at it," said Eddie, kicking a plastic duck halfway across the floor in disgust. "This is our living room. It's meant to be an adult's room but nothing in this house is sacred. No offense, Annabel, but we just don't need an extra person living in the house. Plus the roof leaks. When it rains hard the water comes pouring in and around the glass doors to the deck. And what does Hope do about it? Nothing."

"Well, what do *you* do about it?" I challenged him.

"The point is, I know nothing about this sort of thing. I wouldn't expect Hope to have lunch with boring literary agents and plow through the manuscripts they send you afterward. But houses are her line of work. She knows what she's talking about in this area."

"But she's got too much work to deal with this," I protested.

"That's my point. She's always too busy to deal with the things that matter: her home, her kids."

He didn't come out and say it, but the word *me* hung in the air.

"So what I was wondering," he went on, "was whether you could sort of step in and take over now you're here. You'd be perfect. You must have had experience in house maintenance if you've run a small hotel all these years."

Oh, great. I could see where this was going. And he had a point. What he couldn't be expected to know, of course, was that I'd never dealt with this sort of stuff on my own. I'd opened the door to carpenters and plumbers and builders over the years, said, "Hello, how are you?" and turned them over to Marietta for directions. But there was no point in telling Eddie any of this. It might lead to further uncovering of all the things I was supposed to be able to do and couldn't.

Besides, I seemed to have got the hang of handling Booty. Who knew what I was capable of?

I let him give me a list of what he called the G.C.'s—general contractors—and their phone numbers. So far so good. I knew how to use a phone. I'd start calling them the following week.

But his next request was a little more complicated.

"This is typical Hope. Look, the fridge is virtually empty. What are we supposed to eat?"

I looked at him, dreading what was coming.

"Annabel, would you mind? I have this huge manuscript to read, and it must be done this weekend. Could you take the car and go to the market?"

No, I'm afraid I can't take the car, Eddie, because I don't have a driver's license. Bit of a problem there at the moment. Terribly sorry.

"Or if you want a nice little walk through the woods, there's the Springs General Store ten minutes away. You could take Booty tomorrow in her stroller. They have an Easter Egg hunt and she can run around looking for chocolate eggs. She'd love it. Why don't you do that? You can hang the bag of groceries over the stroller."

That sounded like something I could do, but the phone rang before I told him.

"Who?" I heard Eddie ask when he picked up the phone. "Josie? Do I know you? . . . What? Josie Gardiner? . . . Oh, *Josephine* Gardener. Good God, how did you get my number? . . . No, I'm afraid not. It's just not a terrifically good time. I'm here with my baby daughter, and I have to take care of her."

He held up a hand to silence me, because no doubt he could see the outrage on my face. Taking care of his baby daughter? Since when?

"Oh, you're out here? That's fascinating, but no, I'm sorry. It's out of the question. Terrible shame. Why don't we schedule lunch in the city next week? I'll call you. . . . Excellent. Great. . . . Yup."

I could tell his patience was running out rapidly with whoever it was.

"Jesus!" he yelled, when he finally put down the phone. "What a nerve, calling me here on a weekend!"

"Who was it?"

"An author. A new author I haven't even met. Sounds like she could give me a lot of grief. Her editor left and my boss decided I should take her over for the silly reason that we're both British. It would be quite an important career move for me; her books make money. But the last thing I want is a nightmare author who calls me at home. Have you ever read Josephine Gardiner?"

I wanted to shake him. I recalled his comments the night before about how the Americans were so positive and confident and energetic, but if it meant he'd have to endure a little aggravation in order to further his own career, Eddie was clearly going to run.

And I *had* read Josephine Gardiner. I'd had good reason to. Her books spoke directly to me. Soul-searching, haunting, sometimes very erotic stories about women who fall for unsuitable men. I couldn't imagine someone like Eddie getting past page two.

"I could kill my boss, Clem Springer. He went and told her I had a house out here, gave her the number. She claims she's related to the Gardiners and is basing her new book on them. She wants to come out and stay and do research."

"Who are the Gardiners?"

"Do you remember when we went to the beach, you could look out over the bay and see an island? That's Gardiners Island. Way back in the seventeenth century, a Puritan colonist called Lion Gardiner intervened when one Indian chief's daughter was kidnapped by another chief on her wedding day. He negotiated her release, and in return he got to buy that island for something daft like one large black dog, one gun, some rum, and a pair of blankets. When Hope pulls off a real estate deal like that, I'll be impressed.

"So anyway, it becomes Gardiners Island, and his daughter Elizabeth is the first English person to be born in New York State. The Gardiner family live on the island to this day, but they won't allow anyone else to set foot on it. Sweet Josephine is going to have to have mighty good proof she's related."

• • •

It took me twenty minutes rather than ten to walk to the Springs General Store on Sunday, pushing the stroller all the way. Eddie had obviously never walked there himself. As we approached the store, I saw a large number of small children and their parents gathered there. It was rather a fancy general store. Not the kind of rundown jar-of-Nescafé-and-five-year-old-packet-of-biscuits you found if you ventured within twenty minutes of Rosemullion, it was more of an upscale deli, with imported cheeses and ready-made salads. They served coffee and doughnuts and newspapers, and people sat outside to read and gossip. And to my immense relief they sold fresh vegetables and cold meats and sausages, so with a bit of luck I could do most of my shopping here provided I could train Hope to bring back whatever else we needed from East Hampton. Although I could see I was going to become pretty fit if Hope asked me to get a big order, as there was only so much I could carry on the stroller. I'd be walking back and forth two or three times a day if Hope suddenly decided she needed a lot of groceries.

And how long before someone noticed and commented to Hope that her new nanny seemed to be taking an inordinate amount of exercise?

I picked up some snacks for lunch and wheeled Booty's stroller in between the rows of Jeep Cherokees and Lexuses parked in front of the store. Couples were everywhere. I felt rather conspicuous. Half these mums were pregnant, I realized, looking around me. Summer babies on the way, and my womb was about to pack up altogether. I wasn't part of a couple. I didn't fit in here.

I knew where this could lead. Snap out of it! Get a grip on yourself, Annabel! Marietta's favorite expression when I showed signs of laziness or depression.

I sat on a bench where I could watch Booty, who had

grabbed the little yellow wicker basket I gave her by the long handle and was stomping her way across the grass after a duck, brandishing the basket at it. After a while she stopped and watched the other kids, and then she began to get the picture and rushed over to the bushes to look for eggs.

This is Maud's niece, I thought fondly, yet she has an American accent and she's going to grow up an all-American kid. Maud will have a fit.

Two couples came and sat on the bench next to me. They didn't appear to notice me. One of the men was dominating the conversation, and as I listened I realized he was talking about Booty.

"Hey, that's Hope's kid. Look, over there, down by the water. The father must be here somewhere."

"What's he like?"

"Oh, he's cute," said one of the women. "He's English."

"And he's hardly ever around," said the man. He had what I called a weasel face. Mean. Sallow complexion. Thin pointed features, especially his nose, eyes a little too close together. Snappy dresser. A little too snappy for my liking, especially for a Sunday morning. He looked like he was off to a meeting.

Which, as I discovered, he was.

"He's probably an OK guy. Who knows? But how he can put up with Hope is a miracle. Another nanny just quit on her."

"I don't know why you're so mean about her. I think she's a good broker. She rented our house for us last year, and she couldn't have been more helpful."

"Mark's just jealous," said a blonde sitting behind the weasel. "He wants to match her commissions. He just doesn't have the experience yet."

From this I deduced that Mark must be in real estate like Hope.

"And the bitch of it is," continued the blonde, "he's got to work later today. We thought you guys would be here at the

Easter Egg hunt with Jacob and Rebecca, we missed you at the house, and we wanted to catch you. We can't make lunch. Mark has to show houses."

"It's a real opportunity for me. Hope's gone into the city for the weekend. I overheard her telling someone. I found out who her clients were and contacted them, and while the cat's away this mouse is going to show a whole lot of properties, take some business right out from under her nose."

One of Hope's rivals, clearly.

"So which one is Hope's kid?"

"Oh, she's gone. She was over there a minute ago."

It took a second for the penny to drop, and then I turned to look for Booty.

She was nowhere to be seen.

I had done the unthinkable. I had taken my eyes off her. And as I rushed all around the area surrounding the Springs General Store I realized she had completely disappeared.

9

Right from the start I assumed I would find Booty lying face down in the water. Behind the store was an inlet from Accabonac Harbor. As I set off from the house, Eddie had gone to great pains to describe to me how beautiful it was, how I should be sure to take a look. Booty had been chasing the ducks. The ducks were now on the water. She must have chased them into the water and fallen in. Booty would be drowned and I would be sent back to England in disgrace with the death of a two-year-old on my conscience, not to mention the death of my parents.

How long before they ascertained exactly how the fire at Rosemullion had started? Were they saying, back home in the village, that I had run away? That I could not face up to my responsibilities? Well, they would be right. And now I had gone one step further in the total screw-up stakes.

I ran along the path at the water's edge yelling "Booty!" and people began to move across the grass after me. When I reached the point where the path dwindled to a meager trail leading into thick woods, I turned back to face a small crowd gathering on the bank.

"A little girl, dark curly hair, blue and white dress . . ."

"You're her mother?" someone shouted. At any other time I would have been delighted that someone could have mistaken me for the mother of a two-year-old.

"No. Hope Calder is. I'm looking after her kids." Although obviously not very successfully.

"Booty?"

I nodded. "She was here a second ago."

"Oh, Booty's always running off. Hope should have warned you." A large woman had come out from the store behind the others. "You need to think of her like a puppy, keep her on a lead if you have to. Soon as she could walk, that little one started taking off all over the place. She's probably in the woods. We'll go look. Get your car and follow me."

Get your car.

"I don't have a car."

It seemed like twenty Cherokee and Lexus owners were all staring at me at once. She doesn't have a car. She's a freak. A weirdo. Keep away from her.

"I mean, I don't have it with me," I stammered. "I walked. It's not far."

"Come on with me," said the woman. "Booty moves at quite a pace. Got herself a pair of sturdy little legs. Don't worry, honey. She often does this. Hope comes in to buy a gallon of milk, turns around, and she's gone. Long as she's in the woods, she oughta be fine. It's when she starts going down the road that Hope gets scared."

Oh, thanks for telling me, Hope. Anything else I should know? Like, Does Booty like to swallow bleach? Poke her fingers into electric sockets?

"Everyone go look in the woods," yelled the woman. "I'm going to take this lady—what's your name, honey? Annabel?—I'm going to take Annabel in the car to the bottom of Shipyard Lane and search the woods from there. Meet you back here in ten minutes."

The woman said her name was Cheryl and hurled questions at me about England and where did I come from and the trips she and her husband planned to make to London. I didn't say a word. She stopped her car and led me along a woodland trail, looking right and left, but we didn't see her.

But when we returned to the store there was Booty sitting on the steps. No, she wasn't sitting on the steps, she was lying inert. Even Cheryl seemed to go into a momentary panic, bringing her car to a screeching halt and jumping out.

"She's okay. We found her just a little way into the woods, but she must have fallen over and hurt her leg. There's a big gash on her left knee. We called Dr. Moran already. He's expecting you down at the doctor's office. Better have him take a look."

"Ben, you want to take them? I have a store to run. You'll be okay, honey. This is my son, Ben."

"Could you do me one more favor?" I asked Cheryl. "Could you call her father at home and tell him to meet us at the doctor's? And thank you. Thank you for everything."

"Sure," said Cheryl. "I'll call right away."

Booty came to life and yelled "no!"—what else?—when we lifted her into Ben's truck but on the way to the doctor she snuggled up to me and managed a little smile. Her knee was still oozing blood.

Ben drove us through the village of Amagansett and drew up outside what looked like an old shingled family house with a wraparound porch.

"Doctor's office," he said simply, and carried Booty in for me.

As soon as I saw Dr. Moran I knew everything would be all right.

"You are . . . ?" he asked, as Ben set Booty down on the examining table and slipped out of the room.

"Annabel Quick. I'm Hope and Eddie Calder's new nanny. From England," I added superfluously.

He smiled hello. He was quite short, with a shock of thick white hair that set off his tanned face. His eyes twinkled. They were dark, almost black, and I realized his hair must once have been black too. So he must be older than he looked for his hair to have turned white already. I thought he was around fifty, but he must be closer to sixty. But what a devil he must have been. Still was, in a way. He had an air of authority about him. "Don't worry about a thing," his face said. "I'm in charge now; you can relax." I relaxed. I trusted him.

I have always been too trusting. I'm never prepared for people's nastiness or even their indifference. I guess I'm a bit of a Pollyanna in that respect. I certainly wasn't prepared for Guy and the person he turned out to be.

I like doctors as a breed because I feel you're meant to trust them. That's what they're for. And they're paid to be interested in you, which for someone like me, who has allowed herself to be convinced by her mother that she's not remotely interesting, is always a bonus. I always adored old Dr. Trevelyan back home, even though he drove Marietta mad with his slow, ponderous way of talking.

"I could die before he was through telling me what was wrong with me," she maintained.

Dr. Trevelyan was the only person apart from Maud I ever told about Guy. He sensed I was going through some sort of depression when I went to him with an ear infection, making sure I had his last appointment of the day, because I always enjoyed a chat with him afterward.

"You've always been a healthy girl, Annabel." Only Dr. Trevelyan could call a woman in her forties a girl and get away with it. "Your parents' death was traumatic, but it's more than that. Something else is bothering you. Come on, out with it."

For about five seconds I protested that there was nothing wrong, and then I burst into tears and ruined it all. I left out the more intimate details—there were limits to what I could tell someone who was essentially a friend of my parents—but half an hour later he knew all about Guy.

It wasn't that men didn't interest me. They did. But I'd exhausted the local talent by the time I was twenty-five and failed to meet anyone to help me forget the humiliation of Jasper. Then everyone started settling down and marrying each other, as they do in small communities. A few people imported wives from London or other parts of the country, but there were plenty of attractive young women right in Cornwall, and pretty soon all the eligible bachelors were gone. The folks were pretty traditional in the area around Rosemullion. There were a few lone fishermen who had never married, but they were old salts before their time and held little attraction for any sane woman. People aspired to making a happy marriage, settling down, and raising kids in the old-fashioned way, and as the men ran out I became lazy. In the eighties, when Rosemullion was at the height of its success, Marietta turned the dining room into a full-scale restaurant that gained something of a reputation, following a piece in a national newspaper. The reviewer went into ecstasies about the exquisite taste of fresh fish and seafood brought up by the fishermen and placed in front of you five minutes later—a slight exaggeration, but never mind. It brought in the business for both summer holidays and winter breaks, and for a while we were rushed off our feet. I literally did not have time for romance, or so I told myself.

Guy just slipped into my life without my really noticing what was happening.

He was married. I knew that from the very beginning, so I can't pretend I didn't have a chance to back off before things got out of hand.

He was an unlikely adulterer, or so it seemed to begin with. At the time I met him he was an unassuming—I thought—schoolmaster at a boy's prep school in Oxford. Appearances can be so deceptive: gray jacket, gray eyes, prematurely gray hair. He first came to Rosemullion with his wife, Katharine, and their two boys for a family holiday, an Easter break. Marietta took one look at him and pronounced him boring. But he wasn't. He was, I thought, gentle and funny. He brought me books to read that he thought I might enjoy, music to listen to. He opened up a world of culture to me that I had not previously encountered, and I was flattered that he found my opinion of these things worthy of attention. I began to look forward to his twice-a-year visits to Rosemullion.

It happened on the last day of one of his stays there. I ran into him on the cliffs and we walked together to the nearest village. Rain had begun to pelt down, and we took shelter in a pub. When the rain stopped we retraced our steps along the cliff path until suddenly he took my hand and said, "Come with me."

I knew the hamlet well. The lane from the cliffs was flanked by so many brambles that I avoided it if I could but that's where we walked, to this thatched cottage. By the time we arrived there my legs were covered in scratches.

I'd known the old biddy who lived there until her death. I didn't particularly like the house; it was too cute, too picture postcard. But he was clearly smitten. "I've always dreamed of somewhere like this," I can remember him saying. "A bolt hole. I think that's the real reason I looked for a place to holiday in Cornwall." He was a real romantic underneath the gray exterior, but that was part of the problem. Guy had dreams, but he expected other people to fulfill them. He made no effort to do so himself.

He asked me what I thought of the cottage. I hesitated. I couldn't give him my real opinion, I couldn't destroy his dream, so I said something like, "It's charming, but isn't it a bit small?" I told him I'd been inside and it was a bit cramped. Only two bedrooms upstairs. And then he surprised me by saying, "Oh, it's not for Kathy and the boys. It's just for me to escape to now and then." I was standing there wondering why he needed to escape when he said, "And of course I'll be close to you."

It was a shock. I'd never thought of him in that way, but it's funny, the minute he indicated he was attracted to me, I realized I fancied him too. He had a Jimmy Stewart look about him, the same gangling awkwardness that becomes unbelievably attractive when his attention is focused on you and you realize he isn't such a bumbler after all.

And then he kissed me, and I kissed him back, and it was completely wonderful. Not at all gray!

The back door to the little cottage was open. There was no furniture. We made love on the floor of what I recall was the dining room. As it turned out, the house really did turn out to be only a dream for him. He couldn't possibly afford it, not then, not before he became successful with his books. It was sold to a retired accountant and his wife, a man Marietta charmed into giving her some free tax advice, which resulted in our being invited there for dinner one night, and it was all I could do not to relieve the unmitigated boredom of the evening by describing what I'd done with Guy on their dining room floor.

Our affair went on for years. Not at Rosemullion, although he and Kathy continued to bring the boys twice a year. We met in London. It was sleazy, but of course we didn't think so because it was us. Or at least I didn't think so. I fooled myself into thinking my affair with a married man was different from anyone else's. I imagine many people delude themselves in this way. No other adulterers ever actually fall in love. Just you. You're lucky. You're special.

Maud told me over and over again that he would never leave Kathy, and I always replied that I knew that; it wasn't part of the deal, I wasn't a marriage wrecker, I knew the rules.

But of course I always secretly hoped that one day he'd break them.

Deep down, for all her toughness, Maud is a kind woman. And a good friend. She didn't tell me at first that she had seen Guy in London with another woman after he had begun to go to the same media parties to which she was invited. But then, after she'd seen him with two or three, she did.

I said it wasn't true. She was mistaken. She barely knew Guy, met him once or twice with me because we knew we could trust her to keep our secret. A far as I was concerned, it was more important to keep it from Marietta than from Kathy, although essentially it amounted to the same thing. Marietta would immediately wade in and call Kathy if she found out.

I managed to remain in denial about Guy's other women for about four years. For all I knew, Kathy behaved as I did. As long as she didn't know about them she didn't care. But then I had to face facts. Guy had written one of those semiacademic books about children's emotional intelligence that became a best-seller. Suddenly he was the darling of the London media, and Maud began to run into him all the time. He lectured in America, even took me with him on the odd occasion. But fame has its price. A sighting of him with a woman—not me—was reported in the press. I mentioned it, laughed about it, but the slight hesitation before his tossed-off reply alerted me to the truth. I began to press Maud for details and, wretchedly, she supplied them.

Despite Maud's insistence that it would be the worst possible thing to do, I behaved stupidly and issued an ultimatum. I could see the irony of it. There had been a time when I could have asked him to leave his wife for me. Now all I was doing was asking him to drop his other women and make me his only one. He refused. Furthermore, he said if that was the way I was going to behave we might as well call it a day.

I went home to Cornwall hurt and betrayed for the second time in my life and didn't see him again for two years.

Then came the fire at Rosemullion.

The timing of events in one's life is often strange. Everything seems to be running like clockwork, almost boring, and then suddenly changes hit you—one, two, three—one after the other.

About a month before the fire Marietta made a startling announcement at the breakfast table. She'd had a letter from Guy. He and Katharine would not be bringing the boys for their summer holiday. Well, that was nothing new. Since we'd stopped seeing each other two years earlier, he had written to my mother at the beginning of each year saying they had decided to go abroad but would be returning to Rosemullion one day.

"Where are they going this year?" I had asked casually.

"Doesn't look like they're going anywhere. At least not together. They've split up. He says she's left him."

Considering she thought he was pretty boring, Marietta had always managed to wheedle out of Guy the most amazing confidences, everything, it seemed, except the fact that he was fucking her daughter. There had been moments when I had longed to show her that I knew something she didn't. "But he wants to come and spend some time here on his own. He's booked the Yellow Room for the last two weeks of July."

Has he now? I thought to myself. I wonder what that means?

The news of the fire spread far and wide and he must have heard about it from someone, because he turned up at the funeral. It gave me a fearful jolt when I turned and looked back down to the church in the middle of the service and saw him.

He was staying somewhere in Penzance, and he came out the day after the funeral to see me.

He wanted to pick up where we had left off. In fact, he wanted more. He proposed marriage in a roundabout way. "If I asked you to marry me, what would you say?" Hedging his bets. Not coming right out and proposing. Running scared. Abandoned by his wife.

And my parents barely cold in their graves.

It was insensitive beyond belief. I was shocked. He was thinking only of himself. He wanted me, he needed me, but he didn't seem to be aware of how I might be feeling. Or care.

I couldn't handle it. It was as if the scales of delusion fell away from my eyes and I saw him clearly for the first time. He didn't really want me. He wanted comfort and solace and I was good old Annabel, always there, waiting for him down in Cornwall. Perhaps he had always kept me in reserve, thinking he could reach out and pick me up when he felt like it. And even if I did let him back into my life, I knew I'd be fooling myself. A leopard can't change his spots. I wouldn't feel secure. There'd come a time when he'd begin to feel guilty, not about me but about Kathy and his sons. She might have been the one to leave, but he'd driven her to it. I was amazed at how wise I had suddenly become.

I knew if he touched me my resolve would melt, so I kept my distance. I sent him away, this time for good.

I might have appeared cold to him but inside I was crumbling. I was mourning not only the loss of my parents but also the loss of the only man who had ever offered me a semblance of romantic love. Some kind of ritualistic urge led me back to the pub where we had had our first drink, sheltering from the rain. Driving home, I zigzagged down the road in drunken misery.

When the police caught up with me, it was only a matter of time before I lost my driver's license.

From then on I sank into a deepening depression that manifested itself in the ear infection. It took wily old Dr. Trevelyan to look beyond that and see the unhappiness within.

• • •

Booty was fine. Her knee was cleaned and disinfected and then she was delivered into the capable hands of Deborah, the doctor's assistant, who lived next door and had been only too happy to pop over and help out, Easter Sunday or no Easter Sunday.

Because Dr. Moran said he wanted a word with me.

Uh-oh. Had he spotted me for the fraud I so obviously was?

"Where's Eddie? Where's Booty's father?" I asked, stalling for time. "I asked Cheryl at the store to call him."

"He isn't here. Booty, sweetie, want a pop? Strawberry? Raspberry? Here, give him another call." Deborah held out the phone.

There was no reply. Odd. Maybe he was already on his way over.

"Maybe I ought to call Hope." I was beginning to sound a little desperate.

"Where's Hope?" asked Dr. Moran.

"In New York at her mother's."

"Long distance," commented Deborah, one eye on Dr. Moran.

"That's okay," he said. "Pull Hope's card on the Rolodex. The name's Hofstater, city number. I know her. I'll speak to her, and to Hope. Nothing wrong with Booty, but it'll be more reassuring coming from me, seeing as how you've only just started." He raised his eyebrows at me and I nodded. What a thoughtful man. In a few minutes I would be off the hook, except I still had to find a way to get us home.

I went out to reception to check on Booty, expecting Dr. Moran to call us in to speak to Hope. I could hear him talking to someone.

"What happened?" I asked, when I went back in.

"I spoke to Hope's mother, and they're not staying there. She gave me the number of a hotel where the children's father is staying and said we might find her there. Want to give it a shot?"

I shook my head. What was Hope playing at, telling me she'd gone to her mother? Whatever it was, I didn't want to get involved. Booty was fine. That was all that mattered.

Dr. Moran was looking at me with doctor's eyes, the kind of eyes I automatically trusted.

"The truth is I've taken a job as nanny to Hope's children when I have no real experience," I blurted out. "I was a nanny once, many years ago, but I was only ever really trained to look after tiny babies, and I've forgotten most of what I learned."

He looked a little startled, but then he smiled.

"I appreciate your candor. How long have you been looking after them?"

"I started this week."

"And do you like them?"

"So far so good. They're highly individual children but they're interesting—and interested. And they're fun. I'm enjoying them."

Until I said that I hadn't realized just how much I was enjoying them. From my first day I looked forward to the yellow flash of the school bus coming to a halt at the end of the drive, followed by Harry and Coco running into the kitchen to tell me about their day.

"Well, that's the main thing. Don't worry about it," Dr. Moran advised. "Do what feels right, and if anything happens give me a call. They're basically healthy kids. I'm glad Hope's got you."

I looked up at him surprised. I had been expecting him to wag a finger at me and tell me to keep a closer watch on my charges in the future. "Don't be too hard on her," he added.

I hadn't said a word about Hope. How did he know what I thought about her?

"I guess she forgot to tell you Booty has a tendency to go running off by herself and get into scrapes like this. Probably thought it'd scare you off. But she's a perfectly fine mother in her own way. She loves those kids. She's just one of those women who can't sit still. If she were a hen she'd peck herself to death. If she were a mother hen, she'd peck her chicks to death. And she's faithful to me."

He winked at me and smiled, and his whole face lit up in the most delightful way. His voice had a soft Irish lilt to it. Again I thought he must have been a real Irish charmer in his time.

"Hope's stuck by me when all the other mothers are flocking to my new young partner, Patchett. Handsome guy, I'll admit, and a damned good doctor. I wonder when they'll realize he's gay." He winked again.

"Now Annabel, one more thing." I had stood up to leave, my hand outstretched. I sat down again.

"Yes?"

"If you need to talk about anything, give me a call."

"But—" Hadn't he already said that?

"I'm a pediatrician, I know. But I'm still a doctor, and someone who knows this area pretty well. And you're a woman in a part of the world you probably *don't* know too well. Hope Calder'll grow up one day, and with you in her home it might be sooner than I thought. But right now she doesn't need to know if you've got problems. Do you understand me? You never know when you might need to talk things over. I've seen it happen before, woman your age. Feel free."

How did he know my age?

"Thank you, Dr. Moran."

"It's Ray. Ray Moran."

"Well, there is one thing."

"Shoot."

I imagined the loss of a license through drunken driving was not one of the more common ailments he heard about, especially from nannies, but he seemed to take it in stride.

"Of course I don't have a drinking problem as such," I

blundered on. "There was just this one instance because of a problem I'd had with a man, and my parents had just died, and . . ."

He could tell I was on the verge of tears.

"Whoa, there. Slow down. Take it easy. Tell me as much as you want."

I don't know what he must have thought of me. It was as if I'd taped what I'd told Doctor Trevelyan, slotted the tape into a machine, and hit PLAY. By the end I was crying uncontrollably and Ray Moran was holding my hand.

I snatched it away, embarrassed beyond belief. I was horrified by what I had done. This man, this relative stranger, now knew virtually all my secrets. And it was as if he could read my thoughts.

"I'm a doctor," he said simply. "Okay, I'm not a psychiatrist, but in a way all doctors have to be able to read people pretty well. I could tell from the minute you walked in here you weren't in good shape. And it's certainly understandable. You've been through a lot. But first let's be practical. Here's the number of Amagansett Taxi. The cars look a bit beat up but they're one hundred percent reliable. The money Hope gives you to spend on gas for the car, you spend on taxis. Sooner or later you're going to have to come clean with Hope and Eddie, but they'll understand. Now, dry your eyes, let's get Booty, and I'll run you guys home. It's on my way."

I felt great. I had a friend. I had someone I could turn to. I kept glancing over at him on the drive back to the house. Dr. Patchett might be a handsome young guy but I was pretty sure he didn't hold a candle to Ray Moran. Ray's face might be lined and weatherbeaten, but it was a kind face, and when he smiled his charm was undeniably potent.

I let Booty slip off my lap and out of the car to scamper up the driveway and turned to thank him.

He looked at me for a while without saying anything, and when he did I genuinely didn't see it coming.

"How about I take you out for dinner one night?" Perfectly innocent, acceptable, kindhearted invitation, except he added, "After all, you're not one of my patients."

I was dumbstruck. He was the first man to ask me out on a date since the trouble with you-know-who, and I had already taken note of his charm.

"I'll give you a call," he said, without waiting for my answer.

"I'd better get after Booty," I said, opening the car door, "before she runs off again."

"Eddie?" I called out on entering the house.

No reply.

He wasn't there. I found the note on the kitchen table.

Dear A:
That bloody Josie Gardiner kept calling so I've gone back to New York early to escape her clutches. And I want to take Easter eggs to Harry and Coco, to surprise them and Hope at her mother's. See you next weekend. Kiss Booty.
                                                            Eddie

Great, I thought. He'll get there and find she's not at her mother's. Then what?

10

Hope couldn't believe it.

Instead of being part of an emotional, loving gathering at the cemetery, comforting Maisie, with Craig's arm around her shoulders and the kids kneeling in front of her to put their little posies on Grandpa's grave, here she was, stuck in Craig's hotel suite, with Harry and Coco driving her crazy.

"I'll only be a couple of hours. Three, tops," Craig had told them cheerfully, within minutes of their arrival at his hotel that morning, after two nights at Maisie's. "I have to be at this screening. It's a rough assembly of this guy's latest film. I think he'd be the perfect director for my next picture. They've set up this screening specially for me. I can't not go. You do understand? We'll go to your father's grave tomorrow," he reassured her. "We don't have to do it on the actual day he died, do we?"

Of course we do, Hope thought. That's the whole point of an anniversary.

But then he'd looked at her with that smile she'd forgotten about. The one where he seemed to be looking up at her even though he was at least six inches taller than she was, where he managed to look so vulnerable and pleading that she found it impossible to say no. And then he put his arm around her and she hadn't seen him for so long and had forgotten how good he smelled, how wonderful it felt when he touched her, even if it was just for an instant. When he delivered the coup de grâce—"You look terrific, Hope. What have you done to yourself? You look years younger than when I last saw you. That haircut's sensational, really suits you"— she became instant putty in his hands (even though she hadn't had her hair cut in two months).

Maisie's words last night were ringing in her ears. "You're going to his hotel, you're taking Harry and Coco, you'll be a family again, make the most of every single minute, and I don't want to see you again till Monday morning. Get him back, baby, body and soul. Now's your chance. Don't blow it."

The extraordinary thing was that when she called Maisie in tears to say they wouldn't be going to Mel's grave that day, Maisie hadn't seemed at all put out.

"So we'll go tomorrow," she said cheerfully. Craig's words exactly. Was there a conspiracy going on? Maisie had been beside herself with excitement when Hope had revealed that Craig suggested commemorating the anniversary of Mel's death.

Am I doing this for my mother or for myself? Hope wondered, not for the first time. Because in a way it had been Maisie who had first put the idea in Hope's mind that she should try to get back with Craig.

"I'm always looking at my grandchildren and thinking, Those kids need their father," Maisie would tell her. "I've seen him looking at you, Hope, whenever you hand the kids over. He wants you back, I can tell."

"When have you seen him looking at me, Ma?" asked Hope skeptically. "You've only seen Craig and me together twice in the last five years."

"Well, you know what I mean. I can hear it in his voice when he talks about you."

"When he talks about me?"

"Yeah, when he calls."

"He calls you, Ma? When does he ever call you?"

"I'm still his mother-in-law. He calls. We talk."

"Or maybe you call him?"

"So maybe I do. I like Craig. I always did."

"That is so *not* true, Ma. It was Daddy who liked him. You didn't think he'd make a good husband, as I recall. You thought he was too unreliable, not a safe bet financially."

"Well, he's changed."

"He sure has. I doubt Daddy would even recognize him now."

"Well, at least your father was spared seeing you struggle with that English nebbish."

"Ma, don't start. Daddy would have loved Eddie."

But would he? Hope would never know. And she and Maisie were beginning to have the same conversation over and over again about how a return to Craig would be much better for all concerned.

Hope didn't disagree. She could not deny it was tempting to envisage being part of his newfound success, not to have to worry about money. It was tough not to be sharing in the fruition of the dreams they had started out with. She'd had enough of struggling on her own, feeling that Eddie just wasn't there for her, that she was carrying the load for both of them, not to mention all three kids.

But then she would remember how Craig had dumped them. How could she ever forgive him for that?

Well, here she was in his suite, sitting on his bed, watching his TV, trying to entertain his children—their children—and waiting for him. And the Princess had discovered a new pastime: Room Service.

"Just dial one-one," Craig had said, "and order anything you want."

So far Coco had already placed four separate orders for ice cream, a BLT, more ice cream, and a Coke.

"You have to tip the person who brings you the order," Craig had told her, placing a bundle of dollar bills on the table by the door. Coco, Hope noticed uneasily, was a natural tipper.

"This is for you," she told the waiter solemnly, handing him a dollar, and when he hesitated, probably because he had never before been tipped by a six-year-old in pale pink baby-doll pajamas, she stuffed a few more bills into his hand.

Harry was happy trying to work out the combination of the in-room safe. Hope called Eddie without revealing where she was. Everything seemed fine.

When Craig returned, he called up from the lobby and summoned them all down into a waiting cab.

"Lunch at Michael's," he told Hope. "I've made reservations."

Hope opened her mouth to say they would have been more than happy to go to Burger King and then shut it again. She needed a treat.

She couldn't help noticing the reservation was for three. Hope watched as they quickly laid another place. She had not been expected to join them. To baby-sit, yes, while he went to his screening, but nothing beyond that. Still, he was including her with good grace.

"How was the film? I'd like a kir, thank you."

"It was excellent. This director is going to make it big-time. Everyone wants to be in his next picture."

"Everyone?"

"Gwyneth. Kate. Brad—"

"Gwyneth?"

"Paltrow. Kate Winslett."

"And Brad Pitt. Not Leo?"

"He'll read the script, of course. But Gwyneth's too young for the lead. I want someone with a more mature look. Kim would be great."

Hope couldn't believe they were having this conversation. He couldn't be for real with all this buddy-buddy movie star talk. She decided to play along and see how far he would go.

"Kim Basinger? You know her?" She tried to sound impressed.

"Oh, we go way back." Craig nodded several times, as if he couldn't place enough emphasis on how far back he went with Kim. "Me and Kim. Way back."

"That's terrific," said Hope. "She lives just up the road from us, in Amagansett, so when you come visit her we'll get to see you. In fact, I think she and Alec are having some kind of benefit for Clinton this summer. Surely you're going. If you want to go to the reception, it's only about three thousand bucks."

At this point, she noted, he quickly switched the conversation.

"So, kids, what's it gonna be? The *bollito misto*, or the carbonara maybe? How about some gnocchi?" Harry and Coco looked at Hope. They hadn't a clue.

"Craig, they don't understand what you're talking about."

"Oh, of course. They don't speak Italian. My mistake. Sorry, kids, I'll order for you."

They hated their food. They hated the stiff, formal restaurant. The thick white linen showed up their grubby paw marks. It was not exactly a place where they could get down and run around while the adults lingered over coffee, not a friendly neighborhood Italian but an upscale, fashionable watering hole. They were bored and began to fight, using breadsticks as swords. Craig snarled at them.

"Do you have any idea where you are? I take you to a proper restaurant, and you behave like apes. Coco, give me that. Sit still. Eat your gnocchi."

"I hate it. It tastes like sick. I want a hot dog."

"Are you out of your mind?"

Hope knew the signs. Craig's fingers were drumming under the table on his thighs, thighs encased in well-pressed, pre-faded jeans. He was about to blow. Yet all she could think about was that his furiously tapping fingernails were beautifully manicured. Far better than hers. He clearly took a great deal more care with his appearance now. He'd never worn tasseled loafers when she'd been married to him. And he might have commented on her haircut but it was nothing compared to his. He reeked of money. He emanated signals: I have disposable income. Tap me. And the maître d' and the waiters were buzzing around him constantly. Hope had a fleeting picture of Eddie in the same situation. He'd leave it all up to her. He was hopeless in restaurants, never remembered to tip anyone, never understood foreign menus, and asked embarrassing things like, "What's *mozzarella in carozza* when it's at home?"—an English expression she'd never understood. Yet somehow she never worried about the children and their behavior when she was in a restaurant with Eddie. Hope knew perfectly well that if he'd been with them, he'd have done something excruciatingly uncool like insist the waiter bring Coco a hot dog if that's what she wanted.

Coco was crying now.

"Mommy, I want a hot dog. This stuff is yucky."

"Hope, for Christ's sake, she's so spoiled. Get her to stop. She can't cry here. Please. Do something."

The reservation was for three, Hope recalled irrelevantly. If I were not here he would have to deal with this himself.

Coco's wails were growing louder. People at adjacent tables were looking.

"Craig," said Hope, "order her an ice cream."

"*Gelati, per favore.*" Craig grabbed a passing waiter. "My agent says I'll get two million for this latest script."

"Oh, great," said Hope, wondering when he'd notice that Harry had crumbled his breadstick into the little dish of olive oil and was adding drops of Diet Coke to it.

"I'd run the concept by you, but my agent thinks we oughta keep it to ourselves for the time being, it's that hot."

And I'm likely to run out and tell the world? wondered

Hope. Like I'm not close to you, I'm not someone you can trust?

"Of course I could direct as well as produce and write," he continued, "but I'm going to let this new guy have a shot at it. It's not as if I'm a total control freak."

"When does this picture start shooting?"

"In the fall, I guess."

"So where do you plan to spend the summer?"

"California. Where else? I'll be in preproduction, two–three months. I can't discuss the shooting schedule with you. The location's a secret till the script's a definite go. But it'll be California preproduction."

"So you'll be around to have Harry and Coco in July or August?"

"No way. Oh, sure, I'll be there, but I can't take time off to be with them. You'll have to come out with them or something."

"What about Booty?"

"Jesus! Can't What's-his-name do anything? We went through this last year. I never got to see my kids because you couldn't be bothered to come out and take care of them."

"Craig, that's not how it's supposed to work."

"If we all go out to California I could help you with Booty and Coco," said Harry. He was watching them anxiously, the olive oil concoction forgotten.

"Sweetheart, I know you could, but who's going to look after Eddie while we're gone?"

"Eddie can come too," said Coco.

"No fucking way," said Craig.

"Craig, not in front of the kids."

"What? Oh, I said the F-word. Nothing changes. You were always on me about that when we were married. Kids, does Mommy ever say fucking?"

"Yeah, Mommy says fucking!" they chorused loudly, and heads swiveled all over the restaurant.

"Shhh, for Christ's sake," said Craig. "Hope, think about it. Let me know. Come out for two weeks with them or I can't have them."

Hope was trying to assimilate the information that was being given to her both directly and indirectly: he was inviting her, which didn't necessarily mean that she would see much of him. Still, there would be the evenings. After the kids had gone to bed. But why couldn't he hire a baby-sitter to be with them during the day? Yet if he did that he wouldn't need her. He had asked her to come; she kept coming back to that. Which meant he didn't have anyone else he could ask to look after the kids, he didn't have anyone in his life who was serious enough about him to want to be with his children. He'd asked her, Hope. There was still an opening.

"Well, I'm not coming without Eddie," announced Coco, through a mouthful of ice cream, "and Mommy won't either."

Oh, won't she just, thought Hope, trying to picture Eddie making a stand, for once, and refusing to let her go, and failing miserably. But what was she thinking of? She and Eddie were supposed to take Booty to England to see Mrs. Calder while Harry and Coco were with Craig.

After lunch, Craig suggested a saunter up Madison Avenue. They could pop into Barney's, see if he could pick up some additions to his wardrobe.

Was he mad? wondered Hope. Did he seriously expect Harry and Coco to enjoy watching their father buy clothes for himself?

"I think you might have a better time if you took them to F.A.O. Schwarz," she pointed out.

"How've they been doing in school? Harry, are you a credit to your old man? Hope, don't look at me like that. I know he's only eight, but it's never too young to start. He's gotta learn what it takes to be successful. If I buy him a football I want to hear he's best in his class."

"Yes, Dad."

Hope couldn't bear to see the confused expression on Harry's face. Craig always did this; he always placed the burden of being successful on Harry's shoulders. Because he was the boy. The son. It just wasn't fair.

"Craig, it isn't fair to bribe them."

"How isn't it fair? They've got to learn they have to work for their rewards in life. Truth is I'm doing them a favor buying the stuff for them first. Then it's up to them."

"But they don't really understand what you're doing."

"Coco does. Don't you, sweetheart?"

"Yes, Daddy."

Yes, thought Hope, Coco could read her father just fine. It was dear plodding little Harry who was going to have a problem.

I can't go away in the summer, she thought, trailing around F.A.O. Schwarz after them, it's my busiest season. Summer people want to look at houses. I'd miss thousands of opportunities. But I'm going to damn well try.

Craig kept up a running commentary over his shoulder to her in between what turned out to be an obscene accumulation of toys—why couldn't he exercise restraint anymore?—telling her more and more about his work, how the studio loved him, how everyone wanted to work with him.

"Who would have thought when we were living in that crummy little apartment in the Village that I'd be such a success story? Best thing I ever did, moving to California."

Thank you, Craig, for that little smack in the face.

"And who would have thought I'd be out there in the Hamptons selling properties to all those same movie folk who think you're so wonderful?"

He didn't like that. Didn't want her success to be part of the equation. This was his story. He was the lead. Hers was a supporting role. If she wanted to get back into his life, she'd better not forget that.

Even though he'd been to a two-hour screening in the morning, Craig insisted on taking them to a movie. Hope sat next to him, her elbow touching his on the armrest between them. Suddenly, in the darkness, she felt his fingers intertwine with hers. For the next twenty minutes she didn't have a clue as to what was taking place on the screen. Her body felt like jelly. She turned her head to see if Coco, sitting on Craig's other side, was looking at them, and as she did so he leaned toward her and she felt his tongue slip easily into her mouth.

He kissed her and she kissed him back.

Yet all the time she couldn't help noticing that his eyes were wide open and still looking sideways at the screen.

He'd learned his lesson in the restaurant at lunchtime and let the kids have burgers for supper. I wonder where he'll take me for dinner? thought Hope. I wonder whether he'll talk about anything besides his work? Do I even care as long as I'm with him?

He bores me, she realized suddenly, feeling a little guilty for admitting it. He talks about himself all the time and he won't let me tell him about my life, my work. Yet I still want to be with him. I like the way people turn to look at the four of us. We're a great-looking family. We belong together. We're what I've always dreamed we'd be, what my mother always wanted for me. I've earned this; I deserve this; I'm going to enjoy it.

It was a mantra she'd repeat to herself over and over that night as she sat in Craig's suite, watching the kids once again and waiting for him.

"Hey, what's this? Don't look at me like that. Don't make me feel bad. I never said we'd have dinner. Well, did I? When did I say we'd have dinner? Don't start with the nagging again. You want I should get a sitter from the hotel? Why don't I do that, and then you can make your own plans for this evening. I have to have dinner with these guys. They've come in from London on the Concorde. It's pre-sales stuff; it's important. You know how it is."

Then why doesn't he ask me along? wondered Hope. Because there'd be no one to look after the kids. But he said he could get a sitter. So why doesn't he? Because he wants me here waiting for him when he gets back. But he's not going to come out and say it, not going to accept responsibility for our spending time together. But he's giving me openings. That's what he's doing, he's giving me openings.

Once the kids were asleep in the twin beds in the second bedroom Hope went into the master bedroom, flicked on the TV, and called Maisie.

"Ma?"

"Baby, how's it going? Where are you?"

"Lying on Craig's bed in the hotel."

"And you're calling me? Whatever for? Is he in the shower or what? Have you—?"

"Ma, nothing has happened. I'm here on my own with the kids. Craig's gone out for a business dinner."

"Oh. Well. So he'll be home . . . when?"

"He'll be back when he's through. Who knows?"

"What underwear do you have on?"

"Ma! Jesus!"

"I'm serious. If it's sexy, leave it on. If it's that basic cotton crap, take it off and wait for him naked."

"Wait for him naked? Ma, are you nuts?"

"Has he shown any interest at all?"

Hope had been thinking about the kiss in the movie theater all evening.

"He kissed me."

"He did? Well, there you are, honey. Green light. Go, go, go, take all your clothes off, have a sweet-smelling soak in the tub, and get under those covers."

It was a mistake to call Maisie. She was so basic, Hope was invariably embarrassed. Any minute now her mother would start reliving the sixties in glorious Technicolor, giving Hope a blow-by-blow account of all the orgies she attended. If Maisie met a man over fifty who was stupid enough to admit he'd been in Manhattan in the sixties, Hope knew her mother took one look at him and immediately tried to remember if he was someone she'd slept with. "If you can remember the details, you weren't there," she was forever telling Hope.

If you wanted tales of the counterculture, you could count on Maisie. She claimed to have done it all: marched on the Pentagon, danced in the mud at Woodstock; you name it, Maisie had been there. Hope had once sat down and worked out that her mother could not have done half the things she said she had. It simply wasn't geographically possible. In fact, Hope secretly believed that her mother was a bit of a fraud. She'd never been a free spirit, an artist, or any kind of true counterrevolutionary. She'd probably just watched it all on TV like everyone else.

When Hope, a child of the eighties, embraced money in the form of real estate, Maisie was surprisingly supportive. Any veering off in the nineties toward a more caring, sharing New Age way of life was anathema to Maisie, although she was not above cashing in on it and raking in some New Age money with her skills as a reflexologist. Maisie was an opportunist at heart, and with Craig, flush with his success in Hollywood, she imagined she saw a kindred spirit.

"I can't wait to find out what happens. I'll call you first thing in the morning."

"Mother, please, no! In any case I'll probably be right across the hall from you, tucked up in bed in my old room."

"Baby," said Maisie, "make an old lady happy. Screw your husband."

Hope got off the phone in a hurry. She should never have called her mother. It was fatal to involve Maisie in any form of subterfuge. She always went too far.

She ignored Maisie's advice and with some satisfaction

lay fully clothed on the bed watching TV till Craig came back shortly after midnight.

He blundered in, clearly the worse for drink, and proceeded to take his clothes off in front of her, stumbling about the room as he did so.

Hope froze. What was she meant to do? Creep out saying she'd call him in the morning or hold out her arms in welcome?

As it turned out she did neither. Craig pushed aside the covers in one clumsy movement and climbed into bed before she could say anything. Seeing him naked again after so long was enough of a shock to render her immobile. He was in terrific shape, good well-developed pecs and strong hard abs. She yearned to reach out and stroke the soft hairs on his chest that she remembered only too well.

He was snoring already. And she remembered that too, irritating little grunts that kept her awake for hours. Was there any point in creeping out now? None whatsoever. Why disappoint Maisie?

They were curled up in fetal positions as far away from each other as they could possibly be on the king-size bed when the kids came bursting in in the morning. Hope had stripped down to her underwear, and she hastily pulled the sheet up to her chin. Craig looked across at her for a second and she shook her head.

No, nothing happened. It's okay.

"Sleep well?"

"Yeah!" yelled Harry and Coco, though Hope suspected he was addressing her.

"Coco, get on that phone and have room service send up a full breakfast for four and *The New York Times*. Why don't we all spend the morning in bed like we used to? Then maybe Mommy will agree to come out to California and spend the summer with us."

"I thought it was only for two weeks," protested Hope, and then realized she'd all but agreed to come. "So we'll go visit Daddy's grave this afternoon?" she said tentatively.

"Sure thing, sweetheart." Craig's eyes were closed again. "I'll have to call and postpone a meeting, but I'm sure it'll be okay."

Hope sighed. Somehow she could already see the pattern of the afternoon unfolding.

Coco was in her element, calling room service, but Hope noticed Harry had gotten quiet. He was watching them. She reached out and pulled him to her, more to save her the embarrassment of deciding whether to cross the Great Divide between her and Craig on the bed than anything else.

It turned into a perfect morning as far as Hope was concerned. It was as if they had picked up where they left off, a family once again. Sunday morning with the kids. Craig read the papers. Harry watched TV. Coco played room service, and Hope just lay back and dreamed of where it would go from here.

When the house phone rang just after one o'clock, they were all showered and dressed and thinking about lunch.

"Hello," said Craig. "He is? . . . No, it's okay. Thank you." He put down the phone. "Hope, what game are you playing? Eddie's on his way up."

"What?" Hope was panicked.

"Eddie!" yelled Coco happily, and ran to the door. She pulled him into the room. "What would you like to eat? I can get it for you on room service. Anything. Just tell me."

Eddie looked ridiculous standing next to Craig, thought Hope. Rumpled hair, creased clothes, unshaven. "What's going on?" he asked Hope.

"What does it look like?" said Craig rudely. "I'm seeing my kids."

"And my wife."

"Mine too, once."

"How'd you know where to find us?" Hope asked stupidly.

"Maisie told me the minute I walked through the door. I suppose I should ignore the fact that you never once mentioned you were seeing him."

"Absolutely," said Hope. "I'm just dropping off the kids."

"Eddie, isn't this place great?" Coco was still clinging to his arm. "This is where we eat room service. And through here's where me and Harry slept." She dragged him into the twin bedroom. "And here"—she led him to the door of the master bedroom, where he had a good view of the unmade bed strewn with breakfast debris—"here's where Mommy and Daddy slept."

Hope looked at the floor so she wouldn't see Eddie's face when he turned around.

11

Whoever had delivered the well-known warning that men should take a good look at their prospective mother-in-laws if they wanted to see how the daughters would turn out didn't know what they were talking about, thought Eddie, as he charged along Riverside Drive toward Maisie's apartment house. He was in such a state of pent-up furry that he had the cab drop him off two blocks away so he could walk off some of his rage. Hope was nothing like the blowsy meddlesome witch he was about to confront, the horrible old cow who had deliberately sent him off to see Hope, knowing perfectly well he'd find her with Craig. Maisie had known exactly what she was doing.

Five minutes later he had changed his mind. Hope was as heartless and devious as her mother. Hope had been deceiving him with her first husband for God knows how long. Hope had been using him. He'd served as a welcome haven for her when Craig deserted her. He'd taken her on, along with her two children, and look how she'd rewarded him. He didn't deserve this. How could she treat him so badly? Well, he'd show her he wasn't going to be pushed around. If she expected him to stick around, now he'd caught her out, she had another think coming. He'd move out of her life once and for all. Let her see how she fared with her ex, if that's what she wanted. How long would it be before she found out that once a creep, always a creep?

"What are you doing?" Maisie returned from one of her daily trips from the market as he was throwing his belongings into a couple of bags. Maisie was one of the most restless people Eddie had ever encountered. If she happened to find a spare half hour between her reflexology appointments, she never sat down and read a book or put her feet up. She had to rush out to the market. It was not hard to see where Hope's manic energy came from.

"Getting my stuff together for the laundromat, what does it look like I'm doing?" said Eddie rudely. He wouldn't bother to be polite to his mother-in-law anymore. God knows it had been an effort, and he had only done it for Hope. Now that Hope was about to be history, Maisie would automatically be catapulted to positively prehistoric status.

"You're leaving?"

"Yes, Maisie, I'm leaving. Now you can charge some poor sucker a fortune for this little hellhole. It's a bit late now, but I should tell you that this is the most uncomfortable bed I've ever slept in."

"What d'you expect? It was the maid's bed. Plus, now you mention it, I should have charged you rent. You never once lifted a finger to help me around the house. Not a shelf did you put up for me. Never carried up my deliveries. Never fixed the dishwasher."

"I wasn't here. I was working. And at weekends I was at home with Hope."

"So you spent your weekends installing dishwashers and putting up shelves for Hope? Really? She never told me."

"Maisie, I am not gifted in that area. Words are my métier. I'm an editor, not a plumber. Anyway, now she'll have Craig to be her handyman."

"Words are *not* your métier. What a story you tell. Craig is the writer, not you, and he'll hire someone for Hope. He's rich."

"As Croesus."

"Who's he?" Maisie looked at him hopefully as if she thought he might be a potential suitor for Hope.

"Never mind. I can't believe you would be so cruel as to send me to walk in on Hope and Craig."

"What were they doing?"

Christ, it's disgusting. She sounds almost gleeful, thought Eddie.

"I'll spare you the salacious details. Suffice it to say I am not about to hang around. You've got what I suspect you've always wanted. I am out of your daughter's life."

"You're leaving Hope?"

"Oh, now I suppose you're going to accuse me of abandoning her."

"Well, you don't deserve her, that's for sure, but you don't have to be a coward and sneak out the back door. You weren't going to tell me, were you? You were just going to let me come home and find you gone. When are you going to tell Hope?"

Eddie paused. She was right, damn her. He hadn't planned on waiting for Hope to get back and telling her face-to-face. He'd planned to leave a note for Maisie telling her he was moving out and she could tell Hope. He was too angry to tell Hope himself, too angry and too bloody hurt.

Suddenly he was drained.

"Sit down. I'll make you a cup of tea before you go," Maisie offered, in a surprisingly gentle tone.

She knows she's won, Eddie realized. She can afford to be generous. He finished packing, hearing her clanking around in the kitchen.

"Listen," she said, when she returned. "It's nothing personal, Eddie. You're a nice guy. Too nice, I'm thinking. You don't watch out for her enough."

"What chance do I have?" Eddie protested. "She's always too busy watching out for herself, I don't get a look in. She's always the one who decides what's going to happen."

"That's my point. You can't control her. She was always headstrong. I had a problem with her myself."

"But marriage isn't about control!" he yelled at her, suddenly angry again. "It's about love and respect. I love Hope," he cried, surprising himself with the depth of feeling in his voice, "but right now I don't respect her."

"You never did. You didn't provide for her properly. Financially, I mean. That shows you don't respect her. I want her to have someone who will free her from financial responsibilities, who will let her breathe."

"Oh, and *you* did? *You* let her breathe? Maisie, did you ever ask yourself why she chooses to live way out in Amagansett?"

"Her work took her there."

"Do you seriously imagine there are no jobs for her in New York City? Someone of Hope's ability?"

"You mean she left New York to get away from me?" Maisie seemed stunned. Eddie knew he ought to be thrilled, but he suspected getting away from Maisie had not really been important when Hope accepted the job in the Hamptons. At least not consciously. Maybe subconsciously she'd felt the need to get away, to strike out on her own.

He stood up.

"I don't know, Maisie. Who can figure out what Hope wants? It's possible she doesn't know herself. One thing's for sure: She's not about to slow down and take the time to work it out. You and I do have one thing in common, she's left us both. Okay, maybe *I'm* leaving *her*, but she—and you— drove me to it."

"Well, do you know why she doesn't want you?" Maisie hurled at him. She hates me, Eddie realized. I'm an alien being: not wealthy, not American, not Jewish. Someone outside her experience. Someone she can't cope with. Someone she doesn't know how to control like she has tried to control Hope.

"No, I'm not sure I do. But at least I'm going to try and figure it out, which is more than you'll ever do."

Forty-five minutes later he found himself standing in his office at the Gramercy Press on Easter Sunday. He'd been issued keys and instructions on how to gain access out of office hours, on someone's misguided assumption that he was such a keen young executive he'd be in every weekend working overtime.

He was angry with himself.

The last thing he should have done was storm out of Craig's suite. He should have kept his cool. But then again, how should he have behaved? Shaken Craig's hand and said, "Gee, thanks so much for looking after my wife. I'll take her back now, if you don't mind"? The trouble was he'd done exactly what he knew Hope expected of him. She was always telling him not to be so childish when he was fooling around with the kids, behaving like one of them. She was always saying he should be more of an adult.

But he'd had a shock.

"Here's where Mommy and Daddy slept."

And nobody had denied it. That had been the killer. Until Hope had rushed after him, catching up with him at the elevator, and cried, "Eddie, nothing happened! Nothing actually happened. It's not at all what you think!"

But he'd seen the smug expression on Craig's handsome face and the sad, bewildered look on Harry's. And he had turned his back on Hope as the elevator doors closed.

He went to the office because he had nowhere else to go. Larry and Susie were away for the weekend. Should he call Annabel? Funny he should think of her first. No, he needed time to think. Hope would probably call her and ask if she'd heard from him. Had Annabel been in on Hope's betrayal from the start? Somehow he couldn't bring himself to believe that. Maybe she'd suspected and maybe that's why she'd urged him to fight for Hope, but he couldn't believe she'd condone what Hope had done.

No, he needed to keep them guessing as to his whereabouts for a while, make them worry about him.

Then he had a brainwave.

He flicked his Rolodex and found Arlene's number. Arlene always knew what to do. She'd find him a place to live.

"Eddie?" She sounded flabbergasted. "What happened? Did you lose a manuscript? Hold on, Max is about to swallow a bottle of bleach. Don't do that, Max, give it to Mommy. Can I call you back?"

"I'm at the office."

"At the office? Did I lose a day somewhere? Is it Monday already? Hold on, let me rescue Max, and I'll get right back to you. This I have to hear."

He didn't tell her the whole story. He just said he was fed up with living with his mother-in-law—not something he'd ever kept a secret from Arlene, arriving as he did every morning and bitching about Maisie until he'd had at least two cups of coffee—and he needed to find himself a new pied à terre in the city. Could she help him?

"Have you looked in *The Times*?"

"*The Times*?"

"*The New York Times*, Eddie. It's a newspaper. You know about these publications, I've seen you studying them from time to time. They have listings of places. It's Sunday. Best day to look."

"But I need somewhere tonight."

"Any chance you know what a hotel is?"

"Could you find one and make a reservation for me?"

"No."

"What?" Eddie was dumbfounded. She had never said no to him before.

"No, Eddie, it's Easter Sunday. I'm taking care of Max today. I don't work for you on weekends. I don't work for anybody on weekends. I'm not going to spend the afternoon on the phone trying to find you a hotel room. Look in the Yellow Pages under H for hotel. I'll see you in the morning. We'll start looking for a place for you then. Okay? Have a nice weekend. Goodbye."

Eddie looked up the hotel listings. There were pages of them. He didn't know where to start. Then he remembered that British editors stayed in hotels when they came over on American trips. He flicked through his calendar, which recorded his meetings with them and where they were staying while they were in town, in case he needed to reach them. Within half an hour he had a small list: the Soho Grand, the Paramount, the Royalton, the Algonquin, the Dorset, the Warwick, the St. Regis, the Sherry-Netherland. More recently, since much of New York publishing had moved their offices downtown, they seemed to be staying at the Soho Grand. He called them. The cheapest room seemed to be around $200, but they didn't have anything available. All they could offer him was a penthouse suite at $900. He hung up in a hurry and tried the other hotels on the list. Same story, plus or minus the penthouse suite.

He called Larry and Susie and left a message on their answering machine, but he knew they wouldn't be back in the city before nine or ten. He couldn't hang around until then.

He called Arlene again.

"They're all full for Easter. I don't know what to do."

"Are you whining, Eddie?"

"I'm whining and wheedling and pleading. I'll do whatever it takes to get you to help me."

"And you can't go back to your mother-in-law?"

"Never in a million years. Do you have a spare room, Arlene?"

"I don't have a spare closet."

"No, of course not, I didn't mean it. I wouldn't dream of putting you to any trouble—"

"Don't give me that. Why did you call in the first place? Are you really truly desperate?"

"Truly madly deeply."

"Excuse me?"

"It's a film."

"He's desperate and he gives me movie talk? I do have a couch."

Eddie had a sudden flash of himself lying on a couch with Arlene as his psychiatrist, sitting somewhere behind his head, listening to all his problems. Maybe it wasn't so far from the truth. She was beginning to feel like the only friend he had in the world.

"I'll take it. How much?"

"Eddie, I'm not renting it out to you. I'm offering it to you for the night."

"Yes. Right. I accept. Give me your address. I'll be there in an hour. I'll stop by a grocery store and buy dinner. What does Max like to eat?"

"Potato chips."

"And you?"

"Oh, I have simple tastes. Caviar, champagne, foie gras, that sort of thing."

He bought some smoked salmon, a bottle of champagne, and as many packages of potato chips as he could carry.

When she opened the door to him he didn't recognize her. She'd pinned her overpermed hair off her face with two large barrettes, a face that was surprisingly pretty, devoid of the heavy makeup she wore to the office. He had never noticed the clear gray of her wide-apart eyes, and her lashes, no longer caked in mascara, were soft and feathery. Plus she had a light dusting of freckles across her nose. Eddie had always liked freckles. Her skin was very white. She was wearing a plain white T-shirt and a pair of blue cotton drawstring pants. For some idiotic reason, the thing that appealed to him most was the sight of her bare feet and her toenails, painted silvery pink. He had grown so accustomed to seeing her tottering around on cork wedgies or in her high-heeled boots, it had never occurred to him that inside them she actually had feet.

He was in for another shock when he entered her apartment, because it wasn't an apartment. It was just an L-shaped room. Louvered doors stood open to reveal a kitchen in a closet: undercounter refrigerator, two electric burners, and a sink. Past a half-drawn plastic curtain he glimpsed a shower, basin, and toilet. Stepping into the room, he could see a double bed fitted into the ell with a screen partly hiding it, and there, right in front of him, was the couch: a dilapidated sofa bed.

But what made the room seem so pathetically small was the fact that crowded into every available space were books, balanced precariously on chairs, piled up all over the floor, and lined up on makeshift bookshelves hanging as if by a nail from the walls. An old Royal portable fought for space with her makeup and a propped-up mirror on a table in the corner. This is what she writes her reader's reports on, thought Eddie, suddenly realizing they were always in a typeface different from the Gramercy Press computers. The mountain of manuscripts on the floor beside the table confirmed this. She sits in this little room, with her child presumably pestering her, and she reads manuscripts for me and writes reports on them. Eddie was extraordinarily touched.

"So what are you looking at? I said it was just a couch. I haven't pulled it out yet. If I did we'd have to eat dinner on the fire escape."

How embarrassing. Why had she let him come? The place

was far too small. But if he turned around and left now he risked offending her. He'd have to stay, at least until they'd eaten.

"I bought these." He handed her the salmon, the potato chips, and the champagne.

"Okay, so you're shocked. Not everyone gets to live in the Hamptons, you know? I wanted to be in Manhattan, and this is all I could afford. You know what I make at the Gramercy Press. Out of that I have to take care of Max and my mother in Brooklyn as well as myself. My father died in 'eighty-four, and all she has is his Social Security. But what's that to you? You have your real-estate wife making a shitload of money with her commissions, you have Clem Springer handing you best-selling authors on a plate so you'll be getting a fat promotion any day now. The rest of us have to scrape around for what we can get, even if it is playing step 'n' fetchit for helpless creatures like you. Where do I buy a new suit, Arlene? Where do I get good pizza, Arlene? How do I blow my nose, Arlene? It's amazing you knew how to buy potato chips without asking. So, are you gonna stand there all night or are you gonna sit down, like, on my couch?"

It was the only place to sit.

He sat. Hating himself.

"Listen," she said, more gently, "that was outa line. I'm sorry, okay? You weren't to know. I knew the second I hung up the phone I shouldn't have asked you here. But you know what? I was sorry for you. You're always so helpless, Eddie. Why is that?"

"Don't know."

"Don't want to know is my guess. Won't face up to it. Women always did everything for you, by the sound of it. You got a mother, a sister, a mother-in-law, and a wife, all looking out for you, right?"

"And you." Eddie grinned.

"And you got a nice smile, so you think you're all set. Everybody's gotta do things for you. Well, I'm going to take care Max doesn't turn out like you. My mother spoils him already, and there's nothing I can do about it as long as she watches him while I work."

"Where is Max?" asked Eddie, looking around as if she might have him stashed away in the closet. There was none of the toddler chaos Booty left all over the house—just as well, in a space this size—but a toy truck and a high chair pushed against the sink seemed to indicate his presence.

"He's down the hall with a friend. Which reminds me, I'd better get him."

"I'll have the champagne open when you get back."

"You'll find some paper cups in the closet. Why'd you bring champagne? What exactly are we celebrating?"

She was gone before he could say, "You. And your courage."

She was back in a few minutes, followed by a small boy.

"Hey, who's this?" asked Eddie, leaping up, determined to be friendly.

"This is my son. This is Max. Say hi to Eddie."

"Hi, Eddie."

"Eddie?" Arlene was looking at him. "What's the matter?"

"Hello, Max," he managed to say after a short pause. Why hadn't she ever said? But then, why should she? Was that the reason there were no photos of Max on her desk in the office? Was it awful of him even to wonder?

Max was black.

"You can't handle it, Eddie. You're shocked that Max is African-American."

"I can handle it fine," said Eddie defensively. "I just didn't know."

"How would you? You never once asked me about Max's father, as I recall."

"I didn't want to be inquisitive. It's none of my business who—"

"Who I fucked? You didn't ask because you weren't interested."

"I *was* interested. You've got some weird preconceived notions about me, Arlene. You seem to think I'm judgmental and stuck up, and I don't understand why. You're always so snippy when you're around me."

"Did it ever occur to you that I might be insecure? Did you ever stop to think about that? The fancy atmosphere at the Gramercy Press is not exactly what I was raised for. Everyone dresses a whole lot better than I do. Everyone speaks a different language. Everyone went to private school."

And no one has a black bastard. Eddie thought.

Instead, he said, "How did you get Max?"

"Same way as always. I fucked a black guy. What you mean is how'd a nice Jewish girl like me find herself in that situation? It was the dumbest thing. We got talking on the subway. Don't laugh, but he was reading *Catcher in the Rye.* Yeah, they read too, you know? So I asked him how he liked it and we were still discussing Salinger as we walked out into the street and he asked me if I'd like a drink."

"And one thing led to another, as they say, and along came Max. So where is the guy now?"

"He's dead."

"You're kidding me."

"Why would I lie? Max, where's your daddy?"

"In heaven with tha angels," he said, without looking up from the TV program he was watching.

"I think he imagines it's somewhere in Central Park and we'll meet up with him soon. Erroll's mother fed him that line, and it'll do for the time being."

"But you never mentioned it at your interview."

"Employers don't want mothers of young children. They think we're undependable."

"Well, I'm sure you're dependable, Arlene. I admire you, I really do."

"Don't patronize me."

"I'm not patronizing you. I'm insecure too. I don't know what I'm doing half the time. What makes you so special? I feel like shit. I've dumped myself on you, and I'm the last thing you need."

"Why have you dumped yourself on me? It's time you told me what's going on."

"I found my wife with her first husband. She lied to me. Never told me she was going to see him, let alone spend the night with him. He's a hugely successful Hollywood producer, and he's better looking than Kevin Costner, and I don't have a leg to stand on. I've made a complete fool of myself."

"So you come running to me. Thanks a bunch."

"I said I felt like shit."

"Did you at least open the champagne? What shall we drink to?"

"Let's drink to Max. At least I still have Booty. I mean, I think I do."

"You might still have your wife."

"And Max might just have a suntan."

"That's cheap. I think I like it better when you're snotty Brit pompous. But don't be so negative all the time."

"Sorry. Max, have a potato chip. Oh, you've eaten that package. What's up?"

Max was pointing at the screen in excitement.

"He wants a puppy," said Arlene. "Anytime he sees one on TV or on the street he goes wild."

"Where does he sleep?" Eddie looked around.

"In bed with me. Where else would he sleep?"

Eddie thought of Booty in her cot on the landing. He was about to say they were running out of space at home too, but it wasn't quite the same. They weren't exactly all living in one room.

"He never sleeps on this sofa bed?"

"He likes to sleep with me," said Arlene firmly.

"I'm sure he does," said Eddie, quite sincerely. She turned away, and he realized he'd embarrassed her.

"Max, into the bathroom. Now."

"So what are you going to do?" she asked, when Max was sound asleep behind the screen.

"Dunno."

"You must have some idea."

"I have no idea. That's the whole point. I'm in this city, this country, because of Hope. If she doesn't want me anymore, I might as well go back to London."

"And what about your little girl?"

"I'd take her with me."

"Might not be as easy as you think. Anyway, what about me?"

"What about you?"

Arlene was looking at him in a most peculiar way.

"What would I do without you? I'd lose my job."

"No, no, no. I'd have a word with Clem about you."

"Big deal! Real Mr. Fixit, aren't you? 'Bye, Arlene. Clem'll take care of you."

"You really like working for me? I'm just talking nonsense anyway. There's nothing waiting for me back in England. I might as well stay here."

"Gee, thanks."

"There you go again. You've got a real attitude, Arlene."

"But I'm all you've got going for you right now."

"You know something?" He smiled at her. "That's not far from the truth. Here, let me help you with those plates. Thank you, Arlene. You've done more for me tonight than any of my so-called family have ever done. You've given me comfort. I like being here. Thank you."

He meant it as a quick kiss of gratitude, a peck on the

cheek, but somehow her lips were meeting his and her arms were going around him and he was stroking that milky white skin up and under her T-shirt and feeling her fingers running up the back of his neck and ruffling his hair.

She was clinging to him, and to his utter amazement she was sobbing quietly into his shoulder.

"Hey, what's the matter?" he asked, as softly as he could. "I'm the one in trouble, remember?"

"I've been waiting for this for so long," she said, when she came up for air. "Ever since I first started working for you, you crazy tight-assed Brit. Kiss me again."

He kissed her again for a very long time, and after they'd pulled out the sofa bed they lay on it together for the rest of the night, their arms wrapped tightly around each other. But they didn't go any further because of Max.

In the morning, she fussed with Max, dressing him, getting his breakfast, and casually mentioning at least once every five minutes that her mother was due to pick him up at eight-thirty. Eddie took the hint. He wondered what Max made of the fact that he was still there in the morning. He wondered how often there was someone there for breakfast and whether he even had the right to ask such a question. Whatever the answer, he was gone by the time Arlene's mother arrived.

It was only as he was sitting on the downtown bus, nearing 18th Street and the office, that he realized he'd never asked how Max's father had died.

He'd find out as soon as she came to work. How would last night change things? Was it just a one-night stand? Not that anything had actually happened. Did he want to take it any further? Would she still help him find a place to live? Better take things into his own hands for once, just to be on the safe side. He dialed Larry's office on an inside line.

"Larry? Good, you're there. . . . My weekend? No, awful. Listen, here's the thing. I need a place to stay. . . . Don't ask. Can we have lunch? I'll tell you then. In the meantime, how would it be if I stayed with you and Susie for a while? It wouldn't be for long. . . . Wait a sec."

Arlene had come into his office. Heavy makeup, hoops, Calvin Klein T-shirt, the everlasting leggings, the high-heeled boots, and an expression of blind fury on her face.

Uh-oh. Arlene at the office as opposed to Arlene the shoulder to cry on.

"Someone to see you."

Eddie barely registered Arlene taking the phone from him and saying, "Who's this? . . . Oh. Hi, Larry, he'll have to call you back," before glaring at him and marching out of the office.

The woman standing on the other side of his desk was tiny and fragile looking.

And one of the prettiest creatures he'd ever seen.

She's like Bambi, thought Eddie. Those huge eyes staring at him made him a little uncomfortable. She wore an expensive little black leather jacket and skin-tight jeans. A waif in tough-guy clothing. She came around to his side of the desk so she was standing right next to him and he could smell her musky scent. She held out a hand, dark painted nails, rings on every finger.

"She didn't introduce us. I'm Josie Gardiner."

Outside his office Eddie heard the drawer of a filing cabinet slam shut as if Arlene were sending him a warning.

12

I couldn't believe it. Hope came back from New York City with Harry and Coco on Sunday night and acted as if nothing had happened. I opened my mouth to ask if Eddie had caught up with them but something made me shut it again. Don't get involved. You're here for the kids. Whatever's going on between Hope and Eddie, they have to work it out for themselves.

So when Hope asked, "How's everything been? Booty been a good girl?" I replied, "Everything's been fine. Eddie had a lot of work to do. I took Booty to the Easter Egg hunt today and she ran off into the woods. Fell over and cut her leg, but it turned out to be just a scratch. We've cleaned it up and disinfected it and she's fine."

I breathed an inner sigh of relief. I had handled that pretty well. No point keeping quiet about Booty's accident. Someone at the store would be bound to mention it next time Hope went in. But why had I kept quiet about Ray Moran? Why was I keeping my meeting with him to myself? I knew perfectly well why, and it had nothing to do with Booty.

"Booty ran off?"

"Yes. Does she do that a lot?" I asked innocently.

"Tell you the truth, yes, she does. Worries me some," said Hope. "You have to keep an eye on her. I should have told you. Didn't want to scare you."

Thanks a lot, Hope.

"We stayed in a really cool hotel," volunteered Harry.

I looked at Hope.

"They stayed with their father." Very noncommittal.

And that was all she said.

Except that the following weekend Eddie didn't come home. And Hope just told us, oh so casually, at breakfast on Friday morning, "Eddie's tied up in the city this weekend. He won't be able to make it out here."

Who did she think she was kidding? The look on Harry's face gave everything away. He appeared shell-shocked.

It was naughty of me and I shouldn't have involved him, but I had to know what was going on.

"Shame Eddie's not coming." I just dropped the words into the conversation.

"Yeah. I guess it's because he thinks Dad's going to be here."

"Why would he think that?"

"Because he found Dad with Mom when he came to the hotel."

"He came to the hotel? In New York?" As if I didn't know. "Why did he do that?"

"Grandma sent him over. He came to the city to find us and we weren't at Grandma's like he thought we would be, so she told him where we were. He and Mom had a bad fight outside our hotel room. And I've heard them fighting on the phone. Haven't you heard them, Annabel?"

Hope's shouting was loud enough to be heard in Ireland. I suppose she imagined the kids were asleep. Didn't it occur to her that yelling would wake them up?

"Well, you and Coco scream at each other sometimes," I said reasonably, "and then you're friends again. Don't worry. Eddie'll be home soon. In the meantime, aren't you looking forward to going to the Bradys' this afternoon?"

He was, but I was dreading it.

"We have to go." Coco's voice that morning had risen

higher and higher, culminating in an ear-splitting whine. "Mommy, tell Annabel to take us. We have to go. We always go to the Bradys when they ask us. I love to play with Tara. She's my best friend. Please, Mommy."

"She's just your best friend when her mother asks you for a play date and all of a sudden you remember she lives in a big house by the ocean and they have a terrific pool and they serve you so much ice cream you can hardly move for a week. The rest of the time we never hear a word about Tara."

"But Harry likes to play with Tommy."

"Okay, okay. Enough. You may go," said Hope. "Annabel, it's down on Hedges Lane. I'll give you the number. It's a pretty snotty setup over there, and I'm embarrassed to tell you they like the nannies to drop off the kids and then come back to pick them up. They don't invite you into the house."

Great. Two cab rides. Now would have been the perfect time to tell Hope about the driver's license problem, but once again I balked. I now had another ally as well as Ray Moran. I had decided to let Harry in on the secret. I hadn't told him about the driver's license but I had told him I didn't know how to drive. At first he refused to believe me.

"You're kidding, right? You have to be kidding. All grown-ups can drive."

"Well, I can't. It's our secret."

"We won't even tell Coco?"

"Absolutely not Coco. She'd tell everyone."

"Cool. It's our secret."

"And you have to help me call cabs."

It was outrageous to involve a child in deceiving his parents, but I was right about Harry's reaction. He was thrilled to be in on something with me, to be made to feel special, to be set apart from the other two.

So we took taxis all over the place and the drivers became our friends. How long would it be before they told Hope they were seeing quite a lot of us?

Coco was beginning to smell a rat.

"We're going in a taxi?" she exclaimed later that day, when she heard me calling for one. "I don't want the other kids to see me arrive in a taxi. It looks so dumb."

"No, it doesn't," said Harry.

"I told Daddy we go everywhere in a taxi with Annabel, and he said only maids go in taxis because they're too poor to have a car."

I didn't much like the direction this conversation was going. It was true that just about everyone seemed to have a car, no matter how beat up. Indeed, the taxis were the most beat up of all. I sensed that Coco had a horror of being thought poor. Already at the tender age of six she had picked up the need to project the right image, something that didn't seem to bother a dreamer like Harry. And Eddie's absence seemed to have made her even more insecure.

Because that's what it was, I had decided early on: insecurity. Eddie's nickname for her, the Princess, was perfect. But in a way Coco was just a miniature version of so many terrified women who hide behind a facade of wealth, convention, and designer clothes. It didn't come from Hope, because I could see that Hope had no time for the flashier side of the Hamptons. This need to keep up with the Joneses had to come from Craig.

The Brady house was seriously fancy. A neat gravel drive crunched under the wheels of the taxi, an old station wagon, that bore us up to the house, past excruciatingly manicured lawns with sprinklers revolving over every square inch. But it was a stone's throw from the ocean and once I'd deposited Harry and Coco, I let the taxi go and carried Booty down to the beach. The sea was rough, and the sight of the white crests of the breakers rippling across the water in beautiful straight lines was mesmerizing.

"Here, Booty, we'll bury you in the sand," I suggested, which I knew was the exact opposite of what most people in charge of children would allow. Booty would be wet and sandy and dirty, her clothes might even be ruined, but what the hell, she'd have fun.

Of course, once I'd buried her the first time and she'd wriggled around until she shook herself free of the sand, she loved it so much she wanted to do it again and again, until eventually I left her to bury herself. She was happy as a clam, so I wandered dreamily along the beach, trailing my bare foot in the sand.

I don't think I let my attention wander for more than two minutes, but it was enough.

I looked back and she was gone.

What had I been thinking of?

And where on earth could she be? The beach, stretching as far as I could see on either side of me, was totally deserted. I looked out to sea, and suddenly those breakers looked anything but beautiful. Every one was an instant death trap for Booty if she had wandered into the water. I couldn't see her little head bobbing about in the waves. All I could see were seagulls circling the water and sandpipers scurrying along the shore.

Now I was really terrified.

There was nothing to do but go back to the Brady house and get help.

I ran all the way up the sandy path to the house, up the drive past Latino gardeners who stared at me. I shouted at them and pointed to the ocean but they obviously didn't understand English. They just waved back and smiled. Probably thought I was telling them what a wonderful time I'd had on the beach.

A maid opened the door and I rushed into the house. I could hear the sound of kids playing. The maid directed me to the living room, where a group of smartly dressed women were chatting. God knows what kind of picture I presented to them, bare feet scattering sand, hair windblown, out of breath, shaking all over.

And then one of the women stood up and came toward me, and to my utter amazement I saw it was Hope.

"Annabel, what in the world is the matter with you?"

"Booty's out there. She ran away. She's all alone. I need help. I need—"

"Booty's right here," said Hope, and I looked down and there she was.

I collapsed in the nearest chair. My legs literally gave way beneath me.

"She must have come back through the dunes. She's a tiny tot, but she probably figured out the way easily enough. She's been here before a few times. You came via the road and the path? That takes much longer. They saw her coming back on her own and thought something must have happened to you so they called me at the office—it's only five minutes away—and I drove straight over. I didn't see the car outside. Where did you go?"

It was a relief to tell Hope about how and why I lost my driver's license. I waited till we were in the car driving back to the house. To my surprise, she was totally understanding.

"Why didn't you tell me about your parents? That is *so* terrible. I can't tell you how sad I was when my father passed away. I just couldn't function. I adored him. Were you close to your folks?"

"Yes. No." Marietta and I could not exactly be described as close. "I loved my father too. But Hope, about the driving—"

"Lord, that could happen to anyone. Far better you get drunk in your grief over there than with my kids in the car here. You've been taking taxis? Sure, why not?"

I couldn't believe it. She was completely relaxed about the whole thing. I was taking care of her kids and she didn't care how I did it, provided it left her free to get on with her work. Yet Ray Moran had been right. She loved her children, she enjoyed them, and I could see what little time they spent with her they really appreciated too.

And her joy when a huge bouquet of flowers arrived for her on Mother's Day was unmistakable. The card that accompanied them read *To the mother of my children with my special love, Craig.*

I couldn't help reflecting that it would have helped matters if Eddie had remembered to send flowers too, or at least acknowledged in some way that Hope was Booty's mother. It was now a month since the children had seen him. When Frank Sinatra died soon after Mother's Day, Hope's first comment was, "Oh, poor Craig will be devastated. He worshiped Sinatra." Everything was now Craig this and Craig that. What was going on? Was I supposed to fill in the blanks for myself?

In April it had rained nonstop for almost two weeks and the roof had begun to leak in earnest. Water was seeping in through the sliding doors and they needed to be replaced. I lay in bed night after night and listened to the torrential rain pelting down against the outside wall, and then in the morning I would see a damp patch spreading across the ceiling. The planking on the floor had begun to delaminate. I had to do something. I couldn't leave it any longer.

Once I put Booty down for her midmorning nap, I hit the telephone with the list of general contractors Eddie had given me. I got the answering machine every time.

"Hi there, you've reached Dave Miller of Miller Construction. Please leave your name, number, best time to call, and I'll be in touch the minute I walk through the door."

I found myself leaving a string of woolly, meandering messages about the roof leaking, and often I had to call back when I realized I hadn't even given my phone number.

Not one of them called back.

If I'd only known, it was just a question of learning how things worked in that neck of the woods. It was coming up to the Season, the period running from Memorial Day to Labor Day. Everyone was screaming at the contractors to get their houses repaired before the all-important renters and glamorous house guests descended on the Hamptons for the summer. I couldn't have picked a worse time to make my tentative, nervous oh-so-British requests that someone come to advise on what needed doing.

But after a week or so they had begun to return my calls.

At first I thought they were nuisance callers who had somehow got hold of my name, so familiar was their tone.

"Hi, Annabel, how ya doin'? It's Dave, Dave Miller, ya called me. Got a problem with the roof."

I set times for them to come by during the day when the kids were at school, and suddenly they were arriving thick and fast, tearing up the drive in their trucks, large dogs leaping about in the back. They were invariably grimy and dusty, some with long hair tied back in a ponytail, tool belts hanging from their hips, paint-spattered jeans slipping down their buttocks. Some were bare-chested, some wore sleeveless undershirts, some wore shorts exposing huge muscled calves ending in heavy-duty boots. But they were all open and friendly and full of information, shot at me so fast I barely had time to take it in.

And then I realized my biggest problem was going to be selecting the right man for the job. They all seemed to get a huge kick out of painting a really dire picture.

"Whoever put these sliders in ought to be shot. They're terrible. The caulking sucks."

"When was this house built?"

I hadn't a clue.

"Why'd they put the planks in horizontal on the weather side? No wonder the rain's coming in. They did it just so it looks nice. Crazy!"

Each contractor contradicted the last. "You can't get aluminum siding anymore."

"Aluminum siding? No problem, did a house with it last week."

And their estimates were all over the place. One guy would quote me $8,000 for a new roof and another $5,000, and I couldn't tell why there was such a big difference.

I called Eddie at his office. Waste of time.

"Don't ask me. I couldn't begin to tell you. Run 'em all by Hope. But don't spend more than five thousand. We don't have it."

I was dying to ask him when he'd be home, what had happened between him and Hope. When he asked after Booty I saw my chance.

"She misses you. When can I tell her she'll see you?"

"Who knows?" was all he said. "Give her a kiss for me, will you?"

Hope was in a hurry as usual.

"You're getting the roof done? That's totally terrific, Annabel. You're a star. Gotta run—closing. Be sure to get a bid from Hill Brothers. They're the one people use. Eddie should have told you."

Hill Brothers—only Jonas Hill had shown up—had quoted $9,000.

At my wits' end, I called Ray Moran.

I outlined my problem. Would he think me enormously presumptuous bothering him with something like this?

Not at all, apparently.

"You need a local boy. You need someone who's not going to rip you off. Someone who's going to help you on a regular basis. Hope's husband's never there, is he? Write this name down: Sheldon Bennett. Born and raised right here in Amagansett. Knows the place backwards and forwards. I've treated the family for years. Father died about three years ago. Leukemia. Very sad. Mother took it hard. Three sisters around somewhere. Sheldon took over as man of the family, sold the family house, moved his mother back to New York, and moved himself into a little rented shack over on Lazy Point with the windsurfers. Used to be a surfer himself, one of those guys who travel the world. A bit wild, but I hear he's settled down since his father died. Fixes up houses. Just the guy you need. Give him a call. Kids okay?"

"They're fine." I didn't tell him they were confused and nervous about Eddie not coming home.

"You okay?"

"I will be now by the sound of things, thanks to you."

"So when are we going to have dinner?"

"The weekend would be best. When Hope can be here with the kids."

"When's your night off?"

I hadn't ever had a night off. I hadn't had a reason to want one until now. Unlike my predecessors, I had never sorted out my job description.

"Can I get back to you on that?" I asked. "I need to talk to Hope."

"Sure you can."

It was impossible to talk to Hope. She neatly avoided conversation by insisting we watch the season finales on TV: *Friends, ER, Chicago Hope, Frasier*, on and on they went, night after night. And I sat beside her, wondering how much longer I would be able to stand not knowing what was going on between her and Eddie. Or between her and Craig, for that matter. It seemed as if she was behaving like an ostrich, burying her head in the sand and hoping that if she didn't talk about her marriage problems they'd go away. Not that she was alone in not facing up to her problems. It takes one ostrich to recognize another.

One night everything came to a head.

Ironically, Hope had been sitting there bottling things up too.

She suddenly turned to me as Ross said, "I take thee,

Rachel" to Emily in *Friends* and asked me, "So, what's the deal between you and Maud?"

"What do you mean, me and Maud?" I was completely thrown off guard.

"One of the things Eddie yelled at me the other night was, 'I hope you realize Annabel's a really good friend of Maud's!' And I said, 'What has that got to do with anything?' and he said, 'You'll find out sooner or later.' What was he talking about? Are you and Maud and Eddie all involved in some awful British conspiracy?"

"Wait a minute, Hope."

I lost it. I couldn't help myself. Here was someone who wasn't in the least bit worried that I had been deceiving her about transporting her children but who freaked out because I knew her sister-in-law.

"Stop being so melodramatic and listen to me. I'm not part of any bloody conspiracy, and neither is Eddie. But the truth is I could be. Maud is an old friend of mine. I wanted to get away from England for reasons I won't bore you with. Maud gave me a way to do it, and you're right, she does have an agenda, but I've chosen not to be part of it and you should be grateful for that instead of having a go at me. You and Maud don't like each other, that's no secret; the only thing Eddie's ever done wrong in Maud's eyes is marry you. She thought if she had a friend like me in your household, I could give her all sorts of ammunition against you. But what you have to understand is Eddie is not involved. You can't blame Eddie for anything."

"How can you say that?"

"Because it's true. Think about it, Hope. If I were to go and call Maud and tell her everything that's happened, how do you think it's going to look? You're out all day working, nothing wrong with that, but you barely see the kids because your work eats into your weekends too. And the first opportunity you get, you go rushing off for a tryst with Craig without telling your husband. And the kids are aware there's something going on. I'm especially worried about Harry. He shuts himself away in his room all the time, and when he comes home from school he won't talk to me. He's clearly feeling very unhappy and isolated. What's going on?"

She disintegrated right in front of me. Her face crumpled like a child's and she looked so helpless I reached out and put my arms around her. Oh, well, I thought, now I have five children to take care of. Besides Booty, Harry, Coco, and Eddie, now there's Hope. Marietta never had to contend with anything like this.

"I'm such a mess," sobbed Hope. "I haven't had a reasonable conversation with Eddie since before Easter, and where are we now, late May? He's moved out of my mother's. He calls the kids and we speak then, but only briefly. He caught me with Craig, but nothing happened. I went to New York to see Craig because he had this sweet idea about commemorating the anniversary of my father's death. I stayed the night with him but we didn't make love."

"And you think that makes it all right? You let the kids see you with him?"

She nodded. "Annabel, please don't judge me too harshly. You've found yourself in the middle of an impossible situation and everything you've said is true, but criticizing me is just going to make everything worse. Okay, it's all been building to a head. I'm so busy. Eddie's in the city all week. Craig calls every morning. My mother would like to see us back together. In the beginning we had something really good going for us, and I can't help thinking we could again. Then he jumps down my throat about not being there for the kids and I'm not so sure. It's like it's all right for him to have a career but not for me. Oh, Annabel, I'm so confused."

You have no idea. And what about the fact that you are married to Eddie? Have you forgotten that small detail?

"Well, I know one person who would be happy if I went back to Craig," said Hope. "Maud. I'd have to leave Eddie. That's what she wants, isn't it?"

"You're actually thinking of leaving Eddie?" I was shocked. I wished I'd never had lunch with Maud and got myself involved in this mess.

"I'm going out to California with Harry and Coco when they go to spend the summer with Craig. He's asked me to."

"I'm astonished," I said. And I was—both by the fact that Craig had dared to ask and that Hope had agreed to go. Who was going to tell Eddie?

"Does Eddie know?"

"I haven't told him. The only time we speak apart from when he calls the kids is when he makes these stupid calls late at night. I have no idea where he's staying. When I call him at the office that bitch of an assistant won't put me through. She probably knows exactly what's going on between us. Or, rather, isn't going on."

"But couldn't you at least have discussed it with me?" I protested. "Presumably, you won't be taking Booty to California. Were you expecting me to stay here and look after her on my own?"

Hope looked away. Clearly, that was exactly what she had been expecting, if indeed she'd thought about it at all.

"I was going to talk to you about it when I had my dates from Craig. Right now I don't know if it's July or August he wants us. All I'm asking is that you be here for me, Annabel. I hired you to look after my children. I don't care where you came from or how much experience you had. You're the best thing that's happened to them in years. Don't think I don't realize that. I don't care about references and driving licenses. You tell me the kids are confused about me and Eddie and Craig, but I come home from work every day and all I see is a smooth-running household for once, the kids getting meals on time, the laundry done, the house looking great, and food in the refrigerator. It's home again and it's all thanks to you. I know I'm wired. I know I'm obsessed with my work, but can't you see that I thrive on challenges? Getting Craig back represents a challenge. Eddie's not a challenge, he's just there. Then he's not there when I need him to be. He never gets it right. It's not as if I'm about to run off with a complete stranger. I'm looking to leave the father of one of my children for the father of the other two. It's two against one. Plus Eddie's such a wimp. It's not as if he's making much effort to win me over. Anyway, I have to go to California at some stage to be with Coco on her movie."

This was true. I'd forgotten about Coco's movie. She had arrived home from school one afternoon and announced she was going to be a movie star.

"You amaze me," I had told her, putting a jelly sandwich on the table in front of her. "I always imagined you'd grow up to be a welder or engineer."

She looked at me suspiciously. The thing about Coco, I thought, not for the first time, was that she didn't have a sense of humor. I had a sneaking suspicion the same could probably be said for her father, despite his request that I teach Hope about humor. Craig and Coco were two of a kind; they worked on the assumption that they could get by on their knockout looks and nobody would require them to factor in charm.

"My teacher's going to call you and then you'll see," Coco told me ominously.

She had indeed been spotted by a casting director while on a field trip with the school in East Hampton. Hope had been sent a treatment for the film, a thriller involving a kidnapping, and Craig, needless to say, was over the moon about the fact that his daughter might be in a movie. I disapproved of the whole idea, feeling it would undoubtedly make Coco even more spoiled, but I kept quiet.

"By the look on your face I can tell you don't think it's a

good idea for Coco to do this movie," said Hope. "You and Eddie. He's being really negative about it, and she's not even his kid. Plus he thought Craig's idea that Coco invite friends around to watch *Beethoven's 2nd* on her birthday was terrible. He's against anything Craig suggests on principle. It's a perfect thing for her to do. *Beethoven's 2nd* is actually being shown at seven o'clock on her birthday. What better way for her to celebrate? It's almost as if someone tipped off the network."

"Sorry, but I have to provide the voice of reason here," I said, surprising myself by my sudden desire to take the moral high ground. "She has school the next day, as do all the other kids. They won't get to bed before ten."

"But it's her *birthday*. What's the harm in her having a little fun? Why can't any of us have a little fun? Oh, please, let's talk about something upbeat for a change." She looked mischievous. "Let's talk about sex.

"You know what's so weird? Craig was never that good a lover, if you really want to know. It's the one area where Eddie scores way above him. I think that's the real reason I married him—to have unbelievable sex on tap. Isn't that awful? But now I just can't wait to have sex with Craig again. It's all I'm thinking about after that one night where we didn't do anything. I want him, Annabel, and I'm going to have him. Do you know what I'm talking about? Tell me, does it change as you get older? Do you still want sex as much? Oh, you're blushing. Don't answer that if you don't want to." She laughed.

Was I blushing? I could feel myself starting to relax. Girl talk was fun at any age, and I missed it. Hope might be ten years younger, but I could still talk to her about men. Should I tell her about Guy? Would she understand?

Then I remembered I had to talk to her about a night off. For my date with Ray Moran.

"I don't know what the medical consensus would be on that," I said, by way of introducing Ray's name into the conversation without attracting too much importance to it. "By the way I met your doctor, Dr. Moran, when Booty hurt her knee at Easter."

"Oh, my God, I knew there was something I'd been meaning to sort out. His name and number are taped on the fridge so I knew you had them if you needed them, but I wanted you to go and meet him anyway. Isn't he a sweetheart? I'm keeping in with him because if he ever decides to sell his house I want to be right there. Great property. Much too big for him. Big family property off Springs Fireplace Road. But they won't sell."

"They?"

"Ray and Hannah."

"Who's Hannah?"

"His wife."

His wife. How could I have been so stupid? Of course a respectable pillar of the community would have a wife. What had I been thinking of? He was just asking me to dinner out of kindness to a stranger. Or was he? Whatever he had been planning, I wasn't about to make the same mistake twice.

I called Ray Moran back and told him things were pretty hectic with the kids and I couldn't get away. He talked about a rain check and I brushed him aside, maybe a little harshly. I could tell from his voice that he didn't understand the abrupt change in my attitude.

Well, then, maybe you should have mentioned that you were married, I wanted to say to him, but I didn't.

I was sad. Only now did I realize how much I had been looking forward to spending an evening with him.

And in answer to Hope's question, of course I still wanted sex. But I was beginning to wonder if I would ever find a lover again.

13

Hope was exhausted. She'd been out the night before at a dinner with a client who'd come out from the city and made her drive him around all day long looking at properties, none of which interested him, and then he'd insisted on having a drink with her at the Palm while he waited for the Jitney. Only he'd gotten pretty drunk and missed the bus, and the next one, and by the time she'd got rid of him—and not before he'd put his hand on her knee more than once—it was after ten o'clock. She couldn't allow herself to make an issue of the clumsy pass he'd made, although it had alarmed her considerably. He'd said he'd be back the following week and maybe, just maybe, he'd make an offer on a house and if he did, her instincts told her it'd be a big one.

Because things couldn't get much worse at the moment. She had been asleep for a few hours when the phone rang and a hysterical woman had sobbed that she and her partner had just had a terrible fight and he wanted to pull out of the deal they had been putting together to buy a $500,000 house in Bridgehampton. Another sale down the toilet, thought Hope, as she tried to console the woman. It seemed she just couldn't sell anything these days. Right before Easter things had really been looking up. A number of clients had called, saying they were looking to buy and rent, and then suddenly they'd all gone away. When she'd got back from New York, still on a high from her time with Craig, she'd called them all, expecting to be inundated with people demanding to be shown houses, and no one had returned her calls. She'd waited a week, called again, and finally reached a few of them, only to be told they were fine, they'd found what they wanted, thanks a bunch, they didn't need her anymore.

Then she'd had the most beautiful property fall right into her lap. The brother of an old school friend was moving away from the area and called her ahead of the other brokers to give her the drop. The property was stunning, postmodern, two acres, beautifully landscaped, two-car garage, gourmet kitchen, heated pool. And Hope had a couple all ready and waiting and panting to buy.

She showed it to them.

They offered.

The offer was accepted.

It was almost a done deal when the wife—Hope couldn't bring herself to utter the woman's name—had called.

"Hope," she whined, "I just thought of something. You know the way the house is split-level, you go up to the living room, down to the kitchen, up to the library, all over the ground floor, in fact—"

"Sure," said Hope, "that's a feature of the property. Very unusual part of the whole architectural design, gives a feeling of—"

"But when my parents come and stay they'll find these little steps so hard. It's dangerous. My mother's eighty-one. And if people come for dinner and they get drunk and trip when they go to the bathroom, they'll sue. I can't go through with this deal. We're pulling out."

The next day the house was sold through another broker. This happened all the time in real estate, Hope told herself; deals slipped away as quickly as they appeared. But it did seem like she just wasn't getting any breaks.

And where were all those buzzy young clients everyone

else seemed to be dealing with? Hope was beginning to think she'd cornered the market in geriatrics. For a start, what was she going to do about Hannah Moran? Ray Moran had his pediatric practice, but Hannah was old Long Island money and there was plenty of it. And she'd called saying she wanted to put their home on the market. An old traditional farmhouse, very pretty, perfect for a large family, beautiful old-fashioned English-style garden. Hope went over to have a cup of coffee with Hannah, who seemed fine despite the stories everyone had heard. Lucid. Charming. Asked all the right questions. It was only as Hope was leaving that Hannah said something that triggered alarm bells in Hope's head.

"Johnnie and I have been thinking this place is too big for us for quite some time. We're done rattling around in it. Time we looked for something smaller. You'll find it for us, won't you, Hope?"

Perfectly sound thinking. Except Johnnie had been dead for twenty-five years. He'd been Hannah's first husband, and he'd had the dubious distinction of being killed in a car wreck, driving home roaring drunk, in exactly the same spot where Jackson Pollock had had his fatal accident on Springs Fireplace Road. Hannah had raised a few eyebrows by marrying the young doctor, Ray Moran, only a year later.

Somehow, thought Hope, I'm going to have to find a tactful way of finding out from Ray what this is all about. Why do they want to sell the house, and why hasn't Ray talked to me about it? Something isn't right.

Then there was old Miss Parsons, who needed to sell her little cottage because she was going to be taken in by her cousin's family. She was getting too old to live alone. Miss Parsons was a proud old lady, bent double with arthritis and furious that she could no longer stand up straight. She hadn't a bean in the world except for her home. She was descended from the old Parsons family, some of the original settlers on Hog Creek Road who had made leather goods from the hides of horses and cattle and goats. Her cottage had had nothing done to it in the way of maintenance since the thirties, and while it was clean, it was probably the most unmarketable property Hope had ever encountered. Why Miss Parsons had taken it into her head to select Hope as her broker was a mystery.

"I'm giving it to you exclusively," she told Hope in a confidential whisper when she came into the office. "I've always liked your face. I know you'll sell it to the right people, people who will keep it the way it has always been. I don't want it modernized after I've gone, I want everything left just as it is. I know I can't control this after I've sold it, but please, Hope, make sure the people who buy it will love it and cherish it as I have."

And Hope had promised faithfully. In any case, wasn't the promise academic? Who was going to buy such a run-down place?

But she tried her best. After she'd had the house fumigated to get rid of the smell of cats, dusted off the cobwebs, polished the brass and the antique furniture, and arranged the lighting to show off the pretty faded chintz and Miss Parson's watercolors to their best advantage, she showed it to couples who claimed to want a taste of heritage. She talked up Miss Parsons's family history, made it sound as if they'd be getting an old family estate instead of a two-room cottage whose ceilings were barely high enough to allow an adult to stand up.

The other problem was that, although she had moved out, Miss Parsons insisted on being present every time the house was shown.

"It's her home, remember, has been for many, many years," Hope would tell the viewers. "If there are aspects of it that are not to your taste, please be tactful. Don't say negative things until we're outside."

But they were hard, spoiled Manhattanites and they took one look and ran for their lives, barely bothering to say hello to Miss Parsons and always ignoring her plate of home-baked cookies and lemonade.

"Never mind, Miss Parsons, we'll get there in the end," said Hope sadly, knowing there was more chance of Booty winning the lottery.

As for Anita Mayhew, she had become the bane of Hope's life. Hope had shown her everything she had on her books regardless of the price, and always there was something wrong. Anita Mayhew was trouble, and Hope now knew why.

It was the brown paper bags. They were small, and at first Hope never noticed them. What she did notice was that Anita Mayhew always carried a large shopping bag that did not really fit her image as a rich Texan looking for a million-dollar home. It was in this shopping bag that Hope began to notice the ubiquitous brown paper bag stashed in the bottom.

"You go on ahead and take a look at the outside of the house while I park the car," she told Anita one morning, as they drove up to one of the beachfront properties. Anita left the shopping bag on the front seat. Hope sneaked a look inside the brown bag. As she'd guessed, she found a half-empty pint bottle of vodka. Horrified by what she was doing but determined to finish what she'd started, she took a pen and marked the bag. The next day when she checked there was no mark on the paper bag. Anita Mayhew always had a brand-new pint of vodka with her.

No wonder she had difficulty identifying which house she wanted to buy! She was viewing them all through a drunken haze.

As if her work crises weren't enough, Hope had the social event of the year to organize: Coco's birthday party. Coco never stopped. Hope thought if she heard the words "Mommy, can I ask so-and-so to my birthday party?" once more she'd scream. What she had envisaged as just a small affair, six or seven of Coco's school friends watching *Beethoven's 2nd* on TV and eating birthday cake, had escalated out of all proportion.

It was all Belinda's fault. Belinda was one of the other brokers at Tudor Woods, a woman Hope particularly disliked because she would only deal with rich flashy clients and never went out of her way to help people who wanted to buy the smaller, less lucrative properties. Somehow Belinda, like Mark, managed to subvert the up-call system and only worked with the wealthiest clients.

"You have to make the most of the opportunity. Kids' parties are the perfect time to entertain clients and their children and ask all those people to your house whom you owe an invitation but wouldn't dream of inviting to dinner."

"But it's Coco's party. What about *her* friends?"

"Well, of course you must invite them too. And their parents. Who knows when one of them will want to sell their house?"

Hope had never really thought of the children's birthday parties in that light.

"I don't know how to break it to Coco," Hope told Annabel, "but Eddie isn't coming."

"That's such a shame," said Annabel. "He adores Coco."

"He won't come because Craig is. He's flying in specially. It's a surprise for Coco, so don't tell her. Or Harry. Or Booty. Isn't it just great?"

The next day, to Hope's amazement, Annabel asked if she could go with her to East Hampton to buy some clothes.

Hope was staggered. She'd never thought of Annabel as someone who was interested in clothes. She looked perfectly well turned out every day, but all she wore were jeans, sweatshirts, and the occasional jacket. Nineties nanny uniform.

"Go ahead," she told Annabel. "You can leave Booty with me for the morning. They love her at the office. She can sit at an empty desk and play with the phones and pretend she's me."

When Annabel returned to the office at noon, Doris thought she was a client and Hope saw why. When she'd walked through the door on her own, minus Booty and the other two children, she looked exactly like the kind of rather stylish middle-aged woman who might well be looking for property in the Hamptons. Annabel had been to the beauty parlor and had a complete makeover that would thrill Coco to the core. It gave Hope quite a jolt. Then Booty saw her and rushed over for a hug, and suddenly Annabel was a nanny again.

"I'll run you guys home for your lunch," said Hope.

"Hope," said Annabel, as they were leaving East Hampton, "who was that man with dark hair and a thin face standing by the water cooler? He's another real estate broker, isn't he?"

"Sure, that's Mark. You know him?"

"But he was looking stuff up on your computer earlier."

"So?"

"Well, isn't that confidential information?"

"To anyone outside, yes."

"Mark isn't from outside?"

"No, of course not. He works for Tudor Woods. Is there a problem?"

"I don't expect so. I just thought he must work for a competing real estate company. I didn't realize he worked with you."

Rather than against me, is what she's not saying, thought Hope. "Why?" she asked.

"On Easter Sunday," said Annabel, "while you were in New York, I took Booty to the Easter egg hunt and he was there. I overheard him talking to some friends, about you.

About how you were away and he had the perfect opportunity to make a move on some of your clients. But I never realized he actually worked with you in the same office."

Oh, God, thought Hope, that explains why all those clients suddenly disappeared after Easter!

When Hope checked the computer that afternoon, she found several of the sales that got away had in fact been through Tudor Woods. She'd been a stupid, trusting fool. From now on she was going to have to watch her back at the office. She kept glancing over at Mark all afternoon, irritated by his smarmy patter on the telephone. I'm going to get you, Mark, she thought. As far as I'm concerned, this is war, whether we work together or not. You're never going to have another opportunity to steal another client from me.

But then she remembered her upcoming trip to Los Angeles. What would happen then?

Maybe she shouldn't go.

But she had to go. Craig wanted her to go. Craig was back in her life. Craig cared for her again. Craig was flying across the country tomorrow to be by her side for their daughter's birthday.

Wrong.

He called that night. "Hon?" Good start. He hadn't called her that since they'd been married. "Something's come up. I can't make it. You didn't tell Coco anyway, did you? We agreed it was going to be a surprise. So what she didn't know won't disappoint her."

But what about me? Hope thought.

"But, hey, listen," Craig went on. "There's a pal of mine who's going to be out in the Hamptons. I'd like him to meet you. Can I send him along in my place? It's appropriate he should come. He's producing the movie Coco's going to be in. He wants to take a look at her for the director. His name is Saul, Saul Shapiro. Real player. Nice guy. Who knows, he may even wind up wanting to buy a house out there."

"Daddy's not coming," she told Booty sadly that night. Booty had crept in from the landing and climbed into bed with her. Booty's warm little body pressed to hers was comforting, and Hope had let her stay.

"Daddy's not coming where?" asked Booty.

"Oh, never mind, and it's not your daddy anyway. It's Harry and Coco's daddy and it's very sad for Mommy."

Three o'clock in the morning. The preparations for Coco's party nowhere near ready. Craig wasn't coming. She had nothing in her life to look forward to.

But, Hope told herself, when she woke up the next morning, I'm a winner. I'm not going to be beat.

She marched into Coco's bedroom.

"Coco, my angel, happy birthday. Presents at the breakfast table, and then you're going to help me get everything ready for your party."

No Eddie. No Craig. Once again she was on her own.

Thank God for Annabel.

Nine hours later she was walking around hardly believing what she was hearing.

"What a wonderful party. Too bad your husband couldn't make it."

Coco's birthday was turning out to be a huge success. Well, maybe this was a slight exaggeration, but Hope congratulated herself on bringing together a pretty impressive crowd of people. She'd had the satisfaction of seeing Mark's eyes popping. She had had to invite him, Belinda too. It would have looked odd if she hadn't, given that she had invited so many other people in their business. Some important developers had put in an appearance, and lawyers, and many of Coco's school friends had turned out to have parents who were thinking of selling their houses and buying new ones, and they'd brought friends from the city who were planning to rent next summer. At one point Hope rushed into the house to grab a handful of her business cards, which she proceeded to hand out to as many people as she could.

Too bad your husband couldn't make it. Tell me about it, thought Hope.

Of course, they meant Eddie and she meant Craig.

"What beautiful children. They're adorable. What a great party. Please introduce me to your husband." Everyone had asked that, and she had no husband to produce for them.

It had been a good idea to make it an open-house all-afternoon party, laying out food on trestle tables, drinks on the deck, getting Philomena's cousins to come and serve.

Philomena, it turned out, had gone back home to the Philippines, taking her parents and her brothers and sisters with her.

"She no like America no more," her cousin Tito informed Hope, when he turned up on her doorstep one day with the news, "but you need help, Miss Hope, you call me. Tito."

So Hope had called in a panic on the morning of the party, and Tito had been there within the hour, bringing a team of five Filipino helpers with him. By noon the garden was transformed—crisp white tablecloths, silverware, bowls of salad, the grill fired up, flowers and plants everywhere, glassware gleaming, fish and steaks marinated, bloody Marys mixed, pitchers of iced tea waiting in the refrigerator, hot dogs all ready to be popped into buns.

It was as if the word had spread like a bush fire throughout the area. All afternoon people kept turning up. Hope networked; there was no other word for it. Maybe it wasn't really what she ought to be doing at her daughter's birthday party, but what the hell? You had to grab opportunities when they presented themselves, didn't you?

Annabel's attitude had been the only negative thing about

the whole day. Hope had been aware of her slightly disapproving air as she watched Hope flit from client to client.

Finally she confronted her.

"What's the matter, Annabel?" Hope paused beside her.

"I'm just watching all those presents arrive," said Annabel.

"Isn't it great?" Hope smiled. "Everyone brought a gift. Coco's going to be over the moon."

"We ought to be putting some of them aside. Look at her." Annabel pointed to Coco, sitting on the steps of the deck, opening presents one after the other, almost buried in a sea of wrapping paper and tissue. "She's got so many gifts she's barely even looking at them. That's the way to spoil a child. She needs to learn the value of things. We ought to take some of them away to give to her at Christmas."

Hope didn't know what to say. Annabel was right. It was criminal to see so many toys go unappreciated, but at the same time it made her so happy to see the Princess in her element. Like mother, like daughter, flashed through her mind. Coco's networking as much as I am; she's having a ball just like I am. The Princess is holding court and loving it.

"We'll go through everything later and send as much as we can to charity," she told Annabel.

"Good plan," said Annabel, smiling, to Hope's relief.

"Oh, Hope, is that your husband?" cried someone Hope didn't recognize. A gate crasher! But wasn't it terrific to be giving a party people wanted to crash? Hope smiled. Let them think this fancy creature approaching across the lawn was her husband. What could it hurt?

My God, the crowd's parting like the Red Sea. I feel like I'm at a garden party at Buckingham Palace and the Queen's coming over to say hello. Get ready to curtsy, Hope.

The man had thinning jet-black hair slicked back over his head and very white teeth exaggerated by an incredibly dark tan. He was about six-two and slim. He was wearing a crisp white shirt in pristine starched condition, showing up the crumpled heat-soaked T-shirts of the men around him, and equally immaculate khaki shorts. He's handsome, Hope thought. Yes, I have to admit it. He's a looker.

"I'm so sorry I'm late." He held out his hand. "My flight was delayed in landing at JFK. I had a plane standing by to bring me to East Hampton airport, but first I had to go into the city to see my mother. She's sick."

A plane standing by to bring me to East Hampton airport. Hope could sense Belinda almost drooling beside her, nudging Hope, waiting to be introduced.

Your luck just ran out, Belinda, she thought, and stepped right in front of her, blocking her view of the man.

"Are you Saul Shapiro? You must be exhausted. Come over and have something to drink."

"That'd be great. Could you maybe give my driver something too? I think he's about to expire." He pointed to a man in a chauffeur's uniform and cap wilting beside a Mercedes.

"Oh, look at that car," breathed Belinda behind Hope. "I've been telling Phil to get one of those for months."

"It's a hired car from East Hampton Limousine, I expect," hissed Hope. "Why don't you call them? They'll drive you around in one for fifty-five bucks an hour."

"Yes, I'm Saul. And you're Hope. It's so kind of you to let me come to your party. Where's the birthday girl?"

"Over there," said Hope, pointing to Coco. "There's the Princess."

Coco was wearing her new pink tutu and a tiara made out of pink tissue paper fastened to a headband that she and Annabel had spent all morning making.

"What a star!" He turned to Hope. "I can see just what our casting director saw in her. Now, here, I have gifts. This is from her father." He handed Hope a tiny oblong package. "Pretty light for me to carry, as you can see. And here is something from me. I hope she likes it. I don't have kids so I don't always get it right. What is she, Seven? Eight?"

"Seven. You said your mother is sick?"

"Yes. Parkinson's. I'm the baby. She's eighty-two. Hates that I live in California, hates that I'm not married and haven't given her any grandchildren, says I don't call enough."

A nice Jewish boy, thought Hope. Maisie would adore him. But with a mother of eighty-something he's probably over forty. Is he gay?

"Oh, you shameful boy," she teased. "Where does she live in the city?"

"Riverside Drive and one hundred-and-third."

"No kidding, mine's on Riverside Drive and one hundred-and-fifth."

"Maybe they know each other. So you're Craig Collins's ex. Where's your new husband? Can I meet him?"

"He's not here."

"Where is he?"

"I don't know."

He looked at her and his eyes were sympathetic.

"I'm sorry," he said. "I didn't know."

"Nobody does," said Hope. "Mostly nobody."

"I understand," said Saul Shapiro, putting a finger to his lips. "Now let's give the Princess her gifts."

He gave Coco his present first. It was pretty predictable; a Barbie doll in a pink ballet dress. But of course to Coco it was the perfect present. How had he known? Had Craig told him?

"Oh, thank you, whoever you are!" cried Coco, and flung her arms around his legs. Her tiara got caught in his crotch and he had to disengage it in front of all the guests now staring openly at him.

All of a sudden he looked awkward and surprised and Hope's heart went out to him. This was a sweet man.

"And here's your dad's present." He handed Coco the little parcel. Inside was a turquoise Tiffany's box that matched Coco's eyes. Craig had sent his daughter a silver chain bracelet.

"That must have cost an arm and a leg." Belinda was on the case as usual.

Hope's eyes met Annabel's. This time they were in total agreement. It was a ludicrously expensive and highly inappropriate present for a six-year-old child. They weren't going to say it out loud, but the message was there: Craig's showing off. He must have known the present would be opened in front of a crowd.

Hope thought fleetingly of the little fluffy bunny slippers—pink, of course—that Eddie had sent and of Coco's ecstasy on opening them in bed that morning. They were exactly the right size and now had pride of place beneath her bed.

"I told him I wanted them such a long time ago and he remembered," Coco had told her. "I love Eddie, Mommy. I really love him."

"I know you do, sweetheart," she had replied quietly. Eddie could be a honey sometimes, she thought wistfully.

"Saul, this is Annabel Quick from England," she said briskly, to take her mind off the fact that Eddie wasn't there and to draw Saul's attention away from the oohs and aahs aroused by Craig's present—which, she couldn't help noticing, Coco had discarded almost immediately as if it were a dime-store trinket.

"From England? What an international gathering." Saul smiled at Annabel. "So when's the entertainment?" he asked Hope. "I haven't missed it, have I?"

Entertainment? What entertainment? Oh, shit, I haven't arranged anything except *Beethoven's 2nd* on TV at seven o'-clock tonight, thought Hope in a panic. He'll go back to California and tell Craig I goofed.

"No, you haven't missed a thing," she said quickly. "I'll just go and see what's happening."

She left him talking to Annabel and rushed off in search of Tito.

"Entertainment," she wailed. "Can you juggle? Do magic tricks? Can you get a donkey for rides?"

"I can sing." He pronounced it "seeng." "In fact, we have a band. We play at home together. Good for dancing. You want I tell the boys, they go home and get their guitars? We play for you tonight?"

"Well, if there's anybody still here," she said nervously, praying everyone would have left by then. She had a vision of Tito dressed in Mexican gear, a big hat with tassels, belting out an off-key version of "Do You Know the Way to San Jose."

She couldn't have been more wrong. He and the boys returned, showered and shaved and clad in simple white short-sleeved shirts and black trousers. They plugged their guitars into the outlets on the deck and proceeded to play all the Latin classics everyone knew and could sing along and dance to: "Desafinado," "Guantanamera," "La Bamba," "Tequila," "The Girl from Ipanema," "Bamboleo," and countless bossa novas, salsas, and sambas. Everyone gathered around the deck and clapped to the rhythm, and one by one people got up and danced. Once *Beethoven's 2nd* was over even the kids joined in and jumped about the place.

There was one disastrous moment—although as far as Hope was concerned, it was almost the best part of the whole party. Belinda, weighing in at well over two hundred pounds, insisted on showing everyone what an expert she was at the limbo, attempting to shimmy her wobbling mass of flesh under a pole held by two of Tito's cousins. She might have just made it, Hope thought afterward, if she had had the foresight to remove her ludicrously high heels.

At the last moment Belinda slipped, her ankle turned, and she collapsed with her foot twisted under her full weight. Everyone could see from her face that the pain was excruciating.

Hope saw Ray Moran race across the lawn and up the steps to the deck, surprisingly agile for a man his age, she noticed.

"I'm right here. Don't move. Lie still."

He felt Belinda's ankle and ultimately decided she should go to the hospital. When the ambulance arrived it was rather like a cabaret when she was carted off amid much drunken cheering and whistling. Only Ray Moran kept a serious face. He stayed by Belinda, comforting her.

What a nice man, thought Hope. She looked around. She couldn't see Hannah Moran. Presumably Ray had left her behind. Ought she speak to him about Hannah's plan to sell their house? Did he even know about it? Now was not the time, she decided.

"Thanks, Ray," she said, coming up behind him.

"My pleasure. She's in a lot of pain and I don't have anything with me right now to make it easier. By the way, that nanny of yours is a real find. I'll bet she's terrific with the kids. Good-looking woman," he added and Hope heard the faint note of longing in his voice. Hannah probably hadn't been much of a wife in years. She followed his gaze and saw Annabel dancing with Saul Shapiro. She had noticed him by Annabel's side for most of the afternoon, although every now and then he would come and talk to Hope for a few minutes, outlining the movie, reassuring her that Coco would be well looked after and of course he would be delighted to have Hope along as chaperone.

Hope felt relieved. This man would not make a film that would harm her daughter. Look at the way he had spent all day being polite to the nanny.

Then it dawned on her.

Saul didn't know Annabel was the nanny. She hadn't been introduced as such, just as someone from England. He probably thought she was another of the guests. And by the look of things he was interested in her.

Well, that's just fine and dandy, thought Hope. I'll take her to California with me. Booty too. We'll all go. Annabel can take care of the kids, and that will leave me more time to be with Craig.

And she can see Saul Shapiro. It will be nice for Annabel to have someone special in her life. It's not as if there's anyone for her around here.

14

I was fresh out of the shower, having snatched the opportunity to wash my hair when Booty was asleep, towel-drying my hair and singing to myself, when a glorious hunk with bleached hair and Bermuda shorts appeared from nowhere on the deck. He looked like he'd stepped off the jacket of a Harlequin romance, a pirate with a silver earring in one ear.

Actually, on closer inspection, he looked more like a surfer.

Then I remembered. Ray Moran's contractor. The local boy. What was his name?

"Hi. I'm Sheldon Bennett." He stepped through the sliding doors into the living room. Thank God I was dressed. I often wandered around in just a towel for some time afterward.

Ray must have told him to come by because I hadn't called. I was so embarrassed about Ray. I had gone to considerable lengths to avoid running into him at Coco's birthday party. He must have thought I was very rude. But I didn't know which of the women might be his wife and I didn't want to risk being introduced to her. And I hadn't wanted to take it any further by contacting Sheldon Bennett.

This man was not at all like the ones who had come racing around the house the previous week. He was clean, he

had a good haircut, and his shorts and sweatshirt looked suspiciously designer label. There was no sign of a tool belt. Plus
he was young-looking and blond.

Not my type, I thought. I don't like blonds. I don't like big
men. I like slender, dark, intellectual types. Like Guy. But
Guy seemed a long way away.

"Annabel?"

He looked me directly in the eye and took my outstretched hand.

"Come in."

Those blue eyes were devastating. I didn't normally like
blue eyes. I preferred dark eyes. What was the matter with me?

"Wow! Great house. Beautiful flowers. Whose are all those
books? Is this your place? How long have you had it? Wow!
Great fireplace. Does the chimney work?"

"Wow" seemed to be his favorite word. He marched past
me into the house with an amazing amount of confidence
and began to stride around without asking, opening closets,
looking in rooms, his eyes moving quickly, appraising everything.

And all the time he was firing questions at me and not always waiting for an answer.

"So where's the water coming in?"

"Here." I began to walk upstairs. "Tread quietly, please.
Booty's asleep."

"That's a child? Booty?"

"A little girl. She's two."

"Yours?"

"No. I'm the nanny." Hadn't Ray told him anything?

"Are you married? Do you have children?"

"No. None."

"I have three sisters and three nieces."

"The water comes in here."

"But I'm not married."

All this information coming at me was making my head spin. "When it rains the water seeps down through the roof and under the sliders, and it sort of all trundles along inside somewhere—"

"Trundles?"

He was on his knees at my feet, tapping the wood, and he suddenly looked up at me and grinned. The effect was electrifying. I nearly toppled over.

Get a grip, Annabel, I could hear Maud saying.

"Trundles? You English girls, you have such a crazy way of talking. What does trundles mean exactly?"

I paused. When spoken in isolation the word did sound rather odd.

"Well, it sort of means the sound wheels make when they move, like the tumbrils trundling along toward the guillotine in the French Revolution."

"Tumbrils trundling? The French Revolution?" He was laughing at me and I didn't blame him. It was rather ridiculous to bring up the French Revolution in the middle of a discussion about a leaking roof.

"You got a cellar? Is it dry?"

"We have a crawl space, I think it's called. I've never been down there."

"Frightened of creepy crawlies? I'll go down and take a look. So you're not married?"

"I had a long relationship with someone back in England but I didn't marry him."

Why was I explaining myself to him?

"You didn't? Why not?"

"It was complicated."

"He was married?"

No flies on this boy.

He'd been in the house ten minutes, and already he had me pouring out revelations about my private life.

"So how old was this guy?"

"Fifty-five."

"Oh, old."

I must have made a face because he asked, "How old are you, if you don't mind my asking?"

The strange thing was I didn't mind.

"Forty-seven."

"Are you? You look great. I thought you were in your thirties. You're in terrific shape. Do you work out?"

I know I ought to have been offended by his familiarity, but the truth was I was thrilled.

"I'll be forty this year," he went on. "Getting old."

"You've never thought about getting married?" What a question to be asking someone I barely knew.

"Never. No plans to. Love women. Never want to marry one. Gotta be a big mistake."

Talk about breezy. For a second I had an image of Marietta hiring this guy and trying to keep him in line at Rosemullion. I smiled to myself. Sheldon Bennett might be one person who would have got the better of my mother.

"Never?"

"Nope. I'm a loner."

"So am I," I told him firmly.

"Are you really?"

"The crawl space." Before things got totally out of hand.

"On my way."

The other contractors had been in and out in fifteen minutes. Sheldon Bennett was there for an hour and a half. He found things that needed fixing everywhere he went, all over the house, and one by one he fixed them there and then—a new deck plank, a leaking faucet, holes in the screens, a switchover of the water filter—everything was taken care of, and all the time he pumped me for information about myself.

"So what do you like to drink? What's your favorite color? Where are you from in England? Do you like seafood? Do you like sushi? Why not? Wow! This jalousie door is beautiful, isn't it? They don't make them like this today. So where do you do your shopping? Where do you keep your car?"

"I don't have a car."

That silenced him for a second.

"You don't?"

"No."

"How do you get around?"

"I'm on intimate terms with Amagansett Taxis."

"Intimate?" His grin was very suggestive. I decided I'd better take control of the conversation, so I started asking the questions.

"Where do you live?"

"Me? I got a great place. I rent it. I live over on Lazy Point, across the bay from you. I'm right on the beach. Boats all over my yard. Be easier for me to come across the bay to you in my little power boat than to ride here in my truck. So. The roof. I'll call my roofer and get back to you with an estimate. Whoops, there goes my pager. Can I use the phone to call my service? If you ever get lonely, call me and I'll take you to dinner. Hey, look who's here."

Booty was coming down the stairs on her behind.

"And you're her nanny, Annabel. Nanny Annie, that's what I'll call you."

He checked his pager and made a couple of calls right in front of me, fixing times, flirting, cajoling, laughing, probably making dates with fifteen women.

He stooped and kissed Booty on the head on his way out the door.

Thank God I'm too old for him; no chance of his being attracted to me. The last thing I need is a heartbreaker.

"By the way," he called back as he went down the steps, "I meant what I said about dinner."

Of course, the day he came all the other contractors began to call back with their estimates and when I passed them to Hope, she said, "Okay, we'd better get this show on the road. I hear good things about this guy"—she pointed to a name on my list—"call him and set it up. We'll probably have to move out while they're doing the work. The noise and the smell will be awful when they do the flat roof over the den and the kitchen. Try and get him to come when I'm in California."

"When's that going to be, Hope?"

"Gee, I don't know. I'm waiting for Craig to tell me. I guess it all depends when they want Coco to start rehearsing. School's out June twenty-fifth, so it could be any time after that."

Gee, thanks a bunch for being so specific, Hope. That's a real help.

The more I thought about it, the more I felt I couldn't go ahead with the contractor Hope had selected without giving Sheldon Bennett a chance to submit his estimate. He'd been so kind to me. A little manic, a little cocky, but kind all the same. It was the least I could do. I called him and left a message, and he called back within the hour.

I remembered the way he had checked his service from our house. He'd probably dialed in from somewhere and picked up my message. An image of him sitting in some woman's kitchen having just talked over a job with her flashed through my mind, and to my surprise I felt a tiny stab of jealousy.

"I was calling about the roof, wondering if you could give me an estimate. You see, we've had other bids, and we need to press ahead, set a date."

"Press ahead?" The suggestive tone was there in his voice again. "So how've you been, Nanny Annie?"

Suddenly I realized I was smiling like an idiot at the sound of his voice.

"I've been fine," I told him. "What about you?"

"Pretty good, except my mom's coming to stay."

"Really?"

"Yeah, really. She sleeps in my little spare room, she takes all my phone calls, talks to all my friends, picks up all my messages before I do, and if she doesn't like the sound of the girl or boy, whoever's calling, she erases them. First thing she does, she burns my stash of *Playboy* magazines. She drives me crazy, but what am I going to do? I love her. She's my mom, and since my dad died she's been lonely."

His next words nearly made me drop the phone.

"I gotta be honest with you, Annabel. I'm glad you called. I've been thinking about you a whole lot."

When he said this, I realized that in between packing the kids' lunch boxes and doing the laundry and helping Harry prepare for his field trip, I'd been thinking about Sheldon Bennett nonstop.

"What have you been thinking about me?" I asked, aware that I had injected a bantering note into my own voice, just like his. What on earth had got into me?

"I pictured you sitting on top of me."

Well, I'd asked for that.

"Very funny. I'm forty-seven."

"What's that got to do with it? You look great. I told you. Great hair, great shoulders, great arms, great legs—at least I guess they're great under your jeans. Your breasts too, probably. So don't pretend you don't know it. What do you remember about me?"

"Your eyes," I answered immediately. "Your earring—why do you wear an earring? Are you . . . ?"

"Am I gay? Of course I'm not gay. A lot of my clients are, though, and sometimes I work bare-chested to give them a thrill. No, I love women. I wear an earring because I'm a pirate. My company's called Treasure Cove. So when am I going to see you?"

He was a fast worker. But then was he talking about seeing me as a woman or a client?

"I don't know." I played it safe. "Hadn't you better come over and discuss the roof with my employer, Hope Calder? She's a real estate broker with Tudor Woods in East Hampton."

"Oh, OK. Well, gotta race back. I'm working on a roof. Shingling. I'll call you."

"But—"

But he was gone.

I'd blown it. Now when would I see him?

Sooner than I thought.

Twenty minutes later his truck came tearing up the drive. He bounded onto the deck and scooped Booty up in his arms.

"I've got an hour. Come on, I'll show you my house."

I'd never ridden in a truck before. Inside it was big and wide—like him. The bench seat was wide too.

"Here, we'll put this little girl in between us." He swept aside papers and tools. "I've got this to strap her in." He produced a short length of rope and tied it around her so she was safely secured. "It's what I use for my nephews and nieces. They love going out with Uncle Sheldon. I baby-sit 'em all the time. Now hold on, Nanny Annie. Booty, ya ready?"

Booty squealed. This was a real adventure.

We set off through the woods. Booty clapped her hands when a startled deer ran across the road in front of us. Sheldon stopped the truck abruptly.

"I'm always scared I'm going to run into a deer. I know a guy, lives in the woods, he shoots them from his bedroom window."

"Do you hunt deer out here?" I asked him, looking around nervously for any sign of a rifle. On the one hand I felt like Meryl Streep in *The Bridges of Madison County*, riding around in an American truck with a handsome stranger, but on the other hand there was an air of *Deliverance* too, a wildness, an element of danger. I clung tightly to Booty's hand.

"Me? Never." He was emphatic. "I wouldn't harm a fly. I love animals. I found this kitten in a Dumpster the other day. Someone had abandoned him. He's at my house. You'll see him. I call him Schooner."

We were driving along a road flanked by black pines, tall rushes, and small freshwater ponds with sand dunes hiding the ocean in the distance. We passed cranberry bogs and banks overgrown with salt meadow hay and spike grass. And all along the road were telephone poles tilted at an angle from being battered by the winds coming in off the Atlantic.

We passed a row of rusty iron buildings on the edge of the water.

"That's the fish factory, where you can buy fresh fish. But you don't have to go there, I'll bring you fish. I go out in my boat very early in the morning. What do you like, Striped bass? Fluke? Bluefish? Hey, here we are."

We had arrived at his house. It was located in the most idyllic position imaginable at the end of a point jutting out into a lagoon. On the one side of the point was a tiny island separated from the mainland by a channel running from the sea into the lagoon.

"This is where the windsurfers come," he said, pointing to sails in the distance skimming along the water, reds, yellows, and greens against a brilliant blue sky.

"And here's my house."

It was a small wooden beach shack with sloping roofs and shingled walls and dormer windows like an English country cottage. Some of the windows had little blue shutters and window boxes full of geraniums.

"I planted those," Sheldon said proudly. "I love flowers."

What a contradiction. Big tough guy who loves flowers and rescues kittens. Probably feeds the birds too. And sure enough I saw little birdhouses on poles.

"You built those too?"

He nodded. "And that's Fred up there on the roof." He pointed to a seagull sitting on the chimney beside a beautiful old weather vane with a whale on top. "He never leaves except when I light the stove in the winter. I've got no central heating, just the stove and an electric blanket. You should see it here in the winter with snow on the beach."

There was a flagpole flying the Jolly Roger and boats everywhere. A big motorboat on a trailer towered above us as the truck pulled in. There were several little rowboats lying around on their side, a couple of kayaks. Orange life jackets, paddles, life preservers, buoys, lengths of rope, and fishing nets were hanging on the outside walls. A giant green tarp half covered an icebox on the deck alongside a couple of rocking chairs. A hammock had been strung up between two posts, and a giant barbecue grill stood beside tables and benches. A huge anchor had been driven into the ground and logs of wood had been stockpiled neatly. A motorbike listed to one side. Lumber was stacked up high.

Of course, he ran his business from here, Treasure Cove. As it said on his answering message and on his cap.

Booty was in heaven when we went into the house and she saw the kitten. She tried to pick it up and it broke free and ran away. She chased it onto the deck.

We were alone together, although we could hear Booty talking to herself outside. Suddenly he was awkward and so was I. Inside the house seemed tiny, cramped, dwarfed by his giant stature. I glanced around quickly. It was clear what had happened. I remembered what Ray Moran had told me. When the father died, Sheldon had sold the family house and moved his mother back into the city. She'd probably taken most of the family things, and he'd packed the rest of them—furniture and paintings—into his little shack. There was a beautiful old bureau over in the corner, a small sofa in front of the television, and, looking out through plate glass windows onto the deck and beyond, a panoramic vista of the lagoon and the island. Three cane chairs were placed around a circular glass-topped table with photos underneath. I bent down to take a closer look. Family photos. All-American graduation pics with caps and gowns. Barbecues on the beach. His parents standing arm in arm, smiling into the camera. Over to one side, slipped in under the edge of the glass, was a little black-and-white photo of him holding a surfboard: sun-bleached white hair, a toothy boyish grin, utterly adorable.

He slept in what he told me was his grandmother's old bed, and on the numerous bookshelves were endless sailing books and various editions of *Moby Dick*. The kitchen ran along the wall of the living room—cabinets, refrigerator, electric stove. The surfaces, I noticed, were immaculate. The shower was behind a plastic curtain.

"No washing machine?" I looked around. "How do you do your laundry?" Because his clothes were pristine too.

"Right here in the sink. I take my sheets to my clients and use their washing machines while I'm working on the house."

Used their phones, used their washing machines, probably used their beds when they were away and his house was too cold.

"I'd better see where Booty's got to." I made for the door, noticing its little porthole window.

"Just a second."

He was giving me another of those intense looks. He took a step toward me.

The phone rang.

"Just as well," he muttered.

"Hi, Mom, how ya doing? . . . Okay, I'll be there. No problem. . . . Yeah, yeah, I said I'd be there." A note of irritation crept into his voice. "Listen, I have to go. 'Bye."

He turned back to me.

"My mom. I told you she was coming."

"When does she arrive?"

"Not till next week, but she always has to plan ahead, make sure I'm going to be available to meet her train. Come on, let's grab the little one and I'll take you guys back. Wanna help me feed the birds, Booty? Gotta feed the birds."

I watched him breaking off pieces of bread and handing them to Booty, lifting her up and showing her how to put them inside the birdhouse with its little doors through which the birds could feed.

"You said you made that?"

"I made everything. See those rocking chairs? I made them. Think I'll have a beer before we go. Want one?"

"No, thanks. I don't drink beer." I watched him expertly flip the cap off a Bud with his thumb, something I'd seen Eddie try to do a dozen times and fail. Sheldon was so cool, as Harry would say. I tried to imagine what it must be like to live in this remote spot, surrounded by the sea. I could literally taste the salt in the air, smell the seaweed, feel the damp spray in my hair, and all the time I could hear the hypnotic sound of waves lapping against the boats and the endless clinking of the masts of the sailboats in the wind. What would it be like in a storm, with the wind and the rain howling around and the sea whipped up to lash the house itself?

Right now it was calm and breathtakingly romantic.

For the next few days all I could think about was that house and how much I longed to see Sheldon again. He called frequently, inane conversations that went nowhere, always beginning with his "So how are ya doing?"

I'd tell him what I was making for Booty's lunch or where Coco had gone on a play date. We discussed the weather. He told me anecdotes about people he saw. He made constant references to people who were lonely, with whom he seemed unusually preoccupied. To be honest, I didn't care what he talked about. It was wonderful to have someone who seemed interested in me and my simple life. I longed to tell him about my parents, about my life in Cornwall, but just as I was about to invite him over to lunch or whatever, it was always "Gotta race back, they need me." He seemed reluctant to be pinned down to any concrete arrangement.

And then he turned up again out of the blue one day, just as he had that day he took me to his house, and stood in the kitchen in his shorts and said, "Come on, let's go," and I knew I had to.

"I'll have to bring Booty."

"I know," he said. And added, as he had when his mother's phone call had interrupted us, "Just as well."

We drove to Lazy Point in silence, except for Booty, chattering away to herself. He looked straight ahead and said nothing and I began to panic. I was eight years older than he was. Did it matter? What was going to happen?

"Are you nervous?" he asked suddenly.

"How did you know?"

"It's understandable. I'm nervous and embarrassed. We've only just met. I keep thinking any minute you're going to take a look at me and say, Whoa! Slow down. This guy's way too young and unsophisticated."

"And I keep thinking you're going to take a look at me and think, What am I doing with a middle-aged woman when I could be out with firm thirty somethings with no gray in their hair?"

Oh, brilliant, Annabel, put ideas into his head, why don't you?

"I got thirty somethings. I got 'em all over the place. But all they want is commitment with a capital C, and marriage with a capital M, and kids with a capital K. And I want to live in my little house by the water and take my boat and go sailing once or twice a year in the Bahamas and look after my clients, have a few beers with my buddies, and be left alone."

So what are you doing with me? I wondered. Maybe it's because I'm older and past child-bearing age and you think you're safe.

Again when we were inside his little house, he was awkward.

He's like a teenager, I thought. He may be almost forty but he's shy, like a boy. Yet at the same time he's cocky and fully aware of his sexuality. But he doesn't quite know how to handle me. Lord knows, I haven't a clue.

"I want to kiss you," he said suddenly, and I realized it was this directness that I found so appealing. It was refreshing after years of Guy and his English reserve—but then I had found that charming in the beginning, before all the unpleasantness.

Would there be unpleasantness with Sheldon? And was I completely crazy to be assuming I would have a relationship with this man I barely knew?

"Booty." I pushed the sliding door open onto his deck. "Where's the kitten? See if you can find him."

"She shouldn't be out there by the water on her own," said Sheldon. "Surely she can't swim yet."

Well, you're the one who wanted to kiss me, I thought, suddenly feeling angry and thwarted. But of course he's right. He was more responsible than I was.

"Come," he said, and taking me by the hand he led me out to the deck and sat me down in one of the rocking chairs. Slowly he lowered himself into another rocker beside me, never letting go of my hand. I could feel his thumb beginning to stroke my palm, and I felt like a teenager sitting in the back row of a cinema, waiting for my first kiss.

"Like I said"—he looked at me—"I want to kiss you but not while we're having to keep an eye on the little one. So let's rock awhile, just for a few minutes, before I—"

"Gotta race back."

I smiled at him. It was as if I had known him all my life.

15

Eddie had never felt so confused. And it was always worse when he had one of his rare conversations with Hope. He knew he was always unpleasant when he called, but he couldn't help himself. It was the way she seemed to act as if nothing had happened, the way she was always so cheerful when he was feeling so wretched and hurt and sorry for himself.

It was beginning to worry him that they never really *talked*. If she called it was always to tell him something about the kids, mostly Booty. But whenever he asked to see Booty, she deflected him.

That morning she had called about Harry.

"Don't yell at me." It was almost the first thing she said.

"I wasn't about to. You haven't given me any reason—" He stopped to keep from saying *yet*. "How are the kids?"

"That's why I'm calling. I'm worried about Harry. He's retreated into himself, you know how he does sometimes when he's upset about something?"

"And then you ask him what's wrong and he pretends there's nothing wrong. What's up with him?"

"That's just it. I don't know. He won't talk to me or to Annabel. But they've even noticed he's quiet and withdrawn at school. Maybe you could do something?"

"Like what?"

"I don't know. Call him or something?"

"You think he'd talk to me? Shall I come out and see him?"

"No. Don't do that."

"So, how are you?"

"Oh, I'm just fine." She was always "just fine" when he asked.

"What about Craig? What does he say about Harry?"

There was silence on the other end of the line.

"You haven't spoken to him about Harry."

"I don't want to bother him."

"But he's Harry's father."

"And you're not interested in Harry anymore, just because you've moved out? You know what, Eddie? I think Harry's upset because he misses you, and you don't even care because you're not his real father."

Are *you* trying to say you miss me? Eddie wanted to ask.

Their conversations were always like this. It was as if she called him because she needed him and then she pushed him away before he could ask her what was going to happen with their marriage.

On top of this, he had his relationship with Arlene to deal with. He hadn't actually been aware that they had a relationship until she asked him point-blank what he was going to do about it.

"I worship you," Arlene said simply, after they had been seeing each other out of the office for about three weeks. "You're clever, you're kind, you're beautiful to look at. I love the way your hair falls over your eyes and I have to push it back."

"You don't have to," said Eddie. "I can do it perfectly well myself," and immediately wished he could take the words back when he saw the hurt look on her face. The truth of the matter was that, as much as he smarted from her sharp tongue in the office, it was, he found, what he really liked about her, and the slushiness she indulged in when they were alone was beginning to cloy.

It had been a mistake to give in to her incessant demands to take her to dinner at an upscale French restaurant in her neighborhood. Not because he was ashamed of her and the way she dressed. He wasn't like that, he told himself firmly. Not at all. Although somehow, before their relationship was over, he was going to have to make her understand that the way she dressed at home—no makeup, simple casual clothes—was a zillion times (to use one of her favorite expressions) more classy than the outfits she wore to the office.

Before their relationship was over.

Already he was anticipating this point in their future. Whereas she obviously saw it as a soap opera that would run and run. He could hear the trailer in his head: Will Eddie find happiness with the one who truly loves him? (Although now that he thought about it, Arlene hadn't mentioned what she called the "L" word yet.) Or will he return to the wife who has betrayed him? And will he ever see his baby daughter again? We will return after the break.

And boy, did he need a break!

The problem was, he was becoming attached to Arlene. Although how he could take seriously someone who consulted a plastic toy every day was beyond his comprehension.

"I asked the Magic Eight Ball if it was time we went out to dinner together as a couple, in a restaurant, like a proper date, and it replied, 'Ask again later,'" Arlene told him cheerfully, as he was searching for words to write his tenth rejection letter that morning.

This book is not right for our list.
This genre is not a particular strength of the Gramercy Press.
The author's innate feel for the strife in his characters' lives is poignant but ultimately stifling.
This first novel is not quite strong enough, but I would like to see the author's next work.

Larry had handed Eddie a list of useful sentences to make the agent or author think you actually had some feeling for the work, whereas in fact you probably hadn't even read it yourself.

"Hey, why don't you let me write those letters for you?" Arlene peered over his shoulder. "It's what I'm here for. I mean, after all, I'm the one who reads most of these books you reject. Makes sense that I'd make the letters sound genuine."

"But you do everything for me," protested Eddie. "You read the manuscripts. I rely on you to tell me whether or not I should even look at them, you field my phone calls, you make my reservations, you write my jacket copy, you do my filing, you liase with all the other departments about my books, you more or less do my job for me, and yet you tell me I'm helpless because I let women do everything for me. From where I'm sitting it's not as if I have much choice. And what on earth is a Magic Eight Ball? And before you ask, No, they didn't teach me about it at Cambridge."

"It's this black ball and you can ask it anything you want and you turn it around and around and it gives you one of a whole lot of answers, and it's always right. You should try it sometime."

And this is the person who gives me the most perceptive book reports I've ever seen, thought Eddie. Maybe she reads the manuscripts and consults the Magic 8 Ball. It was bewildering. In among the manuscripts littered about her apartment, he found countless copies of women's magazines whose cover lines all proclaimed in various forms that inside she would learn 24 ways to drive her lover wild in bed, find out if he really cared, know for sure if he was to be trusted, and a zillion other insights into the truth about men.

"What would be really great would be if they just said, 'How to tell from his voice on the phone how big his dick is.' That's it, Arlene! Why don't you write *The Blind Date Handbook?* It'd be a winner."

"Somehow, I don't think it'd be right for the Gramercy Press. Anyway, Eddie, don't be so judgmental. All women read those magazines. I bet your wife has them stashed away somewhere."

"I don't think so," said Eddie, and knew he was speaking the truth.

"Well, then, she can't be very interested in men."

That stopped him in his tracks. Was Arlene right? She saw his face.

"Hey, honey, I didn't mean that. I'm sure she was interested in you. She was probably pretty picky. Only went for the cream."

That was the thing about Arlene. She could be so sensitive. She picked up on his every mood and listened whenever he really wanted to talk. When had Hope last stayed still for more than five minutes, sat down, shut up, and really listened to what he had to say?

"You miss your little girl, don't you?" said Arlene at dinner, as they were looking at menus. "Even leaving Max for one evening with the woman down the hall makes me edgy. I gotta be honest with you, Eddie, much as I love being here with you, much as I begged you to take me to a fancy restaurant, part of me's gonna be sitting here missing my baby, so I can imagine how you feel."

Now she tells me, thought Eddie. "I don't know what to do," he said. "It's been almost two months now. Hope and I aren't really talking. We're not discussing whether we should be thinking about separating formally. I don't know if she's seeing Craig—that's her first husband, who lives in California—or whether he's flying east to see her all the time. I don't know what's happening with Booty. She must be wondering where I am. I wonder what Hope's told her. I asked if Booty could come into the city to see me and she said I could only see her at Maisie's, and I absolutely refuse to go back there. And then I asked if I could go home and see her and Hope said she'd think about it and I haven't heard a word since."

"What about that nanny you liked so much, haven't you spoken with her?"

"Not in a while. I don't want to put her in a compromising position by calling. She works for Hope. Craig pays her—"

"In other words, you're chicken."

"Thanks, Arlene. I knew I could rely on you to set me straight. But on top of everything else there's Harry and Coco. They're not my children, but I love them and I miss them too. I missed Coco's birthday party. I sent her a gift and I had the sweetest little drawing from her saying *thank you*. Annabel must have sent it; it was mailed here to the office."

"Well, you'll just have to decide what to do. You have to see your daughter. You have rights, surely. But you're the one who's going to have to set it up. Have you told many people that you and Hope split?"

That was another thing. He hadn't told anyone. The people who weighed most heavily on his mind were Maud and his mother. Somehow he couldn't bring himself to admit that they had been right all along and that Hope was not the person he had tried to make them think she was. In fact, the only people who knew were Larry and Susie, with whom he was staying. Indefinitely. In a little maid's room off the kitchen, squashed into a twin bed with his feet hanging over the edge.

Larry had proved to be a really good buddy, always willing to sit up and drink far into the night. Occasionally he would counter Eddie's pleas for advice with a tentative reminder. "You gotta remember, I never met Hope. She's on Long Island, you're in the city, and it's not like you guys ever doubledated with Susie and me. It's weird. We brought you together but we don't know her. It seems you two don't have a lot in common, but then neither do Susie and I and we're happy."

"You don't?" Eddie was surprised. "You have your backgrounds, at least. You're both from the south trying to make it in the Big Apple."

"Wrong."

"Susie's from New York?"

"No. I'm the one who's from New York. Susie's from Tennessee. Nashville. Old money. Their place is bigger than the Hermitage."

"What's that?"

"Andrew Jackson's place."

"Who's he? Rich man? You get invited over there?"

"He was one of our presidents. Don't ask me which one, but I know he's been dead quite a while. And I'm telling you Susie's family's place is bigger than his."

"Was."

"Whatever. Only now it looks like a battlefield and I don't mean Shiloh, I mean those pictures you see of World War One battlefields in France where all the trees are cut off halfway up the trunk, all jagged. Or like some ghostly futuristic movie set where half the world's population has been wiped out. I keep expecting to see zombies emerging from the mist."

"What happened?"

"A tornado is what happened. Earlier this year. Really shook Susie's folks up. Swept through their land and destroyed most of their trees, but the house is still standing."

"You go there much?"

"Quite a lot. Obviously, I've embraced the whole southern thing, whereas Susie couldn't wait to get away. But I guess the fact we haven't been able to produce any kids means we won't be inheriting the place when the time comes. That's one of the reasons I don't want to adopt. I think it's meant to be. We can't have kids and we won't be living there. I love the idea of being a southern gentleman on the old plantation, but maybe there's only so far I can take it. I know I landed a job here at the Gramercy Press because they needed a token joker, someone who could take care of all the self-help books and the odd personality book that brings in the money. They know they gotta do 'em occasionally to keep the place going, but nobody wants to sully their lily-white hands with them 'cept me. That's how I met Susie. I had to go to Nashville to see a country singer who was writing a book, and she was visiting her folks. We met on the plane. I love her, man. I'm a complete faker start to finish, but the one thing I don't fake is my love for that little girl, and she knows it."

Eddie was thinking about Larry when Arlene sprang the "So what are you going to do about our relationship?" question on him. He'd been thinking about how nice it would be if he and Arlene could go out with Larry and Susie as a foursome and he was wondering why it was that he had somehow not told Larry that he was seeing Arlene out of the office. Nor had he told Arlene that Larry didn't know about them, so all in all he had managed yet again to get himself into a tangle.

But to say that they had a relationship, that was taking things just a little too far. They hadn't even had sex. She wouldn't allow anything to happen at her place because of Max, and sneaking in a night of passion in Larry and Susie's maid's room was equally impossible. Mercifully Arlene's attention was distracted before he was required to give her an answer.

"Look at that," she said angrily.

"What?" said Eddie.

"That party over there. Twenty women at least. Must be some kind of wedding shower or birthday celebration. They're the pits."

"They are?" Eddie couldn't really see what was wrong with women going out and celebrating their birthdays.

"Absolutely. They're the worst. They'll all order different things. They'll all change their minds a dozen times. They'll all want separate checks, and not one of them will leave more than a sixty-cent tip."

"Ah," said Eddie, enlightened. "Arlene the waitress strikes again. Coming out in sympathy, are you?"

"Nothing wrong with being a waitress."

"So how come you're not still doing it?"

"Everyone should move on, including you, Eddie. When are you going to look for an apartment? Listen, I knew going in that it was going to be complicated with you, but I never figured you'd take this long to sort yourself out. What are we going to do?"

"We, Arlene, are not going to do anything. You're always on me to do things for myself, so I'm telling you: When I'm good and ready I'm going to find myself an apartment, go back to London, whatever."

He knew what he was supposed to say: "We'll look for an apartment for you, me, and Max, somewhere Booty can come and stay for visits." But it had barely been a month. There was no sex. No relationship. The thing about Arlene was she didn't play fair. What she didn't seem to realize was that she was the one who needed the support, but she was always so busy playing the tough girl who could look after herself that she might well end up staying that way if she didn't watch out.

Then, after dinner, after she'd waded in and attacked the women at the next table when they demanded separate checks as predicted—"You do that you're all gonna be here for another hour," she told them, "give your waitress a break; here's a pocket calculator, divide the bill by twenty, what can it hurt?"—after they'd walked down the street for a couple of blocks, she suddenly slipped her arm through his, looked up into his face, and told him, "You know something, Eddie, I owe you so much. You're the first person to take me seriously, the first person I've met who has made me think I'm somebody."

"That's crazy," he said, secretly pleased. "What about Max's father?"

"We don't talk about him. You know that."

And while he was reflecting that each time he tried to raise the subject of Max's father and how he had died, she'd refused to talk about it, she placed her lips on his right there in the street and gave him the kind of soft, tender kiss he hadn't had from Hope in years. And he yearned to be able to take her somewhere and lose himself in her instead of going back to Larry and Susie's.

He did need her.

And she needed him.

Maybe not for the same reasons, but they had unfinished business.

Next morning at the office, unfinished or not, it was business as usual.

"Bambi's on the line," Arlene spat at him. "Namby-pamby Bambi. Shall I tell her you're in a meeting?"

Eddie had made the mistake of telling Arlene that Josie Gardiner reminded him of Bambi.

"No, Arlene, for God's sake, put her on."

Arlene was always after him to get a grip on his career, and here she was trying to separate him from his meal ticket to promotion. Although, to be fair, he had been dreading the moment when he would have to deal with Josie Gardiner again.

She was what his mother and Maud would describe as "a little minx." Emphasis on the *little* in Josie's case. He was definitely attracted to a certain physical type, small-boned and vulnerable, like Hope. He supposed his mother and Maud dubbed Hope a little minx between themselves. Well, they would now anyway.

He'd seen the signs when he'd had lunch with Josie and had done his best to ignore them. She had long, painted fingernails and even before they'd ordered, she began to trail them along the back of his hand in a desultory manner when she wanted to make a point.

"What do you think about my idea to do a novel based on the feud going on in my family, even as we speak, for control of the island?"

Eddie marveled at the way she referred to the Gardiners as her family when she had produced no evidence to support this claim other than having the same—fairly common—last name. The feud to which she referred involved Robert Lion Gardiner, now in his eighties—who had been left the island jointly with his now-dead sister Alexandra by their aunt, Sarah Diodati Gardiner—and the sister's daughter, also called Alexandra. Alexandra married a man who came from a family conceivably even richer than the Gardiners, and the couple maintained they ought to be the sole owners of the island and live in the manor house.

Robert Lion Gardiner didn't agree, and the mudslinging began.

"I would fictionalize the family. I would make the niece a kind of fancy Tina Brown character just to juice things up a bit. I'd put in sex and greed and sugar and spice; it would be a whole lot more commercial than my previous books. Then I'd do an author tour and reveal I'm a descendant and everyone would believe they're getting the real dirt. What do you think?"

Eddie's first thought was that the literary following she had already gathered would be gone forever, horrified by the project's vulgarity. But at face value it had the makings of a definite money maker.

She has tiny teeth, he kept thinking throughout the meal as she continued her story—and he had to admit she was a good raconteur—like little pearl fangs. He watched them sink into a slice of mango as her huge eyes swiveled to meet his.

"I said, Do you like it out in the Hamptons?"

"What? Oh, sorry." Eddie had been imagining the mango sliding down the back of her throat. "Yes, I love it, great place."

"Funny, you don't strike me as the flashy social type. You seem like more of an introvert, a loner." She hesitated. "Like me. I picked up on a sensitive side when I first met you. Was I right?"

"Haven't a clue," said Eddie quickly. "Let's have some coffee. How do you come to be living in New York?"

"Oh, I don't live in New York. I live in London. I'm just here to do research for my book. Clem Springer put me in an apartment on the Upper West Side. I believe it's quite near where you live."

Not anymore, thought Eddie with relief, only she doesn't know that.

Of course they went crazy about her idea at the editorial acquisitions meeting, and Clem Springer summoned Eddie for another drink upstairs.

"How are you two getting along?"

"Fine," said Eddie. Basically it was a case of so far so good.

"That's dandy. Well, don't screw things up, whatever you do. The new novel's gonna be a winner. Make sure she turns it in on time. We need it for the spring catalog. You bring this off"—he made a jerking movement with his left hand and Eddie looked the other way—"you bring this off and we'll think about making you vice president."

"Boy!" said Larry several times, when Eddie told him. "You'd better keep that engine on the right track. Make her whistle blow."

Which was why Eddie always took Josie's phone calls.

But this one was the killer.

"Eddie darling, the time has come for me to go to Gardiners Island. I know there's a patrol keeping people off, I've heard they have guns, but I don't care. Fix it for me, will you? Weekend after next, and I'll want you to come along."

"But you're family, oughtn't you to fix it?" asked Eddie.

"Eddie, don't be tedious. They might be family, but I don't want them to know about this book until I've found out everything I need to know. I need to get onto that island, sniff around a bit, see what I can find out, and nip off again sharpish. So, as I said, fix it."

Something warned him not to appeal to Arlene for help. Instead he called Annabel, the first time he had spoken to her in weeks, and explained his predicament.

"The only ray of light at the end of the tunnel is the thought that if I make it out to the island with her, you could find a way to meet me and bring along the children so I can see them. Booty, anyway. But how I'm going to get this woman onto Gardiners Island is totally beyond me."

But then Annabel produced a bit of sheer Mary Poppins magic out of the air.

"Oh, I don't think that's going to be a problem," she told him cheerfully. "I know just the person to get you there. Leave it to me."

Eddie sat gawping like a goldfish in amazement as Arlene came into his office.

"Shut your mouth, Eddie," she reproved him, "before a fly tickles your tongue. Although while I'm here"—she shut the door behind her and lowered her mouth to cover his—"I might just do that myself."

Little minx, thought Eddie.

Things were looking up, so much so that he decided to put into action a plan he'd been thinking about for some time. He wanted to do something for Max, to whom he had become quite attached. He admitted to himself that Max was something of a substitute for Booty, Harry, and Coco, whom he was missing terribly, especially Harry, after Hope's last phone call. He felt so frustrated by not being able to do anything to help. Well, then, he thought, if he couldn't do anything for Harry, he'd do something for Max.

He went to the pound and got a puppy.

Big mistake!

"Eddie, what is that?" Arlene had returned from the basement, where she had been doing the laundry.

"It's a puppy. A wheaten terrier. His name is Clinton."

"It looks more like a Saint Bernard."

"No, honestly, he's a terrier. I asked. That's what she said at the pound. I said, 'Looks like a Saint Bernard,' and she said, 'He's not a real Saint Bernard.' I freaked. I thought she meant he was stuffed or something, but then she said he was a cross. Maybe that means his father was a Saint Bernard or something. But he won't grow that big."

"Eddie, we are not allowed dogs of any size in the building, and only an insane person would bring a dog into this studio apartment. You'll have to take him back to the pound."

"I'm not taking him back to the pound. I wouldn't be so cruel."

"Well, then, you can take him to the island this weekend when you go out there with Bambi."

It had been a big mistake telling Arlene that he was going to be taking Josie Gardiner to Long Island for the day. She hadn't let it alone for a second, finally arriving at what she thought was a brilliant solution: Take Clinton with them as a present for Booty, Harry, and Coco.

"Does your girlfriend like dogs, by the way?"

"I don't know. I haven't consulted her."

"So she *is* a girlfriend."

"Of course she isn't. She's an author. She's going to do research."

"I don't see why you have to go with her."

"Join the club," muttered Eddie, "although if it gives me a chance to see Booty, it'll be worth it."

"But you're not having a relationship with her?"

"I'm not having a relationship with anyone," said Eddie in exasperation, "not even with my wife. By the way, you just missed Max's father. He called while you were down in the basement."

Eddie had answered the phone on his arrival with Clinton and nearly dropped the receiver when a gravelly voice said, "I wanna speak to my son."

"You want what?"

"My kid, Max. I wanna say Hi."

"He's not here."

It was sort of true. Max was across the hall playing with the kid in 2B.

"Well, whoever you are, get yo' sorry ass away from my child."

There was a click and Eddie had found himself listening to the dial tone when Arlene walked back in and saw Clinton.

"Oh, shit, he's found us," said Arlene.

"I thought he was supposed to be dead."

Arlene put down the laundry basket she was still clasping. "Fell right into that one, didn't I?"

"He's not dead?"

"Jesus, Eddie, you just spoke to him, didn't you? Did he sound dead to you?"

"So you lied to me."

"I lied to you. Big fucking deal."

Eddie had never seen her so edgy.

"Why did you lie to me?" He tried not to sound resentful.

"Because I'm trying to pretend to myself that he's dead. Because I thought it would put you off if you thought he was still in the picture."

"And is he still in the picture?"

"Well, he is and he isn't."

"Arlene, what is going on?"

"Erroll and I got together like I told you. We had Max. Then Erroll's mother couldn't handle the fact that Max was going to be raised as the product of a mixed-race relation-

ship. As I found out soon enough, Erroll listens to his
mother. That woman has him completely under her thumb.
She put pressure to bear on him to get me out of the picture.
If she had her way he'd marry a nice African-American girl
and they'd raise Max together, a nice cozy trio: Erroll, his
mother, and his wife. But where does that leave me? *I'm*
Max's mother. I'm not married to Erroll. I raise Max, and Erroll can go fuck himself. When I kicked him out, Max was
only eighteen months old."

"You kicked him out?" Eddie backed away from Arlene,
who was clattering around in her kitchen alcove. This was
the first he'd heard about her kicking Erroll out. He had always understood it was the other way around.

"Sure. What do I want with a mommy's boy who wants to
take my son away from me?"

"But surely Erroll has a right to see his own son?"

"Yeah. He claims he wants to see Max. He comes looking
for us every now and then, but what am I supposed to do?
He doesn't give me any money. Max doesn't understand who
he is, and if I let Erroll take him out of my sight I may never
see him again."

Eddie recalled the threatening voice on the phone and
conceded she might have a point.

"Is Erroll a gangster?"

"Oh, now don't start romanticizing him. He works at a
gas station, least he did last time we spoke. Eddie, do you see
what I see?" She pointed to a puddle on the floor. "That dog
is just a passing visitor in this apartment."

The following Saturday, Eddie bundled Clinton into a rental
car, warning him that if he so much as dribbled he was going
back to the pound, and drove over to pick up Josie. He was
really rather looking forward to his day out.

The only blip had been Max's sad little face as Eddie carried Clinton down the hall and into the elevator. But now he had Booty's excitement at seeing Clinton to look forward to all the way along the Long Island Expressway.

Josie Gardiner patted his thigh before they were out of the Midtown Tunnel.

"You're adorable. Totally and utterly adorable," she said.

Eddie smiled but kept his eyes on the road. Josie wasn't exactly dressed for a breezy boat ride to an island, but he elected to say nothing. If she wanted to trip across the sand in high heels, who was he to stop her? He was so relieved at her acceptance of Clinton, who had settled into a round ball of fur on her lap, that he was prepared to accommodate her eccentricities.

"I'm not talking about the dog, I mean you. What time are we going to Gardiners Island?"

"We're to meet the man who's going to take us in his boat at three o'clock. That gives us time to have lunch in East Hampton first. Tell me about the research you want to do. Maybe you'll need to visit the Long Island Collection at the library."

"Oh, I'm sorry, I completely forgot to tell you. I have an appointment in East Hampton. I thought you'd probably want to go home right away and see your daughter."

"Very thoughtful of you." Hallelujah! Eddie rejoiced in silence.

"Well, it's extraordinarily sweet of you to bring me out here. I can't understand why you aren't staying overnight with your family, but I'm not going to argue because I'm thrilled you're taking me back again. What I was going to suggest was this: Since we can't do lunch, let's have dinner when we get back to the city tonight. What do you say?"

Eddie was about to plead another engagement when a vision of Arlene consulting the Magic 8 Ball about their relationship flashed into his head. If he'd known that leaving

Hope would mean he'd be sandwiched between two such predatory piranhas as Arlene and Josie, he'd have stayed put.

And fought for her against Craig? What was happening there? he wondered. Had Craig returned as a fixture in Hope's life? Surely Annabel would have said.

"Are you asleep at the wheel?" asked Josie, leaning forward to peer at him with her wide-eyed Bambi look.

"Oh, no, sorry. Look, about dinner. Let's see how late we get back."

"Keeping your options open? I'm looking forward to meeting your wife."

Fat chance, thought Eddie. He supposed Josie must think him a little rude for not extending an invitation to his home, but his private life was none of her business. He wondered what she'd have to say if she knew about his relationship with Arlene.

Except it wasn't a relationship. Was it?

"And your children. How many do you have?"

"One. No, three."

Josie gave him that look again.

"I mean, Hope was married before. We have one together and she has two by her first marriage. Have you ever been married?" he asked, to deflect her attention.

"No way. I don't believe in it. I'm a free spirit. You know the song—I think it's Sting—if you love someone, set them free. I'm too much of a romantic to be tied down."

"You don't believe in fidelity?" asked Eddie, not really interested in the answer. His mind was on how long he would be able to retain his sanity with this nutcase in tow.

"I believe one should be faithful to oneself."

"And a slave to masturbation," said Eddie, before he could stop himself.

The hand on his thigh tightened its grip.

"Not exactly," she said.

"Look, I'm sorry, but you're going to have to remove your hand. It's interfering with my driving," said Eddie.

She ignored him.

"You know, Clem has high hopes for you," she told him.

"And for you and your book," said Eddie.

"As my editor you have a truly powerful role now at the Gramercy Press."

"I know. I'm extraordinarily lucky."

"Actually, I have a little secret to confess," she simpered. She was so maddeningly cute all the time. He conceded she was exceptionally pretty, but the act she put on was infuriating. "I'm so fragile, please protect me" when it was becoming clear she was a manipulative piece of work who had Clem Springer's balls in a wringer.

As it turned out, he didn't know the half of it.

"I asked Clem if I could have you as my editor after I saw you in the office. I'd been watching you for some time. I asked him who you were, and when he told me you were English too I nearly died. Believe me, I had a pretty hard time persuading him you ought to be my editor. He didn't think you were ready, but I played the Brits should stick together line for all it was worth, and here we are. You owe your promotion to me."

"Thank you," said Eddie dryly. "I'm enormously grateful."

"I'm attracted to you. It was a way to get closer. Can't you see?" Again the simpering look. "By the way," she added, before he could respond—although what on earth he would have said he had no idea—"your dog's just peed on my skirt." She lifted Clinton into the air, dangling him in front of the windshield to reveal a damp patch between her legs. "At least I think that's why I'm wet."

Oh, please! She's so nauseatingly arch, I can't stand another second, thought Eddie, abandoning his earlier vow to accommodate her every wish. As he waited for her to finish rinsing her skirt in a gas station toilet, he was tempted to drive away and leave her there. That'd teach the silly little bitch a lesson. Her book had better sell a million copies and secure him the biggest profile in New York publishing as her editor. Too bad he couldn't get Clinton to take a dump on her at some point during the next fifty miles. If he hadn't been on his way to see Booty, he would seriously start thinking about turning back.

"So fill me in on what kind of research you're looking to do on Gardiners Island," he said, as she got back in the car.

"You'll find out soon enough," was the reply, her voice full of innuendo.

They arrived in East Hampton, and the ghastly reality of what he'd let himself in for finally dawned on him when she directed him to the offices of Tudor Woods Realty.

"As I said, I'm looking forward to meeting your wife. I've been thinking about buying property out here, and Clem tells me she's a really hot broker, so of course I called her. I could have had you set up a meeting, but then we don't want her to know you brought me out here, do we? Don't worry, Eddie. If you stay in the car she won't know about us. I just had to meet her, had to see what she was like. Let me out here. Pick me up again at two thirty over there by the bank, okay, sweetie?"

And to Eddie's horror she leaned over and kissed him on the cheek, deposited Clinton in his arms, and opened the car door just as Hope came out of Tudor Woods.

Eddie hadn't bargained for what it would do to him seeing Hope again. She'd put on a tiny bit of weight and it suited her. She was wearing, he noticed sadly, the beautiful Calvin Klein jacket she always wore when she wanted to impress someone she thought would be an important buyer from the city. She'd found time to have her hair cut, and he liked the way it was slicked back off her face. She was smiling, hand outstretched to greet Josie, who would probably only sense a confident, efficient real estate person, but Eddie

could see beyond that. He could see that beyond Hope's natural warmth there was apprehension in her eyes. She was excited but she was nervous. Would she make a big sale today?

Suddenly he wanted her to succeed, wanted to banish the
hint of uncertainty, wanted to reassure her that she would do
just fine and he was right behind her. He had resented her
devotion to her work, her enthusiasm for something in
which he could not share, but seeing her standing there so
anxious to please someone like Josie Gardiner, who would
undoubtedly be the most difficult of clients, he wanted to
rush over and protect her.

But he didn't move. He sat in the rental and let Hope and
Josie walk away to Hope's car. He kept expecting Josie to turn
and point him out to Hope, but for some reason she didn't
and he sat there watching his wife chatting away and gesticu-
lating in the way she did when she was excited about a house.

How long would it be before artful Josie pried out of her
the information that she was separated from her husband?
For Eddie had no doubt that she would. Josie Gardiner, he
now knew, had an agenda all her own, that extended far beyond the professional confines of the Gramercy Press.

16

"Annabel?"

The voice on the other end of the line was familiar but I couldn't quite place it. I was distracted. I had received a letter in the mail that morning from my father's solicitor informing me that probate had finally been granted on Felix and Marietta's will. I was now the proud owner of the blackened ruin that was Rosemullion and all that went with it. And yet the idea that I should now go back to Cornwall, take possession, oversee repairs to the damage, and reopen it as a bed-and-breakfast was becoming more and more of a fantasy as each day went by. This had less to do with the fact that I had convinced myself that I stood a fairly good chance of facing criminal charges upon my return and more to do with the increasing feeling I had that I belonged right here on Long Island.

For the first time in my life I was part of a family. Not my own; we had never been a real family. Marietta had always operated alone, leaving Felix and me to be bossed about as her serfs rather than embraced as her next of kin. Felix had invariably retreated into a world of his own, leaving me to do the same. But here in Amagansett I was part of family life. Harry, Coco, and Booty were becoming as much my children as Hope's, and as for Hope herself, she had all but replaced Marietta in my life. Not as my mother, perhaps, but as the mother figure in the household. She was like Marietta in that respect. Strong, capable, but not one to play the conventional mother role. The difference was that Hope clearly did love her kids, and I had never been entirely sure that Marietta loved me.

"Annabel? You there?"

Now I knew who it was, and I searched frantically for something to say.

"Hello, Ray. How are you?"

Was he going to ask me out to dinner again? Was he upset at the way I had ignored him at Coco's birthday party? I was astonished to realize that I hadn't even thought about Ray Moran in the last couple of weeks. I'd had someone else on my mind. Now what was I going to say?

"I'm good. I just wanted to check. I called Sheldon Bennett, that guy I told you about. The one I thought could help you out with the house. Did he get in touch?"

Did he get in touch? Well, yes, Ray, as a matter of fact he did, but I'm not sure it was quite the way you intended.

"He was wonderful, Ray. Thank you so much. He came over and inspected the house, and Hope's booked him to do the roof." That was a smart move, bringing Hope's name into it. Nothing to do with me anymore.

Except I longed to talk more about Sheldon, longed to ask Ray all about him. Had he ever been engaged? What had his parents been like? Was he seeing anyone now? Who were his friends?

"Yeah, I knew he'd come through. He's a good guy. Bit wild, as I said, but his heart's in the right place. So when are you going to be free for dinner?"

"Well, Hope tells me you have a beautiful house. I'd love to come over and see it one day. Meet your wife. Hannah, isn't it?"

There was a long silence. Didn't tell me you were married, did you, Ray? Now what are you going to do?

"Hope told you about her?"

"Yes, she did."

"It's very sad. For her and for me. I guess I just have to live with it. Not too many folks know. I'd appreciate it if you could keep it to yourself."

Not too many folks know about what? That his marriage was sufficiently on the rocks for him to ask other women out to dinner? Well, no, that wasn't the sort of thing you wanted to know about your family doctor. Well, I wasn't about to tell anyone. Furthermore, I didn't want any part of this conspiracy. I'd had enough of all that with Guy.

"I won't breathe a word. None of my business. By the way, Eddie's coming out this weekend." I wanted to change the subject.

"Comes out every weekend, doesn't he?" said Ray.

"Oh, no, he hasn't been here for ages, not since Easter, when he and Hope—"

I stopped abruptly.

"When he and Hope what?"

Now what had I gotten myself into?

"Well, they've had some kind of misunderstanding. Hope took Harry and Coco into New York to see their father, and she didn't tell Eddie, and he came out here as usual and then went back and found them all together," I blurted out. After all, he had suggested I tell him if I had any problems. "And this is the first time Eddie's coming out since then."

"Maybe he and Hope will sort it out." Ray made it sound so reasonable.

"Oh, no, he's not coming here. He's driving out with an author. I don't think Hope even knows he's coming. I'm to meet him somewhere with the kids."

"Annabel, this doesn't sound good. Be careful. It won't help you to get involved in their marital problems."

So why are you trying to involve me in yours?

"Ray, I'd better run. Harry's standing here trying to tell me something."

"Okay. Give me a call."

Good. I hadn't committed myself to anything.

"What is it, Harry?"

"I think we'd better call Mom." He had a highly disapproving look on his face. He had a right to be disapproving. The bunk bed drama would never have happened if I'd been paying attention to them and not mooning about like a lovesick teenager wondering when and if Sheldon was going to call.

In the end, after two weeks of silence, I'd called him. You're not supposed to do that, but I'd had a good reason. Eddie had presented me with the perfect excuse to make contact when he said he needed to find a way to get to Gardiners Island. Who better to take him than Sheldon?

I left a message on his machine, making a big effort to sound efficient and positive, no hint of "why haven't you called me?" reproach in my voice. A short message. To the point. No reference to any other business between us.

He had responded immediately, almost as if he had been waiting for me to call rather than the other way around.

"Sure I'll take you," he said briskly. No mention of our last meeting. No inquiry as to how I was. "Only takes ten minutes from my house. We'll zip across the bay in my sharpie. You know we're not really allowed to go there, don't you? Private property. Oldest estate to remain in one family in the whole of America. The Gardiners don't like strangers. You have to be careful. Sometimes you have to swim in from the boat, sneak up onto the beach. But if you guys can cope with that, I'll take you. Who else is coming?"

I told him about Eddie and explained about Josie Gardiner.

"Is she pretty?"

"I don't know. I've never met her."

"Probably his lover," he said matter-of-factly.

I hadn't thought of that.

"But if there are going to be four of us, that's too many. The sharpie's too small. And we can't take the kids."

That meant I'd have to stay behind. Well, never mind, I'd still see him when I introduced him to Eddie, and the kids would enjoy his house.

But so far the day had got off to a bad start. An argument had erupted between Coco and Booty over the fire department's Tot Finder stickers. Coco was tired. It was my fault, I'd kept her up the night before to finish writing thank-you letters for all the birthday presents she'd received. Hope had been too casual about it for my liking; I was determined to try and make Coco understand and appreciate other people's generosity. To make up for all the official qualifications I didn't have, I had decided to play the English nanny role to the hilt, and that included keeping a sharp eye on the kids' manners. We were nearly at the end of June, almost a month after the party, and Coco still hadn't thanked everyone.

The row had started when Coco came home from school with her Tot Finder stickers.

"The nurse's office at school gave them to me," she told us proudly. "We have to put them in the windows of rooms where tiny tots are sleeping so the firemen can see where there's a child and go there first."

"Fine," I said. "We'll put them on the landing window so they'll see where Booty sleeps. She's the tiniest tot in this house."

"That's right," said Harry, and he took the stickers and gave them to Booty.

"No!" shrieked Coco. "They're mine! They're to go in a *real* room. Booty doesn't have a room. She sleeps on the landing or with Mom."

I detected a note of jealousy in Coco's voice. This explained a lot about Coco's behavior. No doubt she resented Booty more than Harry did. Booty was a cute little girl who threatened to steal some of the limelight away from Coco.

I watched as she took the stickers back from Booty and put them in the long drawer underneath her new bunk beds.

Booty saw her.

While we were all having breakfast that morning, Booty had slipped into Coco's room and opened the drawer to get the stickers. Coco tried to stop her. The beds were placed in such a way that if you opened the drawer it barricaded the door and no one could get in the room. This was what Booty had done now, and she wasn't letting anyone in especially Coco.

I decided to leave her there for the time being. Harry had reported that he'd gone around the side of the house— Coco's room was on the ground floor—and the bedroom window was open, so if necessary he could climb in there and open the door.

I buttered another slice of toast knowing I—or rather my waistline—would regret it later and watched as Harry began to fill thermos bottles in preparation for our trip. Suddenly I noticed he was pouring vodka into one bottle and topping it up with ketchup.

"Harry, what on earth do you think you're doing?"

"Eddie likes bloody Marys. I thought I'd make one and take it to him for the ride out to the island. Won't he be pleased?"

He looked at me so anxiously I didn't have the heart to disillusion him, but I did make a mental note to warn Eddie before he took a swig.

We were to meet Eddie and Josie Gardiner at Sheldon's house, and when Sheldon arrived to pick us up my heart started hammering in my chest. Every time his truck hit a pothole on its bumpy ride up our sandy driveway, I felt my heart lurch with it. Harry and Coco started yelling, and Booty finally emerged from Coco's room to see what all the fuss was about.

Sheldon scooped her up, deposited a kiss on her forehead, and placed her in the truck.

"Come on, guys, we're going for a ride. How you doing, Nanny Annie?"

He suddenly leaned toward me, and for a moment I thought he was going to kiss me on the mouth. I turned my head at the last minute in a panic and felt his lips graze my cheek.

"This is Harry and this is Coco," I said, introducing them, "and this is Sheldon Bennett, who is going to be putting a new roof on our house."

"Why do you wear an earring?" asked Harry, echoing my earlier question.

"Because I'm a pirate. See the skull and crossbones on my cap?" He bent down so Harry could take a look.

"Cool," said Harry, as I'd known he would.

We piled into the truck, Booty in the middle next to Sheldon, as before, then Harry and me, with Coco balanced on our laps.

"We're going to Napeague," he told them, as we drove along Cranberry Hole Road. "That means Water Land in Indian. Now, they say when the English"—he grinned across at me—"first came here, they found the skeleton of a whale, so one day, Harry, why don't we go look for whale bones in the sand? That sound good?"

"Cool," said Harry predictably.

In the middle of telling Harry all about the treasure buried on Gardiners Island, Sheldon had to brake suddenly when a deer ran across the road and crashed through the dunes.

"Probably off for a swim. Going back to Gardiners Island. They swim across the bay all the time."

He put the truck in four-wheel drive and swung off the road through the thick sand of the high dunes. Once on the beach, we bounced along beside the ocean, the spray blowing through the open windows. The children squealed in excitement as the seagulls waddling complacently along the water's edge were scattered. The sky was a brilliant blue. I fantasized that it would be like that clear across the Atlantic. I hadn't been this happy in a very long time. Sheldon was a quiet presence beside me, occasionally glancing at me out of the corner of his eye. I began to wonder how to introduce him to Eddie.

Should I say, "Eddie, this is my friend Sheldon who's very kindly said he'll take you to Gardiners Island?" Very English and proper but it included the all-important word "friend" if Eddie wanted to pick up on it.

Or maybe I should introduce him as "Sheldon Bennett, who's going to fix our roof," which would put Sheldon in quite a different category.

As it happened Sheldon introduced himself. Eddie was waiting for us at the house, and Sheldon leapt out of his truck to greet him.

"Hi, good to meet you. I'm Sheldon Bennett. I understand you want a ride to Gardiners Island. I've been telling Harry here about Captain Kidd's treasure. Guess you've come to claim it back. Belongs to you English after all."

Eddie barely heard him. He was being attacked by all three children at once. I wished Hope could have been there to see it. How they love Eddie! I thought. They've missed him much more than they let on.

I was pretty shaken by Eddie's appearance. He looked awful. His sandy hair was long and unkempt, and he had the beginnings of a stubble—which gave him a cool throwaway look, but it also told me he hadn't been taking care of himself. There were shadows under his eyes and he'd lost weight.

But when the kids jumped all over him, a bit of his old sparkle returned.

Thank you, he mouthed at me. He looked around him at Sheldon's house. "What a great spot. We followed your instructions, Annabel. Thank God you told us about the Jolly Roger. It stood out above all the other houses and drew us like a beacon. Have you seen that, Harry? This guy's a pirate. Better be careful."

"And he's got a seagull and a kitten and a four-poster bed like the one in the Princess and the Pea in my fairy-tale book." Coco had wasted no time nosing around and was completely won over.

"How'd you find this place?" Eddie asked.

"I rent it," said Sheldon. "You have a pretty nice property yourself. I'm going to be doing some work over there on the roof."

I relaxed. Sheldon made it all so easy.

"Oh." Eddie beckoned to a woman still sitting in his car. "This is Josie Gardiner."

A little birdlike creature got out and came toward us. The first thing I noticed about her was that she virtually ignored the children. Most people try to ingratiate themselves with children, with varying degrees of success. Josie went straight up to Sheldon and all but batted her eyelashes.

"Hello. I'm Josephine Gardiner."

"Well, that's a familiar name." Sheldon laughed easily. "You look right over there"—he pointed across the bay—"you'll see Gardiners Island."

"Yes, I know. I'm a descendant of the Gardiners. Maybe I'll even inherit their island one day." She smiled at Sheldon, and to my intense irritation I found I was a little unnerved by this. She was exceptionally pretty.

"Doubt it," said Sheldon, dismissing her in one quick sentence, which gave me a certain amount of glee. "There's a family feud going on between Robert Lion Gardiner and his niece. They've both been left the island to pass on to their heirs. Only Robert doesn't have heirs and the niece does. Still, both sides think they have a claim. Don't quite see how you'd fit in, Miss Gardiner." I liked the way he pronounced the name as if he clearly didn't think she had a right to it. "Anyway," he went on, "my family's just as old. My ancestor, Samuel Bennett, came to Gardiners Island to work for Lion Gardiner when it was settled, and they were out hunting one day and Samuel's gun goes off and there's Lion lying dead. Maybe you want to watch out, Miss Gardiner. We don't want another Gardiner having an accident with a Bennett."

"Oh, Eddie will protect me," said Josie, and suddenly I felt queasy. There was something a little spooky about this bony little creature clinging to Eddie, ignoring his children and making eyes at Sheldon.

Eddie disengaged himself, looking rather uncomfortable, I thought.

"What boat are we going across in?" he asked Sheldon. "You seem to have quite a few."

"Buccaneer over there. My little sharpie." Sheldon pointed to a little sharp-prowed rowboat with overlapping copper-fastened planks. "Excuse me, but I think there's something in the back of your car—"

The children were there in a second.

"Eddie brought us a puppy!"

I looked at Eddie. Was this true? Had he gone out of his mind?

"Clinton, come here. Heel!" Eddie yelled. The puppy had bounded out of the car as soon as he opened the door.

"Clinton?" said Sheldon, amused. "A presidential dog?"

"Eddie, are you mad?" I asked. "You're not thinking of leaving this here with us, are you?"

"Like who's going to tell Mom?" said Harry, siding with

me as usual, although I could see he was thrilled by the appearance of Clinton.

"Annabel, the kids have wanted a puppy for I don't know how long. You could square it with Hope, couldn't you?"

"And pigs might fly across the bay on jet skis." Honestly, he was impossible.

"If I can't be with the kids, at least they'll have Clinton. That's what I thought," said Eddie. He was trying to look his most appealing.

I have to confess I felt sorry for him. He'd walked in on Hope with Craig. None of this was his fault. He was trying to do something for the kids even though he was getting no encouragement from Hope. Hope might think him a hopeless case, but he was a sweet man in many ways.

"What kind of dog is it?" I asked, hoping he'd realize I was holding out some kind of olive branch and understand that I was happy to see him.

"It's a wheaten terrier."

"Oh, they're incredibly nervy. Always jumping about all over the place. Awful for kids."

Thanks a bunch, Josie Gardiner. What a helpful contribution.

Only she was wrong as far as Booty was concerned. Clinton and Booty seemed to have taken to each other instantly. Booty tugged at Clinton's tail, delighted to have something to play with, and instead of turning on her, Clinton wagged it and moved a pace or two away. Booty chased him, grabbed the tail again, and Clinton wagged it harder. Booty laughed. The game had begun. And when she fell over, Clinton bounded over and licked her head. I was reminded of Nana, who looked after the children in *Peter Pan*. Clinton had a touch of Saint Bernard in him.

"Let's all take Clinton for a walk along the beach," said Sheldon, "and I'll tell you about Gardiners Island. It's on a sandbar and going there is like entering another world. It takes you right back to colonial times. The family's owned it since the sixteen-nineties. One of them even married a president of the United States."

"Which one?" asked Josie.

"Didn't they pass that piece of information down the family line?" Sheldon asked. "John Tyler, it was, Anyway, there's a windmill that's been there since the seventeenth century that's still got all its original machinery."

"Is there a castle?" asked Harry.

"No, they lived in a manor house. There've been a few of them. This one was built in 1949. The one before that burned down when someone smoked in bed, so they say."

It wasn't possible. He couldn't know.

I hadn't mentioned my parents and what had happened to them. Could Ray Moran have told them? Had Sheldon mentioned this deliberately? Was he trying to scare me?

Since that quick cigarette with Hope in the car on my first night, I hadn't smoked at all. No one could associate *me* with smoking in bed. At least not over here.

"They were pretty self-sufficient farmers, grew everything they needed; corn, wheat, barley, flax. There were sheep, cattle, deer, quail, pheasant, wild turkeys, and crazy Gardiners." He glanced wickedly at Josie.

"So what are we waiting for? Let's go," said Eddie.

It was clear that the little sharpie was a bit of a letdown for Josie, who pointed to a white 22-foot Grady anchored in the channel and said, "Why can't we go in that?"

"Because I don't want to advertise our arrival," Sheldon explained.

I stood on the beach with the children grouped around me as Sheldon gunned the outboard motor, and the little boat sped off across the water toward the island. I tried to imagine what it must have been like three hundred years earlier when the first Gardiners went home to their island. I was a little apprehensive. From what I'd seen of Josie Gardiner, it was quite possible the silly woman would do something to attract the attention of a guard.

Coco and Booty, harmony restored between them, set about burying Clinton in the sand. It was an endless occupation, since the minute they covered him he shook himself free and they had to begin all over again.

Harry was quiet. I worried that seeing Eddie so fleetingly would have unsettled him, so I went over to sit down on the sand beside him

"What are you thinking about, Harry?"

"I'm thinking about that island, what's it called?"

"Gardiners Island."

"No, this little island right in front of us."

"Hicks Island."

"Well, I'm thinking up a story about a little boy who lives in this house"—he pointed behind him to Sheldon's shack—"and his parents go away to the city for the day and leave him alone. So he swims to Hicks Island and discovers a whole new magic world just like Eddie's going to discover on Gardiner's Island. This little boy is going to meet pirates and foxes and magic animals and have all sorts of adventures and then he'll swim home and try to explain it all to his parents and they won't believe a word of it, so it will become his secret place. . . ."

He prattled on while I half listened. I wished I had been able to go with Sheldon in the boat. Why hadn't he called me in the last two weeks? He had seemed perfectly happy to see me again, but would he have made contact if I hadn't called him?

I took the kids over to watch the windsurfers, and we picnicked on the beach. Booty got in Sheldon's hammock for her nap and Clinton managed to scramble up too and curl himself into a ball beside her.

I was just about to suggest to the other two that we look

for shells on the beach when I saw the sharpie coming furiously around the point of Hicks Island and into the channel.

When it landed Sheldon leapt out, followed by Josie and Eddie. To my amazement, Eddie whisked Booty out of the hammock, grabbed the other two children by the hand, bundled them into the rental car, and drove off without so much as a word.

Leaving Josie Gardiner behind.

"What's happened?" I asked her. She ignored me.

"Listen," said Sheldon quietly, coming up behind me. "It's okay. He'll drop them off at their house before he drives back to New York. Meanwhile, I have to get this woman on the bus. Slight change of plan. I'll tell you about it later, once I've put her on the Jitney. Sooner the better, believe me."

He lifted Clinton into the back of the truck.

"It's either you or her in the back with the dog, there's not enough room for more than one adult riding up front with me."

"Better be me," I offered. One glance at the defiant little figure shivering on the beach told me she wasn't about to ride in the back of a truck. "What on earth happened?"

"Like I said. Later," said Sheldon. "I'll drive slowly so it won't be too bumpy for you."

I peeked through the rear window of the truck a few times but there seemed to be no communication between Sheldon and Josie, and when we finally deposited her at the bus stop in Amagansett, she astounded me by not offering one word of thanks.

"C'mon, I'll buy you a cup of coffee." Sheldon swung the truck half a mile up the highway. "That's one bad lady," he said, when we were seated in a roadside café. "She's totally nuts."

"I want the whole story, start to finish," I told him.

"As we were approaching the island she suddenly gets to her feet, stands up in the boat, and yells, 'I'm coming home!'

The boat nearly capsizes. Eddie has to hold her down. There's this big beach where I always try to land because it's wide enough that if you land in the middle and there's someone at either end of the beach, you have time to make a break before they reach you.

"This time I can see a patrol car on the cliffs, so I say we have to anchor out in the bay and swim in. Then, as soon we reach the beach, she runs off. I'm standing there thinking she doesn't know the way, she's going to get lost, we're all going to be arrested. Then she beckons to Eddie to follow her and when I go too she says, 'No, not you, just Eddie; leave us alone.' They only got there because of me, and she wants me to leave them alone."

"So what did you do?"

"Well, your friend, Eddie, nice guy, he says, 'It's okay, leave this to me. I'll talk to her, explain we have to stick with you.' So he goes after her and I can see them talking and I'm looking all around in case anyone comes on the scene. And then I can see it's like they're fighting."

"Shouting at each other?"

"No. It was getting physical. He was fighting her off. She was throwing herself at him and flinging her arms around him and stuff and he was fighting her off. And then all of a sudden he comes running back down the bluff, wades into the water, and starts swimming out to the boat. And she won't leave. But Eddie's got the motor started. Looks like he's going without us. What do I do? I can't leave her there on her own. So I pick her up in my arms and carry her, kicking and screaming, out to the boat and throw her in. When I jump in, the boat is already moving. We're halfway across the bay when Eddie tells her that's it; she's making her own way back to New York. You pretty much saw the rest."

"And you don't know what they said on the island?"

"Nope. Saw what happened but I was too far away to hear. Okay, finish your coffee and I'll take you home. You need to get back to those kids. Eddie wants to start back to New York."

When he dropped me off I waited for him to kiss me goodbye but he didn't. Josie Gardiner seemed to have put him off women for life. He gave me one of his intense looks and I was mesmerized by his blue eyes as usual. I felt helpless. I didn't want him to leave. I hated the thought that I didn't know when I would see him again and in a moment he would be gone.

Then he gave me an ounce of hope.

"Tell Harry I'll take him fishing sometime if he wants to go."

"And me too?"

"Sure."

For a second I thought I would have to be content with that. Then without warning he planted his lips on mine in a quick urgent kiss, his mouth dive-bombing onto mine and retreating before I'd had time to respond. I sensed an air of impatience. He was smiling at me but he wanted to be off. He had things to do. He wanted to get back to his other life, his life without me, by himself, wild, by the sea. I had no choice in the matter. I had to let him go.

I thought I was going completely mad. I forced myself to open the door and step down from the truck. I started up the drive, and when I looked back he flashed the headlights quickly and was gone.

I found Eddie slumped at the kitchen table with a glass of scotch in front of him.

"I shouldn't be doing this, I've got to drive back to New York, but Christ, Annabel, I need it!"

And Hope's going to be home any minute, I couldn't help thinking. She mustn't find you here or I really will be in the doghouse.

Plus I have to explain to her about Clinton.

"The kids are upstairs," said Eddie. "I got them a video.

It's so great to be back in this house. You have no idea how much I've missed it. Did Sheldon take her to the bus? Did he fill you in?"

I nodded.

"Thank the Lord. Do you know, she actually thinks we're having an affair. I truly do not understand what goes on in women's minds sometimes. Josie's got it into her head that I am as crazy about her as she appears to be about me, and the truth is I barely know her. I'm just her editor. I've met her in the office a couple of times, bought her lunch, all in the line of duty, and brought her out here because she asked me to— to do research, I believed, in my innocence. But she seems to have translated my organizing this trip as a sign that I care for her, that I'm free from Hope and available. Annabel, I've never encountered this before. She's obviously been sitting at home thinking about me nonstop since she first clapped eyes on me, conjuring up this imaginary romance in her mind out of nothing. It's all in her head. She's totally lost sight of the fact that I haven't responded to her in that way at all. She threw herself into my arms on Gardiners Island and I had to fight her off. When she tried to kiss me, I thought: That's enough. The only thing to do was to push her away with enough force so she would know I meant it—that's what Sheldon saw, me fighting off the advances of a demented woman who imagined we were lovers."

"It sounds very scary," I said.

"Actually, it's very sad. She's ill. Now I've escaped from her, I feel almost sorry for her. She probably believed I found her attractive. Well, with luck I've set her straight. First thing Monday I'm going to tell Clem Springer he's going to have to find her a new editor."

I was struck by an awful thought. Was that how Sheldon thought about me? Had I built our relationship up into something much bigger than it was after only three meetings? Did he just think of me as a woman who needed a roof done? Had I imagined it when I thought he was attracted to me? Maybe I was just as guilty as Josie of fantasizing. Sheldon hadn't called me for two weeks. He'd been in a hurry to get off just now. Maybe he couldn't wait to get away from me. But then again, he'd kissed me, hadn't he? He hadn't fought me off. Quite the reverse.

But were we having a relationship?

"OK. I'd better leave before Hope gets back and finds the dog."

"Eddie, you coward! The least you could do is wait and explain Clinton to her. Although with luck she'll be in a good mood. She was all excited about a new client coming out from the city today."

"Oh, my God! I forgot about that."

"Forgot about what?"

"Nothing. Kids! Come on down. I want to say goodbye."

I could hardly bear to watch. They hugged him and pleaded with him to come again and thanked him for Clinton and ran down the driveway after the car, waving, just like kids in a movie. And of course I was the one who had to comfort them when they came trooping back into the house, Coco and Booty crying openly and Harry on the verge of tears, trying to put on a brave face.

"Well, at least you have Clinton," I told them. "We'll find him something to sleep in for tonight. Then we'll have to ask Mom to get him a basket."

"And food," said Harry. "What are we going to feed him?"

Typical Eddie, I thought to myself, brings us a dog but never thinks to provide food. We didn't even seem to have a leash.

Hope hit the roof.

But not, as it turned out, about Clinton.

"Eddie was here today, wasn't he?" she snarled when she came through the door. "Seems to have seen everyone except me. Was he here?"

I couldn't lie to her.

"Yes. Just for a short while."

"But he didn't have the guts to come and see me. Do you know what he did? He dropped someone off right outside my office and drove off without speaking to me."

I noticed she was extremely upset, more so than I had seen her in some time. She barely spoke to Eddie herself but why was she so upset that he hadn't come to see her? There was more.

"Well, you know what? I soon found out why he was avoiding me. Oh, yes! My client—you know, the one I was so excited about, the lady coming out from the city to look for a house? Big property, she said she wanted. Said her name was Josie Gardiner. I'd never heard of her, but it turns out she's a well-known British author. She tells me Eddie's her editor and they're having an affair. She comes right out with it— boom!—as we're driving along in my car. Apparently Eddie's been too scared to tell me. But she thought I ought to know, even though Eddie and I are separated. Boy, am I angry with Eddie! That woman wasted my entire day. I mean, I was really excited and now I feel like shit."

She was shaking with rage. And hurt. It was more than just the fact that a client had wasted her time. She was trying her hardest not to cry. I thought about opening my arms to her as I had once before.

"Poor Hope," I said gently. I knew what she was feeling. I'd been there.

That seemed to tip her over the edge.

"I never thought Eddie would be seeing someone. Not so soon. It's such a shock."

It's okay for you to fool around with Craig but Eddie has to sit quietly waiting in the wings for you? Double standards, Hope. You can't have it both ways.

But I didn't say any of this. Instead, I hastened to reassure her.

"You couldn't be more wrong, Hope. They're not having an affair. This woman is literally crazy. It's all in her mind. There is absolutely nothing going on between them. It's a strictly professional relationship. She wants more, but she's not getting it, and because of that she seems to be acting out her frustration by telling lies. Don't believe a word of it."

"But you know all about her?" Hope cut in. "Obviously, Eddie's discussed her with you. And you knew he was coming out this weekend and you didn't tell me."

"Hope, I didn't know what to do. Put yourself in my place for a second. You've told Eddie he can't come and see Booty, that he can only see her at your mother's. Naturally, he's angry with your mother: She sent him to find you with Craig, went out of her way to do so, as far as I can make out. So he uses the excuse that he has to bring Josie Gardiner out here to do research for her new novel to call me and ask to see Booty. I thought about telling you. I honestly did. But I thought you would probably say no. I knew the kids would tell you anyway so I thought, Let it happen, let Hope find out afterward, and then I'll deal with it. But you certainly don't have to worry about Josie Gardiner."

"Really?" I could see she wanted to believe me.

"Really."

"I'm relieved," she confessed. "I'm not ready to have Eddie go off with someone. It's weird, I know, but it gave me quite a jolt. If I found out he was seeing someone, that would be it. I wouldn't let him back in the house ever. So it's just as well he isn't. Now that I think about it, I realize he could never get it together to have a proper affair. He's one hell of a flirt, but if anyone ever took him up on it, he'd run a mile."

I wouldn't let him back in the house. Did she mean she had been considering letting him come back?

"I don't see why he agreed to bring this woman out here in the first place," she went on. "Surely it was asking for trouble."

"Because he's a hopeless idiot," I said, without thinking.

"Well, at least we're agreed on one thing." Hope was smiling now.

"But a lovable one," I ventured.

"Don't push it, Annabel. I'm not sure I entirely swallow this Josie-Gardiner-is-nuts story. No smoke without fire. Who knows whether or not Eddie led her on a little. He knows how to use his little-boy charm, don't tell me he doesn't. But you know the thing that really pisses me off is that I thought this woman was going to be such a terrific customer. She sounded so great on the phone. She seemed to know exactly what she wanted. I'd lined up all these beautiful properties for her to look at. I'd gone to a lot of trouble. I'd listened to her real carefully. She said she liked the northwest, the woods, not too far from the water, three beds, two baths, a room to use for her writing. She was so detailed. And then she gets in the car and tells me the real reason she wanted to see me. Yeah, you're right. Maybe she was nuts, but I was so disappointed, Annabel, you just don't understand."

A minute ago I'd had a glimpse of how sad she was about Eddie's possible betrayal. Then, quick as a flash, she was back to Hope the real estate broker. How could she juggle all these different aspects of her personality?

Now she switched yet again, to concerned employer and mother. "Anyway, Annabel, I'm sorry. You're right. You're in a tricky position and you're coping fantastically."

"And you will think about letting Eddie see the kids again? Booty, anyway? They were so happy to be with him, and they're in love with the puppy."

To my amazement she barely registered Clinton, who, as if by some built-in instinct, had had the sense to steer clear of her.

"Can you cope with training a puppy on top of everything else?" was all she said.

And then I got it. It wasn't her problem. It was mine. That was the deal. Well, fair enough, if it made the kids happy.

I nodded at her.

"Maybe I can take Booty into the city to see Eddie?"

"I guess you can. He ought to see her. He's her father. He has rights. Any calls, by the way?"

I pointed to an endless list of people who had called about properties.

"No word from Craig?" she asked.

"No. Have you sorted out your California dates?"

She didn't answer. She had her back to me, and I could see her tense a little.

"Hope?"

She exploded.

"No, I have not heard from Craig about California, if you must know! I haven't heard from Craig for two whole weeks, he hasn't returned my calls, and I am beginning to wonder what on earth is going on. So, yes, take Booty into the city to see Eddie. At least one of my children will get a chance to see her father in the midst of this crazy mess I've created out of my life."

But in the end it wasn't necessary.

I had a call from Eddie at noon on Monday.

"You will not believe what's happened. You will not believe what that woman has done."

"Try me," I said.

"She's told Clem Springer that I made a pass at her on Gardiners Island, that I sexually harassed her, and that if I am not removed from the company immediately she is switching publishers."

"That's not possible!" I was dumbfounded.

"You wouldn't think so, but it's happened and Clem believed her. I've tried to make him understand till I'm blue in the face but he won't see reason. Josie's books make too much money for him to lose her, but I'm expendable."

"I thought she could just move to another editor. You said that yourself."

"Of course I suggested another editor. But she wants my blood. Hell hath no fury like Josie Gardiner scorned. I'm fired. I had to clear out my desk by lunchtime. I'm out of a job, Annabel, and if that's the case I can't afford to stay in the city. You told me Hope was going to California. Well, I'm coming home. You can tell the kids."

"And Hope? Frankly, Eddie, I think you're going to have to be the one who tells Hope."

"Oh, please, Annabel, soften her up for me so she doesn't slam the door in my face."

What did he think I'd been doing for the past month and a half? Suddenly I was furious.

"No," I said firmly. "I've had enough. It's time you and Hope sorted out your own problems."

17

Anita Mayhew was back.

If indeed she'd ever been away.

Hope hadn't heard from her for a few weeks and had hoped and prayed that maybe Anita had abandoned her drunken search for a home in the Hamptons.

But no.

She called that morning and demanded to be shown more properties. The brown paper bag was not in evidence when she got into Hope's car, but there was a faint hint of liquor on Anita Mayhew's breath.

At ten-thirty in the morning.

Hope's mind wasn't on the case. All she could think about was the fact that Eddie had lost his job and was coming home.

In a way, it suited her fine. He could be there with Booty when she went to California to be with Craig.

That's how she thought of it now. She was not taking Harry and Coco to be with their father, she was going out to be with Craig.

But what did it mean about her marriage to Eddie? How dare he just assume he was going to move back in and act as if nothing had happened. He'd been the one to leave in the first place, hadn't he? Was he just going to take it for granted that she would be the sole breadwinner?

And what about Josie Gardiner? What was she supposed to believe about all that?

Besides, she didn't want the kids' lives disrupted any more than they had been. School had been out since June 25, and they'd settled down to a routine of summer activities. Coco was going to painting classes at the Art Barge, a big old ship beached safely in the sand at Napeague Harbor and converted into a gallery. She was returning home happily exhausted at the end of each day, having been on lengthy expeditions through the salt marshes to the beach to paint whatever she found there. And soon she would be going off to start rehearsals for her movie.

Harry was in a country day camp at Montauk, Pathfinders, which specialized in developing camping skills. In addition, Harry was out kayaking and sailing as well as playing softball and basketball every day.

And Booty was at Mother Hubbard's. Her name was Judith Hubbard and she ran a preschool in her garage—the little ones were taught to bang plates together as they went in to scare away the swallows inside—and a camp for toddlers in summer. Booty was out looking for horseshoe crabs and steamer clams, getting covered in mud, feeding ducks on Pussy Pond, and coming home to chatter endlessly about what she had been doing. The kids were becoming delightfully competitive in their eagerness to outdo each other in their activities each day. Maybe it would be a good thing for Booty to have her father there while her mother was away, thought Hope, wondering why she was always so rational. A second or two ago she had been cursing Eddie for disrupting her routine with the kids. Booty adored Annabel but Eddie was her father. Hope knew she must never forget that.

Hopeless though he was.

"That's the house I want!" Anita Mayhew shouted suddenly, as they were speeding along Springs Fireplace Road.

Hope braked quickly. She had already shown Anita three houses, and Anita had turned her nose up at all of them.

"That beautiful house there on the left. Why haven't you shown me anything like that?"

Because you never said you wanted an eighteenth-century farmhouse with a wraparound porch before, thought Hope, glancing at the house.

"Haven't I?" she said, in answer to Anita's question, and then realized where they were. It was Hannah Moran's house, Osprey Farm.

"Is it for sale?" asked Anita, and when Hope hesitated for a fraction of a second, she pounced. "It is, isn't it? I knew it! Stop right now and let's go take a look."

Hope stopped the car. This was a truly beautiful property, with green lawns sloping down to the calm water of Accabonac Harbor. The interior had been lovingly restored with the old wood paneling and the original flagstone floors and fireplaces. Hannah's family furniture looked quite at home. The house had real class. It was far too good for Anita Mayhew. Anita was more suited to one of those massive new custom-built luxury houses they called McMansions that were springing up all over the place, desecrating the landscape.

But they were already at the front door.

To Hope's surprise, the door swung open when they knocked. Inside a strange sight met her eyes. There were notes pinned to the kitchen table, to the fabric of the high-backed armchairs, to the banister of the staircase.

Johnnie, I've gone to the market. I'll be back in an hour. There's meat loaf in the oven for your lunch.

Johnnie, the Martins are coming for drinks. I'm out for lunch. Make sure you're home by 5:30 tonight.

Johnnie. . . .

Countless notes left for a man who had been dead for twenty-five years. Hope removed them one by one. From an upstairs bedroom window she saw Hannah in her vegetable garden down by the water, almost hidden by the tall bull-rushes.

She got Anita Mayhew out of the house as quickly as she could.

"I want that house," said Anita. "What's the asking price?"

"I'm not sure." Hope stalled for time. She had to talk to Ray. Was the house really for sale?

"Is there another offer?"

"There may be," Hope lied.

"Now listen to me," said Anita. "I want that house, and I'm prepared to do whatever it takes to get it. You get me that house and there's two hundred and fifty thousand dollars in it for you."

Hope was shocked. She'd heard that brokers were sometimes offered kickbacks, but it had never happened to her and she had never heard of one as high as this.

"I'm serious," said Anita. "You think I'm kidding but I'm not. I have the money. Hell, I have the money to buy this house whatever the price is. Cash. Imagine that, honey. A nice cash sale that's going to go through real quick. Don't tell me that ain't attractive."

It was more than attractive. It was manna from heaven. And Hope knew Anita Mayhew was speaking the truth. After finding out about the booze, she'd had Anita checked out—discreetly, through connections—and Anita was indeed who she said she was and she was certainly good for a few million bucks. Had she, Hope—and all the other brokers, for that matter—been wasting time showing houses to a penniless lush, it would have been quite easy to tell her to get lost. But Anita had the wherewithal to buy a big property. Although it didn't exactly help matters that everyone who was asked about her financial status felt moved to contribute the additional information that Anita Mayhew was a highly neurotic and unreliable drunk.

That afternoon, Hope drove past the historic building that housed the offices of the Family Medicine practice and made a spur-of-the-moment decision. She swung her car off the road, parked, and walked into the waiting room of the doctors' office, which must have been the hall of the old house a hundred years ago. It was like something out of a Norman Rockwell painting, with patched leather sofas and a partner's desk littered with pharmaceutical leaflets and a jar of lollipops. A mixed bunch of children and adults, many of them in dungarees, sat awkwardly tapping their feet, leafing through magazines but not reading them, waiting to be seen. The beams were so low there were signs saying PLEASE DUCK YOUR HEAD all over the place, with paintings of flying ducks beside them on the walls.

Hope ducked into one of the secretaries' offices.

"You got a crowd out there, Deborah. Any chance of a quick word with Dr. Moran?"

"He'll be having a sandwich in his office about twelve-thirty if you want to stop by then. I'll tell him to expect you. Can I tell him what it's about?"

Hope was about to say "his wife" then changed it to "It's personal."

"Well, it mostly is when a person goes to see their doctor," said Deborah pleasantly, "but I'll tell him all the same."

Hope went home for what she thought would be a quiet cup of coffee, planning to return later. She walked in and frowned. The kids were wearing hideous gaudy swimsuits: lime green, orange, and shocking pink. Annabel had bought them the day before and Hope had nearly thrown up when she'd seen them. But she knew why Annabel had done it. On the beach, with so many children running around, it was hard for Annabel to keep track of three kids all at once. If they were wearing these hideous colors it made it that much easier to spot them. Annabel was right as usual. Better to have the kids safe than make fashion statements.

"I have to go to Amagansett," she announced. "I'll drive you all to Indian Wells Beach and leave you there for an hour. I can pick you up later. No swimming in the ocean, it's far too dangerous, but you can paddle on the edge providing Annabel's right beside you."

On an impulse, after she'd dropped them off, she didn't go back to the car right away but wandered off along the shore in the opposite direction. How long had it been since she'd done this? Although, if she thought about it, it was something she could easily find the time to do every day, and Lord knows it would do her good to take time out, walk by the ocean for twenty minutes, and clear her head. This feels terrific, she thought, as she slipped off her sandals and strode barefoot along the water's edge, scattering the gulls in front of her.

Then she saw where she was. She'd sold the house eventually, not to Eddie's friend, the guy he worked with—what was his name? Larry something—Hope had always thought it ironic that she'd never even met the person who brought her and Eddie together in the first place. The people who had bought it hadn't done much to it. They probably only used it on weekends. Hope took a chance and walked up the beach, through the dunes, and onto the deck. She remembered, ducked around the side of the house, and there it was.

The outside shower.

It all came back in a rush, the way she'd helped Eddie wash the sand off his feet and noticed his instant erection. The game they'd played in the closet. Their first kiss.

Suddenly she wanted Eddie desperately, wanted to slip off the dress she was wearing and have sex with him right there on the deck. And she'd wanted him in another way recently too. When Josie Gardiner had turned out to be a complete waste of time, Hope's first instinct had been to tell Eddie all about her frustration, thinking she had an important new client and how it had all come to nothing. She missed Eddie for that. He had always listened to her stories about clients. He liked people, he was interested in them.

And the more she thought about it, the more she realized that on the day he had brought Josie Gardiner out to the island, he'd made a point of seeing everyone except her.

And then she remembered what Josie Gardiner had told her, that Eddie had been pursuing her relentlessly. And now Eddie had lost his job because of it.

Was it true?

According to Annabel, Eddie was the victim of a crazy little schemer who was getting her revenge by using her influence as one of the Gramercy Press's most lucrative authors to get him fired.

So he was coming home.

And how was she, Hope, going to feel about that?

But she wouldn't be there, would she, at least not to begin with. She'd be in California with Craig.

Abruptly she left the house, put on her sandals, and walked back along the road to her car.

Craig was her future, not Eddie.

"Sorry to hear about your split. I like Eddie," said Ray Moran, when she walked into his office. "Want to share a ham on rye with me?"

"No, thanks," said Hope, wondering who had told him, although it was hardly surprising. Doctors in a small community always knew everything.

"Has he gone for good?"

"No. Yes."

"Well, which?"

Hope shrugged.

"You don't know? You want to talk about it?"

Hope shook her head.

"No? OK. It'll work itself out. Are you sleeping? Is that why you're here? Deborah said it was personal."

"It's not about me."

"The kids?"

"They're fine."

"Because of Annabel."

"Oh, of course. You've met her."

"I've met her." An innocent enough statement but again Hope was aware of the same underlying interest in Ray's voice that she'd noted when he'd spoken of her at Coco's birthday party.

"She's a godsend. I really don't know what I'd do if she left."

"Then we'll have to make sure she stays," said Ray matter-of-factly. "Is she happy out here? Does she get out much? Is there a man anywhere?" A casual question but Hope caught it.

"A man? Honestly, Ray. She's in her late forties."

"Honestly, Hope," he mimicked with a smile, "you'll be in your late forties too one day. Do you plan on giving up men?"

Make my life a whole lot easier, thought Hope. "Oh, I expect they'll have given me up long before then. But no, Annabel doesn't get out much. Maybe you and Hannah could have her over for dinner and I'll stay home with the kids. Actually, I'm going away to California. Coco's got a movie part, imagine that! And Eddie will be back at the house."

"So he's coming back."

Hope explained, leaving out the details about Josie Gardiner.

"So once he's back I'm sure Annabel would be thrilled to come over and see you and Hannah. She needs to be with people more her own—"

Hope stopped, aware she was going down a tricky road.

"People more her own age? Hope, I'm fifty-six. I suppose you could call that close to a person in her late forties. But Hannah's older. I married an older woman. I guess you've heard the stories. Her first husband, Johnnie, killed in a tragic crash; then I came along, young, needing to establish myself with my practice. Did I marry Hannah, twelve years older, for her local name and standing in the neighborhood, not to mention a terrific house and a fair bit of money? Well, the answer, whether you want to believe it or not, is no. Twenty-five years ago Hannah was a beautiful woman, and I fell in love with her. Hell, I still love her in a way. She had to persuade me to marry her. I was happy to go on seeing her secretly until things quieted down following Johnnie's death. Truth to tell, I thought it wouldn't do her any good to marry too soon. Folks loved Johnnie. But we thought, They're going to have to accept us as a couple one day, might as well get on with it. So we did."

"Ray, I'm here about Hannah."

"I guessed as much."

"She's put the house on the market, asked me to handle the sale."

"Now that I didn't know."

"I sort of suspected you didn't. I've been meaning to ask you about it for some time, but it was hard."

"I'll bet. When she do this?"

"Weeks ago. It's a beautiful house. I couldn't afford not to take it seriously. The market's taking a beating. I need all the irresistible properties I can get my hands on right now. But what made me come out and see you this morning was to tell you that I went to the house with a potential client and found Hannah's left these notes all over the place to Johnnie—"

"I know, I know." Ray looked so sad, Hope wanted to go over and hug him.

"How long has she been like this?"

"A while. I'm a doctor. I saw it coming. I just didn't want to believe it. I'm going to have to find someone to take care of her soon. It's not safe to leave her alone for too long in that house. Maybe she knows that. Maybe that's why she put it on the market without telling me. It's her house, you know?"

"Do you want to sell, Ray?"

"I don't know. We do rattle around a bit. It's a big place. What would it mean if we did sell? Move into a smaller place, put her in a home? Or do we keep this place and get someone in to look after her? I don't know anyone who could cope with that. Do you have an interested buyer?"

Hope shuddered.

"I do, but I'd rather die than sell Osprey Farm to this woman. She's crazy for it, though, in more ways than one."

"Well, keep me posted," said Ray. "Don't let her get away without talking to me first. I have to deal with this sooner or later. As for Annabel, nothing would give me greater pleasure than to take her to dinner one night. Please tell her I said so."

"But then who's going to babysit Hannah?" joked Hope, and then wished she'd kept quiet when another look of unbelievable sadness appeared on Ray's face.

The phone rang at eight o'clock that night as Hope was about to put supper on the table for herself and Annabel. By some miracle Annabel had managed to feed the kids by six-thirty and get them all to bed early. Their camp activities were tiring them out.

A deep male voice said, "Hi, honey, it's Saul Shapiro."

Honey!

"Hello," said Hope hesitantly.

"How you doing?"

"Fine."

"That's terrific. How's my little star?"

"Fine also. In bed and out for the count."

"Getting her beauty sleep. That's my girl. Gotta look great for the camera. So listen, I wanted to tell you, I'm sending you a new script."

"You are?"

"Don't take this badly, but we've reduced Coco's part. She won't have many lines to say, if any. But she will be the star. Coco Collins will be the new Macaulay Culkin. We'll see her all the way through the movie. We've decided to cut her dialogue with the kidnapper, that's all."

Hope was secretly pleased. She had been suppressing her anxieties about Coco being part of a violent exploitation movie. She hated to admit it, but she knew she was only allowing it because it meant she could spend more time with Craig in California.

"So she'll be abducted by the kidnapper in the opening sequence before the credits, big action-packed scene; she'll look terrific. The movie will open with her asleep in her bed, head on the pillow, looking angelic; she'll be the first thing the audience sees. Then in comes the masked kidnapper—"

"Masked?"

"Don't worry about it. I've talked to the director. When we shoot it we'll make like it's all a game. Coco's not going to be scared. Trust me on this one. Anyway, once she's been abducted we'll just see her in the background whenever we cut to the kidnapper himself. She'll look great. And then in the end she'll be reunited with her parents, all happy and smiling, the last face we see before the end credits roll."

"That sounds wonderful. When do you want us?"

"Well, that's what I was calling about. There's been a change of location. The script's been rewritten and Coco's now the adorable little daughter of a platinum-selling country singer, which means we're going to shoot the picture in Nashville instead of Los Angeles."

Which means I won't see Craig, was Hope's first thought.

"Are you still there?" asked Saul, when she didn't respond. "That's OK, isn't it?"

"I guess," said Hope slowly, feeling her spirits deflate like a balloon. "Does Craig know the picture's no longer going to be shot in LA?"

"Oh, sure, he thinks it's a great idea."

"Does he really?" said Hope, sinking even further. "Well, then I guess I do too."

"My office will contact you in a week or so to give you the travel arrangements."

"You'll be there? In Nashville, I mean?"

"I absolutely will. I'll be taking care of you, don't you worry." He laughed.

Hope didn't.

She wanted Craig to take care of her.

"Honey?"

What was this Honey stuff?

"Thank you, Saul."

"So I'll speak to you later?"

"Is the shooting schedule still the same?"

"My office will confirm everything. And I'll be in touch real soon."

She got rid of him at last and found she'd completely lost her appetite.

"What's going to happen about Harry?" asked Annabel. "Will he go to California on his own?"

"Unless you want to go with him."

"Oh, no, I don't want to go anywhere," said Annabel quickly, to Hope's surprise. "I want to stay right here."

"You do?" said Hope. "That's great. I thought maybe you might be a little bored, a little restless. Nothing much for you to do, my children driving you crazy. Besides, won't you need to go back to England to recharge your visa or whatever it is you have to do? Your three-month trial is about up. I was assuming you'd want a quick trip home. You left in such a hurry after your parents' death, you must have stuff to sort out. This would be a good opportunity while the kids are away and Eddie can deal with Booty."

"No, I really don't want to go back. I'm fine. I really am."

Annabel seemed strangely alarmed at the thought of going home.

"But your visa?"

"I have to stay here."

"You have to? No you don't. Really. We can spare you for a week or two."

"Can't I fix the visa thing from here?"

"I suppose we can try if we contact an immigration lawyer. Are you saying you never want to go back to England? You want to stay with us forever? In that case maybe we should think about applying for a work permit. Annabel, what's wrong? Why don't you want to go home?"

"I'd rather not go into it, if that's okay with you. Not right now."

Great if she wants to stay, thought Hope. Suits me fine.

"Coco, what are you doing still up?" she asked Coco, who had wandered into the room in her nightie. There was a knock on the door. "Oh, God, who's that? Annabel, take the Princess back to bed. I don't want to hear about any negotiating for another half hour before her light goes out. You need sleep to look beautiful in the movies, Coco, remember that."

Coco went back upstairs like a lamb. She was taking her new role as a movie star very seriously indeed.

It was Miss Parsons at the door in a state of high excitement.

"Hope, I just had to come over and thank you personally. I'm so thrilled. That nice young man from your office tells me he has a fine offer for my house from some very nice people. He said he didn't even need to bring them over. He'd shown them pictures and that was enough. He met with me this morning and we went over everything. I'm so relieved."

"What young man?" Hope was bewildered. She'd been feeling guilty about neglecting Miss Parsons. She hadn't taken anyone to see the house in weeks, mainly because she thought it was a lost cause.

"His name's Mark and he was quite charming." Miss Parsons sounded positively girlish.

"Was he really? Miss Parsons, sit with us and have some chowder. I picked it up at the Fish Farm today. I want to tell you a little about this nice young man."

Hope checked it out at the office the next day. Mark was in the process of negotiating the sale of Miss Parsons's house to a big developer. They would tear the house down and use the land to build something modern and ugly. He must have picked up on the idea after she'd mentioned the house at the weekly update meeting all the brokers attended at Tudor Woods.

"You can't do this, Mark," she told him firmly. "I gave Miss Parsons my word."

"Don't be naive, Hope," said Mark, more or less laughing in her face. "We're here to sell properties, not run a charity for old ladies."

"Mark, I'll make a deal with you. Leave Miss Parsons to me, and in return I'll hand over to you the Anita Mayhew project. That'll be a huge sale. What do you say?"

Wait till he found out that Anita Mayhew was a living nightmare and a drunk.

Saul Shapiro began calling regularly. Why I ever thought he might be someone for Annabel is a mystery, thought Hope, as his tone became more and more familiar. I ought to be over the moon. A handsome, high-profile, wealthy unattached Jewish man is obviously attracted to me, and I don't give a damn.

Finally, after he had said the words, "I just can't tell you how much I'm looking forward to seeing you again," Hope thought she'd better set him straight.

"Saul, I'm married."

"I know, I know, the English guy. But I thought he was out of the picture. At least that's what Craig told me. I mean, Craig's my buddy, he was the one told me about you. Said you were a real looker, and he was right."

"He did?"

"Sure. We have pretty much the same taste. We often trade women. Craig's seeing one of my ex-girlfriends right now, as a matter of fact."

"He is?"

"She's a real honey. Of course, he goes through more women than I could ever hope to handle, but then he's younger than I am."

"He has a lot of women?"

Hope knew she didn't want to hear this, but she couldn't help herself.

"Tons of women. Arm candy is one thing that guy is never short of. Oh-oh, maybe I shouldn't be telling you this. He's your ex, isn't he? I keep forgetting. But there's nothing going on between you guys anymore, right?"

"Oh, absolutely nothing," said Hope. "So what age are these women?"

"Young. He likes 'em way younger than him. They're in their twenties, mostly. I like 'em more mature myself."

"Like in their thirties."

"Exactly."

And how old are you? wondered Hope.

"Is Craig seeing someone special right now?"

"Well, like I told you, there's that girl I dated. I don't know how far that's gone."

I am not going to let this get to me, thought Hope. I am going to tell myself over and over again that Craig is out of my life and I'm not going to see him again. Saul's telling me about Craig's girlfriends was meant to be. The fact that I'm going to Nashville instead of LA was meant to be.

But she did have to speak to Craig about arrangements

for Harry, who was very excited about flying all the way to Los Angeles on his own although Hope was a little anxious about it.

"He'll be fine," Craig reassured her. "Kids do it all the time. They'll hang one of those ID packs around his neck and some sexy flight attendant's going to take his hand and lead him onto the plane and smother him with attention all the way from Kennedy to LAX, probably give him some fixation about flight attendants he won't be able to shake and we'll be devastated when he drops out of an extremely expensive college to become a pilot. Anyway, after our visit I'll bring him to Nashville and deliver him safely into your hands, and you can take him back home. So what are you worrying about?"

"What did you say?"

"I'll bring him to Nashville. Otherwise I won't see Coco at all this summer." There was a pause on the line before he said very quietly, "Or you."

Had he said it? Had he really said it? Maybe she'd imagined it. Wished it. But she couldn't ask him.

The main thing was that even though she had thought it was all over, she was wrong. She was going to see Craig again.

18

"So you're leaving?"

Eddie knew the signs. She wasn't looking him in the eye. She was moving things around the table, picking up the salt, the pepper, her napkin, anything she could find, and putting them down again. He was in for an uncomfortable dinner, wouldn't be able to relax and enjoy his food, would probably suffer from chronic indigestion in the middle of the night. And he was the one with the problem, not her. Typical.

"I am not leaving you, Arlene. I've left the Gramercy Press."

"That's what I said. You're leaving me. Goodbye."

They had been over this time and time again. Arlene had convinced herself that Eddie's abrupt exit from the Gramercy Press signaled an equally abrupt departure from her life. Her insecurity was palpable every second he was with her.

And as if that was not enough, Larry, with whom he was still staying, chided him constantly.

"Get out, man. Perfect opportunity, now you won't be seeing her every day. How you ever got yourself into this mess in the first place is something Susie and I can't figure out."

What I can't figure out, thought Eddie, is why I was ever dumb enough to tell you about Arlene.

It had happened late one night when he and Larry were what Eddie called "tidying up" the last dregs of a full bottle of whiskey.

"You're not serious?" Larry raised his hand as if he were going to slam his palm down on the table and then scratched his head instead. "You and Arlene? What do you see in her? Explain to me what you see in her."

Eddie was a bit taken aback. He hadn't expected to be put on the spot like this. But then slowly, and without really knowing where they came from, he began to find the words to describe how he felt about Arlene.

"She's genuine. She doesn't play games. She always has time for me. She has a pretty rough life. I'm sorry for her, and—"

"You pity her? Oh, boy, that is so not-the-reason to be in a relationship."

"Well, if you're going to be judgmental—" Eddie's drunken state rendered him instantly huffy.

"Oh, no, please, tell me, I'm asking. I want the details."

"Well, I don't pity her, and I don't want you thinking I patronize her because I don't."

" 'Course not," said Larry.

Eddie looked at him fiercely, and he held up his hands in a "not guilty" gesture.

"Stop taking the mick, Larry. I suppose you think I shouldn't take her seriously because she's . . . because she's . . ."

"Blue collar?" asked Larry bluntly.

"Well, it doesn't matter."

"Doesn't matter," echoed Larry.

"She needs me," stated Eddie, "and I find I rather like being needed."

"Arlene needs you? Are you nuts? I've never seen anyone so capable of taking care of herself. I'd believe you if you told me she had an attitude when she was asleep."

"I wouldn't know."

"Excuse me."

"I said I wouldn't know. We don't sleep together. I mean we shared a bed once, but we were awake all night."

"You haven't slept with her?"

"Not the . . ."

"Not the whole nine yards."

Eddie nodded. "Where could we go? She has a kid. And I didn't want to bring her here."

"I believe there are people in your situation who have managed to find a place to have sex. You just don't really and truly want her. It's obvious."

"I respect her a great deal," said Eddie, aware that he sounded pompous. "She's a very brave person. And I'd like to help her. The thing is, Larry, and you won't believe this, when she's at home she's completely different. She doesn't wear makeup, she just loafs around in jeans and a T-shirt, and she looks great. And she's a good cook."

Larry rolled his eyes. "You know what?" he said, leaning forward so his knees were touching Eddie's. He was looking woozily into Eddie's face, and Eddie felt rather uncomfortable. "You know what? She's infatuated with you, and it's turned your head. Listen, it happens. It's totally understandable. You're flattered. She makes you feel good. But you gotta get out before it's too late. And now's the perfect time. Hope know about her?"

"No way. Hope thinks I'm having an affair with Josie Gardiner. Arlene is pretty suspicious of her too. That's the irony. But everyone's way wrong, as you would say. I've lost my job. I've lost my wife. Arlene's all I have left."

"You got me, buddy. Stop feeling sorry for yourself. Any chance you could get back with Hope?"

"I don't know what to tell you. I just don't know what the situation is with Hope. I mean, it's not as if we've talked properly. Every time I think about making an attempt to see her, try to open up some kind of discussion about what we're going to do, that smug fuck Craig's face pops up in my mind and I see red. And I don't call her."

"Craig's the husband?"

"*I'm* the husband, Larry, I'm currently married to Hope. I'm the husband, not him."

"You know what I mean. But let's get back to Arlene. I'm going to try another approach with you in a last attempt to make you see sense. Can you honestly look me in the eye and say there's a chance you'll want to live with her, commit to her, that you never want to get back with Hope?"

Eddie mumbled something. He wished Larry would back off, leave him alone, stop interfering.

"What you have to say to yourself is: If I had a choice, who would it be, Arlene or Hope?"

Eddie stared at the floor. Faced with a question like that, the answer was obvious.

"Hope."

"Well, then, the kindest thing to do is to end it with Arlene now, when there's a natural break, before it goes any further and gets out of hand. Tell me I'm not wrong."

"You're not wrong, Larry. You're fucking Mr. Know-It-All Right."

"Okay, don't get belligerent."

And here I am, two weeks later, still trying to convince her I'm not leaving her, thought Eddie.

He'd met up with Arlene the day after his session with Larry, full of good intentions about letting her down easy, telling her he was not going to see her again out of kindness to her, that it wasn't fair to her, all the things Larry had drilled into his head.

And he hadn't said any of them. She'd opened the door to him and asked him to help her bathe Max and put him to bed.

"I'll warm up his supper while you go and drown in Underwater Mission Impossible. Try to leave a little water in the bathtub. The old lady on the floor below told the super that her ceiling was leaking, and I know why. Max is crazy about you, you know that, don't you? You've got a way with kids, Eddie, whatever else is wrong with you. Max has been a happier little boy since you came into our lives."

Very clever, thought Eddie. Now she's said that, how can I possibly even think of walking out?

Then, when they'd finally got Max off to sleep and mopped up the bathroom, she suddenly turned to him and flung her arms around his neck in that disarming way she had. Before he knew it, her lips were pressed against his and her tongue was making tantalizing little flicking movements from side to side.

"What's all this?" he asked, when he came up for air. All he wanted to do was plunge right back in for another kiss.

"I wanted to say thank you."

"What for?"

"You know what for." She patted him playfully on the buttocks. "Old Springer Dinger called me up to his office and offered me a promotion. Of course, I don't exactly get to replace you. Actually, I think he said they weren't going to replace you. Either you're irreplaceable or you had such a dumb job in the first place they're making it history. But I do get to edit books on my own and I get more money, so I can move to a bigger apartment where Max can have his own room. I mean, it had to be you who put this idea into Clem Springer's head, right?"

"Of course," said Eddie. He hadn't spoken to Clem Springer since he'd been kicked out, but why ruin her fantasy? It had to be Larry's doing.

"No one's ever done anything like that for me before. I love you, Eddie."

Her eyes were shining. Literally. He'd always thought that was just a cliché, but Arlene really did radiate happiness and there was no way he was going to ruin that by walking away.

No way, José, he thought glumly, when two days later her insecurities resurfaced because he showed a reluctance to look at apartments with her.

"Is it because you're worried about money?" she asked. "Don't be. I've got enough to cover a bigger apartment, and when you get another job, which will be soon, you can contribute."

Then: "I'm rushing you, is that it? You're not ready. You've got a lot on your plate. So take your time. I'll find an apartment. You move in later."

She didn't waste any time. Pretty soon he was being hijacked into going around to the new apartment to give it his nod of approval.

"Where's Max?" he asked, when he'd walked through every single room twice and there was no sign of him.

"What do you mean, where's Max? You think he'd add to the decor? You can't tell me it's OK until you see Max in it? There's his room, OK? Tell me how you like my apartment. I mean, it's going to be yours too one day soon, isn't it?"

Uh-oh. Eddie felt trapped. It was probably a nice-enough apartment, but as it was currently almost bare it was rather hard to tell. Maybe she was right, maybe he had no imagination, but all he could see were empty rooms. The pathetic amount of furniture she'd had at her last place barely extended beyond the hallway. He looked around sadly. He could imagine her here, painting the walls herself, cluttering up the place with cheap and cheerful knickknacks. It would probably wind up looking like a teenage den. She'd hang posters on the walls and throw rugs over secondhand sofas she'd find at flea markets. And it would be cozy in the end. Of that he was sure.

"Let's set up your desk," he said, picking up her beat-up card table and placing it in front of a window. "Here. You'll have a view when you write your reports."

"I don't have to write reports anymore, stupid. I don't work for you anymore. I make the decisions now. Maybe someone will be sitting in a little office writing reports for *me* soon."

"Maybe they will." He smiled. "So why is Max at your mother's?"

"So we can be alone."

"Ah. What's this room going to be?" Anything to distract her.

"My bedroom. That's why it's got a mattress in it."

He'd fallen right into that one. There was a new mattress on the floor. Big. Not king size, but certainly queen. It was still wrapped in a plastic cover like a giant present, and as he watched, Arlene began ripping the plastic off.

"Come on, buster. Don't just stand there, give me a hand."

It didn't take long to uncover the mattress and it might have been by accident, but he suspected not, when they found themselves lying on it side by side.

Arlene, as it turned out, was in a hurry.

"Mom's bringing Max here in half an hour," she informed him and knelt astride him, unbuttoning her blouse.

He'd felt her breasts through her clothes but he'd never actually seen them. They were on the small side but high and firm and round. He reached up and felt one, and her skin was so soft he couldn't help himself. He lifted his head and began to suck on her nipple and she began to stroke his hair away from his forehead as he did so. She was gentle, almost motherly. She was cradling his head, nestling it close to her breast. For a second he felt completely at peace, sheltered from the outside world.

"Small craft seek safe harbor," he murmured, remembering the phrase from the coastal weather reports during sailing holidays in his childhood.

That's what he'd been trying to explain to Larry. He felt safe with Arlene. She wouldn't rock the boat. She'd be there for him, whereas Hope kept him constantly on his toes. The problem was Arlene clearly wasn't aware of the feeling of security she gave him. Indeed, she probably never stopped to think that he might be insecure in any way beyond the natural upsets in his life caused by job loss and marital breakdown. She was too busy being insecure herself. This wonderful warm maternal blanket in which she was enfolding him was probably just instinctive.

Arlene was so warm. And so neurotic.

Hope was so driven. And so neurotic. And occasionally the warmest, most loving person he'd ever met.

He had a mammoth erection. He knew she could feel it. She was sitting on it, for God's sake.

She unzipped him and took it out.

If you give me a blow job I'll come instantly, he thought, but he didn't say it out loud because the words were too crude for the moment.

She must have read his mind. She lifted herself off him for a second and lifted up her skirt, and for the first time he realized she wasn't wearing underwear. He wondered how long she'd been wet as she slipped him inside her and looked down into his eyes.

"Hi," she said softly, and grinned.

"Hi," he replied.

"I don't mind if you rush," she whispered. "I'm ready, and Mom's going to be here any minute."

Eddie didn't need telling twice. He pulled her head down so he could kiss her as he came inside her and felt her shudder and begin to weep.

"Hey, what's this?" he asked, holding her to him afterward.

"I always do this. I don't know why. Release of tension. Don't mean nothing."

"Well, give me a smile or else I'll worry."

She smiled, and her eyelashes surrounding her large gray eyes glistened with tears.

Who would have thought that underneath the warpaint and high heels and bravado she took to the office there would be such a vulnerable little kitten? he thought. And who would have imagined such a sex kitten at that?

"We've started something, haven't we?"

She wasn't pleading. Well, not quite.

"This changes things, doesn't it?"

"Yes," he admitted, "it does."

There was no time to say any more and he dressed hurriedly, not wanting to be there when her mother arrived.

He thought about it that night as he lay alone in the twin bed in Larry and Susie's tiny maid's room.

Should he move in with Arlene? At least he'd have a more comfortable bed. Well, he could think about it while he was in England with Booty, visiting his mother.

Damn. He'd left his jacket at Arlene's apartment, he'd departed in such a hurry. His tickets were in the jacket pocket. He'd stop by tomorrow to collect them.

Arlene flung them at him when he opened the door.

"They slipped out of your jacket pocket. Max picked them up. You weren't going to tell me, were you? You lousy no-good bastard. You're going back to England. You were leaving me. Those tickets are for next week. You weren't going to tell me."

She slammed the door in his face, and by the time he boarded the plane with Booty in his arms she still hadn't returned any of his phone calls.

The one time she'd picked up he'd gabbled that she'd got

it all wrong and he was just taking Booty to see her grandmother, he did it every year, and she'd screamed, "I trusted
you! I was crazy!" and hung up in the middle of his sentence.

The stewardess helped him settle Booty and handed him
a large scotch. He drank it swiftly and found that as the plane
climbed into the air and headed out over Long Island, for
once he wasn't thinking of Hope, now directly below him,
but of a pair of huge reproachful gray eyes, how bad he felt
about making their owner unhappy and how sad he felt
about leaving them behind.

19

There were times when I could see exactly why someone would employ Maud for advice to the lovelorn. She came across as a shallow person, concerned only with appearances, someone who didn't care, but this was not the real Maud. Once she had taken you on as her friend, she was undeniably loyal, often to the point of interfering on your behalf and poking her nose into areas of your life you wished she'd stay out of.

Her telephone call this morning had alerted me that this was one of those times.

Indeed, it alerted me to much more than that.

Maud had been back to Cornwall for the first time since she was a girl. I had been half expecting to hear from her since I had learned from Eddie that they planned to visit Rosemullion. It didn't sound at all like Maud to go wandering down memory lane on some nostalgic journey, but then Eddie's behavior made it sound as if he too had gone off on some weird tangent.

I simply could not understand it. He kept calling from England to ask if anyone had been trying to reach him.

"No. No one's called. Who, Eddie? Who were you expecting?"

"Oh, just a friend I forgot to give my mother's number to." Eddie was curiously evasive.

"Well, why don't you try calling this friend and leaving your number now? How's Booty?"

"She's fine."

"Does she miss Hope?"

"Actually, she asks about *you* quite a lot. My mother is very intrigued. She keeps asking, 'Who is this Annabel?' Sooner or later I suspect she'll put it together that you're the Annabel from the B and B we stayed at in Cornwall. Whatever happens, I don't fancy your chances of anonymity once Maud starts blabbing. But I'm afraid if I'm going to be really straight with you, the one Booty misses most of all is Clinton. I'm beginning to wish I'd never brought that dog home. She asks me every single day when she's going to see him again. I had no idea he had made such an impression on her. How is he, by the way?"

"Driving me nuts," I said, and it was true. Clinton of course was still a puppy, with boundless energy and a constant desire to go running off through the woods. Harry and I took him for walks on a leash along the beach every day, but he never seemed to get enough exercise.

"You can imagine how confusing it is for my mother to hear Booty chatter incessantly about Clinton."

"How has your mother reacted to you and Hope breaking up?"

There was a silence on the other end of the line.

"Eddie?"

More silence.

"You haven't told her?"

"No."

"Eddie, for God's sake!"

"Well, Booty's too young to be able to spill the beans, and anyway it's early days. It's only a temporary separation. Who knows what's going to happen? Why rock the boat?"

Why indeed? Maybe this was a good sign. Maybe this meant he was seriously thinking of finding a way to get back with Hope. Or maybe he was just being Eddie the coward.

But who was I to pass judgment? Now I was behaving like a coward, wasn't I?

"Annabel, I think it's time you came home," Maud told me. "They're saying some very peculiar things about you in Cornwall."

No preamble. No "How are you? How's it going over there?" That was the funny thing about Maud. Her loyalty and concern manifested itself in unexpected ways. She was the one who had been responsible for my new life on Long Island but not once had she bothered to call and check how I was doing, and out of loyalty to Hope I hadn't called her. So this was the first time Maud and I had spoken since I had arrived. And now she was suggesting I come home again.

"Who's they?"

"The villagers who live around Rosemullion. The fishermen. That old Mrs. Thing who's supposed to be looking after what's left of the place. Waste of time if you ask me, she's deaf as a post."

Well that was true enough. Old Lucy Trebethick, whom Marietta had insisted on retaining as our cleaner, never wore her hearing aid, but I couldn't see how that affected her ability to pop in every day and check the place over.

"Start at the beginning, Maud. You and Eddie took Booty to Cornwall for a holiday and you made a pit stop at Rosemullion, at least that's what Eddie told me you were going to do. Any particular reason?"

"Eddie's idea. Pure nostalgia. I think he had the notion that since he enjoyed a bit of bucket and spade there once, Booty would too."

"And did she?"

"Who can say? I left them on the beach and went and had a drink at the pub. Then I walked about a bit, through your grounds and into the house. It was wide open, by the way. I met quite a few people en route and as soon as I revealed I was a friend of yours they all started nattering about you."

"Saying what, for heaven's sake?"

"That you'd run away. Been dumped by a married man. They knew all about Guy. You thought your mother didn't know a thing about it, but you were wrong. Nothing got past Marietta. She knew what was going on, told quite a few people in the village too. Sorry to be so blunt, sweetie. I think your mother was a bitch to gossip about her own daughter, but there you are. Not that any of that really matters. It's the other things they're saying that I'm worried about."

I knew what was coming. I couldn't bring myself to say anything, just waited for Maud to tell me the worst.

"There's an awful lot of speculation about how the fire started. The thing is, your mother wasn't the only one to gossip. Mrs. Trebethick told everyone about how you smoked and how it drove your mother crazy because she was trying to run a nonsmoking establishment. They all had a good laugh about it. You know how they talk in small communities."

I know only too well, although I didn't quite understand how Maud was such an expert on small communities.

"To be honest, I'm not sure they really liked Marietta very much. I think they rather admired the fact that you defied her by smoking in your room. Mrs. Trebethick waxed lyrical about emptying your ashtrays. But what they're all wondering is whether you were smoking that night."

To my surprise I felt relieved when she said those words. At least I could stop wondering what they were saying. Now I knew. I could almost relax. I knew what I was up against.

"Of course I told them to go to hell," Maud told me, sounding very proud of herself for defending me. Knowing Maud, she'd probably made matters a thousand times worse, insulted people, come across as the city person she was, and tried to tell people who'd known me all my life what I was really like. On the other hand, she never once asked me if I had indeed been smoking that night, if there was a chance that I had started the fire. If I had been responsible for the death of my own parents.

She took it for granted that I was innocent.

But she thought I ought to go home. "It just doesn't look good, your not being here."

"But Maud, you were the one who sent me away."

"Oh, I know, but can't you just come back for a bit when Eddie returns? I have to tell you, Annabel, you've worked wonders on my brother. He's hardly mentioned Hope at all. Whatever's going on?"

She had a point. Hope and Coco had gone to Nashville. Harry was going to California. Eddie would be back with Booty. The three months Immigration had granted me to stay in the country were almost up. I could go home and come back before school started again. For the time being, I had no reason to stay.

Except one.

I could see him through the window, patiently showing Harry how to measure a plank of wood.

Once everyone else had taken off and I was left with Harry, Sheldon had begun work on the house and adopted Harry as his unofficial apprentice. Harry was thrilled. Every morning he rushed out onto the deck and stood waiting for Sheldon's truck to come up the driveway. I noticed him perking up a bit and deliberately kept my distance, allowing a bond to develop between them. Soon Harry was his old self again, chattering away.

Now and again I caught snatches of their conversation.

"So what if the little boy goes to Hicks Island for the day and it comes time for him to swim home across the channel because his mom and dad will soon be home from the city—what if he doesn't want to? What if he wants to stay on the island forever?"

"He can't," I heard Sheldon say. I realized they were fleshing out the story Harry had begun on the trip to Gardiners

Island. "We can't always do what we want. The little boy has to come home from Hicks Island because it will make his parents happy to see him safe and sound. If he's not there, they'll worry."

"Yes," said Harry slowly. "I hadn't thought of that. What do you have to do that *you* don't like doing, Sheldon?"

I froze. This was a private conversation, and Sheldon probably wouldn't be happy knowing I was listening in.

"Harry, you have no idea! I have to spend a lot of my time—time I would much rather spend on my boat, sailing or fishing—seeing people and listening to them complain to me because doors won't fit or windows are leaking. And I have to be nice and polite and smile when all I really want to do is tell them not to be rude just because they have money to throw around."

"You don't think Annabel's like that, do you?"

"Not at all. Annabel's one nice polite lady. I'll work for her any day."

I hugged myself.

"And you never make your parents worry?"

"My dad's dead, and he's probably looking down on me and worrying all the time when he sees what I get up to, but no, I'd never do anything to hurt my mom. She worries about me because she's the worrying kind, but it's not because of anything I've done. She's just like that. I've grown used to it."

"When your dad was alive . . ."

"Yeah?"

"Did he and your mom, I mean, did they love each other and stuff?"

"Sure. They adored each other. They had a really happy marriage. That's why it was so sad when he died young."

"I don't know if my mom and dad love each other," I heard Harry say. "They broke up, and my dad lives in California now. Eddie, my stepdad, *he* left, and now I don't know what's going on."

"That's a tough one," Sheldon said. "I guess you'll just have to wait and see what happens. What you have to remember is, whatever happens between your mom and your dad, and your stepfather, they'll never stop loving you, and you have to love them back more than ever at this time. They need you while they're having this trouble. Do you love your mom?"

"Sure I do."

"And your dad?"

"I guess. I don't see him very much. I'm going across the country to stay with him in a couple of days. Tell you the truth, Sheldon, I'm a little scared."

I could hear the tremor in Harry's voice.

"Why's that?"

"My dad wants me to be a big successful guy like him, and I don't understand how to be that guy. I always feel so small beside him. I feel good about taking care of my mom and stuff, but my dad doesn't seem to care when I tell him about that. He just always wants me to be the best in my class at math or sports."

"Listen," said Sheldon gently, "dads are like that. They always want the best for you. You just have to ride it out and then, when you get older, you'll know how you want to be and your dad will have to respect that. Want me to take you and Annabel fishing before you go to California?"

"Wow! Yes, please!"

"You'll have to get up real early. I get no time off from this work of mine. It's a twenty-four/seven vocation, on call all the time like a priest or a doctor, so we'll have to go out at five-thirty in the morning. I'll come and get you because Annabel doesn't drive."

And he did.

It was as near perfect a morning as I'd had since I'd been there. It was exciting to set the alarm and get up at 5 A.M. with

Harry and be ready and waiting when Sheldon turned up in his truck, just as it was exciting driving along the pre-dawn coast roads with the sea mist still lingering all around us.

We'd wrapped up, because Sheldon had warned us it would be windy going out, and he was right. Standing at the wheel, he looked preoccupied. The boat moved very fast over the choppy water, spray coming hard at us.

"Look for birds, Harry. When you see birds circling, it means there's fish below."

I could tell he was impressed that I knew how to cast. He watched my line as he was showing Harry.

"Here, Harry, put your forefinger on the line, flip the bail over, flick your wrist, and cast the line out as far as you can. Who taught you?" he asked me.

"My father," I told him, remembering Felix patiently giving me lessons.

"You're a natural. Watch Annabel, Harry. Hey, fish on Annabel's line. Look in the water, Harry, there he is; see him down there? He's hooked, he's thrashing around. See how Annabel's reeling him in and letting him bite and then just when he's thinking of getting free she knows when to reel him in again? Get the net, Harry, we're going to land him. That's our job, you and me together. But don't put your fingers anywhere near his mouth. He's a bluefish, and his teeth are really sharp. You have to hold him by the gills so he won't bite."

And if Harry falls in the water, which one of us is going to jump in and save him? I couldn't see a life jacket anywhere.

I found myself worrying about this until we were safely back on land and hurtling home in the truck. Stupid, but I couldn't help it, even though my anxiety had ruined the last half of what had started out as a perfect trip.

So it was all the more ironic that the accident happened right at the very end and had nothing to do with the water.

I was convinced I had shut Clinton in securely and there was no way he could get out. It was something I had to attend to every day, so why would I have screwed up and left a window open today?

But I had. Maybe it was because we got up so early and were in a rush. I suppose I should have been grateful that he was still running around in the woods.

But we weren't expecting to see him, and when he came shooting out of the driveway, Sheldon wasn't prepared. He saw Clinton at the very last minute and swerved quickly to avoid him. Too quickly. We hit a tree.

Harry was riding on my knees. He shouldn't have been. He should have been sitting between us, properly secured with Sheldon's rope, but we were all so cheerful on the way home, singing raucous songs at the tops of our voices, that I hadn't even thought of it.

Now, on impact, he was thrown forward, out of my arms, and his head hit the dashboard.

He went out like a light, and when he didn't come to I lost it.

Concussion. Brain damage.

Sheldon swung the truck around and headed back down the road, and after a while Harry came to, rubbed his eyes, and looked at me.

"Don't move," said Sheldon. "We're going to get you checked out."

"I'm fine," protested Harry, trying to sit up. He did seem to be okay, but I knew Sheldon was right. We had to get him looked at.

Then it dawned on me where we were going.

"Are we going to the hospital?" I asked.

"Dr. Moran's closer. He'll take a look at him. We're almost there."

Sheldon drove into the courtyard in front of the doctor's office and jumped out of the truck. He ran around to my side and lifted Harry out of my arms. I followed as he carried him into the building. It was a touching sight, this big man carrying the small boy in his arms. Is it just the image I'm attracted to? I wondered. His beauty, the romantic location of his house? Is this what happens as you get older? Instead of becoming wiser and more realistic, do you fall prey to fantasy? Why was I in such a muddle?

But then I thought how patient Sheldon had been with Harry around the house and on the boat. This was a sweet man, a decent man.

He was talking to Deborah, telling her what had happened. He had placed Harry on a sofa in the waiting room.

"I'll tell the doctor right away," said Deborah. "He'll be with you shortly. Don't worry. I'm sure it's nothing."

"I'd like to stay, make sure he's okay"—Sheldon turned to me—"but I'm late already. I have to see this guy at ten, a new job, give him an estimate—"

"Go," I said.

"I'll call you."

He bent his head and kissed me on the lips. In front of Deborah.

Beyond Deborah I saw a door open. Ray Moran stood there. How much had he seen?

20

Of course Harry was fine. Just a bump on the head. Ray ran tests, to be safe, and I called both Hope and Craig and told them what had happened. Ray also spoke to them and reassured them that it would be fine for Harry to travel to California.

"Oh, I wouldn't worry about that," I heard Ray say. "He's a responsible fellow. Wouldn't have been his fault. No way." He was speaking to Craig, I realized he must be talking about Sheldon. Craig didn't know Sheldon.

I had avoided mentioning Sheldon's name to Ray. It hadn't come up. Had he seen Sheldon kiss me? Deborah had even if Ray hadn't. Would she say anything?

Whether he'd seen us or not, Ray persisted with his invitation to dinner. Only this time he put a slightly different slant on it.

"Come to the house once Harry's gone. When does he leave? Wednesday? Then come Thursday night. About seven o'clock. Hannah and I usually eat around seven-thirty. Love to have you."

So maybe he *had* seen Sheldon kiss me. Or maybe I had only imagined that he wanted a date with me in the first place. Maybe he was just being kind. Any notion of his thinking of me in any way other than as a stranger to the neighborhood to whom he and his wife should offer hospitality was all in my imagination. Like everything else.

I had no idea what was going on with Sheldon, and when Harry left for Los Angeles I was even more confused. I went with Harry to JFK to see him safely on the plane in a hired car organized by Hope before she left, and on my return I was alone in the house with Sheldon.

Suddenly he became elusive again. I couldn't help noticing that since our first kiss he was now almost reserved, in marked contrast to his initial bravado. It seemed as if our relationship had inched back a notch or two instead of forward. Now it was like drawing blood out of a stone to get him to put his arm around me. Of course, he hadn't been able to embrace me and kiss me when Harry had been around, but it didn't seem that he was in any hurry to take advantage of the fact that Harry had left.

Our relationship—if indeed it was a relationship—was no straightforward affair. For a start I could never reach him directly by phone. He never picked up; he screened all his calls through his answering machine. When I challenged him about this he mumbled he'd had enough of girls calling him all the time. He told me to call his pager, but then it was often hours before he called back, if at all.

Sometimes I watched him at work, noting the slow deliberate way he carried out practical tasks, never hurrying, always thorough, immensely patient. It was certainly at odds with the whirlwind speed with which he charged about the place, the "Gotta race back" Sheldon who couldn't wait to hang up the phone, on the odd occasion that he did call me, and be off somewhere in his truck.

I imagined this was how it must feel to be a housewife as I watched him trot into the kitchen off and on during the day, grab a can of Budweiser from the fridge, or pick at something I was in the middle of cooking. But then at the end of each day, instead of staying to eat supper with me, he disappeared in his truck.

Where did he go? Why had he come on so strong in the beginning only to maintain so much distance between us now?

He was graceful when he worked, I reflected, watching him execute small intricate movements with his large hands. Like many big people, he might be a surprisingly good dancer, for he was particularly nimble on his feet. And in direct contrast to the suggestive bantering Sheldon frequently directed at me, the swift repartee, the taunts, there was, I discovered, a quieter, more serious side to him.

More than once he spoke of his old surfing life.

"I miss it," he said wistfully one day, staring at the ocean when he dropped me off for a walk on the beach. "And I miss being on the water in my boat. I never get much of a chance these days. So much work. It's like I'm sucked in."

"Why don't you make time?" I asked him.

"You don't understand," he told me. "It's like a drug, working. Then I have to have dinner with my clients. I have to be nice to them, be polite. But I'm a loner. All I want is to be alone on my boat. On the water."

Where does that leave me? I wondered. Where did he go when he wasn't with me?

"Why don't you just take off on your boat, if that's what you want?" I asked him frequently, more and more aware of the restlessness inside him.

"I just might," he said, giving me that intense look. "I just might one day."

As much as I wanted to know more about this other side of him, I knew I couldn't probe. It was enough that he even felt able to let me see it occasionally.

Then there was the fact that he could be so disarming. He was as upfront about his insecurity as he was cocky about his sexuality.

"I was so nervous when we first met," he told me candidly.

"My heart was going a mile a minute, I was so shaky. I didn't know what to say to you. You looked so classy and confident, way out of my league, but I was really attracted to you. And then I didn't know whether to call you or not. I didn't know if you had a guy you were dating. And I didn't dare lay a finger on you—although I wanted to. I thought you might report me to the Board of Contractors for harassment."

"Oh, I will," I said, laughing, "right away. Just give me their number."

But could I believe him? Was this really how he'd felt or was it only a line?

And when I was about to dismiss him as a bastard who was stringing me along, I'd recall what he'd told me about what he called his Golden Club, the old ladies he did things for.

"Old Mrs. O'Rourke, she's so lonely since her husband died. She calls me a lot to fix things for her around the house. I had to race over there one night last winter. She was in a real panic. Sometimes they'll call and I'll find it's just a light-bulb they can't reach needs changing. But this time she had a burst pipe. It was like Niagara Falls. But all I did was call her plumber, something she could have done herself. Some old women, they're so helpless."

Like me, I couldn't help thinking. I wondered how old Mrs. O'Rourke was. Seventy-something? Or merely fifty-something. Was that how Sheldon thought of me, just another lonely woman who needed help around the house? Waiting to join his Golden Club?

Except he wasn't coming to the house much anymore. And days went by when he didn't phone.

So when Maud called unexpectedly, she caught me at a low ebb.

"What's up, sweetie? Lonely? Eddie will be back soon to keep you company. Pity you haven't found yourself a man out there."

"Well, as a matter of fact—"

"Annabel, I don't believe it! You've got a lover?"

"Well, not exactly . . . I'm not sure whether he's a lover or not. Thereby hangs the problem."

"Thrilling! Wait a second, let me pour myself a drink and then you can tell me everything. I don't want the edited version. I want the whole story, first kiss, first fuck, first discovery that he snores. Don't leave out a thing."

I didn't, including pointing out that we hadn't actually had a first fuck. I told her about the *Playboy* magazines I'd seen lying around his house, the caller ID I knew he swore by. The kissing. The fishing. How he'd been sweet to Harry. The reluctance to issue dinner invitations. The kindness in fixing things around the house.

"He's an operator," stated Maud with authority, when I had finally run out of details. "Oh, boy, I feel a story coming on. He's got you totally hooked. You're obsessing about him. Rugged nature boy saves jaded sophisticate aching for love from the cynicism of her urban career and puts her back in touch with the real world. Except of course you're not remotely sophisticated, darling, and you don't exactly have a career, but never mind. It's still—oh, so *Horse Whisperer*. Just as long as you understand that boys in the country are a law unto themselves. They don't behave like boys in the city."

"Well, just as long as *you* understand that I've never lived in the city so I wouldn't know," I retorted, "and he's a boy by the water, not in the country."

"Same difference. That's exactly my point. You're an innocent."

"How is he different?" I was beginning not to like Maud's take on Sheldon.

"He can get away with more in the country—or wherever—and it sounds suspiciously like he's got a whole load of women he's seeing all at once. Why else would he not see you in the evening?"

"Because I'm busy with the children? Because he's busy with his clients?"

"Oh, Annabel. Grow up. He's racing around from one woman to the next. He knows exactly what he's doing."

He's racing around, all right, I thought. "Gotta race back" was his favorite phrase. I'd always thought it was to his work. But maybe not.

"But he came on so strong in the beginning, he was so keen, and—"

"And now he leaves two weeks between calls?"

"How did you know?"

"Sweetie, the man's a positive cliché. A walking commitophobe."

"A what?" I could never keep up when Maud started spouting magazine-speak.

"He's a dance-away lover. All over you to begin with, then he realizes he can't follow through, he's terrified of commitment, so he dances away and only calls every now and then. Although that's pretty standard in any man. A day is like a week to them."

Everything Maud said had a depressing ring of truth. Was Sheldon really an out-and-out operator? Was I being taken for a ride?

"Well, never mind, dearie. I'm sure he thinks about you. Not very often, I suspect, but I'm sure when he does think about you it's with great fondness. But he's predatory, Annabel. If he's reached forty still unmarried, he's an operator. Face up to it. Tell you what, have a peek at *Men Are from Mars, Women Are from Venus* for an insight into men. Phenomenal best-seller. Sounds like you could use it."

"You've read it, Maud?" I was astounded. Tough, worldly Maud with a manual for lovesick women?

"Only in the line of duty, of course," she said quickly. "It's extraordinary, really, like reading a romantic novel—or what

I imagine reading a romantic novel is like. This nonfiction self-help how-to-understand-your-man book has become the new romantic novel for women who wouldn't be caught dead reading Barbara Cartland, yet they think it's OK to read some baloney by some man just because he's got a PhD. Take care with this guy Sheldon. You could be in for a rough ride."

The thing is, I thought to myself, she sounds like she's speaking from experience. Maud, I suddenly understood, had probably suffered at the hands of a string of operators.

But was Sheldon really leading me on? That wistful sensitive side to him—didn't that show sincerity? I could trust him, couldn't I?

Maybe I was trusting him because it made me feel better. Well, from now on, following Auntie Maud's words of wisdom, I would trust him with my eyes open. If that was remotely possible.

What would Maud have said about Ray Moran? I wondered as the taxi drew into the forecourt of Osprey Farm. I was struck by the dignity of the building. Not only was it extraordinary to find an old house so well preserved around here, but the rambling structure of the building was almost English country house in feel. It was a far cry from the tacky pseudo-historical architecture that was springing up all over the Hamptons, not to mention the ghastly giant McMansions. Ray Moran's old farmhouse was the genuine article, evoking the period when the first British settlers had arrived in East Hampton over three hundred years ago.

I rang the doorbell.

"Merry Christmas, I'm Hannah Moran," said the woman who opened the door. I smiled. It was a warm July evening.

But she wasn't joking.

She was a good-looking woman, tall and slim with fair hair streaked with gray, pulled back, and fastened in a loose knot. Her eyes were pale blue and large and childlike and her mouth was very wide. She was wearing a beautiful close-fitting blue wool jersey dress that matched the color of her eyes, with a cashmere shawl thrown around her shoulders.

In July.

As I entered the house I stopped dead. There were Christmas cards everywhere, a tree in the corner with decorations and lights, and a pile of gift-wrapped packages stacked around its base.

"Johnnie told me you were coming for Christmas. I'm so happy to have you. We haven't been to England for years, and you can fill me in on what's been happening. Tell me your name again."

"Annabel Quick."

"Johnnie, Annabel's here."

Ray appeared in the doorway.

"Hello, Annabel, come into my study and I'll give you a drink. I'm in the middle of my call-backs but don't worry, the turkey's in the oven. Hannah, honey, you'd better check the table, make sure I put out the right wineglasses."

"What are you drinking?" he asked me, once I was inside his study. It was like a library, lots of shelves filled with books, most of which I could see were medical tomes. An old partner's desk was placed at the window with a spectacular view down to the water. There was a beautiful wooden mantelpiece above the fireplace but I was relieved to see no Christmas fire burned in the grate. I could imagine how cozy this room must be when it really was Christmas, with a roaring log fire going and soft lighting from the pretty lamps. There was an almost feminine feel about this room, I thought, as I sank into a giant sofa loosely covered in an unusual print of fading red poppies on a white background. Suddenly I realized why I liked it so much. With its wood paneling, it was the first room I'd encountered since I'd been in America that felt really old. It reminded me of Rosemullion. I felt at home.

"I'll have a glass of sherry, if you have it." It seemed appropriate to drink something genteel in this room.

"It's rather good iced, even though it is Christmas," Ray said, smiling at me and looking at me for my reaction. "I thought Hope told you about Hannah. She's having a bad day today, I'm afraid. A bad week, really. But it's given her a sense of purpose thinking it's Christmas. Thank God I hung on to last year's Christmas cards so she could put them up. Be back in a minute."

He returned from the kitchen with ice for my sherry and reported that Hannah was busy making cranberry sauce.

"From local cranberries, as you can imagine. Will you excuse me while I return a few of these calls before we sit down to dinner? Part of a doctor's evening, I'm afraid."

I listened as he sat at his desk and telephoned patient after patient, giving them the results of tests, answering their queries, soothing them, reassuring them, always managing to end the call by making them laugh and giving them hope.

And yet here he is, I thought, with a sick wife, on his own and no one to give him comfort. No wonder he wanted to have dinner with me!

"So how have you been?" he turned to me and smiled. "It's good to finally have you here, although I would have thought you would prefer to go out to a restaurant, get out and about a bit."

"I don't want to go out and about," I said crossly, to cover my embarrassment. How awful that I hadn't known about Hannah. That's what he had meant when he'd said it was very sad and he'd just have to live with it and I had been foolish enough to think he had been talking about his marriage disintegrating. "I mean, I'm very happy to be here," I added quickly, "but I enjoy my own company, and after a day with those children I've been more than happy to have an early night, believe me."

"Oh, I do, I know exactly what you mean. My patients tire

me out completely. That's when I come in here for a bit of solitude. Nothing like having a place to think your own thoughts without having everyone else's crammed down your throat. Problem is, Hannah likes company. She always has. I worry that I've let her down. I'm out all day and I'm often called out at night or I'm in here with the telephone. It's almost as if she's reverted to being married to Johnnie to give herself some company. When she's like this she's in her own world, and I just go along. She seems happy enough. Who cares if we have Christmas in July? I could have done without stuffing the turkey this morning, but—"

"You cooked the dinner?" On top of everything else.

"Sure. It's not safe to give her the complete run of the kitchen. I do all the marketing and cooking—we have someone in to clean but basically I'm running the house."

And your medical practice, I thought.

"I'm so glad to have you here, someone different to talk to. Folks never say anything, but I've noticed a distinct decline in the amount of visitors at the house since Hannah got—sick. I've tried to keep it quiet, but word's got around and no one knows what to say to me. It's odd, I'm tired out at the end of the day and I welcome coming home to this room, but sometimes I get lonely. This is my room. I created it. It used to be used for coats and storage, nothing more. Just a room off the hall where people came and took off their coats and warmed themselves in front of the fire before going through to the reception rooms. This is the one room that is mine. Everywhere else in the house I find myself pretending to be Johnnie, because that's who Hannah seems to think I am half the time."

Even in bed? I wondered. Do they still share a bed? Why am I even thinking of that?

"So here I am, talking about myself nonstop. Let's hear about you. What news from Cornwall?"

"None as yet." I didn't tell him what Maud had said. "I expect the fire report any day now, and then we'll see. I suppose I'll need to go home just as I've begun to settle in here. It's going to be interesting to see what happens between Hope and Eddie when Hope gets back from Tennessee and Eddie from London. You heard Coco's in a movie being made in Nashville? They'll be a family again for the first time in months, and I have no idea how it's going to work out. Given that Hope was fooling around with her first husband, Mr. Success, before Eddie left, and given that Eddie now has no job, I don't see how he's going to win her back. Hope's at that stage in her life where appearances really matter." How did I know any of this? When had I ever bothered to stop and think about stages in a person's life before? I sounded like Maud and her magazine-speak. Still, now I'd begun pontificating, I might as well continue because what I said had the ring of truth. "The outward signs are important. Her career's going great. She's putting a lot into it. She wants a husband to match. But she loves her kids. . . ."

As I spoke, I realized how indiscreet I was being about Hope and Craig, but I knew their secret was safe with Ray Moran and it was good to share it with someone.

"But now she's found you."

"Yes, well, I suppose she has. This stage will pass"—I warmed to my theme—"and in about ten years' time, maybe less, when she's slowed down, she's really going to need a loving husband. But you can't just tell her that. The next few weeks are going to be crucial. Hope could well come home on a high, take one look at Eddie loafing around the house, and kick him out. I'll just have to keep the kids out of the way and hope they sort it out between them."

"Not much fun for you," said Ray. "Tell me why—"

"Johnnie." Hannah wandered into the room. "I've done nothing about the Christmas dinner. I'm just going to the market to get a turkey."

"No need," said Ray. "I brought one home. One of my patients gave me one, remember?"

"Well, we'd better get it in the oven if we're going to give this dear lady something to eat."

"Better had, Hannah, better had." Ray led the way into the kitchen. "Sorry we couldn't find any holly for the table, Annabel."

I felt a terrible urge to giggle. The table was laid with lines of red ribbon trailing between the place settings, beautiful bone china, and plenty of gleaming silver, and the centerpiece was a little wooden crèche surrounded by fishing boats.

"Hannah's folks were whalers way back when. This has been handed down through generations. It makes her happy to see it. Light the candles, would you please, Annabel? We'll have to leave the French doors open to get some air."

Beside the cradle scene was a tall vase of Canterbury bells, skillfully arranged. So Hannah was still able to do something, I thought. Ray saw me looking at them.

"I'm getting pretty good, don't you think? Amazingly therapeutic. I make sure I spend half an hour each day giving all the vases clean water and rearranging the flowers. Hannah wakes up to new flowers every morning by her bed, although I confess I don't bother in *my* room."

Well, that answered my question. Was there no end to the surprises in this kind and gentle man?

Apparently not. His cooking was first rate and just as well, since the conversation at dinner didn't exactly flow. Hannah smiled sweetly from time to time, ate like a horse, and repeatedly reminded Ray that the Melvilles were coming for a drink.

"Are they?" I mouthed at Ray, surprised that anyone would be asked to the house so late.

"Oh, sure," said Ray, "they're our neighbors. They always come for a drink on Christmas Day."

"You mean . . . ?"

"December twenty-fifth. They won't be here for a while yet. . . . Glad you reminded me, Hannah. I'd forgotten."

When he left the room to fetch dessert, Hannah turned to me and asked, "Where's Johnnie? Is he dead?"

Now what do I do? I wondered. Tell her the truth or say he's just next door? This is what poor Ray has to put up with all the time.

I said nothing but just smiled at her as pleasantly as I knew how, and Hannah suddenly embarked on a long story her grandmother had once told her about how one of her ancestors, out whaling, had slipped his gold into his boots when his whaler had been pursued by a Confederate ship and how that gold had kept her family going for several generations.

She ought to be telling Harry stories like this, I thought. He'd love them. Or Sheldon.

And then I realized to my surprise that this was the first time I had thought about Sheldon all evening.

Ray drove me home. He wouldn't hear of my calling a taxi.

"I can leave Hannah. Lord knows, I leave her for most of the day."

Then I had a shock.

I saw Sheldon's truck coming toward us as we turned off the Old Stone Highway. In seconds we would pass on the road. I was almost home. Had Sheldon been to the house?

I don't know why, but I didn't acknowledge Sheldon as he passed us. And Ray gave no indication that he had seen him.

But Sheldon had seen me. I saw him look sharply at me and then past me at Ray.

"You can drop me at the end of the driveway," I told Ray. "It's such a beautiful night, I'd enjoy the walk up to the house. Thank you for a wonderful evening."

In the rearview mirror I could see Sheldon's truck had stopped at the top of the hill. He was watching us.

"Well, thank you for being so understanding about Hannah. It's rare I get a chance to talk to someone about her. It's done me good. I'd like to do it again sometime. We can go out. Would you like that?"

"Yes," I said. "Why not?"

"Great. I'll look forward to it." And he leaned over and kissed me softly on the cheek.

Very different from Sheldon's lightning kisses but very pleasant all the same.

When I checked the rearview mirror, Sheldon's truck had gone.

"One more thing," said Ray, as I got out of his car. "Watch yourself with Sheldon Bennett."

This was so unexpected I stood with my hand on the roof of the car for a few seconds before leaning in and asking, "What do you mean?"

"Just watch yourself. Don't let yourself fall for him."

"What are you talking about?"

"He'll hurt you. He won't mean to, he's a decent boy, but I've seen many girls set their cap for Sheldon over the years, and they're always disappointed. He's not one for marriage, keeps himself to himself, and probably doesn't even realize he's a heartbreaker. But every year there's two or three more. I wouldn't want you to be one of them."

"I'm not a girl, Ray," I said sharply. "I'm a woman." And then I realized I'd more or less admitted my involvement with Sheldon.

First Maud. Now Ray.

Well, I couldn't say I hadn't been warned.

Not that I needed warning. I'd already had my heart broken by Guy. I had sense enough to avoid repeating the experience with Sheldon.

21

"When are you coming home again?" Maud asked Eddie repeatedly as she drove him and Booty to the airport to catch their flight back to New York.

"I'm going home now," Eddie pointed out. "Long Island's my home." What in the world was wrong with Maud? She had never before been so concerned about when she would see him again. And her behavior when he kissed her goodbye at the gate was even more unexpected. She flung her arms around his neck and clung to him. He could feel her body heaving and realized she was crying.

"Maudie, what's up?" He had called her Maudie when they were children growing up together.

"Why do you have to live over there, Eddie?" Maud had called him Eddie only when they were children. Once he was grown up it was always Edward. "You don't belong there. You're English. You ought to raise Booty here."

"But her mother is over there," Eddie insisted patiently. "Booty is to all intents and purposes American. Take comfort in the fact that Annabel is there to look after her. There is nobody more English than Annabel." He laughed, hoping Maud would cheer up.

But she looked even more glum.

"You don't get it, do you, Edward? Mother's getting old, as you've seen. You're the only family I've got."

"Well, that's not—" Eddie had been about to say it wasn't his fault but stopped himself. For one awful second he saw Maud as she might be in twenty or even in ten years' time: a miserably lonely woman, still grumpy and irascible, in fact probably more so, battling to keep afloat in the harsh media world she had chosen to inhabit.

"Maud, do you have any kind of pension plan?" he asked her, feeling suddenly rather guilty about leaving her looking so bereft.

"Oh, for Christ's sake, I'm not in my dotage yet. Of course I've got a bloody pension scheme. Got 'em all over the place, as a matter of fact, but I'm not quite ready to retire just yet, if it's all the same to you. Since when did you become so responsible as to start thinking about things like pensions? Do they have a good one at the Gramercy Press?"

He had been relieved to see her perk up at the chance to berate him over his inability to sort out his own pension plan. He allowed her to tell him how hopeless he was, relieved to see the old Maud emerge once again. Although once on the plane, once he had finally got Booty off to sleep, he began to worry in earnest. If he had had a pension plan with the Gramercy Press—and Maud was quite right, he was too hopeless even to know if he did or not—wouldn't he have lost it now he had been let go? He looked down at Booty lying in his lap. He was her father. Whatever happened between him and Hope, he had a responsibility for this little girl he loved so much.

Before long his mind switched to another problem he was going to have to deal with: Arlene.

She was so sweet behind the tough exterior. He'd never met anyone quite so giving. She had no pretensions, no hidden agenda. What you saw was what you got. What he had was a girl who boosted his ego when he needed it but who was so emotionally dependent and needy and insecure that it almost made him yearn for Hope's bossy self-sufficiency.

He knew he ought to call Arlene the minute he reached New York. When he had stopped calling her from London it must have sent her into a panic. After the initial discovery about her private life and Max and her courage, he could almost program her every move. And it bored him. Just a little.

He also knew that one look into those big gray eyes and he would immediately want to pick up the sex with her where they had left off.

Back home with Annabel and Booty, Eddie stayed put, waiting apprehensively for Hope's return from Nashville. What would happen? Would she drop the kids, turn right around, and disappear with Craig the Creep into the sunset? Well, no, she had to work and the kids had to go back to school in Amagansett. So would she throw him out instead? Surely she would have suggested that by now? She knew he was going to be there when she returned. Maybe she was as confused as he was about where they were going to go from here.

He could sense Annabel watching him, probably wondering the same thing. A few days after his return they were walking Clinton along the beach and he could tell she was gearing up to tackle him about Hope. She had made several references to Clinton and the question of where he was going to sleep when Hope returned. (At the moment he slept on Eddie's bed.) At Booty's insistence, he had been sleeping in a basket beside her cot on the landing. Would Hope allow that to continue?

What she really wants to know is will Hope and I share a bed and will Clinton be allowed to go on sleeping on it, Eddie realized. To throw her off the track, he asked her, "Annabel, how well do you know my sister?"

She smiled. "Oddly enough, I've been asking myself the same question recently. If you'd asked me when I first arrived, I'd have said we were old friends who had virtually nothing in common anymore. And to be honest, we don't, but I realize that Maud and I know each other pretty well in spite of that."

"Well, do you think she's happy?"

"Why do you ask?"

"I'm worried about her," said Eddie, and described to Annabel what had happened at the airport.

"Oh, I wouldn't worry about that. Maud's quite capable of taking care of herself," said Annabel.

"I'm not so sure," said Eddie. "I'm beginning to wonder whether I ought to start thinking about going back to England if Hope and I get a divorce."

Annabel yanked Clinton's leash and turned to look at him.

"Is that in the cards?"

"Don't ask me. It's up to Hope."

"I'm asking you, Eddie. It's up to both of you. If you want to stay with Hope, you have to say so. To her, I mean. When she gets back, if not before. Do you want to stay with her?"

"I don't know. Maybe."

"What's stopping you?"

"A number of things, beginning with whether she wants me back. Given that I don't have a job. And then there's—"

"What?"

He had been on the brink of telling Annabel about Arlene.

"You want to know what I think about Maud?" she asked, relieving him of the decision.

"Go ahead."

"I think she's one of those women who are only really happy if they've got something to complain about. Maud needs to be on edge. If all her prayers were answered—say, if you split up with Hope and went home to England—she'd have no reason to bear a grudge against Hope. You may think I'm crazy, but I think you'd be depriving her of something important in her life. Much of Maud's energy goes into criticizing and arguing. It's the fuel she runs on. Dissipate that and she'd become deeply depressed. If she decides she wants to be near her family, let her move to New York and get a job here. Meanwhile, you set your mind on making Hope happy when she gets home."

All very well for you to say, grumbled Eddie to himself.

But then he was thrown an unexpected lifeline. He was offered his job back.

Clem Springer called one night and summoned him into the city to have lunch at the Four Seasons, no less, one of the fanciest watering holes in town.

After the obligatory small talk about the Knicks' chances against the Pacers, during which Eddie winged it as best he could since he hadn't the first clue about basketball, Clem poured Eddie another glass of chardonnay and said, "I owe you an apology. And you owe someone called Sheldon, period. This Sheldon, whoever he is, witnessed what happened with Josie Gardiner. Why didn't you ever mention him to me? Anyway, you told Larry Fredericks, and Larry tracked him down. The woman really must be insane; Sheldon said she attacked you. The thing is, the Gramercy Press doesn't publish her anymore. She's apparently unable to work. That wonderful idea she had of writing about her so-called ancestors—she hasn't written a word of it. It was all a complete fantasy, an excuse to get you out to Long Island and into the sack, as far as I can make out. So, so long, Josie, hello, Eddie. Welcome back."

"Welcome back?"

"To the Gramercy Press."

"What about Arlene and her new job?"

"Doesn't make any difference. She's doing fine, and in any case Larry said you ought to work in Publicity."

"He did, did he?"

"Sure. What do you think?"

"I think I'll think about it and let you know."

"Don't you want to know what the job is and what it pays?" Clem was looking at him as if he had gone mad.

And maybe I have, thought Eddie. Here I am being offered a solution to my problems on a plate and I'm not even interested. I want time to think. Being offered his old New York life back made him realize that he did not want it. Living in Manhattan during the week would mean he and Hope would be back where they started.

Working things out with Hope would take time. He needed to be around her as much as possible. He needed to prove to her—and to everyone else—that he meant business. Of course, she might be poised to bring Craig into their home, but he needed to be there too, at least to make a stand against its happening.

And one small area of his life still had to be sorted out.

Arlene opened the door to her apartment and catapulted herself into his arms before he could say a word.

"I knew it, I knew it, I knew it! I said to Max, He'll come back to us, I know he will. Come in. Where are your bags? Are you moving in tonight?"

Eddie felt suddenly exhausted. This was going to be hard. He wasn't even sure what he wanted to say. Seeing her again was a mistake. No, not a mistake. It was wonderful to see her again. She was real and fresh and vulnerable and brave all at the same time. And she so clearly wanted him.

But he'd thought a lot about Arlene, and he had worked out that life with her would be a zillion times harder than with Hope. He wouldn't get to see Booty as much as he wanted. He'd have to contend with the menacing presence of Max's father in the background, and while Craig might be a creep, he didn't pose any real danger. Financially it would be hard, too. He'd have to contribute to Arlene's household as well as pay child support for Booty. He'd probably never see Harry and Coco again.

Suddenly the thought of moving in with Arlene was terrifying.

He knew he would be behaving like the coward everyone claimed he was by dumping Arlene, but he also knew he had one last chance to show that when he wanted to he could be a fighter. If he dug his heels in when Hope came home and made her take him back, that would be going against everyone's expectations.

"Sit down, Arlene. Let's talk."

"Okay. Sure. Let's talk. What's the deal?"

"There's no deal. That's what I want to talk about."

"I don't like the sound of this. Max is across the hall. Our neighbor is a real honey. She lets Max play with her little girl whenever he wants. But you know what, he'd never forgive me if he didn't see you the minute you came back. You're not moving in tonight, but you'll stay and eat dinner with us, right? I made—"

"Shut up, Arlene, and sit down."

"Don't get heavy with me just because you went to Oxford or Cambridge or wherever it was. Doesn't give you the right to think you're better than me."

" 'Course it doesn't. How's the new job?"

"It's so great, Eddie. I'm getting manuscripts sent to me and the letters that come with them, they're written to me! *Dear Ms. Kowalski. Dear Arlene Kowalski.* I'm somebody!"

"Hey, we're going to be a publishing couple. We can read manuscripts in bed together. You got your job back, didn't you? I told Larry, and he said he'd speak to Springer Dinger."

"Yeah, I had lunch with him. I'm thinking about it. He suggested I work in Publicity, but the truth is I'm not sure I want to stay in the city."

Now she sat down. "What are you saying?"

"My wife's coming back from Tennessee soon, and I want to try again with her."

"Your wife's coming back and just like that we break up? I'm toast? What about us?"

"There is no 'us,' Arlene. There never really was. In your own way you're living as much a fantasy as Josie Gardiner. Only there's one big difference. I'm attracted to you. You're smart. I think you're incredibly brave. I admit I'm very fond of you."

"You say all this and yet you're going to say we can't be together. I don't get it."

"There's nothing to get. Sometimes you can write everything down, and on paper it all seems like the perfect plan yet you know it won't work. It's because of—I don't know, circumstances. I'm married to Hope. It's a done deal. I have to be there for her."

"But we have something going for us. It's not fair."

"Life rarely is. There's no point expecting fairness. We had something going for us. Had, not have. Yes, we did. And I shall always remember it. You must too."

"Looks like it's all I'm going to have. Memories."

"Don't be bitter. There's always someone in the picture who loses out, or thinks they do, whose time hasn't come. This time it's you. I couldn't be more sorry."

"You're going to start with that crap about how I deserve someone better than you. That I'm a wonderful person and the right man's going to come along. I just have to believe in myself. Give me break."

Eddie grinned. The old Arlene was surfacing. This wasn't going to be as bad as he'd feared.

"I mean, look at you," she went on, "going on about how you have to be there for your wife. How come you don't have to be here for me instead? Because you're a coward, Eddie. Little wifey's coming home, and it's easier for you to go back to her and carry on as if nothing had happened. Leaving her and coming to me would mean rocking the boat, and that would be too much trouble. Listen, I'm not a fool. That part you got right. I know I was not much more than a convenient piece of ass for you. I amused you, but I knew that ultimately it wouldn't work out. I kinda liked you, Eddie. That's all. So if you're not going to stay I'd like you to scoot before Max comes back, because he really has begun to love you and it would break his heart if he saw you and then you left again. So go on, get out of here!"

No kiss goodbye? Suddenly Eddie rather wanted her in his arms one last time.

"Are you nuts? You think I'm going to roll over like a damn puppy dog every time you ask me? Out! Now! Nice knowing you. Walk through that door and down the hall and hit the elevator button before I *really* lose my cool."

She means it, Eddie thought. She's mad as hell at me. She really is tough. Her face is like steel.

He was astounded. Here was Arlene, whom he had come to believe was deeply sensitive and vulnerable underneath, barely turning a hair when he came to tell her it was over between them. She was virtually shoving him out of her life.

But then when she'd slammed the door behind him and he was halfway down the hall to the elevator, he heard her. They could probably hear her in New Jersey. Loud, heart-wrenching sobs were coming from Arlene's apartment.

As he pressed the DOWN button, Eddie wondered if he would ever figure women out. They seemed to act one way and feel another.

But right now he was going home to Hope. No more Manhattan. He'd tell Clem Springer to take a running jump off his Springer Dinger board. He winced momentarily at the Arlene expression.

But then he thought about the fact that he had the chance

to make a new start. It was as if his marriage were beginning all over again. Things were looking up.

Then he got back to Amagansett to find Annabel almost hysterical with worry.

"Eddie, thank God! Clinton's run away. We haven't seen him since you left this morning. Booty cried all day. I've just rung Hope to tell her."

"No need to worry Hope. Now I'm back, let's take the car and go look for him."

"No, you don't understand! I asked Hope to speak to Booty, calm her down, tell her Mommy would be home soon. Then I spoke to Hope some more, and when I put the phone down Booty had gone too. She's gone to look for Clinton, and it's dark!"

Well that's going to be a great start to our reunion, thought Eddie. I have to tell Hope our baby's missing.

22

Saul Shapiro was anal-retentive, if that was what it was called; Hope couldn't remember. It was something like that, wasn't it, when a person was obsessively neat, folded up their clothes just so before going to bed, leapt ten feet across the room to pounce on a stray speck of dirt on the floor even if they happened to be in the middle of a passionate embrace on the sofa at the time.

And his clothes were always so immaculate, shirts so sparkling white they almost blinded you and shoes so shiny he could probably look down and see the hairs in his nostrils reflected in them. Hope smothered a giggle.

Then she frowned.

What had made her do it? She hadn't really wanted to go to bed with him, and when she'd seen him neatly folding his underwear and placing it on the chair, she'd known she wouldn't be able to go through with having sex with him, if indeed she'd ever wanted to in the first place. She listened to him cleaning his teeth in the bathroom, followed by several seconds of gargling and discreet spitting. When he lowered his body next to her in his freshly laundered pajamas and prepared to give her a Listerine kiss, she had turned away, feeling mean and wretched. Saul was a nice man and she wasn't being fair to him. She'd led him on, given him clear signals that taking her back to the hotel after dinner might lead to a night in bed, and now she was going to make a run for it—all because she wanted to make Craig jealous.

Why do we do this, she asked herself, act like we want the opposite of what we're really longing for? Craig arrives, suggests dinner, and I turn him down when I've been dreaming about spending time with him for weeks. Instead, I ask him to take the kids because, I tell him, I've got a date. Then I engineer it so I have dinner with Saul in the place where I know Craig's going to be taking the kids. I know Craig's going to be there early, but I make sure we overlap so Craig gets to see me with Saul.

And all the time where I really want to be is over at the other table with my ex-husband and my kids.

I could be. Craig asked me. But I said no.

Of course, she could have dumped Saul at the end of dinner, but some perverseness made her go through with the whole farce of pretending she wanted to spend the night with him. She envisaged Craig delivering the kids back to her hotel room in the morning and discovering she hadn't spent the night there.

Poor Saul. He had even obliged her by falling asleep quite quickly after she'd turned away from him, pleading tiredness. She thought she might have even caught a glimpse of a look of relief on his face. Maybe, now that she thought about it, Saul probably didn't like sex. Maybe he found the whole thing rather distasteful. It would, after all, mean rumpling his pajamas and maybe the ultimate horror of a semen stain on the sheets.

Suddenly she knew she couldn't stay there. How could she have even allowed herself to think of letting the kids discover she'd spent the night in someone else's bed? She got up carefully, took her clothes to the sitting room of Saul's suite, and dressed there. As she did so, she pictured Craig trying to sleep in his king-size bed in his suite down the hall with Harry and Coco thrashing about either side of him. For that was what he'd agreed to do when he took them for the night. He didn't have an extra bedroom. They'd all have to sleep together.

Well, at least there wasn't room for a woman.

For that was what had prompted her to lead Saul on, to try to make Craig jealous. Saul had continued to paint a disquieting picture of Craig as a womanizer. Yes, she could blame it all on Saul, if she tried. That would be very convenient, if a little inaccurate. It wasn't as if she'd had much time even to think about Craig when they'd first arrived in Nashville.

For a start, Nashville itself was a surprise. Hope knew her expectations of rhinestone cowboys serenading her on every street corner were a little over the top, but she hadn't been prepared for so urban a city—high-rises, hospitals, office buildings.

Then she had to come to terms with the fact that she was hopeless as a stage mother. Or maybe screen mother would be more accurate. Whatever, Hope was not cut out to sit around all day on the set clutching a bag of needlepoint and chatting with other mothers. She had never stopped to think how boring a movie set might be. There often was only a few minutes of action all day, and the rest of the time was spent hanging around.

Hope was no good at hanging around. She needed nonstop action, speed, achievement.

For once, the fact that the Princess was such a little prima donna was a plus. She kept Hope on her toes along with everybody else. Coco was more demanding than any of the other children in the film. She had the star role, but that wasn't the only reason.

From the get-go the other mothers hated Coco. Hope soon realized that the professional screen mother pushes her child to the fore at every opportunity. Hope didn't need to do that. Coco was perfectly capable of grabbing the spotlight herself.

She had no lines to learn—and in any case, as Hope quickly discovered, it didn't work like that. The director talked the kids through their scenes and then told them what to do at each step while the camera was rolling.

Coco was in heaven. She had her own trailer with her name on the outside by the door and a bag of warm Krispy Kreme doughnuts with pink icing delivered to her every morning for breakfast.

The opening of the movie had been rewritten yet again. The first scene now involved Coco's being kidnapped at the Tennessee State Fair where her father in the picture, a country music star, was performing. He was being played by a genuine celebrity on the country music scene, so the re-creation of the State Fair (the actual event would not take place until September) had drawn huge crowds of extras.

Coco basked in the singer's reflected glory as hundreds of pairs of eyes watched her accompany him on a tour of the fair, holding his hand and grappling with a giant stick of pink cotton candy. She was wearing a white dress with what she called a "frilly out" skirt, and Hope had to admit she looked adorable. Perched on top of her white-blond hair was a miniature turquoise Stetson.

Coco adored Hair and Makeup.

She didn't actually need very much, but she made sure she had an hour-long session every morning, and when they said the turquoise Stetson would bring out the beautiful color of her eyes, she was putty in their hands. It was only a matter of time before Wardrobe was able to persuade her to slip her tiny feet into a pair of little white rhinestone-studded cowboy boots.

Although they were only taking care of tracking shots of father and daughter moving about the fair through the mule barn, the swine barn, the cattle barns, the poultry and rabbit barns, and the livestock show arena, Coco was constantly aware that the camera was on her.

"She's a natural. Normally whoever was playing alongside her would have to involve her at all times so her attention wouldn't wander, but that little Coco's on the ball every second," Hope heard the director tell someone on the set. "Kid's got a future. Who's her agent again?"

"Doesn't have one. We made a deal with the father. Ten thousand bucks," he was told.

This was news to Hope. Craig had said nothing about Coco being paid. Was he pocketing the money?

"Craig Collins? We paid that shit ten thousand? Not that it goes to him. He had to deposit the check in a designated bank appointed by the city. Court guardianship. It just bugs me to give him a dime, whatever he does with it."

"Why? You don't like him? He's a friend of Saul's."

"I suppose he's a nice enough guy. The only real beef I have with him is he stole my girl coupla months ago. Me and this woman were hitting it off pretty good. She made it clear she was ready to make a commitment. Hell, *I* was ready to make a commitment. Then along comes Craig Collins and sweet-talks her right out of my life. I'm like, 'Baby, I thought we had something going.' She goes, 'Oh, honey, I'm sorry, I thought we did too but I've fallen in love with Craig; what can I tell you?' I say, 'You can tell me goodbye.' Month later Craig takes off with somebody else, and my girl is toast."

Hope backed away. She didn't want to hear this.

"Mrs. Collins, they need you on the set. They're having a small problem with your daughter. She doesn't want to judge the Diving Piglet contest."

"My name is Calder . . ." Hope began. After what she'd just heard, she wanted to avoid the name Collins. "OK. I'll be right there."

When she arrived at the scene she soon saw what the problem was. It wasn't a question of Coco's not wanting to judge the Diving Piglet contest. It was the fear of getting her cowboy boots dirty that had made her back off.

"Mommy, I don't want to get all muddy," she complained.

"Coco, do not whine. I don't like it at home and I don't like it here. Hank"—Hope turned to an assistant director—"where is Coco going to be standing in this scene?"

"Up there," said Hank, big, beefy muscles bulging, "on that platform. See the hatch up there? The little piggies, they're going to come scooting out of that hatch, run along the plank, and go diving down into the tank of water. First one to scramble out onto that lower platform there wins the prize. All your daughter has to do is look down and see which little piggy comes outa the water first."

"So she won't get her feet muddy?"

"No, ma'am." Hank winked at her as much as to say, I get the picture. "C'mon, little lady, let's lift you up on that platform all ready for the director."

"Coco, honey," said Hope firmly. "You're going up there on that platform and Hank will lift you up so you won't get dirty. It's like a stage. Everyone at the fair will be looking up at you."

Coco almost threw herself into Hank's arms.

"Ready to go, Harvey!" Hank yelled at the director.

"Good, good. Coco, you look great," called Harvey, looking through the camera. "Barney," he shouted at the country singer playing Coco's father, "I'm only picking you up as far as your balls. Ya need to bend down beside her. That's it. That's better. Now, Coco, sweetheart, what you're going to do is, when I call *Action!* you walk to the edge of the platform and look down, but keep holding Barney's hand because we don't want you falling into the water, do we, sweetheart?"

"Don't call me sweetheart," said Coco.

"What is she, politically correct? Going to sue me for sexual harassment?"

"Wouldn't surprise me," said Hank.

"OK, sweetheart, I mean dumpling—sorry, Coco—move in farther, look down, that's it, now, camera, action! See those piggies? Good, good, clap your hands a little as they go

by, that's perfect, that's beautiful, get this in the master shot
I'm going to be a happy man. Wanna make me a happy man,
sweetheart; sorry, pumpkin? No, what's her name? I got shit
for brains; I knew it twenty seconds ago." He turned to Hank.

"Coco," whispered Hank.

"Coco, wanna make Daddy a happy man?"

"You're not my daddy," yelled Coco. "Neither of them!"
And she stamped her foot, confused the audience, and ruined the shot.

"Who needs kids?" Harvey shrugged. "Child pictures are
very soft in Japan anyway, so they tell me. What am I doing,
making a picture with kids? I hate working with kids, it ain't
worth it. Now, Coco." He peered through the camera again.
"Mistress Collins, if you please. I call *Action!* The piggies
come running out. You clap your hands. You watch 'em dive.
You look down, and when you see one of 'em scramble out
of the water you go, 'That one, he's the winner!' loud as you
can. Let me hear you say it."

"*That one, he's the winner!*" screamed Coco.

"Shirley Temple in the making," said Harvey, beaming.
"All right, everyone, stand by, going again. Camera! Action!"

Coco didn't move.

"Mrs. Collins?" Harvey looked at Hope beseechingly.

"Coco darling, what's the matter?"

"Mommy, I think it's cruel to animals for these piggies to
have to dive into the water."

"Jesus!" muttered Harvey. "Hank, what's the next scene?"

"We're back in the crowds and the kidnapper grabs her as
her father's presenting the prize for the best banjo solo."

"Good," said Harvey, "set it up. That kid needs kidnapping."

After this, when Hope drove out to the airport to meet Craig
and Harry's plane from Los Angeles, leaving Coco in Hank's

capable hands, she was ready to tell Craig what a pain in the butt his daughter was, but Craig beat her to it in true Craig fashion.

"Your son's a serious wimp," he whispered to her by Baggage Claim. "Won't surf. Hasn't touched the mountain bike I bought him. Can't hit a ball on the tennis court. All he talks about is some guy called Sheldon who took him fishing. He and this Sheldon are writing a book together. You know that? Spends his whole time scribbling in a notebook."

"Well," hissed Hope, "your daughter's driving everyone nuts on the set."

"Naturally, she's the star." Craig grinned. "Maybe I can find a vehicle for her for my next picture. Have her come live with me in LA. Great Hollywood profile: a father/daughter team. Meanwhile my son's turning into a faggoty writer."

"You were a writer once, as I recall," said Hope. "I'd assume that's where Harry gets it. I'm relieved to hear he's your son again, but keep your voice down. Harry's very sensitive."

"Exactly. That's my point." Craig nudged her playfully. He was in a very good mood. "A sensitive faggoty writer in the making. Gotta knock it on the head early. He's gotta grow up tough. Be a player. Look at his parents, for Christ's sake. Two mega-successful people. He can't let us down."

"Dad said you weren't too happy with your outdoor activities in California," said Hope gently, when she had Harry on his own. "What happened? You had a great time at camp this summer. I thought you were all set for that kind of stuff."

"It wasn't the stuff, it was Dad's girlfriend. He was busy in the office all day so I had to be with her. She took me to the beach and biking and stuff, and with anyone else it would have been really neat. But I didn't like her at all. She was cool-looking—young, much younger than you, pretty, blond—but she put me down all the time. Acted like she was talking to a kid."

Hope smiled. The "much younger than you, Mom" was a

bit of a blow, but it was good to know the girl's looks hadn't impressed Harry.

"But his *new* girlfriend seems like she might be OK," added Harry, spoiling it all.

"What do you mean, his *new* girlfriend?"

"Well, he dumped the first one the last few days I was there."

"Overnight?"

"Pretty much."

"So how old was the new one?"

"Mom," said the older, wiser California Harry, "believe me. You do not want to know."

The good thing about film crews, Hope had already decided, was that they were great at entertaining kids. It amused her to see that by now Hair and Makeup were treating Coco like a doll, playing with her, passing her around, winding her up and setting her off like a robot, prompting her to sing the songs she had learned at school and perform her ballet steps for them. The Special Effects guys whisked Harry off to show him their tricks, and the camera crew promised to let him pull focus and clap the clapper board. And when Hank and the script girl invited both kids to go for a burger, it left Hope free to go to dinner with Craig when he asked her.

She said no.

She didn't understand why. Why was she angry with herself for falling under his spell again so quickly? What did she expect? She had spent the entire summer plotting to be with him. Driving out to the airport she had been panting to see him, but then after his few supercilious comments about Harry she was furious. When Harry told her about his LA harem, she was all set to walk away from him. Yet within hours she was dreaming about spending an evening with him.

But a little voice said, "Don't make it easy for him," so she didn't. She said no thanks, she already had a date.

She thought about a present Annabel had brought her from London and smiled. It was a chocolate figure called The Perfect Man. *He's rich, he's smooth,* read the caption on the box, *and when he gives you grief, you can bite his head off.*

Why was it that the way a man's eyes were set in his face, the way his hair lay on the back of his head, the way he walked and the sound of his voice could make you forgive the words you heard and make you want to put your arms around him? Physical attraction, thought Hope. That's all it's ever been with Craig, his energy and his looks, nothing else. I'm not even sure I like him anymore but I want him and I want him to want me.

The only problem was that after she turned him down, Craig wasn't forthcoming with anymore dinner invitations. At least not intimate dinners à deux. For the next three nights he was busy organizing group dinners for Saul and the upper echelons of the crew, the director, the assistant directors, the production designer, the costume designer, and the cast. Hope was never seated anywhere near him and found herself watching as he held forth with a never-ending stream of anecdotes. He liked an audience, relished being the center of attention. Well, he always had.

But as she watched, miserable, disappointed, she detected a growing boredom in the expressions of the people around him. They were being polite. He was their producer's friend. He was a producer himself. He might even employ them one day soon. They had to be careful. But she could see their interest waning.

Saul was by her side every night, attentive, polite, gentle. Did she want the meat and two veggies or some pasta? What kind of wine did she like? Did she enjoy being on the set? Were things all right at home? Was she missing Booty? Was she losing out on any work? All the things Craig should have been asking if he still cared about her. But Craig was too busy showing off, oblivious to her. Which was why, on the third night, she found herself responding to Saul's attentions with a little more interest than before, brushing her hand across his arm, whispering in his ear, encouraging him just a little, knowing exactly why she was doing it and hating herself for it.

But it worked.

She saw Craig glance at them once, then twice, and by the coffee stage she knew he was watching them. She turned to Saul and asked him if he'd mind giving her a ride back to the hotel.

Craig watched them leave.

I should feel triumphant, thought Hope. He's noticed. He could even be jealous. But I feel awful.

She got away with a good-night kiss. Saul probably thought she was just playing hard to get because he asked her out the following night, and this time she engineered it so that Craig took the kids and ran into them in the restaurant.

Twice he had seen her with Saul. How was he to know that nothing had happened either night?

He didn't.

And he bit.

He asked her out himself. This time she didn't say no.

He presented himself at her hotel promptly at seven-thirty, barely seconds after Hank had picked up the kids. They were embarking on the ultimate adventure of spending the night in his Winnebago.

The phone rang just as Craig was ushering her out the door.

"I have to get that. Wait," said Hope.

"Let them take a message." Craig was impatient. "I'm starving. After dinner, why don't we go hear some Bluegrass, try a little two-stepping?"

That would turn it into a late night, was Hope's first thought, and who knew what might happen?

She reached for the phone.

"Hope? It's Annabel."

"Annabel, what's up?" Hope heard Craig sigh with impatience in the background.

"It's Clinton. I'm afraid he's run off somewhere. Eddie's in the city and I can't go looking for the dog. The thing is, Booty's beside herself. I was wondering if you could just have a word with her, say good night, calm her down."

"Come on, Hope." Craig was cracking his knuckles, a habit of his she had always loathed.

"Of course," she told Annabel. "Don't worry about the dog. He'll turn up. . . . Hi, sweetheart. . . . What? . . . No, he'll come home soon. All dogs do. He'll be fine. . . . What's that? . . . Love you too, Booty. Love you very much."

"C'mon, honey." She felt Craig nuzzle her behind the ear with his nose, and her heart started thumping. "C'mon, I haven't seen you in ages." She felt him take the receiver from her hand and replace it as he pulled her face to his and kissed her.

As the tip of his tongue touched hers she heard a click and imagined a little voice saying, Mommy?

It stayed with her throughout the cab ride downtown to the restaurant, right up to the moment when they were seated at a secluded corner table and Craig asked, "Hope, what do you want to drink?"

When she didn't answer he snapped his fingers in front of her face.

"Hey, is anybody home? I said What do you want to drink?"

"Sorry, what? Oh, I don't know. Whatever you're having."

"Hope, what's your problem?"

"I'm worried about Booty. The dog's run away and she's all upset, I should call back. . . ."

She stood up.

Craig grabbed her by the wrist.

"Sit down. She'll be fine. Don't be so boring. Here I am, giving you a night out away from the kids, and all you want to do is run to the telephone. Those days are over, honey. Harry and Coco are fine. We know they are."

"I said I was worried about *Booty*." Hope was aware she sounded tense.

"And I say you're making way too much of a fuss. I say you should relax and give me a smile. I say you should let me tell you about this script I read today because it has the perfect part in it for Coco, and if I set it up to shoot in LA you could come be there with me."

She had been staring down at the table. Now she looked up at him as he reached out and gently drew her face toward him. This was the old Craig. They could almost be sitting at the little breakfast table in the kitchen of their old apartment in Greenwich Village, trying to figure out a way to solve their financial problems and inevitably coming to the conclusion that all they had was each other and their kisses to keep them warm. And then, in the same instant, she thought, How can he think I can just give up and go live in LA and leave all my clients in the lurch?

"OK," he went on, "so I'm just looking for an excuse to lure you to LA. Or maybe that slimeball Shapiro has already asked you. What's going on with you guys? Jesus, I couldn't believe it, I thought the guy was supposed to be a friend of mine, but then he starts making a play for my wife right in front of my eyes."

And from what I've heard this is not a practice totally unknown to you, thought Hope.

"I'm not your wife, Craig," she said quietly.

"Honey, what is it?" His voice was very soft, very caring. She had never been able to decide if his concern was genuine when he spoke to her like that. She didn't understand herself at all. She'd played a game with Saul to get Craig's attention. Well, now she had his attention and she found herself doubting his sincerity. She'd wanted to be a success so Craig would want her back, and now he wanted her back and all she felt was that she was some kind of trophy. Why did he only want her back because someone else wanted her? Why couldn't he want her for herself, for who she really was, for the person she'd been when he married her? If she really thought about it, she hadn't changed all that much. She'd always been a fighter, she'd always known she wanted to succeed at what she did, but that didn't just mean her work. She understood that now. It meant succeeding at being a wife and mother too. And she hadn't been a successful wife for Craig. That's why he'd left. Maybe that was the way it was meant to be.

"It's nothing," she told him. "It doesn't matter." It was pointless to discuss it further. Clearly he didn't understand how she felt about Booty. She wasn't his kid. Why should he let it spoil his evening?

I knew going in what I'd be getting with Craig if I went out with him this evening, she thought. So why did I do it? Isn't it time I started facing up to the fact that he's egotistical and self-obsessed and doesn't understand how important it is to me to be a good mother?

And I *can* be a good mother, she determined. I love Harry and Coco and Booty as people. Craig loves Harry and Coco because they're extensions of him; he sees them as his clones and wants what they become in the future to reflect well on him. He doesn't really care about them. Why on earth did I marry him in the first place?

She found she could answer that question with surprising ease. It had been the excitement of the future that attracted her to him, the potential for them to grow together. She loved his stubborn determination to sit in a cold bare room and write a screenplay, come what may, while she went out and took care of business. It was the fact that he had needed her that had made her fall in love with him.

I need to be needed, thought Hope. Or do I? I pretend to myself that my husband and my children need me because I don't want to accept that I need them, that my need is probably greater than theirs. But it should be a two-way thing.

Craig doesn't need me anymore.

But then he surprised her.

"Listen," he said carefully, reaching out to take her hand. "I understand you have a choice to make if you come out to be with me in LA for any length of time. I can appreciate that. You're quite a hotshot now in the real estate business. I'm proud of you. I guess I knew all along that you were going to make a success of yourself. Don't forget, I was the one who used sit there all alone in that little place we had in the Village, thinking about you while you were out earning our daily bread. Don't think I didn't appreciate it. I did then, and I still do. I want to make it up to you, Hope. I've been a shit. Hey, we could get a place in the Hamptons as well as California. That's a big movie scene in the summer."

"I already have a place in the Hamptons," Hope pointed out. She dared not look at him. She couldn't have wished for him to say such wonderful things if she had written the script herself. And yet somehow it didn't make her feel as good as she had always imagined it would.

"Yes, but that's with What's-his-name. If you're going to leave him, you'll probably have to buy him out, so give him the house."

"Just like that?"

"Just like that. I can't bear to see the way he's letting you down. You're like me. You've struggled, you've made something of yourself, and for what? To be dragged down by a loser? Look at me, Hope. You know what I've been thinking? What would your father say if he could see you now? He never even met Eddie. He's up there thinking I'm his son-in-law. And that's exactly what I am. We had a little hiccough. It happens. We caught it in time."

He's being so sweet, thought Hope. Does he mean it?

"Are you saying you need me, Craig?"

"I'm saying I want you."

But have I been wanting you just because Eddie's been driving me nuts? wondered Hope. Why am I so perverse? Why, when I have within my reach the very thing I've been wanting for months, do I feel so hesitant?

What about Eddie?

But Eddie's so helpless, always has been, he's always needed me to direct him. Is that why I married him? Because he needed me—or someone like me?

And my children have Annabel. Do they need me?

She only had to think of Booty's little voice on the telephone.

I need to be needed by Booty whether she likes it or not. I'm her mother. She's my baby. There's no doubt in my mind.

"Excuse me, do you have a pay phone I could use?" she asked a passing waiter.

"There's one outside the ladies' rest room," he told her.

"Hope," said Craig, his voice suddenly harsh, warning her.

She left him sitting there.

"Thank God you called." This time she reached Eddie, and he sounded odd and shaky. "We tried to reach you at the hotel. They didn't know which restaurant you'd gone to."

"Why? What is it? What's happened?"

"It's Booty. She's wandered off in the dark into the woods after Clinton."

"Call the cops, Eddie. I'll take the next plane home. I'll take the Jitney from the airport and let you know when to meet me. But call the police, Eddie. Do it now."

"The police?" Craig had come up behind her.

"Booty's missing." Hope was shaking. She put her arms out, expecting him to hold her.

"What's-his-name fucked up again?"

It was strange. She hadn't thought of it like that until Craig mentioned it. The snatched conversation with Eddie had been two parents frantic with worry about their child. It wasn't a question of apportioning blame.

"I have to get to the airport. I can stop by Hank's Winnebago to pick up Harry. You'll take over from here with Coco, right?"

"You're not serious?"

"What do you mean?"

"You're not leaving just because he called and said she's missing. It's only been a couple of hours. They'll find her before you get home and you'll have left for nothing."

"Craig, I have to go."

"What about us? We were just starting to work things out."

"We can do that another time. Now I've got to get to the airport."

"Have you any idea how much of a hassle it was for me to schlepp all the way to Nashville to see you? I was in the middle of a pretty hefty negotiation in LA and I would have preferred to do it face-to-face. But no, you want me to deliver Harry personally, so I get on a plane and come see you. And what do I find? You're making a fool of yourself with Saul, and now you go running back to What's-his-name at the drop of a hat."

"I'm not going back to Eddie. I'm going back for my child."

"But she's not *my*—"

He stopped.

She looked at him. She could hardly believe it. He'd been about to say, But she's not *my* child.

The man was a monster, a self-obsessed monster. As frantic as she was about Booty, Hope couldn't help but acknowledge that she'd been in denial about Craig. He'd probably always been like this, but he'd been smart enough to always stay one step ahead of her.

He'd left her when it was convenient for him. He had been monitoring her career rise. He probably figured she'd be useful to him now. He'd always known she was a sucker for the family image. He'd reeled her in with that spiel about the anniversary of her father's death. He'd probably never had any intention of going anywhere near her father's grave.

She'd fooled herself into thinking Craig was the one who knew her so well, that he was the one she wanted, when all the time he'd been playing on her vulnerabilities. But the one area where he had failed was the area on which she placed the most importance: her kids.

Craig had screwed up. He'd tried to make her think she was a bad mother by working so hard she neglected them.

Wrong.

She could honestly say to herself that not once had she felt that her kids had turned against her.

Whereas Harry was scared of his own father. And Coco was in danger of becoming permanently spoiled simply because she was successfully acting out the role her father had chosen for her.

I'm going to save Harry and Coco before it's too late, Hope found herself thinking. Craig is their father, but the less they see of him the better, and if I'm clever I can make sure he sees them very rarely.

They love Eddie. They've been happy with Eddie. How could I have been so blind as not to see that until now? Craig created for me an idea of how I wanted to live my life and I swallowed it.

But it was just an idea.

What Eddie has always delivered is the life I really do live, for better or for worse. And if I'd only bothered to stop and think, I'd have realized I have become truly successful in my work only since I've been married to Eddie. Craig would never have allowed me to spend so much time working. Eddie doesn't like it but he accepts it because he knows it makes me happy.

Eddie wants me to be happy.

Craig wants me to make him happy.

I'm going to save Harry and Coco, but meanwhile I am going home to save Booty.

And my marriage.

23

Freedom, I learned, comes when restraints are finally lifted.

The letter I received from my father's solicitor left me feeling liberated. There was no other way to describe it. All the questions hanging over me had been answered. There was no reason for me to look back unless I chose to do so. I had never imagined that it could bring such relief.

Following the telephone conversation with Maud in which she had revealed what the villagers were saying about me, I had written to the solicitor asking him to make inquiries about the progress of the insurance investigation. I realized I had been waking every morning expecting some kind of bombshell to hit that would, in all likelihood, prove too much of a shock for me to absorb. I was learning how to pace myself now that I was on my own. In Cornwall I had let Marietta dictate how I spent my day, and I had become lazy enough to allow her to influence the way I reacted to anything that happened. She would deal with any problems that arose. I didn't have to worry. I had become lulled into such an extraordinary sense of false security that when I now faced unpleasantness, I was too stunned to cope.

To an extent I had confided in Ray Moran (although he did not know about my smoking in bed), and of course Maud knew the position I was in, but I had not wanted to burden Hope with my problems beyond the fact that my parents had died recently. Or was it that I thought she might not be sympathetic, absorbed as she was with her own problems? One thing I had learned was that you have to be discriminating as to whom you can entrust your confidences. Not from the point of view of discretion—otherwise, of course, I would never tell Maud anything—but you have to be sure they are the kind of person who will understand you or you will wind up feeling more lonely than ever. But, as I was rapidly beginning to realize, you can only really trust yourself—and your instincts.

And now my instincts were telling me to go forward rather than back to the past.

So in a way it made sense to seek help and information from someone who was completely detached—like a solicitor.

His Letter of Freedom, as I dubbed it, was short and to the point. It told me in blissfully succinct phrasing that the insurance people had completed their investigation and my claim would now be addressed. Almost as an afterthought, he informed me that the fire department's report had revealed that the fire had started as the result of faulty wiring. Apparently the wiring in the west wing—where my parents had their bedroom—although newly installed last year, was found to be a faulty piece of work. If I had only stopped to think for a second, I could have worked out for myself that if the cigarette I had been surreptitiously smoking in bed that night had indeed slipped out of my hand as I fell asleep, and started the fire, I would have been the one to be killed, not my parents, whose room was at the other end of the house. I recalled the electrician who had been responsible for the new wiring in my parents' wing. I had not liked him. He was a newcomer to the area. Marietta had insisted we employ him instead of continuing with our old electricians, who were reluctantly having to raise their prices in line with inflation. The newcomer undercut them by a third and Marietta had fallen for it.

And paid for it, I thought.

I called Maud and told her the news.

"Well, there you are, sweetie. She should have handed things over to you years ago. I always thought it was utterly ludicrous the way she bossed you around."

"How do you know she bossed me around?"

"You told me. Every time you came up to London you complained about your mother. It was obvious to anyone that you were actually running the place. She managed to make you think she was in charge, and you were such a ninny, that you believed her. She was a classic control freak and you let her get away with it. You know how to organize a household perfectly well. Look at what you've done with my wretched sister-in-law. Edward told me he'd never seen the place look so good and run so smoothly. All due to you. But don't let Hope become the new Marietta in your life."

"Well, you dumped me right into her lap," I mumbled. Why did I always get irritated when Maud pointed out a few home truths, especially when I knew she was right.

"Yes, but look at how much good it's done you to get away. You should be thanking me," Maud retaliated. She always had an answer, which was even more infuriating. "Anyway, I'm mellowing on that score. As I told you, Edward doesn't seem to be so much under her spell as he was, and he seems cheerful enough. So when are you going to come home and get Rosemullion back on its feet?"

"I don't know."

"Want to stay with the Seahorse Whisperer?"

"Ha-ha. Very funny. He's not that important to me."

How much truth was there in that throwaway remark? I'd tossed it off in response to Maud's teasing, but since I had learned that my problems in England were being solved, I had begun to wonder just how much Sheldon really meant to me. Now I was experiencing odd moments of real confidence, whereas before I had been perpetually vulnerable.

Perhaps the time had come for a little self-preservation. I had not slept with this man, even though I was violently attracted to him. If I did sleep with him I would surely be hurt, if Maud and Ray were to be believed. They probably thought I already had. It was foolish to expect too much from Sheldon. I'd probably be better off thinking of him as just a friend who fixed the roof. A hard, cold, unemotional approach, totally unlike me, but deep down I knew it made sense. Despite my newfound maturity, there were still a few things I didn't feel like confessing to myself just yet but needless to say Maud set me straight.

"Well, that all sounds very grown up," she said. "Perhaps you're finally beginning to realize what a hopeless picker of men you are. Jasper. Guy. This Sheldon character. All of them have a million other agendas in their lives besides you. They all have other women."

She's right, I thought. Even Ray. Ray has Hannah. Now why had I included Ray in the list? At least Maud didn't know about him. Not that there was anything between us, of course.

"Very bad for your self-esteem, sweetie," Maud continued. "Find someone who cares about *you*."

"Easier said than done," I said grumpily. Where are all the men who care about *you*, Maud? was the question I never asked. Maud was probably incredibly lonely.

I thought wistfully of Sheldon and how sweet he was with Harry, how kind he'd been to me. I thought he had cared about me but no one seemed to agree with me.

Sheldon or no Sheldon, I wanted to stay here. It was when Maud had asked me when I was coming home to sort out Rosemullion that I realized it was the last thing I wanted to do. I had been freed from Rosemullion and all its constraints. Rosemullion represented my past. For some reason, my future here, seemed to be on Long Island, and if I sold

Rosemullion, I would have a bit of money of my own for the first time in my life.

Money to give me freedom.

But for the time being, I had a few more immediate responsibilities to take care of.

Booty had wandered off in search of Clinton, but as usual she hadn't gone far. About an hour after we'd discovered she was missing, Eddie and I found her battling her way through the woods, woods she knew well—given her frequent excursions in the past—and where she was unlikely to encounter any danger, even in the dark. By that time, however, Hope had left Nashville and was on her way home.

That was not a bad thing, I reflected. Now Eddie was back, Hope needed to be there too or everything would fall apart again. Besides, once Booty came home and discovered Clinton was still missing, she would not be consoled.

It wasn't just a "no!" day, it was a "no!" hour, a "no!" minute, a "no!" second, and on top of everything else of course she wanted Hope.

We told her we'd call the dog pound, the Animal Rescue Fund. We'd even call the local radio station to get them to broadcast Clinton's disappearance over the air. But of course Booty didn't understand any of this.

Even Eddie couldn't do anything with her, in spite of her initial delight in having him back in the house. Even though she had spent time with him in England, Booty seemed to understand that he had now come home. In the beginning she had followed him around the place, imitating his every move. If Eddie brushed his teeth, Booty wanted to brush hers. If Eddie put his feet up on the sofa for forty winks, something he was capable of doing several times a day, Booty followed suit, which was often the perfect way of getting her to nap. Only when I saw her about to take a slug of scotch did I step in and halt proceedings. But whatever had happened when father and daughter had been over in England had been a good thing. A closeness had developed between them that I realized was in no danger of being broken now that Eddie had elected to remain home on Long Island.

He confided to me on the first evening that he had been offered his job back but he gave no indication as to why he had not accepted it, and I decided not to inquire too closely.

And when Hope arrived home I took Booty and Harry off as much as I could so she and Eddie could be alone together.

I don't know what happened while Hope was away and it wasn't my place to ask, but from what I could see she and Eddie were on the brink of reconciliation. They were still somewhat tentative around each other, but they were back to sharing a bedroom and a couple of times Hope asked me rather sheepishly if I would mind taking Booty downstairs to sleep in my room to give them a bit of privacy.

In addition, I was surprised to note that she seemed to be spending more and more time at home. Showing houses seven days a week seemed to be a thing of the past.

When I commented on this, she winked at me. "I've told them at Tudor Woods that I can't be there for them every second of every day. They have to remember I have a family. Besides, you remember Mark? The guy you saw at the Easter egg hunt?"

I nodded.

"Well, I had problems with him, as you know, and I decided the only way to work things out was to get him to work with me rather than against me. He's smart and energetic and competitive, as he should be. I have many more clients than he does, more than I can handle if I'm going to make more time for my family. Anyway, half the people I rush around showing properties to don't come through with an offer and it's time wasted. I did a little thinking and figured out if I handed some of them over to Mark, especially the ones I felt just might be people out for the weekend amusing themselves looking at houses—pipe-dream people, I call them, and believe me, I can spot 'em—then he could work on them. Who knows? He might succeed where I wouldn't, and feel good about it, and I could spend more time at home. And he'd owe me. So I took him to lunch, schmoozed a little, and suggested we work together. For a start, I told him to stay away from Miss Parsons. I still haven't found a solution for her, but at least I know Mark won't sell her house to a developer who'll level it."

We were sitting on the deck having a cup of morning coffee, enjoying the sun. I felt she was as relaxed as she'd ever be, which pleased me. Coco, who had been delivered home from Nashville by one of Saul's assistants, was playing with a doll, a kind of Barbie with black hair and big boobs she had named Monica.

"Her father's idea of a joke," said Hope. "He bought it for her. You know, Annabel, she's just like Craig. Even at six you can see she's ambitious and work-obsessed. I thought she got it from me, but now I see Coco's got a ruthless streak in her, just like her father. You should have heard the conversations they were having in Nashville. You would not have believed your ears. I overheard Craig explaining to her that they have to get her agent to fight for better billing for her next movie."

"I didn't know she had an agent," I said.

"She does now. Craig wasted no time there. What I didn't know was that she already has another movie lined up. It's going to amuse me, watching Craig and Coco come up against each other over the next few years. I have a sneaking feeling Coco might get the better of Craig one day."

"Coco's your revenge on Craig?"

Hope laughed. "You could say that."

I waited for her to elaborate, but she didn't.

So where does that leave Harry? I wondered. Although I couldn't believe the change in Harry since I'd first known him. I was proud to think that maybe I had been responsible for boosting his self-confidence, but there was no question that the one person who could really take credit for toughening Harry up was Sheldon. In the time they had spent together—indeed, ever since Sheldon had come into our lives—Harry had acquired the closest thing he would ever have to an older brother looking out for him.

The roof was done and I could see Harry missed Sheldon who, true to form, had not called me for two weeks.

"Where is he, Annabel?" Poor Harry didn't understand why his new friend had suddenly disappeared, didn't understand why I wouldn't call him.

"He could help us look for Clinton in the truck," Harry said reasonably.

Clinton was still missing. It sounded harsh, but we hadn't really had that much time to get attached to him. Even Booty had stopped asking where he was. We preferred to think that some weekend people had found him wandering around and, instead of taking him straight to the pound, had kept him and taken him back to New York, where they would pamper him and take him for long walks in Central Park. It was quite possible, Hope pointed out with a certain amount of logic. He was a good-looking dog, and wheaten terriers were very popular. We knew we were probably deluding ourselves, but the alternative—that he was lying dead in the woods, his corpse devoured by foxes—was too horrible to contemplate and certainly X-rated as far as the kids were concerned.

"Well, you call him, Harry," I said eventually, in exasperation. "Here's the number."

But my plan backfired and confused Harry even more.

Sheldon reappeared at the house the very next day, slipping in through the kitchen door and kissing me quickly on the mouth.

An electric current sizzled through me. I was aware that I was shaking.

I didn't look at him. The sight of those blue eyes would be my undoing. I'd be quite safe, we'd have Harry with us, and he wouldn't be able to do anything with Harry there.

But Sheldon had other ideas.

"Just taking Annabel, I'm afraid, kids. Too much stuff in the truck for me to fit any more of you in, and you remember what happened last time, Harry. Big bump on the head. Wouldn't want that to happen again."

"Absolutely not," said Eddie. "The kids can stay with me. We'll be fine."

"Truth is I wanted you to myself," he said, once we were off in the truck.

"Uh-huh." Be noncommittal, I told myself. Look straight ahead. Keep watching out for Clinton. That's the only reason you're here.

"Yeah, I'm really glad you called."

"It wasn't me who called." I knew I sounded rather churlish. "It was Harry. He wanted to see you again. He wants you to look for Clinton."

"Oh." I could sense him looking at me. He was clearly thrown by my attitude.

"Thank you for what you've done for Harry," I said, by way of compensation. "It was sweet of you. I was worried about him."

"Any time." He sounded more cheerful now. "Don't worry about him. He's a loner, like me. That's why we get on so well. When I gave him a job to do, something small, nothing he couldn't handle, we worked together in silence. There was no need for chat. Oh, we talked in between, sure. Had some great conversations. He's only a kid, but he understood that I needed my space from time to time. Listen, if he stays around here, maybe when he gets through school he could be my apprentice."

"What about college?"

"What about it? I'd be teaching him a skill. He can earn

his living with it any time. Hell, he can take over my business. He can be my right-hand man and run Treasure Island, and his dad will be proud of him. That's what he needs, that kid, someone to be proud of him."

"I have a feeling that might not be the case," I said, "although Eddie might understand. Why, are you thinking of retiring?"

"Well, someday, sure. What's left for me? Actually I'm going to start thinking about my future pretty soon. I'll be forty soon. I can't be racing around putting on new roofs and shingling when I'm fifty. There's gotta be more to life than this."

"What about your old ladies? What about your Golden Club? They'll need you," I teased him.

"Oh, I know I'm in their wills," he said with confidence. "Millions of dollars coming my way."

"Well, what are you worrying about?"

"I don't know. I just have to be successful in my own right somehow. I mean, look at you. Don't you want more out of life than just being a nanny?"

That hurt, but then the truth often did. He'd hit the nail on the head, carpenter that he was.

"What about kids?" I was straying into uncharted territory here, but he seemed in a mood to confide in me. "Don't you want a son of your own? Your own Harry?"

"I don't want kids," he said firmly, and I could tell he meant it, "but I do want to bring something to this world, to leave behind something I can be proud of."

I thought he sounded almost scared of mortality. Probably as a result of his father having died relatively young.

"Where is this damn dog anyway?" He sounded angry for the first time since I'd known him. "He's been gone too long. We'll never find him now. Let's just stop and have a cup of coffee. There's a flask down there by your seat. Here, I'll get it."

He reached across me. It was just a ruse to move closer and start kissing me. I felt my arms go up and around his neck. I was kissing him back and he was pulling me toward him so that I was half lying across him, in his arms. We were parked on a deserted road with wetlands on either side and salt hay blowing in the wind. Occasionally I heard the mocking caw of a seagull as it flew overhead, as if it were telling me, "See? Didn't take you long to fall back into his clutches."

"So, you been seeing any good doctors lately?" he asked, when I came up for air.

"What were you doing that night? Why were you over by our house so late?"

"Had a job I was finishing up nearby. Thought I'd come by and see you. Didn't know you had a date with the doctor."

"It wasn't a date," I said crossly. "I just went over to have dinner with him and his wife."

"And that kiss he gave you?"

"He was just saying goodbye. A kiss on the cheek." Why was I explaining myself to him?

"Not like this."

He kissed me again on the lips, his mouth devouring mine.

"Guy's too old for you anyway."

This made me angry. "What on earth do you mean? He's a good-looking man. And he's not much older than I am. Maybe you're too young. Maybe you're just a boy. How do I know there aren't times when you confuse me with your mother?"

"You think I kiss my mom like this?"

"No, but you care a great deal about your mother, I can tell. You respect older women."

"I care a lot for you too."

I care a lot for you too. Just talk, probably. I didn't say anything.

"You think I'm kidding? I admire you. You're your own

woman. You might wonder why I haven't been rushing things, but I figured I'd take it slow. Truth is, I thought if I slept with you right away I might fall in love with you. I'm a loner. Right now I have control of my life, but if I get involved with you, that would change."

"Well, nothing's happened, so you're quite safe, aren't you? I'll be going back to England soon. You won't have to worry about me anymore."

He let go of me, then gripped me by the upper arms and looked me straight in the eye.

"Forever?"

"For a while. I have a few things to sort out."

"You going back to that guy you were in love with?"

"No."

"Then why?"

"Got a house to sell back there."

"You'll have money?"

"I can be part of your Golden Club," I teased him.

"No, you can't," he said fiercely. "You're Nanny Annie. You're different."

"I appreciate all you've done for me, Sheldon. Perhaps you'd better take me home."

He didn't take me up the driveway but stopped the truck at the end. His kiss was the tenderest I'd ever had from him.

"I'll call you before I go."

"Whatever."

I stood beside the truck holding his hands through the open window. He stared at me for what seemed like an eternity. That intense gaze, all the more powerful when he wasn't smiling.

Then he put his cap on his head, adjusted the peak so I could no longer see those penetrating blue eyes, and began to back the truck away from me. I let go of the door.

"Sheldon!"

The truck stopped, but not for me.

Harry was running down the drive, followed by Eddie.

"Did you find him?" Harry yelled.

"No, not yet, but hop in and we'll look some more, if you want," said Sheldon, without looking at me.

"Wait a second, take Annabel too, would you?" said Eddie. "Ray Moran just called and asked if she could come over. He sounded very upset. I'd take her myself but we've got a problem. My beloved wife appears to have forgotten that she has invited her mother to stay with us, and the wretched woman is arriving on the next Jitney. Someone has to go pick her up, and since Hope's nowhere to be found, that someone has to be me. The place is a terrible mess. If Ray hadn't sounded so desperate, I'd beg you to stick around, Annabel, and help me clear it up. My mother-in-law will no doubt blame me for every speck of dust she lays her eyes on."

I hated to leave him there looking so dejected and I can't pretend it was a comfortable ride over to Ray's.

When we drew into the forecourt of Osprey Farm, Sheldon leaned across me and opened the door.

"Have a good trip," he said, before he drove away.

"Sheldon!" I shouted.

He looked back once, with an expression of unbelievable hurt on his face.

Then he was gone.

"Hannah's had an accident." Ray met me at the door. If he'd seen Sheldon's truck, he didn't mention it.

"What's happened? Is she hurt?"

"No, no, she's fine. A little shaken but no harm done. Except to the kitchen." He led me into his study and sank down on the sofa. He looked exhausted. His shirt was rumpled, his trousers loose, and his white hair was badly in need of a cut.

He needs looking after, I thought. He's not taking care of himself.

"Thank you for coming," he said, squeezing my hand. "The mailman alerted me. The mailman, of all people. He smelled smoke when he delivered the mail and called the fire department. And me. Hannah had left a saucepan of milk on the stove and wandered into the garden. She remembered that she had to get her planting done but forgot all about the milk. We figure she was outside for half an hour before the mailman turned up. She was still out there when the fire department showed up. The kitchen's a write-off, but at least it didn't spread to the rest of the house and Hannah's OK."

"I suppose I should say something like 'That's all that matters,' but it's more than that, isn't it?"

"You were the first person I thought to call," Ray said quietly. "Don't ask me why. As the local doctor I must know just about everyone in the area, but I felt you'd understand best. What's happened means things have got to change. I can't go on leaving her here alone. I'm going to have to find someone to look after her. Either that or make Hope a very happy woman by giving her Osprey Farm to sell."

I was surprised by my reaction. Listening to him, I had felt flattered, warmed by his admission that I had been the first person he thought of. But now, I felt bitterly let down. He had called me not because he wanted someone to confide in but because he needed someone to look after his wife. He needed a nanny for Hannah. Who better than I?

Yet I couldn't help feeling sorry for him.

"If I don't sell I'm going to be trapped in this house with Hannah forever, and yet I love this house as much as Hannah does and I don't want to sell it."

I recognized his dilemma. He had come to a turning point in his life just as I had. Something had to give. Neither of us could go on as we were.

"You're at a bit of a crossroads, aren't you?" I said. "I know. I am too."

"How come?"

I told him about the fire report at Rosemullion and how I no longer wanted anything to do with the place.

"Kind of a different slant to your story," he said. "You want to be shut of your place; I want to hang on to mine. Any ideas about what you're going to do?"

"Go back home and sell the house. Then maybe I'll return here and see what happens," I told him. Saying it, I realized it was indeed what I was planning.

"What do you want to happen?"

"No idea." I laughed. "That's the beauty of it. For the first time in my life I have no notion of what the future holds, and it feels great."

"Whereas my future is staring me in the face, and if I want it to change I'm going to have to take action."

"Well, when I come back maybe I can help you sort it out," I said gently.

"Would you?" he said, and his face lit up with pleasure. I was amazed at how good it made me feel to make him smile. It was something I wanted to do again sometime.

He drove me back, and when I walked into the house I could sense the changed atmosphere before I'd even entered the living room.

A small elderly woman with too much makeup and dyed black hair was sitting in Eddie's favorite chair by the fire with Coco placed squarely on her knee. If this was Eddie's mother-in-law, I didn't envy him. One of the advantages of not being married was that you didn't have to contend with in-laws.

And what was Hope doing here in the middle of the day? This was unheard of. Must be a family crisis. Had one of the kids fallen ill? Had Sheldon run off the road and knocked Harry out again?

"Ray OK?" asked Eddie, as I walked in.

"He will be. Hannah had an accident, but she's fine."

Everyone was looking awkward, including Eddie.

"I'm Annabel Quick," I said, holding out my hand to Hope's mother. I could see a slight resemblance, something around the set of the chin and the oval-shaped face. Maisie Hofstater might have been quite pretty once, I conceded generously. "We haven't met, but we've spoken on the phone. I'm the nanny."

"I know who you are," said Maisie. She ignored my hand. "I don't know why you needed to go and hire an English nanny for Hope, Eddie. We have nannies in America, you know."

"It was Hope's idea to get a nanny from England," said Eddie wearily.

"Well, if you'd given her more support, she wouldn't have needed a nanny in the first place." Maisie was on her feet now and rolling up her sleeves, Coco dumped on the floor. Any minute now she'll advance on one of us like an ugly little prizefighter, I thought.

"I'm not sure I understand what you mean."

"Money. That's what I'm talking about. What do you bring to this marriage? Tell me, I'd like to know."

"Ma," said Hope, "don't start."

"I've already started," Maisie shouted, clearly very angry, "and I'm going on till I finish! Even when he had a job he was making barely half what you do, Hope. And he can't even keep a job. How are you going to afford a nanny now? I'm sorry, but there's no way they're going to be able to keep you on," she said to me, with a rather unpleasant baring of her teeth that I understood was an attempt to smile.

"Don't talk to Annabel like that," said Eddie unexpectedly. "She's done a damn sight more for the kids than you ever have, Maisie. They love her. They really do."

"And they don't love me? Is that what you're implying? I'm their grandmother. How can you compare me to a nanny? Hope, tell him to take a walk. You know I always visit you this week of August. You weren't expecting me?"

I looked at Hope. She'd said nothing to me about her

mother arriving. Could it be that she'd forgotten? And where was Maisie going to sleep?

"Ma," said Hope, "I told you. We don't have room anymore. Now Annabel's here, we don't have a spare room. I told you. It must have slipped your mind."

"She's got a mind like a steel trap," Eddie pointed out.

Hope glared at him. "Ma, we'd love to have you for the day. What say we all go to the beach and then to Gosman's for a fish supper? I'll take the day off."

"You forgot about me." Maisie was determined to feel sorry for herself. "I came all the way out here to see if you were all right, now your husband can't provide for you, and you forgot about me."

"Ma, that's enough. I didn't invite you. You're making this up to make me feel guilty. Eddie's had some bad luck, that's all. He doesn't need you dumping on him right now. And he's right about Annabel. I would have been lost without her these past months. She's one of us. She's not going anywhere. Eddie and I need her."

"Eddie and you? What do you mean, Eddie and you. You're separated. You left him."

"Actually, Ma, he left me."

"What about Craig?"

"He's in Los Angeles."

"But you and Craig—"

"Are divorced. You know that. And we're staying divorced."

"You're keeping this one as your husband?" Maisie nodded at Eddie, who was looking decidedly more cheerful. I had a feeling this was the first time Hope had really stood up to her mother.

"I sure am." Hope put her arm through Eddie's.

"So who's Arlene?" asked Maisie.

I saw Eddie withdraw his arm in a hurry.

"Who?" said Hope.

"Girl called Arlene," said Maisie, looking straight at Eddie, eyes gleaming. "Came to see me. Said she was a friend of Eddie's, brought some of his stuff back." Maisie produced a shopping bag and proceeded to remove things from it. "A sweater, a pocket calculator, a photo of Booty."

"You remember Arlene," Eddie said, rather too loudly, I thought. "She was my assistant at the Gramercy Press. I must have left those things there. Sweet of her to bring them over."

"And this," said Maisie. With a flourish she withdrew an electric shaver from the bag and tossed it at Eddie's feet. "How do you explain that?"

Hope looked at him. I saw she looked nervous.

"My razor?" said Eddie. "I used to shave at the office before I had to go to functions in the evening. Lots of guys do."

Arlene, I realized, must be the mysterious person Eddie had asked me about when he went to England, the friend he thought would try to reach him. What had happened between them? I was not sure I wanted to know.

And neither, as it turned out, did Hope.

"I don't know what you're suggesting, Ma, but I don't want to hear it. I think you'd better go back to the city now and I'll bring the kids in to see you another time. I've got to get back to work. I'll give you a ride into East Hampton and put you on the Jitney there."

Unfinished business. Clearly that was what Eddie had with this Arlene, and Hope knew better than to go raking it up.

What about the unfinished business I had with Sheldon?

I didn't have the nerve to call him; besides, he never answered his phone. What if he didn't call back?

And I didn't want anyone driving me there. I wanted to see him on my own.

Finally, I announced one morning that I was going to go

for a long walk around the bay to see if anyone had seen Clinton. We hadn't sounded out the fishermen. We'd assumed he'd gone off into the woods. But he might have taken the coastal route, run along the water's edge, been swept out to sea.

It took about an hour to walk along the bay to Lazy Point, and by the time I got there I was exhausted.

At first I walked right past the house without realizing what had happened. I hadn't recognized it. His beach was totally empty.

No boats, no buoys, paddles, life jackets, oilskins, or any of the other paraphernalia that had been strung up around the house. The rocking chairs and the barbecue on the deck were gone, as was the hammock. The deck was bare except for the lone birdhouse perched on its pole. I glanced up. Fred the seagull was no longer sitting on the chimney. And as I stepped across the deck with a sinking feeling to peer in through the glass doors, I knew what I would find.

The inside of the house was empty. No furniture, no pictures. He had even taken down the fishing net suspended from the wooden ceiling, in which he had entwined a mass of fairy lights that twinkled up among the beams, casting tiny dots of light all round the room.

I stumbled back down to the beach and collapsed in shock on the sand.

He'd gone.

"Missed the tag sale, did you?" said a voice from a rowboat bobbing on the water. An old fisherman in waders jumped out and pulled the boat up onto the beach.

"Tag sale?" I repeated.

"Sheldon. He had a tag sale before he left, sold some of his stuff. He'd have sold the house, only it didn't belong to him. And he didn't sell his cat. He left old Schooner with me. I got instructions to deliver him to some woman."

"I'll bet," I said, under my breath. "When did he leave? Where has he gone?"

"He's just gone sailing. That's what he told me, and that's what I've told everyone who's come looking for him."

Girls? I wanted to ask, but stopped myself. Now I would never know if Sheldon was what Maud had called an operator or if I had really meant something to him. Maybe it was better that way.

"You don't know where he's gone?"

"Nope. Shouldn't think he knows himself. That's the whole point. He's free. He's drifting somewhere out on the ocean. Who knows where he'll land? He's been wanting to do this for a long time. I've seen it coming. He's a pirate at heart. He's restless."

"Will he be back?" I asked.

"Oh, sure," said the old man, "but I doubt it'll be this century."

"One more thing. Was he alone?"

"Far as I know. He's fearless, that boy. Crazy with it. But I knew he'd be off again one day. Being on the water and surfing. That's all he's ever lived for. Nice guy. I'll miss him."

You and me both, I thought.

My foot hit something that rolled away in the sand. I picked it up.

It was a pencil with the words Amagansett Building Materials and a phone number. He'd always had a pencil stuck behind his right ear, the one without the earring.

I tucked it behind my own right ear and walked slowly home around the bay, my vision blurred not by the mist blowing in off the sea but by my own salty tears.

Eddie was in the kitchen when I walked in. He put his arms around me.

"What's wrong?" he asked, full of concern. "Your parents?"

"No. I mean, yes, always. It'll take me a long time to get over their deaths, but it's something else. Eddie, could you run me over to Ray Moran's in about an hour or so when he's finished work? I need to see him."

"Sure," said Eddie. "Good guy, Ray. Glad you two have become friends."

I could have confided in Eddie about Sheldon and he would probably have understood but I had qualms about talking to someone younger. I needed someone my own age. I needed Ray.

"How's Hannah?" I asked, when Ray let me in a couple of hours later.

"The fire was a shock, but she'll get by. For a split second every now and then she realizes she was responsible. It's awful when that happens—and it does happen at some point each day—that moment when she understands the state she's in, when she remembers Johnnie's dead and everything she's been saying is rubbish. I dread to think how she feels when I'm not here for her to turn to. And I can't tell you what it means to have someone to talk to about it. I didn't call you the other day to ask you to come and look after Hannah, although that's probably what you thought and why you left so soon. I called you because I needed you, I wanted to be close to you and tell you my problems, and now I guess by your face you've got problems of your own."

I told him about Sheldon. About his going away.

But I didn't tell him about the tentative effort Sheldon had made to tell me that he cared about me. I was afraid Ray would tell me I had imagined it.

Which I probably had.

"So are you going back to England soon?"

"I don't have a green card. I'll have to find a reason to come back. Why do you ask?"

"I don't want you to go."

"You don't?"

"I'll miss you."

"Ray, you barely know me."

"Well, you barely got to know Sheldon Bennett, as far as I can make out, but it looks like you miss him. Or you think you do. I want to get to know you, Annabel. I've been trying to make that clear ever since you first came to see me about the kids, and that was months ago. I saw you at Coco's birthday party and I thought you looked like a million dollars. If that stupid woman hadn't twisted her ankle, I'd have done something about you then."

"What do you mean, done something about me?"

"I don't know. Asked you out."

"What about Hannah?"

"What about Hannah? Hannah's my wife. She's not going anywhere. I love her, but she's out of it. You've seen what she's like. I'm never going to put her in a home. I'm never going to leave her. But I want a life. I'm entitled to one. Hell, so are you."

"What exactly do you have in mind, Ray?" I asked, as he moved closer to me and put his arm around me.

"This," he said, and very slowly placed his lips on mine and kissed me. To begin with I shut my eyes and saw Sheldon in his boat, tousled blond hair, broad chest, Bermuda shorts resting on his hips, a beer in his hand.

And then gradually the image faded and I found myself responding to Ray with a surprising urgency.

Till he pushed me away.

"Easy does it. Slow down. We've got plenty of time. I've got to sort out what to do about Hannah and Osprey Farm before I get carried away here. So if you've got any suggestions for the future, I'd be happy to listen to them."

I regarded him thoughtfully. It hadn't been anything like kissing Guy or Sheldon, but I was pretty sure I'd like to do it again.

"Ray," I said, "I do have an idea. How many bedrooms do you have in this house? And before you ask, it's not what you think."

. . .

The next morning the old fisherman from Lazy Point turned up at the house.

"Oh, it's you who was on the beach," he said, when I answered the door. "I didn't know. I just had an address and instructions like I told you. He wanted his cat to go to a lady. Weird name. Nanny Annie. You know her?"

I nodded, choking.

"Well, here's Schooner. He loved this cat, so I guess whoever he left him with had to mean something to him, you want my opinion. 'Course, he never said nothin'. But anyway, he's left a bit of himself behind with this damn cat, and he's left it with you. Be seein' you."

Nanny Annie.

It occurred to me that Sheldon had probably never known my last name. I'd seen him once going through his electronic organizer, looking up a number when he'd checked his answering machine and had to call someone back. Women's names came up one after another—just the first name and a number.

But he'd left me his cat, and that meant he'd thought of me before he left.

I hugged Schooner to me. Who knew? Maybe one day he'd be back.

For Schooner.

24

Hope went downstairs to the kitchen at seven-thirty on a Monday morning and encountered an unfamiliar sight.

All three children were sitting, dressed and ready for breakfast, at the kitchen table.

And Eddie was cooking.

There was a terrible smell that made her want to gag.

"I'm cooking the kids a full English breakfast. Best thing to set them up for a hard day's work at school."

Coco pointed her finger down her throat in disgust.

"Can't you give them, like, just half?" Hope pleaded, as the smell of bacon, sausage, fried bread, fried eggs, and grilled mushroom and tomatoes assaulted her senses. "Or even a quarter?"

"No way," said Eddie. "Has to be the Full Monty. They can't go off to school without a full breakfast inside them. Harry, I smell burning! What's happening? You're supposed to be Johnny-on-the-spot with the toast."

They managed perfectly well before you took over, thought Hope, but she knew she wasn't going to win her argument. To give Eddie his due, he'd managed to get them out of bed at six-forty-five and downstairs, dressed, half an hour later, and for that he deserved a medal.

"Where's Annabel?" asked Hope.

"Still asleep. It's her last day. We're taking her breakfast in bed," said Coco.

"Yeah, we're taking her the Full Monty. Rah, rah, rah!" yelled Harry, and the others began to giggle hysterically.

Hope smiled.

Whatever her reservations about their unhealthy, greasy breakfast, she had to admit the children had fun with Eddie. They were happy with him back in the house full-time. It had softened the blow of Annabel's leaving.

Oh, God, what was she going to do without Annabel?

She had determined to spend more time with her children. And she would, providing Eddie would do his bit too.

Annabel couldn't go on being a nanny forever. In a way Hope had known that the minute she first saw her. And it wasn't as if Annabel was going far. She would still be in the area. She could see the children regularly. She would be around to baby-sit.

Oh, no, thought Hope, I mustn't think like that. It's not fair to her. I've got to let go. I've got to let her get on with her life. But I can find her somewhere to live. That's the least I can do.

A house on Lazy Point had recently come on the market, and she was excited about it. It wasn't anything big or spectacular, but the location was a big draw, right on the end of the point, surrounded by water, with its own beach and mooring rights and beautiful views out over the bay. With some clever renovation it could be magical. Just the ticket for some overworked Manhattanites looking for a summer beach house. Maybe if Annabel sold Rosemullion she would have enough money to buy it.

The owner was in a quandary as to whether he should sell or not. He had been renting it for the past few years, but the tenant had disappeared overnight. Rent fully paid up, nothing underhanded, but no word as to when or if he might be coming back.

"It's a great little house," she told Annabel, following the kids into her bedroom as they carried in her breakfast tray. "I'll find a buyer in no time at all, but I was wondering if you might like to take a look at it before I start showing it officially?"

"It's on the market?" There was an odd look of shock on Annabel's face as she shooed her cat off the bed and the children settled the tray on her knees. "Thank you. This looks delicious."

That was another thing. Annabel had suddenly acquired a cat. It was named Schooner. The children were holding their breath, hoping she would leave it behind for them. But where had the cat come from? It wasn't even a kitten, yet the kids seemed to know it, even Booty. All very strange.

If Annabel did decide to take Schooner with her, at least the kids could console themselves with Clinton—the new Clinton. They had been almost hysterical when Eddie had returned home one evening with Clinton.

Only one quick glance told Hope that it wasn't Clinton.

"Eddie," she had hissed in his ear, "what's going on?"

"Same pound. Same litter of puppies. Same Saint Bernard cross. Are they going to know the difference?"

Harry and Coco weren't fooled for long, but as far as Booty was concerned, her beloved Clinton had come back to her and that was all that mattered. Harry and Coco were sworn to secrecy, although Hope didn't trust Coco for one second.

God knows it would make life easier if one pet or the other was not there, thought Hope. Clinton chased poor Schooner all over the house, and if he caught up with him, Schooner promptly spat at him and tried to scratch his eyes out. If she could persuade Annabel to buy the little Lazy Point house and take Schooner with her, that problem would be solved.

"Sure," she told Annabel. "It's on the market at a very reasonable price. Little shack on the end of Lazy Point. You know the place? Got a weather vane in the shape of a whale on the roof."

"And a birdhouse on a pole outside. It's for sale?"

"Or rent."

"Oh, please rent it. Don't sell it."

"Why? Do *you* want to rent it, Annabel? I thought you might be looking for something to buy, since you're staying here."

Hope was intrigued. Annabel had never shown any interest in real estate before. And now Hope had found her the perfect house, hadn't she?

Yet Annabel was adamant. She didn't want to live at Lazy Point. For some reason the mere mention of the place seemed to upset her. But she didn't want Hope to sell it either. Hope must rent it to someone, Annabel insisted, in case the person who had been living there ever came back.

"But that person wouldn't have any special rights to it," Hope pointed out. It was no use. Annabel didn't want to listen.

Hope wondered if all the others stopped to think about it as much as she did, how much all their lives had changed in the last six months. They'd all moved on, but perhaps none more so than Annabel.

Annabel had changed countries. She was living here full time now and had applied for a green card, sponsored by Ray Moran. In time she would probably become an American citizen.

And she had a new job.

The job was at Osprey Farm, and it was while Hope was driving Annabel there later that morning that a solution was found for one of Hope's more outstanding problems: what to do about Miss Parson's cottage.

"Give it to me," Annabel suggested out of the blue, as they were driving past. "Rent it, I mean. It couldn't be in a better location for me."

Miss Parsons's cottage was within walking distance of Osprey Farm. And Osprey Farm was where Annabel was going to work, ostensibly as a carer for Hannah Moran during the day until Ray came home at night, but bigger plans were afoot.

Osprey Farm was to be converted into a bed-and-breakfast, and a highly exclusive one at that. There were only six bedrooms, but the idea was to model it on an English B and B. It was going to be called the Osprey Farm Inn, and there would be a small dining room serving a full English breakfast in the mornings and simple English food like shepherd's pie and bangers and mash in the evening. Annabel was having antique furniture and paintings shipped from Rosemullion in Cornwall that would be in keeping with Osprey Farm's eighteen-century hewn beams, and she and Eddie were in constant discussion about the redecoration of the "guest suites," as they were now referred to (much to Hope's irritation), so they would look like those in an old English manor house. Hope was forever coming home and finding her own furniture draped with swatches of cabbage-rose chintz. A brochure was being designed for a mailing before the summer season. Then there was the renovation of the kitchen so it could be commercially approved. And so it went, until Hope thought if she heard the words *Osprey Farm* once more she would scream.

But for Annabel to move into Miss Parsons's cottage on Pussy Pond made total sense.

"Why shouldn't I sell the house on Lazy Point? What reason would the owner have to hang on to it?"

"None, I suppose," Annabel replied, but she still looked sad. Hope couldn't figure it out.

Things would have to change once she found a suitable buyer for Miss Parsons's cottage if that day ever came. But presumably by then Annabel would have moved into Osprey Farm.

And that too made total sense, thought Hope. Sooner rather than later. Ray Moran was besotted with Annabel, any fool could see that. Except perhaps Hannah, who was deteriorating fast. Just as well, maybe. But how did Annabel feel about Ray? Eddie thought they made a perfect couple. He had been observing them together. He was often over at Osprey Farm, Annabel too, and returned much later than he did, often cooking Ray's dinner. The inn was to be a three-way enterprise between Ray, Eddie, and Annabel. Ray owned the premises, and Annabel and Eddie would supervise the running of the B and B. Hope knew she should be pleased that Eddie had found something to do, something that he seemed to be really excited about, but she couldn't help feeling left out.

"Larry always said I ought to work with people, that I was a good communicator," he'd told her. "He meant in publicity at the Gramercy Press, but I'm going to be communicating with people on a daily basis when I'm welcoming guests at Osprey Farm and looking after them. Think about it, Hope. All your clients can stay there while they're out here looking for properties. We'll have details of Tudor Woods listings exclusively in reception. None of the other realtors will get a look in."

He was full of ideas; so was Annabel. Where does that leave me? Hope wondered. When the inn finally opens they're going to be there every night, and I'm going to be left home with the kids.

Still, she couldn't deny she was happy with the way her life was going. Having Eddie home again took her back to the time when they were first married—the great sex, the constant teasing, the romping with the kids.

Eddie was fun. She'd forgotten that.

My problem is I've always wanted to impress people, thought Hope. I've always cared far too much what other people thought about my life rather than focusing on what I wanted my life to be. What impressed people ultimately, she had come to realize, was when you were happy and they could see it was for real. You could be married to the richest, most successful man in the world who could provide you with the most enviable lifestyle, but if that man was a competitive, self-obsessed shit who ignored you half the time, you would be miserable inside. And unless you were prepared to work hard to hide that misery, unless all that mattered to you was what kind of outward appearance you created, unless you were prepared to live your life for others, what was the point?

More and more often she remembered her father's words: "You should want whatever it takes to make you happy. Not what makes other people happy and not what they think makes you happy."

What makes me happy is seeing my children happy.

What makes me happy is someone who laughs with me at the end of the day, someone with whom I can relax, someone with whom I don't have to watch myself every second to check that I'm projecting the right image.

I have to work so hard to make a good impression during the day, when I come home at night I want to be loved for myself.

And Eddie does just that. He's so laid back himself, he doesn't expect much of me and he's grateful for whatever I give him.

Sometimes she wondered about the woman who had gone to see Maisie with his things. She never asked Eddie about it because she realized if she uncovered a betrayal she would be bitterly jealous. Best not to know and assume it was in the past.

But it told her something. She had known all about Craig's arm candy, but it hadn't really bothered her much. Yet here she was admitting she would be jealous if Eddie strayed. At the end of the day, in more ways than one, she realized, Eddie meant much more to her.

I thought I married Eddie on the rebound, but the truth is I married him for love. It just took me awhile to realize it. I'm a lucky girl, she told herself.

But she was still a hungry girl.

The estate that Doris told her about when she walked into Tudor Woods one morning was a real estate broker's dream come true. It had imagination. It had class. It had space. It had historic value combined with impressive architectural design. It had something for everyone. A renovated potato barn standing in eleven acres of former potato fields, there were five bedrooms, five bathrooms, extensive decking and porches, cathedral ceilings, tennis court, two-car garage, heated pool and pool house, plus two one-bedroom guest cottages away from the house. All this, and five minutes from the ocean. Asking price well over a million and a half.

Hope was positively salivating. She could almost feel her $50,000-plus commission check rustling in her hand.

"I'll go take a look right away," she told Doris.

"It gets better," Doris replied. "There's a couple coming out this afternoon. He's in advertising, she's on Wall Street, they make a million and a half between them. They're desperate to buy. Three kids: a teenager, a nine-year-old and an afterthought, a little one. It'd be perfect."

"Speaking of little ones, guess what?"

"Booty? You got her this afternoon? Oh, no, Hope, not again. I'm real busy here."

Hope had made it a golden rule never to show houses on the afternoons she had Booty. It didn't look good, turning up with a kid, and besides those afternoons were for her and

Booty, so every now and then she left Booty in the office with Doris and disappeared for an hour or two.

Or three or four. Doris had clearly had enough.

"Oh, what the hell. I'll take her with me. It won't matter just this once."

In fact it turned out to be a plus. As Booty ran around the lawn chasing butterflies, the wife of the couple turned to Hope and said, "It's perfect for the kids. We have a little girl just about the same age as yours. I can see her running around out there safe and sound just like your daughter is doing now."

"And the pool's far enough away from the house to be no danger at all," said Hope, pointing out yet another selling point. "Let's go inside and I'll show you through. Booty, we're going inside, sweetheart. Come with us, please."

Booty led the way, her sturdy little feet stomping up the steps and across the front porch into the house. Hope called out to her every few minutes as she showed the couple around the house so that, when Booty answered, Hope knew she was all right.

That afternoon Doris called in a high state of excitement.

"They called and offered the minute they got back to the city. They must have discussed it throughout the drive back. And the best news is that they've even gone over the asking price to be sure of getting it."

Booty brought me good luck, thought Hope.

But she didn't. Quite the opposite.

When she went to the office the next morning, Doris could barely look her in the eye.

"There's a problem."

"They pulled out?"

"Not yet. But they will."

"Why? They were so set on it. You told me."

"The caretaker called. There's been a flood. The whole second floor is ruined."

"But it hasn't rained for a week," protested Hope. "It didn't rain last night. Did a pipe burst?"

"You're going to say I'm crazy, but he told me the bathtubs overflowed, all five of them. Hope, what were you doing over there?"

"Doris, do you seriously think that I took a bath in each of five bathtubs and let them all overflow while my clients waited downstairs? You saw me come back with them."

"So what happened?"

"It's a mystery."

"You can say that again," said Doris.

The mystery was solved that night when Hope told everyone over supper what had happened.

"Booty!" said Coco and Harry in unison.

"Booty?"

"Eddie was telling us how when he was a little boy he used to play tricks on Auntie Maud and go into the bathroom, put the plug in the tub, turn on the faucet, and leave it running. Then he'd tell his mom his sister had done it. Isn't that cool?" Coco whooped in glee.

"But I still don't see what this has to do with Booty."

"I showed Booty how to do it. She can climb into the tub and she kneels down and puts the plug in. Then I pretended it was my fault when she ran over the bath," said Harry. "But it's OK, Mom. We caught her in time. I would have mopped it up, I swear. Did you take Booty to that house yesterday? Did you check the bathrooms before you went downstairs? Was Booty with you all the time?"

"Well, I could hear her, but I couldn't actually see her. Are you seriously telling me Booty went upstairs and climbed into all the bathtubs and filled them with water and let them overflow? I don't believe it. Have you any idea what a big house sale I've lost because of that flood? What on earth was Eddie doing, even telling you about such a stupid trick? Eddie . . . ?"

But Eddie had slipped out the door to Osprey Farm for more discussions with Annabel and Ray.

Here I am, thought Hope. Suddenly I'm the one who's out of the loop. I want back in. I love Eddie. I love my kids. But it's crazy to compromise my own chances for success. The kids don't need me twenty-four hours a day. I'll go nuts if I keep on like this. I never thought I'd see the day, but there's something I have to do.

She dialed a number in London.

"Maud? Did I wake you? Listen, there's something you can do for me. . . ."

25

I was astounded. Ray only waited two months after Hannah died before proposing.

Hannah went out in style, I'll give her that. She'd been having these strange little strokes for some time, and Ray had become resigned to the fact that another might mean the end. Then he woke up one morning, went into her room as he always did first thing, and she wasn't in her bed.

They found her down by the water, slumped in a rowboat. She had got herself all dressed up, God knows how. An old-fashioned sun hat with ribbons tied under her chin, a silk dress, and a fair amount of jewelry, none of it paste. She had sprayed herself with Chanel No. 5, the scent Ray had always given her.

But she was barefoot. A pair of satin mules had been placed neatly on the lawn at the edge of the wetlands that led down to the water. She must have waded through the bullrushes to the rowboat, untied the rope, and clambered in. Fortunately there was no wind, the water was calm, and the boat was still bobbing close to the bank.

Sitting there in her finery, she'd had a final massive stroke and it had killed her.

So, as I said, I was astounded, but not because Ray proposed so soon after this happened, indecently fast as it might seem.

I was astounded—hurt, devastated—because he didn't propose to me.

Still another man in whom I had placed my trust had betrayed me. For the first twenty-four hours after I learned what had happened, that was how I saw it. But then I began to calm down and take a more rational view of things. To be honest, it was more a question of my pride being hurt than my heart. I had come to accept that Ray and I were a couple, as much as we could be while Hannah was still alive. We had been very circumspect in our behavior. Hope and Eddie knew, simply because we were working so closely with him every day.

It was wonderful to see how Eddie had really come into his own working at Osprey Farm. We'd been open for nearly a year, and already people were coming back for a second visit. Much of this was due to Eddie's charm. It certainly had nothing to do with me; I stayed very much in the background. I played a big role in the day-to-day running of the place, making sure the rooms were exactly how they should be and the bathrooms well stocked with the kind of miniature goodies people love to steal. I organized the breakfast menus—breakfast was served on trays in the rooms—and made sure the right newspapers were available, not that it was a huge choice: *The New York Times*, the *New York Post*, or the *East Hampton Star* once a week. Sometimes people asked for *The Wall Street Journal* or *The Washington Post*, and I had to alert Eddie to pick them up on his way over.

And I arranged the flowers in the rooms, flowers plucked from the gardens at Osprey Farm. That was the part I liked best.

I walked there every morning from Miss Parsons's cottage. I now had a U.S. driver's license, but I hadn't got around to buying a car. If it was pouring with rain, Eddie picked me up on his way to work and dropped me off on his way home.

I loved my little cottage by the duck pond. I'd had it painted throughout, vibrant colors that startled my visitors. For example, my sitting room had bright turquoise walls with a white ceiling. This was a color that really showed up Marietta's extensive collection of little Cornish seascapes in their gilt frames. I was bold with the choice of color for the kitchen too: scarlet. I loved the way these strong modern colors sprang out between the old beams of the house. I went a step further and painted the shutters on the windows a wonderful powder blue. I could do this because the house had escaped being listed on the national register of historic places in spite of having been in Miss Parsons's family for several generations.

I didn't own the house, I rented it, but this in no way detracted from the pleasure of having my own home for the first time in my life.

This was one of the reasons I hadn't moved in with Ray.

One of the reasons. There were others.

We'd only had sex a few times and it had been a disaster. Admittedly, I was out of practice, but even so, Ray and I in bed together didn't work. I liked him so much. I could see he was still extremely good-looking. But somehow I couldn't put the two things together and come up with attraction. There was just no chemistry as far as I was concerned. Being held by him was nice, being kissed by him was nice. But who needs nice? I wanted sparks and uncertainty and elation. I wanted an adrenaline rush, nervousness, passion, and the feeling of being more alive than I had ever felt before. Ray was tender and gentle, but he wasn't exciting. He was safe. Too safe. He was probably exactly what I needed, but he wasn't what I wanted, and try as I might I couldn't respond. What I found comforting in a doctor I didn't necessarily want in a lover. At least not yet.

I might be forty-eight but I didn't feel middle-aged. I felt the need to make up for all the time I wasted, buried down in

Cornwall under Marietta's thumb. I wanted to spread my wings. Ray already had a pipe-and-slippers approach to life. No edge. Nothing remotely dangerous about him anymore. After four or five hours with him, I began to feel like a child who has grown tired of adult company and yearns to escape.

Of course, none of this came to mind when he told me he was going to marry Eloise Walters. *Eloise*. The name says it all: so affected. I must have been going around in a totally blinkered state because I should have seen it coming. She was one of our guests at Osprey Farm. A divorcée—I think she was an interior designer—who arrived one weekend with a pile of books and magazines and disappeared into her room for twenty-four hours. The housekeeper couldn't get in to do the room, and in the end I had to go and knock on the door and politely inquire whether she wanted supper brought up on a tray. I had visions of reading about the Scandal of Osprey Farm in the *East Hampton Star*, how they had found a woman who had starved herself to death without anyone's noticing. No, she said, she'd come downstairs and have bar snacks. We didn't have a bar, but I knew what she meant. Eddie served her sandwiches and a bowl of chowder and sat and chatted with her by the fire, so when she returned again and again I assumed it was he who was the big attraction.

Eddie told me later she had made a beeline for Ray, who had gone down like a ninepin almost immediately.

"I suppose I should have said something," he muttered sheepishly. "It's just that since it was clear as day to everyone else what was going on, I assumed you knew."

"But he's only known her four months! And it's only two months since Hannah died. *Two months!*"

"It's awful to say so, but we all know Hannah was effectively dead long before that."

"Don't make excuses for his behavior, Eddie. Do you actually like her?"

"I think she's right for Ray," he said, surprising me.

"You can't be serious."

"I'm totally serious. Ray needs someone like her desperately. He's had years of caring for Hannah, and when Eloise focused all her attention on him, it must have been like getting hooked on a new drug for him."

"What do you mean, focused her attention on him? Where? When?"

"She sat up late into the night with him after you'd gone home. She laughed at his jokes, told him how wonderful he was, bought him little presents, fixed him drinks. She showed him she was crazy about him and he was putty in her hands. I knew someone who was obsessed with me recently—this is something that need not get back to Hope—and it was irresistible, especially when I hadn't exactly been top priority with Hope for quite a while. Eloise made him feel special."

"And I didn't?"

"I don't know, Annabel. Did you?"

No, I thought, I didn't. I was too needy myself. I was almost as much a burden to him as Hannah. I let him play the good doctor role and lapped it up and now when it's too late and I've lost him, I have the nerve to feel miserable and foolish.

It was only a matter of time before I realized something else.

I couldn't go on working at Osprey Farm. Eloise moved out to live there, and even though nobody ever came out and actually said anything, pretty soon it became clear that she would take over my job. In any case, it was awkward between me and Ray now.

"You're probably not going to like my saying this," said Eddie, "but I think it's for the best. Hope and I were talking about it last night. In a way, by working at Osprey Farm you're replicating your life in Cornwall. When you left us you were taking a step back instead of a step forward. The only reason I didn't say anything was because we hoped that one day you and Ray would work something out. And of course we needed your organizing skills to get the B and B off and running in the first place."

"Oh, thanks a lot!" I told him, outraged, but after I'd calmed down I had to admit he had a point.

And to think at one stage I had even had the ludicrous idea that I might be a carer for Hannah. Luckily Ray had stepped in and hired a nurse for her, telling me I had too much to do running Osprey Farm.

Well, not anymore.

Ray turned up one day at Miss Parsons's cottage. It was the first time we'd been alone together since he'd told me he was going to marry Eloise. When I opened the door to him it was like we had been set up on a blind date. We knew why we were there but we didn't know what to say to each other. I spent far longer than was necessary making him a cup of coffee. He waited until I set it in front of him and then said, "You know it wouldn't have worked between us, Annabel."

"Do I?" I said perversely. "Why wouldn't it?"

"You didn't want me. I was interested in you from the first moment I saw you, you know that. But as soon as we began to see more of each other I could tell you found me boring."

"Oh, Ray, I don't—"

"I don't mean as a person. We rub along very well and we make good business partners, which is why it's so sad you're leaving, but I totally understand your reasons. It's just you remind me of Hannah when she was younger."

"And you're going to tell me Hannah found you boring?"

"No. Not me. She was hooked on me, that I do know. The one she found boring was the distinguished older lawyer everyone thought she would marry. You really are a lot like her, same independence of spirit. She couldn't settle down with a boring old lawyer. She wasn't ready for that when Johnnie was killed. That's why she shocked everyone by marrying me, a much younger man. I was quite wild and dangerous in those days, even though I was playing the role of respectable young doctor. You would have fallen for me then. Relationships. It's all about timing. You can meet someone, fall in love, but if it's the wrong time, forget it. It ain't gonna happen. With Hannah and me it was the right time, and it worked. Until she got sick, it worked very well."

He looked so sad I reached out and patted his arm in a rather useless consoling manner.

"Do you love Eloise?" I asked.

"Always the romantic, Annabel." At least I'd made him laugh. "No. I can't put my hand on my heart and say I'm head over heels in love with her, but I know she can make me happy and I'll settle for that. But you wouldn't, Annabel. Maybe you'll settle down one day but not yet. Right now, you want nothing less than high-octane passion."

"Backed up by tenderness and affection," I added.

"So what are you going to do, go back to being a nanny? I hear Hope's new girl out from England is driving everyone crazy."

This was true. Maud had excelled herself by sending someone as unlike me as she could possibly find, a ditzy nineteen-year-old called Tiffany from Liverpool, whose accent was incomprehensible to everyone in Amagansett. But she had huge breasts and already had the local youths dancing around her like flies.

"Now I have to baby-sit my own children night after night," Hope grumbled, when I went by for supper, "but Tiffany's a tough little worker during the day. Gets on with the job. If I told you that Coco now makes her own bed and is downstairs for breakfast before anyone else, would you believe me?"

"No way."

"Well, it's true. Tiffany is the oldest of seven children, and she's kept her little brothers and sisters in order all her life.

She wouldn't take any back talk from Coco from the get-go. She's good with Booty too."

"And Harry?"

"Harry misses you the most, Annabel. You ought to stop by and see him more."

"I will," I promised.

"He still asks about that guy Sheldon who did the work on our house last year."

"Ah," I said. Very noncommittal. "Whatever happened to his house?"

"How should I know?" said Hope.

"But you told me you had it on your books, for sale or rent. The little house on the end of Lazy Point."

"Oh, that," said Hope. "I didn't know it was his house. You never said." Hope looked at me sideways.

"It wasn't his house. He rented it from the owner."

"Well, it sold," said Hope flatly.

"*Sold?*" I nearly screamed. "Who to?"

"No idea. Nothing to do with me. The owner sold it— what—a couple of months ago. Not through Tudor Woods. The new owner's moved in, I heard."

Well, that was that. I was more or less back where I started: no job, no man, no family—for in a way I had come to look upon Hope, Eddie, and the kids as family and now I was no longer with them.

But while the blows had hit me hard, they in themselves were softer. I'd made progress. I had my little house. But I had to find a way to earn my living and ironically—although in this case indirectly—once again Maud was the one who came to my rescue.

Maud had dropped a bombshell on us all six months earlier by suddenly calling up and announcing she was getting married. Eddie and I went back to England for the wedding and got the shock of our lives. We'd anticipated that her Rupert would be someone working on the cutting edge of the media, but to our amazement he turned out to be a rather shy and soft-spoken antiques dealer in his late fifties whom she had met when she had taken a mirror into his shop to be valued. They were an odd couple—she bossed him around and he let her—but they clearly adored each other. In the preliminaries to their small wedding I had lunch with Rupert alone one day, and that was when I saw he had an entrepreneurial side that brought him very much to life. He was passionate about his work, and when he heard I still hadn't done anything about the paintings and furniture from Rosemullion that I hadn't been able to fit into either Osprey Farm or Miss Parsons's cottage, he insisted on driving me all the way down to Cornwall to take them out of storage. He became quite excited when he saw what he called "the booty," little realizing the pun he was making with regard to his soon-to-be-wife's niece, and assured me he could sell everything for me.

Then he had a better idea. If he could sell it, so could I. And rather than let it sit around in London waiting for American tourists to wander in and see in his shop, why didn't I take everything back to America and sell it on the spot? So we went into partnership together. When he and Maud came to stay with Hope and Eddie (marriage had softened Maud to the extent that she was prepared to spend a week under Hope's roof) for a summer break, Rupert took one look at Miss Parsons's cottage and pronounced it the perfect place to open an antiques shop.

So now I'm in antiques, long distance, so to speak. I don't buy, I sell. I have long since exhausted the spoils of Rosemullion, and now I am dependent on Rupert to send me watercolors, oils, books, antique furniture, anything I can fit into the little wood-paneled front room. Genuine English antiques sold by a genuine English antique, as Eddie teases. But it's a success and Rupert and I split the profits. Hope makes a point of stopping by with people on her way to show them houses, and I proffer lemonade and cookies just like Miss Parsons used to do and they invariably buy something. Eddie tells people about me when he's serving drinks at Osprey Farm. It's amazing, the impression an English accent still makes on Americans.

Harry comes and helps on Saturdays. I give him my filing to do and he's really rather good at it. He has such an orderly mind and he's so conscientious. But we still talk about the morning we went out fishing with Sheldon, and I know there's a side of him that yearns for a little more outdoor excitement, something Eddie can't quite get it together to do. Harry is still working on the story he and Sheldon began, the one about the little boy who goes to Hicks Island. It's growing into a book. My dream is that one day Eddie will be able to use his influence with his former contacts in publishing to find Harry a publisher. Maybe I have an undiscovered bestselling writer working in my shop.

"Did you know Sheldon's house sold?" I told Harry.

"It did? We should go check him out."

"Check him out? How do you know it's a him?"

"Has to be. No woman would live in that house. It's too dangerous, so close to the water and so exposed to the winds," said Harry dismissively. "No, I think we should check out the new owner and make sure he's going to keep the house like it ought to be kept. For Sheldon's sake. It's special, that house. We don't want the new owner making it all fancy and adding stupid extensions and ruining it, right?"

"Absolutely right, Harry. Shall we take a walk over there? Pick up Clinton and walk around the bay."

"Cool. Pity we can't take Schooner, show him his old home. But you can't take a cat for a walk, can you? We'll come home and tell him all about it."

The first thing I saw as the roof of the house came into view was that Fred the seagull was back sitting on the chimney. Well, if Fred thought it was safe to come back the new owner must be a nice guy, I told Harry, but I could see he wasn't prepared to be convinced that easily.

As we drew closer I reeled back in astonishment. Whoever the new owner was, he went out on the water. The yard was littered with rowboats and outboard motors and splashes of color, green and blue kayaks and paddles and yellow life jackets and orange diving suits just as it had been when I used to go there last year. But now everything looked new and fresh. The house had been painted. The shingles were still the same beautiful weather-beaten gray, but the shutters had been given a fresh coat of powder-blue paint. That was where I'd got the idea for the color of my own shutters. I hadn't realized it at the time.

Harry was running around the house, peering in the windows.

"Harry, come away from there. Don't snoop. You're trespassing. It all looks fine. Let's go back before the tide comes in."

But Harry wouldn't come away. I sat down on a rock and looked out across the channel to Hicks Island. It was a crisp winter day and the sky was a brilliant blue. It could have been a summer day except I knew if I put my hand in the water it would probably freeze. There was ice on some of the rocks nearer the water. It would probably snow tonight and when the new owner awoke he would look out onto a white beach.

I heard the sound of an approaching car.

"Harry!" I called. "For God's sake come away from the house! We can't be caught snooping."

He joined me reluctantly.

"Let's just stay and watch from the beach. I want to see what he looks like. He might be a cool guy. He's got a lot of the things Sheldon had. He's got a telescope just like Sheldon's. And a desk. And—"

"Shhh. The car's stopped. He'll hear us. Now we really

can't move or he'll see us. Keep as still as you can, and then we'll creep away."

We crouched down behind the rock and heard the car door slam and then the wooden door of the shack. I confess I was curious. I was dying to see who had bought the house that had once meant so much to me.

And then Harry blew our cover by getting to his feet and waving!

"Get down," I hissed. "He'll see us."

"He has seen us," said Harry. "That's why I'm waving." And to my horror he rushed up the beach toward the house.

Oh, great, I thought. How am I going to explain what we're doing here, trying to hide ourselves on his property. Probably get arrested.

"Need a hand, Nanny Annie?"

I needed a bulldozer. I couldn't move. I was rooted to the sand in shock.

"What are you doing out here? It's freezing. Come on in the house and I'll make you a hot drink."

I looked up.

Same penetrating blue eyes. I'd forgotten how wide apart they were. Hair shorter than it had been, almost a buzz cut with a few tufts sticking up on top where his cap had ruffled them. It made him look sweet, like Tintin. The silver earring was still in the left ear.

I'd forgotten how strong he was. He picked me up and carried me up to the beach to the deck.

Harry was jumping up and down.

"I was trying to tell you, but you kept making me be quiet! I could see his truck! I knew he was back."

"Have you come back to get your things?" was all I could think to ask when we went into the house and I could see the desk, his grandmother's bed, the giant birdcage standing in the corner, the fishing nets with the fairy lights draped over a chair waiting to be strung up, the pictures of sailing ships stacked up on the floor against the wall. "Hope said some-one's bought the house."

He nodded. "Tea? Coffee?"

"Tea. But you had a tag sale. The old man said—"

"Sure, but only for the garbage. You didn't think I'd get rid of my grandmother's bed, did you?"

"So you had everything in storage? Are you selling it to the new owner?"

"You just don't get it, Annabel." He reached out and drew me to him. "I *am* the new owner."

"*You* bought the house?" I couldn't believe it. He was back. He was hugging me. It was too much to take in all at once.

"I bought the house," he confirmed, speaking slowly as if to a child. "I've been away for almost a year and I've made quite a bit of money. And I've sold my yacht. I had enough for the deposit, so I went ahead and got a mortgage."

"Will you want Schooner back?" Harry was looking very worried.

"Is he living with you guys? I left him for Annabel."

"No, he's with her, but I get to see him when I go and work at her antiques shop."

Sheldon looked down at me. He was still holding me in his arms, with Harry watching us as if it was the most natu-ral thing in the world. Which, in fact, was how it felt.

"I heard you'd set up a little store. Good for you. No, sorry, Harry, but Schooner's going to have to come back to me, but I'll tell you what. I'm willing to share him with Nanny Annie. We'll have joint custody. He can spend a week with her and a week with me. How's that?"

"And you'll take us fishing?"

"Sure. Whenever you want."

"How long have you been back?" I asked him.

"Couple of months. I've been staying with a buddy while I sorted out buying this place."

"Why didn't you—" I stopped, aware I was sounding like a nag.

"Why didn't I get in touch? I wanted to get this place looking great and then bring you over here, surprise you, but you beat me to it."

"Are you going to invite Annabel to come and live here with you?" asked Harry. I could have throttled him.

"No, I'm not. I don't want anyone living here with me, but that doesn't mean I don't want to see her."

"Why did you come back?" Harry persisted. And this time I really did want to know the answer.

"It's where I belong," he said simply. "And I wanted to come back for Nanny Annie."

He was laughing, winking at Harry, teasing me, but there was an element of sincerity in his tone.

"Here's your tea, Annabel. Have a seat in the rocker. I need Harry here to come give me a hand getting some wood out of my truck and loading it up on the deck. That OK with you, Harry?"

"Sure," said Harry, delighted.

I sat in the rocker. I sipped my tea. And I watched him through the window.

It was simple when I thought about it. I was meant to wind up with someone like Sheldon. He wasn't solid, safe husband material. He might have got himself a mortgage, but he wasn't going to change. He would never be a conventional partner. But that wasn't what I wanted. At least not yet.

Sheldon and I are two of a kind. We know how important our freedom is to us. There is no asking price high enough. Freedom is priceless. Sheldon understands that.

But it doesn't mean you can't fall in love.

He was smiling at me through the window, blowing me kisses.

He's younger. He'll probably lead me a fine dance. It's risky. But I've escaped from the past and I'm still ready for adventure. He brings out the romantic in me. He's bought the house. He'll be here. And I'll be there, over at Miss Parsons's cottage. I can have Sheldon, and I can have my freedom. What have I got to lose?

He came bursting through the door.

"Listen, I've got to go over to the lumberyard, pick up some stuff I still need. I could drop Harry back at his mom's for you. Why don't you stay here, and then when I get back I can tell you all about my travels. How's that sound?"

I smiled up at him and took his hand and squeezed it.

"It sounds perfect."

"I wish I didn't have to leave you, but this stuff's important and"—He bent his head quickly;

I knew what was coming—"I gotta race back."

He swooped. A dive-bomb kiss on my lips. The intense look into my eyes. Then he was gone.

It was as if he'd never been away.

For Passionate Romance and
Searing Family Drama,
No One Compares to

Barbara Delinsky

THE CARPENTER'S LADY	0-06-103024-4/$6.99 US/$9.99 Can
FAST COURTING	0-06-100875-3/$7.99 US/$10.99 Can
FINGER PRINTS	0-06-104180-7/$6.99 US/$9.99 Can
FOR MY DAUGHTERS	0-06-109280-0/$7.99 US/$10.99 Can
GEMSTONE	0-06-104233-1/$7.99 US/$10.99 Can
AN IRRESISTIBLE IMPULSE	0-06-100876-1/$7.99 US/$10.99 Can
MOMENT TO MOMENT	0-06-101099-5/$7.99 US/$10.99 Can
MORE THAN FRIENDS	0-06-104199-8/$7.99 US/$10.99Can
PASSION AND ILLUSION	0-06-104232-3/$5.99 US/$7.99 Can
THE PASSIONS OF CHELSEA KANE	
	0-06-104093-2/$7.99 US/$10.99 Can
REKINDLED	0-06-101097-9/$7.99 US/$10.99 Can
SEARCH FOR A NEW DAWN	
	0-06-100874-5/$5.50 US/$6.50 Can
SENSUOUS BURGUNDY	0-06-101101-0/$5.99 US/$7.99 Can
SHADES OF GRACE	0-06-109282-7/$6.99 US/$8.99 Can
SUDDENLY	0-06-104200-5/$7.99 US/$10.99 Can
SWEET EMBER	0-06-101098-7/$6.50 US/$7.99 Can
A TIME TO LOVE	0-06-101100-2/$5.99 US/$7.99 Can
TOGETHER ALONE	0-06-109281-9/$6.99 US/$7.99 Can
VARIATION ON A THEME	0-06-104234-X/$7.99 US/$10.99 Can
WITHIN REACH	0-06-104174-2/$6.99 US/$8.99 Can
A WOMAN'S PLACE	0-06-109505-2/$7.50 US/$9.50 Can

....

Available wherever books are sold or please call 1-800-331-3761
to order.

BD 0202